Our Heroes Return

Betty Rose

DEDICATION

'Our Heroes Return' was written after requests from the readers of 'A Week in Time', a WWII home front novella that focused on how my little group of neighbours- Frances, Eliza, Ruby, Norma and Lizzie- had fared as the war progressed and came to an end.

'Our Heroes Return' is a full novel and it follows the many changes that the war brought- social, political and emotional.

I enjoyed writing and connecting once again with my feisty band of working-class women, because my roots are born from the same ilk, and I'm proud of such.

I dedicate my story to the brave men and women who fought and to those who lived their own battles on the streets and in their homes.

I'd like to thank my dear friend, Kate Oman, who is an author of nine books herself, for her encouragement as well as her editing and support in publishing my fourth novel at a time when I was having a few doubts and wondering if I should publish again.

Books by the same author:

'A Week in Time'- WWII home front novella on Amazon

'Keep Them Close' and 'Alone It's Okay' on Amazon, Waterstones, Goodreads, and Pegasus Elliot Mackenzie publishers.

CONTENTS

Prologue	4
Introduction	6
Chapter 1	8
Chapter 2	39
Chapter 3	62
Chapter 4	101
Chapter 5	129
Chapter 6	179
Chapter 7	227
Chapter 8	251
Chapter 9	273
Chapter 10	283
Chapter 11	299
Epilogue	329

PROLOGUE

VE Day: 8th May 1945.

At long last; victory in Europe, after 6 long years of conflict.

Church bells rang out throughout England, marking the formal acceptance of Nazi Germany's surrender to Britain and her allies.

At 3pm, Tuesday, the 8$^{th\ of}$ May 1945, Winston Churchill, in his unmistakable grave authoritative style, spoke to the nation from number 10 Downing Street.

"Yesterday morning at 2.41am, at general Eisenhower's headquarters, the representative of the German High Command, signed an act of unconditional surrender of all German land, sea and air forces in Europe, to the Allied expeditionary Force.

Hostilities will end officially at one minute after midnight… but in the interests of saving lives the cease fire began yesterday, to be sounded all along the front. The German war is therefore at an end…

We may allow ourselves a brief period of rejoicing but let us not forget for a moment the toils and efforts that lay ahead. Japan, with all her treachery and greed, remains unsubdued…

Advance Britannia.

Long live the cause of freedom!

God save the King."

The surrender of Imperial Japan was announced by the Emperor Hirohito on August 15, 1945, and formally signed on September 2, 1945.

The United States accepted Japan's surrender.

Emperor Hirohito went on the radio at noon -15 August 1945.

"We have resolved to pave the way for a grand peace for all of the generations to come by enduring the unendurable and suffering what is unsufferable."

FINALLY, THE HOSTILITIES OF WW2 CAME TO A CLOSE.

INTRODUCTION

VE celebrations, a day the residents of this small English town had longed for and imagined. That such a day would ever happen had been dismissed as a beautiful fantasy or pie in the sky by the pragmatic amongst them. Only, the dreamers knew different. Their only way through this hell was to cling onto the possibility of better days and victory. Hungering for a time when they could live out their days free from the fear of the devilish bombs, no longer scrunching in terror as the Doodlebugs flew unmanned over their heads. Their aching hearts longing for the day when they could send their children off to school, knowing they were safe to playout their childish dreams and pranks. Where they could walk to school hand in hand, no longer carrying the sinister masks whilst clinging to their mother's hems. Remembering and yearning for the times when as the evenings drew in, they'd once again sit with a cup of cocoa by the fire and climb the stairs and be safe in their beds.

Would their lives ever be the same? They hadn't all made it home, how could they? And of those that did? In one way or the other, most were marked from what they'd seen and what they'd had to do to survive. Although the deep shadows of war were not always visible to the naked eye, few escaped them, in one way or another. Their souls were marked by the terrible sights and deeds committed by others or themselves in the name of rights or freedom. And some of those returning home, found those they'd left behind were also inexorably changed. They pretended to laugh as their kiddies ran from their open arms, hiding behind their mam's skirts at the sight of the returning stranger.

Neighbours Frances, Lizzie, Ruby, Eliza and Norma, had survived the horrors and hardships of the past 6 years, their experiences bonding them together in such a way they'd become intrinsically the entwined, a strong effective family unit. Their neighbours, who also called these long narrow streets home, the bricks scarred and blackened by fire and blood, were now extensions of this tight, supportive unit. It was as diverse in background as a bunch of conscripted soldiers, but they were intrinsically welded together by need and experience... family!

How had they fared during the long six years of conflict; a war that involved more than thirty countries? WW2 was identified as the biggest and deadliest war in history. Years filled with danger, loss, deprivation, but also excitement, empowerment. It had provided a window that invited and offered so many other possibilities and choices, that had never before been open to them.

Who was damaged and who had blossomed?

Would they be content to slip back into their past roles, and way of life?

Or do they want more? Better?

CHAPTER 1

Brinklow Street VE party; Wednesday, 9th May 1945.

"Mam? I want jelly."

"It's for the little ones."

"It's not fair."

Norma Watling was at her wits end. It was hot, already the sweat was gathering uncomfortably under her heavy bust. The dust was blowing over from the rubble of bombed out Whittle Street and clinging to her lips and nostrils. She rubbed her face with the corner of her pinny and sighed.

"Come on now Mary, stop complaining. Today of all days, you should be happy."

"Oh, but…?"

"No!" Norma turned towards her eldest daughter. *"I don't want to hear any more about it. Please, for me? Be a good girl and help us out with the youngsters. You're nearly fifteen now;*

I was working in Martins' shoe shop at your age, bringing money into the house."

Mary's bottom lip trembled. *"I only want some jelly. The red jelly looks so lovely, and I'm really so very hot."*

Norma relented. *"We'll see."* They had been through so much. Exhaling, she wiped the tears from Mary's face with the corner of her pinny. Yes, they had all been through hell, in one way or another, and it wasn't over yet.

Churchill's announcement yesterday was clear about that. The German surrender was a Godsend, but her old man, Reg, he was still out there, somewhere in the east with his regiment, and the Japs hadn't surrendered yet. Her stomach churned at the thought of Reg being hurt, killed, or even worse in her eyes, taken prisoner. Gawd help him if they ever got their hands on him; she'd heard such stories.

Suddenly dizzy, she plonked herself down on the nearest chair and looked along the length of tables at the kiddies, squashed together like sardines. It had been a job and a half getting this lot together at a moment's notice; mostly women helpers, as was the norm. There were few men returned home yet, and those that had, well, some weren't in a particularly good way, mentally or physically. Only yesterday, as she'd stood in the queue at the butchers, Mrs Atkins was regaling them, in a stage whisper, that her old man, recently discharged from his unit, wouldn't touch meat!

"I put a plate of nice gravy and potatoes and a pork chop in front of him and he was all of a tremble. Pushed it away from him. Said it smelt of death. You'd think I was trying to poison him. I said to him, 'Give it here then, and you can have me veg!'"

Her stomach had tightened inside her like a vice, and she'd had to rush out. What was Reg seeing? What was he going through?

She looked along the line at the excited faces. God love them. Some of them had been up since first light, and out playing in the street at the crack of dawn; it was no wonder they were all a little fractious. Still, they'd pulled it off... sort of! A cacophony of odd chairs and stools made an up and down snake of differing heights. The tables were decorated with the best white tablecloths that hadn't seen the light of day for the war years---well---there hadn't seemed any point; they'd had very little fancy stuff to grace them. On some tables they'd made do with starched white sheets. The kids didn't mind, all they cared about was the party food, and the hats, and the blowers, of course. They were puffing on these with the full capacity of their lungs.

It had been a hoot really, a happy chaos, getting the party together; an instant reaction to Winston's announcement of yesterday. The few blokes that were around? They had cheerfully hung the bunting up along the whole length of the street, whilst the women ripped the blackout curtains down from the windows. And then? Oh, it was glorious! The church bells had rung out for the first time since the beginning of the war.

They had danced. Oh, how they had danced and jiggled and sang and laughed! Kicking and jigging in long swaying chains of totally uninhibited abandon. The children had watched in amazement, looking on from their bedroom windows as the celebrations carried on into the night. The brave had dared to slip back downstairs and sit on their front doorsteps, hiding in the shadows. More than a few would have awkward questions ready for their mums the next morning.

Those that had Union Jack flags hung them out of bedroom windows, others draped them around their shoulders or waved them along as they high kicked amongst the crowd. That night few cared for propriety; although some took it to excess maybe and would bear the consequences at a later date.

The chaps lit a bonfire on the waste ground nearby and they kept it burning for most of the night. No more blackouts! Norma had gazed at the orange flames and the sparks flying into the dark sky; staring into the blaze hoping for a sign, any sign that Reg was safe. The fierceness of the fire brought a release, a release from pain and fear, finally. Tearing herself away, she crept back into the house and washed the smoke from her hair in rainwater from the water butt. She climbed into the sanctuary of her sagging bed, trying not to roll on top of her two youngest who didn't murmur, dreaming the dreams of magic and childhood. As soon as her head hit the pillow she slipped down into the pure slumber of exhausted body and strained mind.

At first light she'd woken as bright as a lark, leapt out of bed and got to it. And now the party was in full sway! She'd been busy since 4am and, to be truthful, she was jiggered. Perhaps Mary would keep her eye on her other three, just for half an hour? Or maybe not; it didn't seem fair. They were good girls. Mary, almost fifteen, she could hardly believe it! Susan was thirteen, Gracie twelve and little Margaret just ten.; she featured her dad. Why, she'd been, almost six years old when Reg had enlisted. What would their dad think of his girls when he came home?

A nagging tug from her belly reminded her---what if he didn't come home? Taking a quick glance down the table she decided to nip into the kitchen for a second. She brushed her hair back from her face and took a long draw of water from the mug. Oh, what she could do with a hot cup of strong tea and a quick fag. No time for that this morning. Oh Reg, what if you don't make it? She couldn't imagine being on her own with the girls for ever. Yes, she'd managed, but it was lonely, and tough, financially and every which way.

The sudden slam of the back door cut rudely into her thoughts.
"Susan? What on earth?"

"Mam? Tommy Smith just pulled my hair and stuck his big fat tongue out at me---I don't want to sit opposite him."

Emboldened by the presence of an adult close behind her she ran to the door and bellowed, *"I hate you, Tommy Smith! You stink, and your house stinks too!"*

Norma sighed, wiped her face on a flannel. *"No rest for the wicked."* She took a lookout onto the street, but it all seemed to be swinging along. Pointing her finger at her enraged child she heaved a sigh, *"Now listen young lady, that's a terrible thing to say. "*

Susan's face was scarlet, her eyes blazed with indignation. *"Don't care!"*

"You will do in a minute young lady. Now then! Get yourself back out there and behave."

The object of Susan's rage was unrepentant, not showing any signs of distress from the spiteful words hurled at him a minute earlier. *"Susan's got fat ankles"* he yelled. The cheeky grin on his grimy face was too much for Susan and she burst into tears. Norma rushed back outside and caught Tommy by his collar. *"Now then Tommy, leave our Susan alone. Picking on little girls, a big lad like you. You should be ashamed."*

"Didn't do 'nuffin'," he sniffed. Norma raised her eyebrows. Susan's undone pigtail was evidence to the contrary of his boyish exuberance...

It was all too much for Susan, whose tears quickly disappeared. *"Liar."*

Leaning over the heavily laden table, she stabbed her finger in Tommy's dish of red jelly. That was it! Tommy leapt forward, keen to reciprocate but the weight of his elbows on the flimsy table caused the fragile legs to give way, and a landslide of jellies, pink blancmanges and paste sandwiches slid into the laps of those unfortunates who were sharing the nearby table.

"Oh lord help us!" bellowed Norma. Seizing Susan by the intact pigtail, she led the struggling child back to the open door of their house. Mary looked on in horror. *"Oh no! That lovely wiggly red jelly!"*

Norma turned and raised an eyebrow. *"Mary, let it go."* Gracie and little Margaret did their best to stifle their giggles behind sticky hands. For a moment Tommy froze like a rabbit in the headlights, then made a supersonic disappearing act. Shoving a sandwich into each of his trouser pockets and a whole fairy cake into his mouth, he shot off on his thin scabby legs; evidence to all that not all the children in these streets had come through this war unscathed.

Norma started to laugh, her shoulders shaking with an almost desperate abandon whilst her children looked on with amazement. Then her laughter seized in an abrupt emergency stop.

"Mam?" queried Mary.

"Oh Christ." she muttered, *"Never mind me duck, I think I've had too much sun."* How could she explain how she was feeling? Her brain was like that bloody red jelly, it was all too much, too wonderful, so terrible.

Ever since Winston's announcement, all she'd heard was the other women babbling on- wondering when their old men would be demobbed, how nice it would be to share a bed, what would he look like, etc. All she could think of was the unfairness of it all with her Reg; his war wasn't over yet. They'd looked at her expectantly. *"I haven't got a sodding clue where or when!"* she'd hollered.

Put on a brave face Norma, she thought; keep a stiff upper lip, keep smiling. *"Bugger it! Today,"* she glowered, *"I've just about had enough."*

Unaware of the awkward silence around her, she began collecting the broken dishes and scooping up the mess of jelly and blancmange. A soft voice cut into her thoughts, *"Come on duck, there are enough here to sort this lot out. Let's go and have five minutes."* She felt an arm wrap around her waist. The scent of lavender and sweet rosewater, along with the calm quiet strength of the voice behind her, gave the game away.

"Lizzie? Oh, how glad I am to see you."

"Now then, sit yourself down Norma. I'll brew us a pot of tea. If I'm not wrong, you've been up most of the night and not taken a bite of food."

Norma blew her nose. *"I couldn't eat a thing, not at this minute, but thank you for the offer, Lizzie. VE Day! I didn't think it would ever happen, did you? Everyone was so happy last night, dancing, jigging around. Of course, I'm happy, but for me it was a hard day. It's not fair, he should be home with* me and the kids. I won't touch a drop of alcohol until I hear from my Reg, not until he's back here with me, where he should be. It doesn't feel normal, y'know, me celebrating without him."

Lizzy sat still, hands in her lap, brown eyes a shining darkness. *"These are not normal times, Norma. War is not normal, or God help us if it ever becomes so. Normal rules don't apply I'm afraid."*

"The truth is, I'm jealous, and envious too. I want my husband home here, where he belongs, with me and the girls. Is it so wrong to feel like this?"

Lizzie stood slowly, paused, and took a deep breath. *"I'm going to put the kettle back on the stove. Take your pinafore off, nip into the scullery and splash your face with cold water. I'll take a look at the cards for you if you like?"*

Whilst Norma tidied herself up, Lizzie cut into a brown loaf and a basin of brawn and made up two plates.

"Reg wouldn't want you being maudlin like this. Either way, whatever happens ducks, your girls have survived and right now they still need you. Your Mary is nearly fifteen, she's a young woman now, it's not as if they are babies."

Norma nodded, as she caught Lizzie watching her. She smiled apologetically, *"Thank you. I hadn't realised how hungry I was. I do feel a bit more like myself now. Our Susan and that Tommy Smith? Little tykes. I didn't know where to put myself. The kids have run a bit wild during this lot and this behaviour is the result. Reg would have tanned our Susan's arse."*

Lizzie's eyes opened wide. *"Your Reg? Never! Not once did he lay a hand on those girls, you know that. As for your Susan running wild? No, don't be silly. She's as sharp as a pin that one, and she won't let anything pass her by, I'll give you that. You don't need to fret about her, or any of them. You've done a good job of being both mam and dad."*

"Oh Lizzie, I do hope so. She wants piano lessons; can you believe it? Where am I going to find a piano? Never mind being able to find the money, even if I do."

Lizzie didn't answer, pursing her lips in thought she sat fiddling with her wedding ring. She gazed at a photograph of Ruby, her lodger, perched on the mantlepiece.

Norma didn't wait for a response. *"Oh, dear Lizzie"* she smiled regretfully, *"I'm being a pain, aren't I? There are many much worse off than me. That poor little sod, Tommy Smith? He lost his mam to the bombing, then his dad's sent home missing a leg. How's he going to find work Lizzie? God help him."*

"No, don't be daft, Norma. I was trying to think where we could get our hands on a piano for your Susan. As for work? There'll be plenty of work, believe me. This country has to be almost rebuilt--- housing, factories, shops, schools, the docks. Where will the government find the money? Well, that's a different matter. And, from what I've heard, Tommy's dad is doing all right, going the right way if you take my meaning. He's being well looked after at that convalescence place at Brighton."

Norma brightened. *"Of course. I'm glad the Hilary's have taken Tommy in; they're good folk. We might see a bit of meat on the lad now, he's dreadfully thin. I've been thinking, I could try a bit of charring, it would help with those piano lessons she's after. The piano though? God knows where that will come from."* She sighed, *"Reg wouldn't like it, but he's not here, is he?"* Rubbing her hands on her pinny, she turned to her friend. *"Lizzie? Charring: honest work, honest money. It will do me good."*

Lizzie inclined her head. *"We can ask around. You never can tell after all. It never fails to surprise me what people chuck out these days. So? Do you want me to read your cards now?"*

Norma's eyes took on a faraway look. *"We all have a lot to be thankful for, strange as it seems, to be saying that. At least Herr bloody Hitler didn't make it to these shores."*

"Norma?"

Stretching her bare legs in front of her, Norma looked down at her stout brown shoes. *"When this rationing comes to an end, I'm going to wear stockings every day. I'm going to buy the girls a pair of soft leather sandals too, white ones, the ones they always wore at Easter. Reg used to buy that white shoe dip; it cleaned them up a treat. And I'll dig out those pink flowered curtains; they're about the only ones I didn't cut up for dresses."*

"I take that as a no then? The cards?"

Norma's eyes opened wide. *"Oh, sorry! I think I'll go back outside. And Lizzie? Thank you for being such a good friend. What the ------? Blimey, those children are making a racket out there, and we've still to give out their new mugs and liquorice sticks. I'm off into the fray then. I know I should count my blessings; some have lost everything. I'm not alone- never will be, not with four daughters. Are you joining us?"*

"I'll be with you in a mo." She pulled her cardigan off the back of the chair and wrapped it around her shoulders.

Norma gave her a strange look, for it was baking hot outside. *"Alright Lizzie?"*

"Yes love, a sudden shiver that's all. Think someone just walked over my grave."

"Well… if you are quite sure?"

"Yes, now get yourself outside. It sounds as if their murdering each other out there."

"TTFN then."

"Tara for now luv."

Lizzie just wanted a few moments to herself. Scorning the tea pot, she reached for the bottle of parsnip wine. It was a treat to stand at the window looking out. No more black-out curtains, thank goodness. The May sunshine beamed into the windows, glancing off her thick specs and momentarily blinding her. Wiping her watering eyes, she tutted at the streaks of dust exposed by the glare. A job for later, she mused, but not today. Today was special, to be savoured, remembered. There are the Thompsons, music blaring from the open doorway, little Jack sitting on the step mauling a mangy looking ginger cat. There's Bill Buckley in his element, performing a jolly tune on his squeeze box, swaying along the long line of red-faced kiddies, who, jammed together at the tables, elbow to elbow, who are wriggling and prodding and squealing in excitement. This is a good day.

Sipping the amber liquid, savouring the heat as she swallowed, she thought back over the years. What would her mam and dad have thought of Hitler and this war? How old would Dorothy Anne be now? What a comfort she would be to her now. Why Lord? Why did you take my daughter from me? She sighed. It wasn't to be. And she'd lost Jack her old man too, not long after. He was a grafter, a bit too fond of his booze, like many of the men back then. A twelve-hour day, then off to the pub, before finally back to the missis. Still, he never strayed, and if she kept her tongue quiet when he staggered home then he was no trouble really. She'd learnt early on in the marriage that he wouldn't abide her giving him lip about another cold dinner left on the side. He had been a good provider, a good dad. Dorothy Anne was always tucked up in her bed by the time he made his way home. She was none the wiser that her wonderful father was inclined to deal out an occasional slap to her mother. The booze had finished him off- a sudden heart attack- gone like the flick of a light switch. He'd left the house to her in his will, not much else but it had provided an income; she was never short of lodgers. And during this war, the house, still standing thank the lord, had welcomed the new breed of women, who were suddenly independent and enjoying the autonomy of earning a man's wage. Ruby was the present one.

Dear dad, in his starched white collar and trousers pressed to a knife edge, a Sunday chapel goer, evening sinner, —what would he have thought of the goings on? He'd been in the WWI. Like many, he had hoped it would be the last.

What a terrible, wicked loss of young lives, so many fine young men, and it hadn't stopped with them had it? No, the bombing of the home front; families, kiddies, women, the elderly, blown to kingdom come; concentration camps all over Europe. She stretched her neck to get a better look out of the window, caught the gaze of Bert and gave him a nod and a wave. *"Look at them all, God in heaven, it's a miracle we weren't all trampled under the Nazi jackboots."*

What would happen to them all now? The newspapers warned the country would be bankrupt after this war and there were five million men and women waiting to be de-mobilised back into civvy street. Gawd, it didn't seem possible. Did that mean the women would be forced to give up their jobs in the factories? Of course, it did. It was a man's world still.

Change! One certainty in this life—that and death- couldn't be avoided.

Where will I and my friends be in a year from now? There was Norma and her four girls, and Reg? Who knew? Perhaps it was a good thing that Norma hadn't sat for a reading today, although…

Then there were Frances and Joseph. Well, he was back home. He had almost lost his leg, but he'd done his bit. Thank God he'd been spared.

Ruby? Although she'd never set out to hook up a husband from the Yanks like some, well, she did, and was set on a new life with John Parker overseas.

And the rest of them? Who knew better than she, from her years of predicting and reading the signs, that even when the cards and crystal ball forewarned and hinted, fate was only a small part of it? People were unpredictable, often setting themselves on a totally different course to the one they'd set their heart on. Sometimes she grew weary of the many expectant pleas to tell the future, of offering sensible advice, always having the answers. Hadn't she always bore this responsibility, this gift of foresight which at times was a burden? But cards or not, for some reason her senses had always been overstrung, highly tuned to another dimension; it was who she was. From a young scrawny motherless girl with about as much grace as the last wall flower to be offered a dance; she'd had to learn to manage and shoulder this responsibility.

Well just for today, this glorious day, she was going to let her hair down and enjoy herself. Just for today, she was going to snatch at this moment in time and stop trying to put everything right for others.

A raucous shout from number 10 interrupted her musings, *"Come on gal, get moving, join the merry throng!"* It was Bill Wilson, the local milkman, seemed he'd started the celebrations earlier than most, or carried on from last night. He made his way over to her doorstep, his marked limp causing him to lurch one sided like an injured crab. *"Got 'some-fink' for you duck".* He winked.

"Oh," Lizzie waited. He handed her a brown paper bag. She peeped inside. *"Beetroot."* He said proudly. *"The first lot from the allotment."*

"Oh, thank you Bill, how lovely. I've a drop of vinegar I can steep them in after they're boiled, haven't had a bit of beetroot for ages."

"Say no more luv, we have to look after our own." He tipped his cap and turned.

"Bill? Leg giving you some jip, is it?" she asked, concerned.

"Can't complain. Joining the throng?"

"Try and stop me," she laughed.

There was one thing she was going to do first! She was going to clear out her hidey hole under the stairs. Grunting in exertion, she worked clumsily in the gloom under the stairs, haphazardly slinging out almost any item that came to hand. As was her habit, she voiced her annoyance and thoughts out loud, whether there was a recipient to hear her or not. *"Oooo, ow, I should have a torch under here somewhere. Broom, well, it's seen better days; mop bucket; gazunder? well, I won't be needing that anymore, wonky stool. Half a packet of humbugs? Well, I never, how long have they been there? I'll have one of them later."*

A crocheted throw and a bit of old carpet followed, joining the chaotic heap behind her. So engrossed in the long overdue tidy up she didn't hear anyone come in behind her.

" Cooeee! Can I come in?"

No answer.

Frances leant forward, bellowed into the darkened space that enclosed Lizzie. *"Hello? What are you doing?"*

Startled, the older lady shot upwards, cracking the back of her head on the door frame. *"Gawd, I'm seeing stars."*

Frances giggled. *"Sorry to frighten you Lizzie, but whatever are you up to?"*

"You don't sound very sorry," moaned Lizzie.

"Oh, come on. Why are you doing this now? it's beautiful out there, and I've come to join in the celebrations. Joe's outside, and we've brought ginger beer. It's so hot and the kiddies are having a lovely time. Bill Buckley is playing that old accordion again, and they're trying to organise a three-legged race for the adults, want to do it with me?"

Lizzie raised an eyebrow. *"Me? Don't be daft. Come on in then and mind your step. I'm looking for my blinking gas mask. It is going on the bonfire, and jolly good riddance, I will never put one of those things on my face again, ever! The smell of the rubber, I could never abide it."* She scratched her head. *"Can't think what I've done with it."*

Frances helped her straighten up. *"Leave it for now. Come on, hurry."* She pulled a hairbrush from her handbag. *"Here, quickly, comb your hair, then we can join the others."* Making a dash in front of the parlour mirror Lizzie pulled the brush through her new Toni home perm, carefully tweaking the frizzing curls, avoiding the tender bump that was growing bigger at every second. She patted and twirled the ends of her hair proudly. *"Do you like it?"*

Frances tilted her head, considering. *"Did Betty Brown do it for you?"*

Lizzie turned, *"Yes, she always does a good job."*

Frances avoided making a straight answer. *"Ruby and John Parker are waiting. You'll want to see what he's brought along for the kiddies, and Ruby had some news."*

Lizzie gave her a knowing glance. *"I have an inkling about Ruby's news."*

Frances pulled on Lizzie's arm, impatient to be outside.

"Just a jiff." Reaching into her pantry Lizzie grabbed a jar and plopped a splodge of Vaseline onto the back of her head and rubbed it in." *Ouch."*

Frances opened her mouth wide. *"Know about Ruby?"* She sighed, *"Of course, why am I surprised?"* Then thoroughly impatient and exasperated, she gave a moan, *"Oh Lizzie, whatever are you doing?"*

"It's good stuff. It will dull the pain; you gave me a fright; I nearly knocked my brains out."

"Ready Lizzie?" For a second Lizzie turned as if she'd forgotten something. *"What now?"* Frances rolled her eyes, found herself giving Lizzie a gentle push over the doorway. *"Mind the step,"* she said, feeling a small stab of guilt at her impatience.

Lizzie stepped out, raising her hand over her brow, shielding her eyes from the strong sunlight. *"Oh lore."* The bright rays reflected on the thick lenses of her round glasses, giving her an- other worldly air. Leaning on the door mantle to steady herself she attempted to give John an explanation. *"I've been under the stairs too long, you see John."*

He gave her a quick smile. How the heck did he answer that? Stepping forward, he opened his hands. *"Here you both are, at long last."*

Lizzie patted her hair, waiting for a compliment. He gave the old lady a questioning glance, what was that stuck on the top of her head? Frances gave him a sideways glance, smiled, made a silent shush with pouted lips. John raised an eyebrow and took the hint. He had a soft spot for this odd lady Ruby had such an attachment to.

Lizzie took off her spectacles, wiping her watering eyes with an immaculately laundered handkerchief. Before she knew what was happening, Ruby dived on her, knocking her specs out of her hand.

"Gawd Ruby, my goggles, don't break them; can't see a thing without them. Here, let me sit down a second; you clamped onto me like a carpenter's vice. You've crushed the air from my poor old lungs."

John bent quickly and handed Lizzie her glasses. *"Ma'am."*

Ruby stepped back. *"Oh, I'm sorry Lizzie, it's just that I can't wait to tell you."*

Lizzie caught hold of Ruby's hand. *"Alright duck, we'll have a conflab later."* Ruby nodded. Lizzie smiled up at John. *"Packing up, are you? At the base? You boys going home soon?"*

"We still have some loose ends to tie up yet ma'am---There's some finishing off in the east—but yes---soon, I hope." He gave a weary sigh. *"Home, sure sounds good. We should be shutting up shop very soon. I'm only-----well----."* He turned. It was Norma. Catching sight of Francis and Ruby, she pushed a plate piled high with multi-coloured iced cakes into Mary's hands and bounded over, giggling like a schoolgirl, *"Oh, it's bloody marvellous to see you all together."*

The look of surprise on their faces brought her to a sudden stop. Lord! Tears this morning; one moment up, the next down, then charging at them as if she hadn't seen them for months. She reddened. *"Sorry, I don't know what's got into me."* But she did; everything was changing, the times they'd all shared together were coming to an end, and there was more than a fair chance she'd find herself a widow. Ruby was off to America, Frances had her Joseph home, Eliza had the support of her mam and dad and the farm, and not forgetting her very considerable charms to help her over the loss of Tommy. As plain as a church mouse, Reg had always made her feel special; yes, she had her daughters, but when well-meaning friends pointed this out, she wanted to poke 'em in the eye! She was scared. Her moods were up and down like the kid's yo-yos. Could be 'the change' but she didn't want to acknowledge that possibility, not yet, so she pushed the thought away.

John coughed. What is it with these Brits?

"Been at the parsnip wine Norma?" laughed Ruby. Norma blushed. *"Ah, I'm only joking,"* apologised Ruby. *"Come, sit here with us."* She tapped an empty chair beside her, empty because one of the legs were rickety. *"You look done- in."* Norma lowered herself down tentatively as the chair rocked unsteadily beneath her.*" A bit,"* she acknowledged.

"Aye up," cried Lizzie, her brown eyes shining. Norma's abrupt entrance jolted her memory. *"I have an idea. Here, John? When you Yanks clear off--- I mean go back to the States--- I don't suppose you'll be taking your furniture and stuff back overseas?"*

Ruby was aghast. *"Lizzie?" What was she up to?"* She shrugged her shoulders, looked at John, *"Hell, I don't know where this is going."*

John raised his eyebrows. *"Well --- I -----"*

Lizzie jumped in. *"I mean, I believe you have a piano over there---- at the base? From what Ruby tells me? And I know someone who is very keen to buy one for their daughter."*

Norma reddened.

John scratched his head, paused. *"I believe we can help you out ma'am."*

At long last. The tables were cleared and returned to their rightful owners. There may be a little to put right in the morning, but it could wait. Ruby, Frances and Norma sat in companionable silence. They had been through too much together to feel the need for constant chit chat, especially when all they needed right now was a little time to reflect and relax.

Norma, for one, was more than glad to have a few minutes to herself; tugging off each shoe she stretched her feet in front of her and rubbed her ankles. *"Excuse me ladies. Oh, this is heaven. Well, we gave the little blighters a good party, and the spread wasn't too poor either."*

They both nodded. *"Mmm."*

The street was almost empty now. It had an air of quiet forlornness; apart from the distant voices of the few stood around the bonfire on the waste ground, relit for a second day, there was little to remind them of the occasion. Frances coughed. The smoke drifted slowly on the still air. Despite being low on wood and paper, the fire was still burning, although not so intense. It was very probable that some would regret their impulsive discarding of nick-nacks in the morning.

Frances glanced down at her watch, hanging loose on her slender wrist- 8.00pm. She glanced at Ruby's new roundness of stomach and her heart lurched with a sudden longing. Despite their love and closeness there was still no sign of a 'little un' for her and Joseph. Maybe God felt she had been given enough of his blessings; hadn't her husband survived and returned home to her despite all the odds against it? She sighed, sweeping her long hair up and off the back of her neck.

It was still wonderfully warm, and the ghost of today's revelries had left a vibration of sadness all around. It was if the earth was reminding them that the end of hostilities was still not completely over. A brief respite, Churchill said.

How she adored living here in this little home place, with its community. She never wanted to move away into the countryside like some. No! She and her Joe would build up their little business, amongst their friends and neighbours, watch the children grow, and perhaps, one day, have a few of their own. A son for Joseph who could help his dad out in the store; Joe would need help.

 The doors and windows in the street were wide open. The children, exhausted and satiated with cake and jelly, were tucked up in their beds; the older ones bribed with a comic or two. Norma's girls each had a Bunty, a Dandy or Beano, whilst Mary was engrossed in a copy of 'Gone with the Wind'. It had been slipped into her satchel by her very best friend Marjorie Peacock, who saw herself as frightfully sophisticated and too mature for comics.

 John sat on the step of a nearby house, his long legs stretched out in front of him. He was engrossed in a lively debate with Alf Higgins from three doors down, speculating if and how the Japs could be brought to heel. Every now and then John would take a furtive glance at the strange apparel Alf wore on his head. A retired coalman, he still wore his close-fitting leather skull cap, a necessary protection for the many years he'd humped coal on his back through the terraced houses into their backyards. It was still attached to a long flap hanging down his back, which had protected him from the weight of the sacks. When he wanted to strengthen a point, he pulled the cap off and waved it above him. It was rumoured that he slept in it!

Ruby lit up and passed a cigarette to Frances. There was an easy silence between them as they shared it back and forth. Norma had moved herself a couple of feet away, sitting on her front step, so she could listen in to her girls. Lizzie weaved her way up and down the street, chatting with the few who weren't quite ready to settle back in doors.

Old Thomas Zackery had dragged his rocking chair outside. Drawing deeply on his pipe, he wasn't going to dwell on the hell of the last few years; he'd given up trying to make sense of it all. His lad had gone down with his merchant ship in the early years of the war when the German U Boats were hunting in packs. His only sister and her four kiddies had been taken in the last few months of 1944 when the Nazis had launched a tirade of VIs on the southeast coast. A widower for many years, he was the only one left from his family; he was going to savour every taste and smell and sight of these celebrations. Winston had cautioned there was still difficulties ahead, so he was going celebrate and be damned. Squinting against the sun he waved to Lizzie and raised his pipe.

"I've been saving this wedge of baccy for a day like this, never thought it would come." She stopped and handed him a wedge of home-made toffee wrapped in greaseproof paper. *"Here Tom, get your jaws around this, it's my last piece."*

Joseph had turned in. He'd been helping out with a few other blokes from early in the morning and his leg was giving him jip. Knowing he was lucky to keep it, didn't always make things easier. What was lucky about being lame, for pity's sake? Tonight, it was bloody painful; it was grinding him down. He hoped it would be easier in the morning after a night's rest. But then, if he was honest, it wasn't only his leg that gave him trouble; in the darkness he still found himself straining to hear the footsteps, back in time, injured and hiding from the Gestapo, in dread that someone had 'broken'- betrayed them. He fears he will never be right, whatever right is. He'd tried to hide the pain to Frances, the last thing he'd wanted was to spoil the day for her; he adored his wife.

Declining the offer of a cigarette from Ruby, Norma disappeared into her house. She emerged a few minutes later, balancing a tray with three mugs of tea. Frances reached out and grabbed the flowered cup, handed it to Ruby, then took the tray from Norma and placed it down on the step at the side of them. She explained, *"I'll have mine in a jiff, it's a bit too hot for me."* Ruby handed her a half- smoked cigarette, *"Want to finish this off Frances?"* Frances nodded an affirmative and Ruby handed her the cigarette. *"Oooo, this isn't one of our self-rolled ciggies, it's lovely."* She took a long drag and inhaled the smoke deeply, then offered it back to Ruby, who took a quick drag then tossed it into the kerb. Apart from the tea, nothing further passed through their lips for a good five minutes, sipping the hot brown liquid gratefully. They were all lost in their own thoughts and wanderings of future possibilities. Norma was the first to break the silence.

"Oh, would you just look at that." She pointed upwards to the sky above, a glorious orange and red blaze. *"My Reg calls this the golden hour, just before sunset. I wonder where he is now. It doesn't seem right somehow, me celebrating and him God knows where."*

"I know darling." Ruby squeezed her friend's hand. What would she say? What could she say? How did she answer her? It would be wrong, and an insult too, to offer platitudes. Norma was right to be concerned. John had told her some terrible stories about the Japanese army and their fierce warrior contempt of prisoners. She looked sideways at Frances; their eyes locked. The words unsaid, sat like a third person between themselves and Norma.

Norma looked from one to the other. Their discomfort irritated her. *"You're my best friends, you don't have to tiptoe around me. I know how it is."*

Frances looked down at her feet, couldn't meet her challenge. Ruby took hold of the 'baton'. *"Alright then, I won't bugger about. I would be as worried as you Norma. But there is no easy answer, is there? For the last six years we've all lived with uncertainty, death, and we've got through it all somehow. It's no different now, not really. If one wears a hair shirt and stays in bed all morning, what does it achieve? You have been strong throughout all of this, you still are. I'm not going to preach that you should be thankful that the girls are safely through it, you must be sick of hearing that. I can't make any promises, I wish I could. But what I will say, is that you aren't on your own; we have your back, just as we've always done. Come on, I've one cigarette left, you can have it."*

Norma whipped out her cigarettes. *"Have one of mine."* She attempted a smile, a mechanical widening of the mouth that had little or no connection with her heart. *"Ere should you be smoking?"*

Ruby pulled a face, *"Bloody hell, word gets around like wildfire! No ta, you have it."*

Frances gazed at them both thoughtfully. If she were pregnant with Joseph's baby, she wouldn't be sharing that fag. It couldn't be good for the little one, surely? Still, Ruby was Ruby, she had her own way of doing things. *"The truth is Norma darling you have to hold on tight. I had constant nightmares about Joe, he was missing presumed dead for nearly two years. There were many who thought I was crazy, some even told me so, but I never gave up hope. Sometimes I did wonder myself, you know? Was I losing my mind? And then, one night he just 'sort of appeared'. Sitting on my bed he was, as large as life, like the genie in the lamp had finally given me my wish."* Frances sighed. *"I was so alone during that time. I know we all had each other, but I needed my man. I totally understand where you're coming from. I always felt guilty too, you know, if I went to the pictures, had a nice time. You mustn't give up hope."* She looked at Norma, the lights in her eyes were dull, weary. She remembered how it was when friends tried to reassure her with glib cliches when Joe was missing. Good intentions or not, she'd always had an urge to poke them in the eye.

Norma took a deep drawer on the cigarette and handed it sideways; Ruby waved it aside. Norma threw it down and ground it under her heel. *"Right! Enough. I don't want to put any more of a damper on the day. Don't know what's got into* me these past couple of days. Reg would be first in line for the celebrations if he was here. Old Churchill pulled us through, didn't he? And if I know him, he'll carry on until the jobs finished. He's a stubborn old bugger. And I can be too."

"*That's the spirit!*" cried Ruby. "*Wasn't he marvellous? I had goosebumps when I heard Winston's speech. What was it he said? 'We must allow ourselves a brief period of rejoicing, and then let us not forget the toils and effort that lay ahead. Japan, with all her treachery and greed, remains unsubdued.' Magnificent.*"

"*Yes, it was some speech,*" said Frances. "*I think we should be drinking something stronger that a cup of Rosie Lee. What do you think, ladies?*"

"*I guess. But I wasn't going to have an alcoholic drink until my Reg is home.*"

"*Oh Normaaaa!*" they chorused.

Their squeals brought on a fierce irritation, but she didn't have the energy to justify herself. "*Just one then.*"

An unexpected kiss on the back of Ruby's neck caused her to fly around, ready to give someone a mouthful for their cheek. Her voice was sharp. "*Lieutenant John Parker. You gave me a fright!*"

"*Sorry honey*", he drawled in his lazy American accent.

Ruby's voice softened. "*You big ape.*"

"*I heard the request. Something stronger? I think I can help you out with that.*"

Out of nowhere Lizzie shot forward, like a ball out of a cannon. *"I'll fetch some glasses."*

Norma guffawed. *"Blimey Lizzie, have you got bats ears or something?"*

Lizzie nodded. *"Something like that."*

Ruby gave her auburn hair a side sweep and patted her stomach. *"I'll just have a tiny drop please John."*

He leant over her shoulder and placed a kiss on her forehead. *"Would you rather have some candy?"*

Frances craned her neck. She raised her eyebrow, caught Ruby's eye, *"Candy?"*

"I've been eating barley sugar Fran, you know, for the morning sickness." She twisted around to John and reciprocated his affection, planting a long, drawn-out kiss, full on his lips. Ruby had never been shy of expressing her emotions. *"No thanks darling, a small drop of something special will be lovely. I'm sure it won't do any harm. We've all waited so long for something good to happen. So, let's celebrate."*

Giving a triumphant smile, he held a bottle up for their approval.

Frances was aghast. *"French brandy! Oh, my giddy aunt!"*

John looked puzzled. *"Giddy aunt?"*

They all laughed. *"Just a saying John,"* chortled Frances, *"don't ask us to explain it."*

"French brandy? Yes please," they chorused.

"My Joe will be sorry he missed this," grinned Frances.

"It can't be as potent as Lizzie's parsnip wine," giggled Ruby.

Lizzie stuck her chin out. "*I'll 'ave you know that my parsnip wine has helped us through more than a few sticky situations.*"

John stood tall in front of them, looking from one to the other. "*Yes sir, only the best for you girls. So? here we go. Hold your glasses up ladies. Say when?*"

He poured the golden amber liquid into their glasses, and it splashed onto Lizzie's outstretched hand. She popped her fingers into her mouth. "*Waste not want not, I don't think I've ever tasted real French brandy, it tastes sweet, a bit fruity.*"

Norma held her glass up in front of her, sniffed the glass. "*Don't suppose one will harm.*" She grinned widely, "*It smells lovely and spicy.*"

"*I used to pinch me mam's cooking sherry when I was a nipper,*" smiled Lizzie. "*She always blamed my dad. I can't think why because he was a strict chapel goer.*" Her brown eyes took on a faraway look. "*The Lord took her early when I was still a girl; I've never stopped missing her.*"

John looked at Ruby. "*Cooking sherry?*"

"*It's a rough sherry, we use it in our fruit cakes, for celebrations, Christmas, weddings, and christenings.*"

"*Oh. Well, I hope this is as good as your cooking sherry Lizzie? I'm sorry we don't have any ice, but I believe it's not something you Brits have a taste for anyhow- cold drinks.*"

"What? Water this beautiful brandy down John? That would be sacrilege!" cried Norma. She took another tentative sip. "Although it does make feel rather hot."

"I think we should all make a toast!" cried Ruby. "Who's going first?"

"Me!" Norma jumped to her feet. "To the safe return of all our soldiers overseas."

They chorused together, "Cheers!"

Ruby stood. "To Frances and Joseph's new business venture. To the success of their hardware and ironmongery shop."

"Cheers!"

"And lastly," shouted Lizzie, "To Ruby and John's new life in America, and good health to the little baby they're expecting."

"Cheers."

"Oooo!" cried Lizzie, "Don't let's forget- let's all raise our glasses to Churchill and King George."

"Cheers! To Churchill and King George!"

CHAPTER 2

Joanie tugged her apron over her head, smoothed the wisps of her hair from her forehead and had a quick peek in the mirror. Fifty years old, and didn't she feel it! The finish of her 'monthly friend' and the start of hot flushes during the night, meant that some mornings she was wearier than when she'd climbed into her bed. Now her old man, Arthur was a good fourteen years her senior, but he never stopped. Always on the go was Arthur, especially since their lad Gordon had been discharged from the RAF--- when was it? About ten months ago now. That day she'd seen the state of his hands for the first time, she'd almost fainted! The burns had healed up to a point. They'd done the best for him at the specialised burns unit, nevertheless, she hadn't expected him to be in such a mess; scarred skin, stiffness maybe; not ugly stumps of skin and bone in place of his once beautiful fingers. She'd thought her heart would stop.

He'd talked to his dad about it mostly, wanting to spare her the details, but Arthur filled her in later on. How they'd dragged him out from the plane, and at first, he thought he'd got away lucky, and then, it hit him, the stench of burnt flesh. Looking down he saw the skin hanging in shreds from his hands. How come he couldn't feel any pain? He remembered starting to shake violently, and then he'd blacked out. Shock, a killer in its own right! He'd been treated with other severely burned airmen in their own little unit away from the main hospital. Brave young men, with their war over, desperately wondering what the future held.

Joanie had begged him to confide in her, and when he did, she almost wished she hadn't. *"I'm so sorry; I didn't visit you!"* she wailed. *"Why ever didn't you tell me and your dad? All alone, with this pain? I didn't have a clue. Oh son, it must have been a terribly lonely time for you."*

"Mum, listen to me. This is exactly why I wouldn't let James tell you. The nurses would have written you a letter if I'd asked them, only I couldn't cope with your distress as well as my own. Many of the chaps had horrific facial burns too. Can you imagine the terrible shock they experienced on waking to find themselves so disfigured? It's one thing to have this awful damage to a body, but to a young man in his prime, to find himself without a nose? Or the side of his face melted? I'm telling you mum; we couldn't have coped with visitors."

"Oh, I see." Joanie's voice quavered; she was offended. *"Gordon, I can't see how a visit from those who loved you would have hurt. Your father and I were worried sick. Surely family would have helped?"*

"No. The nurses were our family. I had to come to terms with what happened and seeing you and dad upset would have made things more difficult. Don't forget, we are all young men. Some of the chaps were, are, very brave men, much more than me." He sighed. *"I suppose our youth and arrogance pulled us through, and we didn't want pity, that was the last*

thing we needed. And of course, they made a few allowances that we wouldn't normally have had on a routine ward."

Joanie raised an eyebrow, *"And what were they?"*

Gordon had laughed. *"Concessions. A regular, on tap, supply of beer. Yep. And a piano and radio. Nothing was too good for us mum, we were spoilt. Being nursed and treated together, meant that we weren't stared at like freaks. We were still a part of the fighting fraternity which was so very important to our self-respect. A couple of our chaps went back up in the air again."*

"Beer? What with medication? I would have thought bed rest would have been the best treatment?"

Eventually he tired of her eager interrogation, he took a deep breath to manage his irritation, but his words still came out abruptly.

"Now listen up mum. I'm not going to make a habit of chewing over these times. My war is over, done."

Joanie blinked. *"I thought it's good, to talk, you know, to your mum. You can tell me."*

"Telling won't help. Not for me anyway. It's like this: some poor buggers didn't make it, and some did."

"I see."

He relented. *"Sorry about the language mum, but really; coming up to discharge I thought long and hard about civvy street. Since design and engineering are no longer a practical option, I settled to take up the teaching profession. It was good enough for dad, and good enough for me. It provided dad with a long and respectable working life; he always provided well for us, didn't he? His family? Some of the chaps in the burn's unit have useful connections, and with the support of the head doctors and the RAF psychological services, I believe I'm sufficiently recovered, physically and mentally. I'm ready to take on the challenges of taking on a rowdy, probably undisciplined class of lads. I mean, they are bound to be a handful, it goes without saying."*

She'd sensed her son's overconfident air didn't somehow match what he was truly feeling. His hands were shaking, and he warned her. *"I don't intend to waste time brooding. My futures in front of me and I plan to embrace it."*

Joanie wasn't so sure of her son's choice, he hadn't inherited his father's genteel nature, or his patience. He had a quick mind, she'd give him that, but he'd always been more of a 'doer'. Still, he'd made his choice, only time would tell, and she admired his dogged determination to take life back on fully, instead of wallowing in self-pity like some. It would be good if he had a nice girl to see him through the ups and downs that would inevitably face him. His disability and the mastering of a career he may not be particularly suited to, would not make it easy settling back into civilian life. She believed he would make a decent, reliable husband, and she would feel so much better if he married. He hadn't inherited his father's tall lean build. He featured her side, the Simpsons, stocky and sandy haired, but he was a decent lad, kind, good natured.

As for Frances? Well, Frances's husband, Joseph, was home now, and even a blind fool could see how happy they both were, and busy starting up a new business together. Gordon had held a light for that young lady since his early teenage years, only Frances had never held any romantic notions for him, other than valuing their friendship. Thank goodness he'd finally seen the light and had the sense to keep his distance from them both. Before Joseph and Gordon had been called up, there was always a rivalry between the pair of them, and Frances hadn't really helped at the time, silly madam.

Now James, her other son? He was a different kettle of fish- tall, lean, deep! She had no idea whose side that came from. It was difficult enough gaging what was going on inside that lad's head before the war. On his last leave, well, he'd been stubbornly unforthcoming to any motherly enquiry about his doings. Arthur had warned her, *"Stop picking at him Joanie, let the lad be. We don't know what he's been through, or what he's seen. Leave things be."*

All he would say was the RAF weren't ready to discharge him yet; he would be staying on in the service for the foreseeable future. Very hush hush! But it hurt her to be shut out. After such a long stretch away, she'd been keen to spending some time with her sons. She had an inkling that his dad knew a bit more than he was letting on too and it annoyed her. On this occasion Arthur wouldn't share the information with her.

So be it! She took a deep breath, glanced around the kitchen. She tried to remind herself- be thankful for small mercies. It was very quiet in there? She shouldered the door and burst into the parlour.

"Chess! I should have known. All my lovely food is getting cold."

Gordon dropped his chess piece, startled by her noisy appearance. *"Blimey mam, you gave me a start. I hope you don't mind, I'm not really very hungry. Heavy head, you know? I'm still a little jaded after last night's celebrations. Victor Brown was very generously filling our glasses with that home brew of his. I think it was a bit stronger than I realised."*

Arthur's brow furrowed. *"No son. We'll not be wasting good food that your mother's prepared, particularly on the back excess alcohol."* He turned to Joanie. *"I'm sorry mother, we were rather lost in the game. Give us a minute to wash up and we'll be at the table."*

Joanie frowned. Why did he always insist on calling her mother when the lads were around?

Gordon protested. *"But dad, I don't think I could."*

"Your mother's gone to a lot of trouble, come on, be sharp. I could have warned you about Vic Brown's brew, it's had me on my uppers on more than one occasion."

Gordon attempted a weak smile. His stomach lurched. *"This looks smashing, mam."*

Joanie gave a satisfied nod. *"I hope you can do it justice. I queued up for an hour at the butchers. It will be a good day when I can just walk into a shop again without standing in line. Shop, shop! Get washed up then."* She avoided looking down at his hands.

They rolled up their sleeves and scrubbed up under the cold-water tap. *"Mam is still so particular,"* whispered Gordon. *"How am I going to plough through this lot, dad?"*

Arthur gave the table a sideways glance. *"Do your best."*

Gordon reluctantly pulled his chair under the table.

"Here you are," beamed Joanie, *"A good slice of pie, this will put a lining on your stomach."*

Gordon thought it could have the opposite effect. He would have to put on a good show, there was no other way out of it, other than upset mam. Why did women get so affronted when you refused food, as if you were rejecting them personally?

Arthur gave Gordon a conspiratorial wink. *"Dig in son, egg and bacon pie. I bet you didn't have anything like this served up in the Naffi? Here, have some potatoes and pickle."*

He dutifully speared the pie with the prongs of his fork. *"Mm-mm, nice."*

Joanie covertly observed the webbed scarring on her son's hands and wrists. She swallowed hard. To look on helplessly as the food slipped away from his grasp was torture. Nervously, she gave Arthur a quick pleading glance, a signal, *'For goodness' sake, Arthur, please help him! He's struggling.'*

Gordon caught the expression of panic.

"Mam? Please don't fuss. I'm alright with this, really! I've accepted the way things are now. I came out of this war a lot better than some of my 'flying' mates." He tried to lighten the mood. *"Do you know? I lost my eyebrows too, they've never grown back properly, have they? Looks like I've plucked them, like Betty Grable."* He smiled at Arthur. *"Thanks to dad, here, insisting that James and I had a good education, I've managed to find good employment. Things are looking up, don't you think? It's not so awful teaching, although some of the lad's behaviour is a lot to be desired."*

Joanie reddened; she could feel a hot flush coming on again. Rushing over to the window she threw it open, flapping a hanky in front of her face. Keeping her back to them both she carried on in conversation over her shoulder. *"Why don't you try for a post at the local grammar or a privately funded school? You wouldn't have to put up with that nonsense then. Parents paying good money want results, they wouldn't stand for that sort of nonsense."*

"Mother, we've been over this already, ----it's------." He stopped mid flow, raised a quizzical eyebrow.

Arthur held up a warning finger. *"Shush, she's having one of her women's 'doos' again. Don't pay any heed to it, you'll only embarrass her. She has got a point though; it would be easier and more rewarding."*

"No! I'm afraid I don't see it like that at all. When I served in the RAF, I became acutely aware of the class distinction in this country. I want to do something about this dad. I want to help others, from all walks of life, make this country a better and fairer place to live in. Education, what better place to start?"

Arthur placed his hand over his son's. *"Haven't you already done your bit son? Risking life and limb for your country?"*

"No. I did what we all had to do: our duty. Other men were burned worse than me. My mates pulled me out of that plane at great risk to themselves dad, the fuel could have ignited at any minute. I don't believe I was spared to sit back on my laurels. I got off light, believe me. And, while we are on the subject, I may as well tell you. I've joined the Labour party and I shall vote for them in the July elections."

Arthur moved his hand, knocked his fork from the table. *"Is that the reward Mr Churchill deserves for pulling us all through this lad?"*

"He was a wonderful war time leader; I'll give you that dad. Only, you must know how things stand in this country now. His lot are against progress dad! A health service for all—free—can you imagine it? His lot rejected the Beverage Report on welfare, turned their noses up at the 1944 Education Act, and the 11 Plus examination! You were a teacher dad. These kiddies have been through an awful lot. I look forward to a time when there will be opportunities for all of Britain's youth to have an equal chance of a decent education. It's important to me." Gordon's eyes shone. *"A Britain where we can start to do away with our bloody class system. Can you imagine it?"*

Joanie turned, alarmed at Gordon's raised voice.

Arthur refused to react. He coughed politely. *"We should let Mr Churchill finish the job. I do not believe the majority of British people feel the same way, they won't reject him. Why? It would be a shameful betrayal. There is still a lot to be done, as you well know. We still haven't beaten the Japs. Hold your horse's son, wait, give it some thought. That's all I ask."*

Joanie piped up. *"The lad has a right to his opinion, Arthur."*

"Now mother," said Arthur.

Joanie reddened. Why did he insist on calling her mother when the children were around? Sometimes she resented him. She was fiercely aware of her own encroaching years and Arthur was fourteen or so years ahead of her. She wanted to scream at him, sometimes. --- I'm not there yet-don't suck my life away! We are not in the same decade. When I am, I'll powder my face and slick on my pink lipstick and make the most of it. Only now, I will jealously protect the moments of womanhood I still have.

Gordon growled his response. *"I had plenty of time to give it some thought, as you say, when I was stuck on my back in that damn hospital."*

"Enough, both of y'---" cried Joanie, stopping short by a shrill whistle and excited barking.

Keen to move on, Gordon pushed himself forward, and the two of them stretched their necks to see out of the window.

"Oi!" he shouted, *"I'd know that whistle anywhere; Harold you old dodger, what's going on?"*

The elderly gent pulled up sharp. *"Gordon? You're home then! Scoffer's just spotted that mangy Tom cat that's been hanging around, and he's going damn near mad to get at him. He's got him cornered. He'll come off worse, he always does."* Harold hollered again, *"Scooo—ffeeeer-----".*

The unfortunate moggie was hissing and spitting, showing no sign or inclination to retreat. Gordon shot out of the front door waving a chunk of sausage in front of him. *"Here boy, here boy, Scooooffeeer!"*

The scent of the meat was enough to momentarily distract the mongrel… just long enough. Harold caught hold of Scoffer's collar and dragged him away, providing sufficient time for the hissing Tom cat to make his escape by clawing up the fence and making an opportune exit. As Harold turned, his shabby brown overcoat flapped open displaying a pair of corduroy trousers tied up with a piece of string, and a once pale blue shirt missing a button. *"Good to see you lad. Couldn't catch hold of him."*

Joanie despaired. Following her friend Violet's passing two years ago, Harold had made himself a makeshift home in an old caravan. He had, like many, lost all inclination to set up a proper home, especially after being bombed out and losing his wife. Harold's two sons, Eric and Clive, were overseas still with the First British army. She knew they would see their dad right, but it was anybody's guess when they would return home.

She looked on fondly at Gordon making a fuss of the old dog, stroking and petting him. He was completely unaware of the tuts and stares of the few who had been brought out of doors by the noisy spectacle.

Joanie, ever vigilant as ever with anything that remotely involved her son's welfare, noted how Harold suddenly stiffened. It was clear that he'd spotted Gordon's hands and was trying to disguise his shock with mock cheerfulness. It made her heart sore.

"You're back then?" shouted Harold. "And as for you lot? I'm sure you all have homes to go too?" The onlookers slowly dissipated. He straightened his cap and waited. *"I'll be off myself then, although I wish I could say I had a home to go to. Tara for now."*

Joanie's heart went out to him, he looked a lonely old soul. Poor Harold. Well, she wasn't having any of that nonsense. There was enough food on the table for another mouth, and she would never forgive herself if she let him wander off like that. Violet was always the first to help out if anyone was ever in a scrape. Besides, she hadn't caught sight of Harold for a while, and she hadn't seen him at the celebrations either. *"Harold? Where are you going? Come on in and join us for a bit of tea."* Harold's face brightened.

She pointed at Scoffer. *"You'll have to put that hairy beast in the yard while we eat."* Everybody around here was well aware of that dog's reputation for pinching food off the table. *"I'll put some fresh water out for him and find him a few scraps."*

Harold pulled off his cap and folding it in front of him, stepped inside.

Joanie was relieved to have company. The head of the Pickering household, Arthur, was normally a calm, considerate man, content to listen to others' views with consideration and equanimity. But lately, when he and Gordon brought up the subject of politics, it became very heated, and she always ended up with an agitated stomach. She didn't profess to have a keen interest in the workings of the country, staying alive day by day during the past six years had given her enough to think about. Gordon had expressed some strange views since he'd returned from service, and despite Arthur's usual forbearing stance, he was struggling to comprehend his son's point of view. She really didn't want them to fall out. This war had a lot to answer for. She glanced at Arthur. Him being a good- few- years older than her, she was usually happy to defer to his explanations on topics that she considered out of her limited schooling experience. After all, he'd taught at some of the best schools during his teaching career. Only, sometimes, her emotions took a strange turn. She gave him a tentative smile, which he returned. Poor Arthur, still, what he didn't know wouldn't hurt him!

Harold was standing just inside the door, obviously ill of ease, scuffling from one foot to the other. She moved forward. *"Come on Harold. Don't stand on ceremony, we've known each other too long for that. Give me your coat; you can wash your hands in the kitchen."* She gave Gordon a nod. *"Will you take Scoffer outside please love? Give him a bowl of water, and there's a ham bone that I used for the soup yesterday, he can have that."*

Joanie handed Harold a towel. *"Never know what nasties that old cat could have been carrying."* Harold nodded. Arthur smiled, though it disturbed him immensely to see how Harold had deteriorated since Violet had passed. *"Good to see you, Harold. Take a seat."*

Gordon sat beside him. He was surprised, Harold was usually so chipper, but right now the old gentleman seemed a little down at the heel or down on his luck. *"I didn't see you at the street party Harold, everything alright?"*

Joanie bustled between them, handed around the plates. *"Dig in,"* smiled Gordon.

He gave Joanie an embarrassed smile. *"Thank you."* He carefully lifted a slice of pie and some pickle, took a large bite, chewing steadily. *"Well Gordon, the street party?"* He struggled to speak through a mouthful of pastry, *"I did have a wander around, only I've become a bit of a hermit since Violet passed, and the lads being away still. For me, it will be time to celebrate when they are both home safely."*

Joanie handed him a mug of tea. *"I'm going to leave you all to it for a jiff, just remembered something."* She crept out into the yard and closed the door behind her quietly. Scoffer was gnawing on the bone. Sipping her tea, she sat herself down on the stool in the corner of the yard. Aahhh, hot and strong, just what the doctor ordered. The men's voices reached her through the open window. Looking upwards she watched the pale shadows of cloud rolling across a darkening sky, delighting in a fresh breeze blowing up. Closing her eyes for a minute, she made a mental note to bring her washing off the line.

Scoffer's soft whiskers tickling her leg woke her with a start. She must have dropped off. This seemed to be happening rather too much lately. She made a mental note to pop into the herbalist shop a few streets away and treat herself to a tonic wine. She hurriedly smoothed her hair down and spoke softly to the indignant pet who was clearly put out at being left in the wet. He pressed behind her as she opened the kitchen door. Hastily drying off her face with a flannel she gave the old dog a rub down with a clean floor cloth and poked her head around the living room door. *"Want another brew?"*

Arthur frowned. *"Are you alright?"*

"Yes. I closed my eyes for a minute and fell asleep," she laughed. *"And yes, in the rain!"*

Gordon looked up. He loved his mum, always been closer to mum than dad, only he knew her too well, he'd had to draw a line. *"Never say no to a cuppa, mum, I've a thirst for England."*

She quickly scanned the table. Harold was sitting back with his hands across his stomach, Arthur sitting forward listening to the commentator on the radio, and Gordon again softly relating some story to Harold that was making him smile. They'd made short work of the food and she suspected her son had hardly touched his share, although he'd made a show of pushing his food around on his plate.

Returning with the tea, her hands shook as she struggled to put the heavy brown tea pot down on the middle of the table.

Arthur didn't notice, still intent on the news. Harold did. *"Here, let me give you a hand."* She looked into his face and was surprised to see him looking upset.

"Arthur?" queried Joanie." *What's going on?"* He switched off the wireless. *"Going on?"*

Gordon answered softly. *"Harold was telling us about Len Skinner."*

Harold blew his nose on a non-too clean handkerchief. *"He's gone strange."*

Joanie scratched her head, puzzled. *"Whatever do you mean?"*

"Just as I said, he's gone strange. Shell shock or somethin' like that. He only talks in whispers and then stutters so much I can't make head nor tail of what he's saying, it's all very awkward. His missus gets no sleep with him." Harold's eyes rolled. *"He gets these nightmares, terrible they are. Wakes

her up screaming and whimpering---soaked in a cold sweat."* He paused to emphasise the horror and drama.

Joanie knew who he was talking about, the whole street knew, there were few secrets around here. Folding her arms across her chest she gave Harold a stern look. *"Now then Harold. Len Skinner is not the only one to come home the worse for wear, and if I know Constance Skinner, she'll see him right. She's packed in her job at the factory and is hell bent on getting him back to his old self."* She paused. *"Maybe it's a good thing they haven't a family just now."*

Harold wiped his mouth and chin with his grubby handkerchief. *"I'm not so sure he'll mend. Darn it, Joanie! What sort of a life will he have after what he's been through? He's lost his marbles. I've seen it all before, in the last war. He'll be no good to her or himself, poor chap."*

Joanie shook her head. *"No Harold. His words may be slurred, or difficult to recognise, but he can understand well enough. I sit with Leonard when Connie has to pop out on an errand. He's a bit of a sight, I'll warrant that; his trousers are held up with braces and it's as if there's nothing solid inside of them. Connie has to mince his food up like a baby's, he can't manage it otherwise. And you know something? She wouldn't have it any other way; he's back home. She'll nurse him to health; you wait and see. He adores her, sits in that chair holding her hand as if he never wants to let it go."* She wiped a tear away.

Arthur leant forward. *"Now mother, tears won't see us through."* He turned to Harold. *"Harold! He was a prisoner in one of those hell holes in the east until it was bombed by the yanks and rescued. What they found, doesn't stand to be repeated, especially at the tea table. Joanie is correct, I also* believe he'll pull through. If that lad could last two years in that camp, then he's stronger than he looks. A man's strength to survive depends on much more than his physical ability. Hate can carry a person through, and a determination to see justice done."

Harold took another sausage roll. *"Strewth. I hope that's so then. I'd like to see him well, he deserves better."*

Arthur stared ahead, thoughtfully. *"I've sat with him and had a simple game of draughts, not always successfully; he doesn't have the concentration yet."*

Joanie's eyes met Arthur's, then she looked across the table at Gordon and Harold. *"Connie told me a little,"* she whispered, *"They said she needed to understand what her husband had been through."* Harold raised his eyebrows, anticipating. *"No Harold, I'm not going into details. It was an awful place, too terrible for words."*

Gordon spread his hands out on his lap. *"We've all lost someone or something of ourselves in one way or another. Len and me? At least we have a chance of life. I bet he thought he'd never see Blighty or Constance again. And if it wasn't for the chaps risking their own lives to drag me out of that cockpit, then I wouldn't be here, sitting at this table with you. It was damn near minutes from exploding. The surgeon was amazing, grafting my hands, mum."* He gave a slow smile. *"It was darn painful, but the pretty nurses couldn't do enough for me."*

"Anyone in particular?" asked Harold, expectantly.

"Yes, as a matter of fact there was one, a right smasher. But I couldn't ask any girl to pal up with me at the time. I didn't know how things would turn out. it wouldn't have been fair,

what with my hands and all. I mean? What sort of future could a chap like me offer her?"

Joanie plopped her teacup down into the saucer. *"You never mentioned a girl?"*

"Why would I mum? I never walked out with her, and we lost all contact when I moved to another rehab for physio." Gordon paused, looked down at his hands. *"I have thought of her since though. I really do think she liked me."*

"Then why don't you write to her? What was her name?"

Gordon raised his eyebrows in mock horror. *"Here we go, dad. This is why I didn't mention her. Oh, crikey mum, I knew you'd make a big fuss."*

Joanie hmphed, indignant. *"I'm only taking a motherly interest."*

"I can see that. Listen, if you must know; her name is Gwendoline and her family are from Wales, the valleys. Funnily enough, her mother was a teacher like dad, although she never moved on from the local school, I believe."

"Gwendoline?" Joanie clutched her hands together. *"Such a beautiful name."*

"Yes, and she's stunning mum. When the war broke out, she volunteered for nursing. They got her and the other volunteers through their training pretty sharply, soon put them through their paces. What those nurses saw and had to do for us mum, you wouldn't believe."

Arthur gazed steadily at his son. *"A Welsh girl then; and her father?"*

"Yes, he's a miner, reserved occupation."

"A miner's daughter, with an education?"

"Her mam was a teacher don't forget, and she insisted on teaching, even after she married. Gwen's maternal grandfather was a vicar, he always thought his daughter married beneath her. Not the usual miner's family I suppose., but her dad supported his daughter having a good education, wanted to make a point to the old man."

Arthur nodded.

Joanie eyed Gordon over her teacup. "*You seem to know a lot about her considering you never took her out. It sounds as if you were more than pals.*"

Gordon yawned. "*I do, and I didn't.*"

Arthur guffawed; Joanie protested. "*Stop it! What's that supposed to mean?*"

"*It means mam, to answer your question, that I didn't take her out, and I do know her quite well.*"

"*Sounds like you're coming under friendly fire,*" laughed Harold.

"*Some of the nurses returned to the ward when they'd finished their duties and sit with us lads; Gwen was one of them. At the beginning I was in a lot of pain, angry, frustrated! She helped me a lot mam. She read to me; my hands were useless for a long time. She has a beautiful voice. ---- I liked to hear her stories about her community, her family. Her dad was very strict chapel, didn't believe in women wearing makeup, painting, he called it, or drinking any sort of spirits. The pubs in the valleys are not like they are around here; they are for men only."* Gordon rocked back on his chair, gazed out of the window. *"She doesn't need to put slap on her face, she is perfect as she is."*

Joanie gave Arthur a sideways glance.

Harold reached out and helped himself to another sausage roll. *"Her grandfather is a vicar you say?"*

Gordon nodded. *"Yes, that's right."*

"Well, I never. Is this real sausage meat Joanie? Only it tastes so grand. My Violet was a good cook, wasn't she?"

"It's sausage meat mixed with grated carrot and breadcrumbs Harold; it makes it spread a bit further. "

Harold's cheeks bulged. *"Well, it's smashing."* He turned to Gordon. *"If you really like her, I'd get in touch pretty quick, before some other bloke steps forward."*

Gordon eyed him speculatively, considering. Of course, he did have her address, and he had promised to write, but she'd never written to him. Then again, how could she? He'd deliberately forgotten to leave his address for her. He'd been in a strange mood when he'd taken his leave of that hospital. However, things hadn't turned out so badly, not really. His hands had responded fairly well to treatment; they were as good now as they ever would be. He had work. Why ever not, go for it, old chap. He looked across at his father.

"I'll think on it." He wouldn't let on yet; his mam would never give him a minute's peace.

"Just one thing young un."

"What's that Harold?"

"An important one. Can she cook?"

They all chorused together. *"Harold!"*

"Strewth! No need to shout!" He stuck his chin out. *"I'll say it again. I'll own, I'm not a particularly sentimental man like some; like you Arthur, but me an' Violet, we did alright together. Only, at the beginning, the very beginning, well, she couldn't cook for toffee. Said her mam never taught her, can you believe it?"* He paused for effect. *"Said her job as the eldest had been taking care of the little uns in the family."*

"Yes, Your Vi' was the eldest of nine siblings. Her poor mother was never in good health after the last one," sighed Joanie.

"Her poor mother?" Harold was incredulous. *"I was fairly clammed for the first few months of marriage. My own mother had to step up, showed Violet the ropes, so to speak. I must be the only fellow never to have gained weight when newly married."*

"Oh dear," laughed Joanie.

"Drat it, Joanie. What I'm trying to say is, these sorts of things are important. We had more than a few rows, I can tell you." He leant forward. *"Do you know? She made me Yorkshire pudding one Sunday. Carried it in, proud like. I said to her. Ere, there's something wrong with this Vi', it's flat. Not like my mam's. You know what she said to me? 'Well take you and your belly off to your mam's, I'm sick of hearing about it'. That's what I got, yes sir, me a hard-working chap. Turns out, she hadn't put an egg in it! Can you ever believe it?"*

Gordon tried to straighten the smile that was threatening to spread across his face. *"The very thought of it, Harold. When I write----"* He stopped short when he caught Joanie's eager expression. *"If I write----and we do meet up, I'll be sure to ask her, if she can cook."*

Harold nodded. *"If I had my way---"* Scoffer's sudden frantic woofing broke into Harold's protestations, and Gordon was quick to take advantage of the interception.

"Do you know? It's a wonderful evening. Any objections if I take the old chap out for a walk Harold? A stroll along the canal bank should clear my head some. Alright if I leave the table mam? I really couldn't eat another bite."

Joanie nodded. At least Harold had appreciated the spread.

Harold gave a loud belch. *"Beg your pardon! Yes lad, by all means. Only, keep a tight rein on his lead when you reach the rough ground, this time of the evening the wildlife will be about, and he has a penchant for chasing the rabbits. He's not grabbed one for a while --- he's like his owner, getting on in years, and a bit grey around the muzzle."*

"Super." Bending and kissing Joanie on her cheek, Gordon pulled on his cap, and disappeared out of the back door, calling back. *"Just a spot of rain. Thanks Harold, I'll have him back in a couple of hours."*

With Gordon's exit they all relaxed, the tension disappearing from around the table. They listened as Scoffer's eager barking gradually fading away, accompanied by a solitary rendering of *"Run rabbit, run rabbit, run, run, run."*

Arthur loosened his collar. *"He'll be fine, Joanie. Try not to worry; he's a good head on his shoulders. Anyway, time to take ourselves away from the table. Fancy a game of dominoes Harold?"* He gave Joanie a questioning glance for her approval.

"Of course, Arthur, shift yourselves so I can clear this table."

Harold rubbed his meaty hands together. *"Ready for a thrashing again?"*

"Hmmm, we'll see about that. Joining us for a quick game Joanie?"

She couldn't think of anything worse. *"No, thank you. When I've finished the dishes, I'm going to sit in the backyard, and get on with my knitting. Gordon's quite right, just a spot of rain. I think it's stopped. It's a beautiful evening, be a shame to waste it."*

Chapter 3

"Come here—sit with me. It's been a long day." He waited. ---*" Sweetheart?"*

Frances hesitated, swallowed. *"Joseph, I think I'll put a light on the stove, heat up some water--- I need a long soak in the bath before bed."*

Josephs' eyes darkened, hurt. *"Here we go again. Fran? Are you avoiding me? I've hardly set eyes on you all day. You're as slippery as an eel. What is it?"*

She bent her head, pulled out the clips and shook the long black lengths of smoothness loose. *"Give me a minute to put the water on and I'll come and join you. It's just been one of the days."*

He leant back into his chair and waited until his patience ran out. He stood slowly. *"Frances?"* Walking into the scullery he was surprised to find it empty. The pans of water were bubbling away on the stove. Maybe she was out in the yard, it was a warm evening.

He was right. There she was, hidden in the shade of the coal shed, curled up like a little girl, fussing Midnight, who was purring and stretching in ecstasy from her touch. Sensing another presence, the cat shot away; Frances looked up at him, attempted a smile, and failed. Her green eyes were glistening with tears.

"Crikey Fran. What is it?" He leant over her, stooping to take her in his arms he winced as she swiftly leaned away from him. He stepped back, hurt. *"You can tell me anything darling, I won't talk, I'll just listen. It may help."*

Frances wanted to be alone, have some time to think. How could she explain it, didn't want to upset him, didn't understand herself sometimes? She touched his hand. *"Leave me be for a while Joe, please."*

"Right, if that's what you want." He snatched the tin bath from the nail on the outside wall, wobbled awkwardly into the kitchen. *"I'll leave you to it."*

His limp was always more noticeable when he was tired and upset. *"Joe? Darling? I'm sorry. Don't be angry---I've been with Eliza this afternoon. She's not doing so well. The truth is, I'm all over the place. Forgive me? Love me?"* Dropping the protesting cat back onto the chair she followed her husband inside, flinging her arms around his waist and buried her head into the warm safety of his chest. *"Love me?"*

He dropped a soft kiss onto the top of her head, smelt the sweet perfume of her dark hair. *"I'll never not love you."* Wrapping his arms around her tightly he felt her lean into him.

"Oh Joe. Eliza always believed Thomas would come back home. She was so sure of it, used to say he was one of life's lucky ones. It's been two years since his merchant ship went down. What with the nipper to keep her busy she seemed to be getting over it, settling down? Oh Joe, you should see the little one, such a pretty little thing and so like her dad. She has his brown curly hair and cheeky smile. And now? All of this? VE

day, the celebrations? My good friend was breaking her heart, and I couldn't find the words to comfort her."

Although it wasn't only this that was really troubling her, but she couldn't tell him. She was ashamed. Seeing Eliza and hearing her chatter about her children, she'd been resentful. Why couldn't she appreciate the gift she'd been given, three healthy nippers? How she would adore to have a baby in her arms. Why wasn't it happening for her? Hadn't Joe paid his price? His leg had been smashed to bits, and God knows what else he'd been through during his time in France, he stubbornly refused to share it with her.

She remembered Lizzie's words; *'Resentment is a terrible emotion, very destructive, it's dark and will eat you through and through if you give into it.'* Only it was difficult not to feel this way at times, and this afternoon had been one of them. Joseph believed there was a solution to any problem, if it was faced head on. But to find an explanation to their childlessness, it would require a compromise from both of them, and he refused to meet her halfway on this one. All she asked was for him to visit Doctor O'Connor with her, have a chat. He wouldn't budge. Every conversation around the subject ended in same way- retreat and a loss of hope on her part. And this afternoon, resentment was her companion; towards not only Eliza, but him too. Oh, Joseph, why won't you?

Joe pondered. What did he say? What could he say? He realised her distress was not only her inability to comfort her friend. *"Drat it, Frances. I'm not stupid."* He rubbed the back of his neck. *"We can't go on like this."* He sighed. *"Eliza will cope in one way or another. Only, at this moment, I'm more concerned about us. Maybe we'll go and talk to the GP."*

Frances raised her head, *"Joe?"*

"Come on love. I saw your face when you held that toddler on your lap earlier."

How could he tell her? Tell her of his guilt. Hid by the Resistance whilst his injuries slowly healed, he'd become close to them, and one of their number, Collette, had offered him more than food and medication. They had comforted each other. Perhaps this was God's punishment for his unfaithfulness. Maybe it was something he'd picked up? Only he'd had a medical before discharge from the ranks, everything had been in working order, well, other than his leg.

"Joe? You promise?"

"Yes. I promise. Now then, let's get the bath filled and you can have a long soak. I'll sit here, by the side of you and keep you company whilst you tell me all about it." He gave her a hankie. *"Here, sort yourself out and I'll tip the water in."*

She quickly stripped down to her under slip and dipped her toe into the water. *"Strewth Joe. Anymore and the water will tip over the sides when I climb in."* Tugging off her slip she lowered herself down into the water. *"OOO, lovely."*

He pulled up a stool ---" *It's a shame in a way. You know--- What you were saying? Going in for another kiddy, what with all ready having the twin lads and all? With Thomas away she already had her hands full. I mean; Tommy will never see little Mary Rose, will he?"*

"No. The last one wasn't planned, Joe. That last leave they shared together? You know--- When he jumped ship? That's when Mary Rose was conceived. Those last few days they had, those memories? They will stay with her forever. She believes that little Mary Rose is a blessing, a comfort given to her from the Almighty. It was Tommy's time. At least when he had the official leave, when we had that little get together at Lizzie's, all of us neighbours---just before you came home? That's when he heard that their little romantic interlude, when he jumped ship? ---that he'd made Eliza pregnant. He was so proud Joseph. He returned to his ship and his duties looking forward to better times. Two days after that second leave, his ship was blown to smithereens, right out of the water. A nearby naval vessel picked up a few survivors. As we all know, he wasn't one of them. His luck had run out. He's with his mates, at the bottom of the North Sea."

Joe trickled water down her back. *"Among the many other brave souls Fran. Many of those merchant ships were old rust buckets. They were poorly equipped, wouldn't stand a chance from a direct hit. They took many losses, and Britain would have been in dire straits without them, they carried what we needed to keep up the fight, and food?* We could have starved without them too. *In my book, they are the heroes, not only the Royal Navy, with their shiny buttons and top draw accents."*

"Yes, I think so too. Only, she was inconsolable today. Her mam and dad are at their wits end. I mean really, they thought she'd settle down again, once the celebrations were over. It's two weeks since VE day and she still hasn't picked herself up.

We all know how fond Sam and Kathleen were of their son-in-law too, I'm sure they were thinking of him on VE day, and the boys? Hopefully they will remember something of their father; it's all so sad."

She turned quickly. *"Oh Joe, how could I have been jealous of her today? When she was crying! Because I was. I resented the fact that she had three children, and me none. What a cow I am."*

He leant forward over the ridge of the bath. He didn't answer her. It was maybe time for him to tell her, only not now. *"Sit forward pet, I'll wash your back."*

Closing her eyes, she slipped under the water. It sucked in around her; its silky warmth held her close.

"Leave it a minute. Joe? Will you be a darling and tip in another saucepan, before it gets cold?"

"Anything to oblige." He poured in the water, testing it first with his finger.

"The thing is? Seeing her like that? It brought it all back to me. The two years you were missing, the day I received that telegram. Missing in action! The uncertainty, the not knowing, the pitying looks. It was hell. And poor Eliza? She'll never really know exactly wat happened. Was he trapped inside the ship? Did he drown? Was he burned alive? She keeps reliving it all. I am so very lucky Joe, to have you here with me. But when I'm with her I feel so dratted guilty. For my jealousy, and for my luck in having you home."

Pushing herself up she caught hold of his arm, then made a play of slipping backwards, sloshing water over the sides of the bath.

"Here, you've wet my trousers."

"Whoops a daisy." She gave a suggestive smile. *"Better take them off then Joe."*

" What then?"

"I think I could make room for you at a squeeze. Climb in."

"Ere, move along, my knees are stuck under my chin."

She splashed him. *"Stop complaining Joe."*

Eliza was restless. *"Mum, how will we all go on now? All these families broken up, people with nowhere to live? So many lives sacrificed, my darling Thomas among them."*

Kathleen frowned, looked over at Sam, whispered, *"Leave us."*

He was quick off the mark. *"Come on then you three perishers, let's us three take a walk in the sunshine. We can pick a few daffs and tulips for your mam and your gran."*

Little Mary Rose took hold of her grandad's hand and wrapped her soft fingers inside his hardened grasp, hardened by work and life. Michael and Charlie were out of the door before he'd even finished his sentence, eager to escape their mum, she was different now and her misery confused them.

Eliza watched them disappear. *"I'm sorry mam. Three children in the house. At your time of life, when you and dad should be taking things easy. The boys are a handful, aren't they? I can't thank you and dad enough, really."*

Kathleen pulled an embroidered handkerchief from her cardigan pocket and handed it to her daughter. *"Listen to me. There is barely a day when I don't think of your Thomas, he was like a son to me and your dad. You know he was. Only----This won't do Eliza. You have to find your strength from somewhere and I might suggest concentrating on your children again instead of moping around all day. You were doing so well and all. The children are healthy and loved, well fed and housed in a secure home. The twins adore helping their grandad here on the farm, and Mary Rose is a little treasure, a gift from God if ever there was one----an image of her father. Now----enough is enough. And while we're at it, let's get one thing straight, once and for all. You and our grandchildren are not a burden. Why? You're a good help to us, usually---- And your dad? He's not getting any younger, neither of us are, only I can see your dad's beginning to feel the strain more than me. The lads will be a Godsend in a few years; why they even muck in now don't they?"*

"You don't understand mum. It hurts so much. All the couples making merry, dancing, canoodling, making plans.VE day wasn't a celebration to me, it was a reminder of what I'd lost. Me and Thomas? We had such plans. I miss him so very much."

"I know love, I understand."

"No, you don't mum!" Eliza wailed. *"How can you? You never really loved dad in the way I loved Tommy, not even for a day, not in the way we loved each other."*

Kathleen reddened. *"Stop it! That's neither here nor there. My marriage to your father has been good and steady. Everyone's relationship is different Eliza. What does matter though, is that you have three young children who need their mam. They need you to be strong and set an example, to raise them so your husband, and their father would have been proud of them."*

Eliza lit a cigarette, pouted. *"But Mum..."*

"No buts! I don't want to see you lying in bed of a morning anymore. VE celebrations are over so you can't use these as a reason for hiding away anymore. The country is still on its knees and there is much to be done. There are many lads still overseas, fighting the Japs. Your father has indulged you enough, and poor Frances yesterday? You cried and wailed until she didn't know what to do or say."

"Oh mum, it's just that-----"

"No. Enough excuses. Upstairs, scrub your face, put a nice frock on."

Eliza stubbed her cigarette into her saucer. *"What for?"*

"Do I have to come over there?"

"Blimey mum, I'm a grown woman."

"Then start to act like one. I mean it Eliza. I've always found that doing a good deed for another takes my mind off my own troubles. You can take this basket of eggs and wedges of cheese down to the church hall. The hens are laying well at the moment. I'll give your father a shout and ask him to nip you over on the motorbike."

Eliza paused on the stairs.

"Go on then. Get yourself spruced up. The little 'uns' can stay here. If I know Sam, he'll have worn them all out. Little Mary Rose will be needing her nap and Charlie and Michael can settle with a jigsaw. It will be good when the school is up and running full-time again. Part-time lessons are not enough for them and I'm no teacher, I haven't the wherewithal, or the patience."

Kathleen yanked open the door and gave a long whistle. *"Sam? Are you finished?"* She waited for an answering call… nothing! Tugging off her apron she made her way through the long grass to the barn. *"There you all are. Didn't you hear me whistle, calling?"*

They didn't answer. *"Well, I don't know,"* she protested.

There they were. Kneeling in the corner of the barn, bent over in a huddle. Leaning forward she could hear something, and just about see a squeaking wriggling mass.

"Oh grannie!" they chorused. *"Look! Minnie has had her kittens, come and see."*

Sam pulled himself up slowly. *"She's hidden them away well this time Kathleen, they are a couple of weeks at least. Come away now children, leave the mother to rest, you mustn't worry her. Don't touch her kittens yet, she wouldn't like it."*

Protesting, but not resisting, they all complied. When grandad spoke, he meant business; only they adored him, all the same.

Taking note of Kathleen's flustered expression, he frowned. *"What is it, Kathleen? We were about to make our way anyhow."*

"I'm hot, been baking. Can you take our Eliza over to the church hall? We can spare a few eggs and that butter will go rancid if it's not used up: there's a little cheese too. Also, Sam, I don't want to see anymore of you coddling our daughter. Sam? You're not helping, not now. Please?"

"Fair enough."

He snatched up each grandson and tucked them, wriggling, under each arm, whilst their sister clutched at her gran's skirt, pleading to be lifted too. They made a slow way back to the house, Sam huffing and puffing loudly. Kathleen quietly observed but didn't say a word, expressing her disapproval of his daft behaviour with a raised eyebrow. When will he accept it? He's not a young man anymore?

He ignored the scathing look and dropped the boys in a wriggling heap onto the sofa. Mary Rose's eyelids were already drooping and heavy with the need for sleep and Kathleen swiftly lay her down on the nearest armchair.

"Make me a cuppa missis and we'll be off; I'll have a quick splash under the cold water tap while the kettle boils."

Sam was washed, refreshed with two mugs of tea and a jam tart or two, and dressed in his wool jerkin and heavy leather gauntlets in no time at all. *"Where is she then?"*

Kathleen shrugged, tutted, *"Up the stairs."*

He paced to the stairwell, bellowed upwards. *"Eliza? Are you ready yet?"*

Kathleen tucked the soft blanket around her sleeping granddaughter. *"For goodness' sake Sam! You'll wake the dead with your hollering."*

Sam continued to call out. *"Eliza? Daughter? If you're not down these blinking' stairs in a minute, you'll not be going anywhere."*

He could hear her muttering to herself above. *"As if I care."*

Sam was about to answer her when Charlie began to yell, his eyes wide. *"Wake the dead? With hollering'? Can you do that grandad? Really? Wake the dead? Will they hurt us?"*

Before he had the opportunity to answer, Eliza was down. Taking the stairs two at a time, she kissed her boys, giving her father a sulky frown.

"This was mam's idea if you must know dad, And mam? Fancy scaring the boys like that. Charlie? Grandad can't wake the dead. Once you're dead, you're dead!"

Kathleen brushed passed her. *"I'm not sure Lizzie would agree with you on that one! Listen, I've wrapped the eggs up well in newspaper, they're in the back saddlebag."*

She looked at Sam. *"Off you go then. And Sam? Don't forget what I asked you earlier."*

"Ta-- raa", they chorused.

"Thank gawd". She settled the twins with a jigsaw and tucked herself into the corner of the sofa with her knitting.

Kathleen made little progress with her knitting; she was lost in thought. It was strange. Sam and her daughter had always argued like cat and dog before she'd married Thomas. He'd always been overly protective and strict, harbouring on severeness at times, but since their son-in-law was lost at sea two years ago, well, he'd changed so much. For the most part, he was ready to listen to her now, and he willingly indulged his grandchildren. It warmed her heart to see how he softened when they were around. Let's face it, he loved having them all about, filling their home with laughter. Goodness, how would he react if Eliza eventually met another man? She still had her beauty; her blonde hair and cornflower blue eyes were as bright as they'd ever been. Her daughter was well aware of the power she wielded with her shapely figure and prettiness. There was one drawback though, there wouldn't be many young fellas overly keen to take her and three young children on. Maybe an older man, she mused.

Eliza straightened her frock, smoothed her hair and took a deep breath. The door was ajar as usual. *"Can I come in? Hellooo--- Lizzie?"* She took a small step inside the back door. Lizzie never locked it; it wasn't the 'done thing' in this neighbourhood. *"It's me, Eliza---can I come in?"* She heard the shuffling of feet.

The door flew open. *"Yes ducks. Come on in. I've been having forty winks---was a little off colour this morning, to tell you the truth of it."*

Eliza's smile froze. What was Lizzie wearing? Trying to hide her astonishment she gazed around the room. *"You've been polishing, I love that lavender you use."*

Nothing got past Lizzie. She gave Eliza a meaningful look. *"Yes, I am dressed a bit strange. It's like this. I had a mishap with the teapot this morning, smashed it and spilt its contents all down my lovely dressing gown. This arthritis in my hands is becoming a right nuisance. Anyway! This is a boxer's robe I do believe. Ruby brought it back from the base, some sort of souvenir. I believe the last owner was a famous celebrity boxer over in America."* She gave a bow. *"It's just the job, isn't it?"*

"It's certainly very swish," gasped Eliza.

Lizzie stretched out her arms, did a turn. The black and red velvet robe hung down to show just enough of spindly ankles. A small hair curler wrapped around her dark grey hair hung loose over her narrow forehead whilst a heavy hood almost reached the bottom of her pointed nose.

Eliza exploded in snorts of laughter.

Lizzie was affronted or pretended to be. *"Aye! It's not that funny. It's grand--- here, feel the fabric--- how soft and it is-----"* Then she stopped short. Eliza's laughter was infectious.

"Crikey, blimey Lizzie, you're a tonic! OOO! Can I use your lavvy? I've had so many cups of tea down at that church hall. I'll pee my knickers if I don't move quickly." Eliza didn't wait for an answer but made a smart disappearance to the lavvy in the backyard.

Lizzie took the opportunity to speed up the stairs and remove the offending robe. She quickly tugged on her woollen underwear. *"Don't cast a clout until May's out"* she muttered under her breath, her haste making her all fingers and thumbs. Pulling on a brown and beige flowered frock, she took a quick glance in the dressing table mirror, tutted, and discarding the dangling roller, pulled a brush through her freshly washed hair.

"Hellooo? I'm back. Are you up there?" called Eliza.

"Down in a minute. Do you like my frock? I whizzed it up on the Singer."

Eliza stared. *"It's smashing. Where did you get the material from?"*

"I cut up an old pair of curtains that I picked up from the jumble sale. It's lovely and soft. Feel the material."

Eliza squeezed the hem of the skirt. *"Clever clogs."* It wasn't the time to let on; that dress had graced her bedroom window at the farm in the form of curtains since she was a girl. She thought they had long gone. Her mam was such a hoarder, kept things for years.

"Not bad for an old dear, am I? So? Sit yourself down then. What brings you this way?"

"I thought I'd pop in while I am around this way, only I'm sorry I've disturbed you when you're poorly. Mam gave me a few eggs and butter and cheese to share out, at the church hall. The hens have been laying like billy-o. Here, I've saved a bit of butter for you. Dad will be here to collect me in a little while, so I won't keep you."

Lizzie gave Eliza a sharp glance. *"Hmmm, I think it's you who has been under the weather, if I'm not wrong."* She took hold of her hand, gave it a squeeze. *"It's lovely to see you duck. I'm fine, I've been blessed with a strong constitution. Now* then. *If you don't mind me saying, you're looking a little peaky?"*

The floodgates opened. *"Oh, dear Lizzie. Thomas promised me he would survive this war; he swore he would return to me. It turned out he was wrong---so very wrong. It's not fair, I need him. Damn the Royal Merchant Navy- all show and nothing but rusty buckets of ships for the men to sail in. Tom was full of the romance of the sea, telling me of waves as high as the heavens. And at what cost? Here I am with three young kiddies and no man."* She took in a deep breath to steady the hammering of her heart in her breast. *"I'm not strong. I'm not the sort of woman who can be a widow and raise a family on her own. It's not fair!"* She stamped her foot, shaking the cup and saucer in her hands.

"Come along now; life often isn't fair, you're old enough to know that." Lizzie took the cup and saucer and carefully placed it back on the table. *"My best crockery, all I have left of my mum."* She gave Eliza an encouraging smile. *"Now then, listen to me."* Leaning forward she grasped both of Eliza's hands. They were sweating, trembling. *"You don't really have any choice duck. You ARE a widow, with three children to raise, and they need you. Thomas would want you to be a good mother to them. You have to face your future with resolve and determination. There is no other way! Build a future from the bottom up, like a brick wall, a row at a time, a day at a time."*

"I'm not a dratted builder! I'm not strong like you are. And I don't want to be!"

"You've no choice. Thank your lucky stars you aren't left on your own as so many others are. Sam and Kathleen are here for you and the children. You have a roof over your head and food in your belly. You have to build on what you have."

Eliza pouted. Lizzie handed her a lace handkerchief. *"Here, wipe your eyes."*

"You think I'm wrong don't you, like all the others. I know what folks think of me, say about me," she snapped. *"Flighty Eliza, flirty Eliza. It's true, right now I'm behaving badly. Mam is at her wits end. Surely you must see how it is. The last two years since Tom's ship went down, I was getting through the day, safe on the farm with my parents, the children. Little Mary Rose was, and is a comfort, and the boys? More than a handful but keeping me busy. There I was, hid away there, protected, pretty much away from others. Then, wham! VE day!*

"Tom and me? We had such plans," she groaned. *"We'd saved well. He wanted us to have our own pub, landlord and landlady of-----we talked for hours, choosing its name, where would it be? We were building our own wall, our future. It's rotten luck, that's what it is. And VE day? Everyone celebrating, couples everywhere, dancing, singing, laughing, drinking. Dad even found Doris Crompton, making out with a yank in our barn. I saw them too, loving each other. And I want that too, the closeness. I was jealous, and I screamed at her. 'You whore!' I'm ashamed. I was jealous. Realising how sterile my life had become without Tom, without his kisses and caresses. I've been so damned angry ever since, can't shake it off. My mind is full of a rowdy complaining classroom of thoughts. It seems any minute as if my head will explode with these headaches. I'm not old Lizzie. I can't sleep, it's unbearable. I seem to have lived the past two years in hibernation and I've woken up. Is it wrong to want more? I'm suffocating on that farm, God help me."*

Lizzie sighed, took a long swallow of her tea, her voice cool and measured. *"You're lucky Doris didn't give you a fourpenny one."*

"She was otherwise engaged!"

"As you said. Listen, you're still a young woman with a lot of life ahead of her." She threw Eliza the tea towel.

"What the? -------"

"You can help me with these dishes."

"Oh. So? Lizzie, what do I do?"

"You carry on. That's what you do. Spruce yourself up a bit. You are smart, and pretty, only you're not a girl anymore. It's time you conducted yourself as a woman. Work hard, make it happen, shine your light."

"And how do I do that?"

"Listen Eliza. I don't have all the answers. This is for you to work out love. The country is still in dire straits. We haven't beaten the Japanese army yet, although I do believe it's in sight. Talk to your parents, see if you can come to some sort of an arrangement. Maybe find work for a couple of days a week in town, as long as your mam could cope with the children. There will be plenty of work now, I'm sure of it. I can ask Ruby, perhaps she could get hold of a typewriter, then you could practice." Lizzie raised an eyebrow. *"Everything is not lost. Do you hear me?"*

"Blimey. Got you, loud and clear!" She took a long breath. "Well, thanks for listening. I suppose I should be ashamed of *myself. Umm, Lizzie? ------ Do you think? --- Do you think you could read my cards? Please? Or the crystal ball?"*

Lizzie frowned, considered. This was the last thing Eliza needed at this moment. This young woman was one of many who found themselves in similar situations, and the best thing for her right now. It was encouragement, yes, but also help to accept her circumstances, however terrible they were; it was the only way. VE day had momentarily topped her equilibrium.

"Not today ducks. I've been under the weather, as I said."

"Another day then?" Eliza pleaded.

"I don't see why not. I'm sorry, I can't magic everything better pet. Nonetheless, I hope it's helped, talking to a friend. Because I am your friend, and it's difficult talking with family sometimes, isn't it?" She handed her a thin slice of cake. *"Here, it's currant cake without the currants."* Eliza giggled. Lizzie wagged a finger.

"Now then. Did I tell you? I've been given a budgerigar. I'm going to call him Winston. What do you think?"

Before Eliza could answer there was a knock on the door. It startled them both. She must look a sight! Pulling out her compact, Eliza dabbed some powder on her nose, hastily retouching her Victory Red lipstick. Lizzie stood and straightened her new frock. They waited.

"The knock was followed by a tentative *"Anyone in?"*

Lil stepped in from the back door. Noticing Eliza, she hesitated. *"Oh, I'm very sorry Lizzie, you've got company. Shall I call back later?"* She glanced at the box of tarot cards on the table. *"Are you busy?"*

"Not at all. It's nice to see you. Sometimes I can go days without company and a good natter. It seems I'm the bees' knees today. Are you on your own Lil?"

Patrick poked his balding head in the door. *"No, she's brought her old man with her. I'll sit in the yard and have my smoke if it's alright with you? Leave you ladies to it."*

Lil turned quickly. *"Patrick?"* She spoke hurriedly in an undertone. *"Eliza is here. Is our Jimmy already on his way?"*

He raised his eyebrows. *"Strewth."*

Picking out a match from his Swan Vesta box, he struck it sharply on the outhouse bricks. *"He popped into the off licence. I'll finish my Woodbine and head him off."*

Lil heaved a sigh. She hoped to God he would be able to find him. Her nephew Jimmy had always had a thing for Eliza, from way back when he'd helped out at Sam's farm when he was a lad. Everyone knew that Eliza hadn't actually discouraged him, and she'd dallied with him much later on when Thomas was on ship. It riled Lil still, --- everyone knew she'd only ever really been serious about Thomas, but she'd still encouraged and enjoyed Jimmy making a fuss of her. In Lil's book it hadn't been the thing to do, and she'd made her thoughts on the subject clear to her nephew at the time. *"Messing with a married woman will only bring grief, leave her alone."* Jimmy had always insisted that they were only good mates. He'd swore he would never push himself on her, and she was happily married. Besides, he protested, allow me some integrity aunt Lil, I wouldn't stoop so low as to pinch another man's wife while he was away fighting for his country, or in Thomas's case, doing vital work on the merchant ships. She'd always thought he protested too much, if you had her meaning!

As far as she was aware now, they had seen very little of each other since Thomas's death. Jimmy had been much in demand as a skilled engineer in his reserved occupation, whilst Eliza had had been pretty much holed up at her parents' farm, rearing her three children and helping out her mam and dad.

This afternoon she'd hoped to have a quiet natter with her friend, only seeing Eliza here had certainly upset the apple cart. Here she was, as large as life---dolled up to the nines--- blonde hair piled up high, scorching red lips, and her frock in cerulean that carefully set off her wide cornflower blue eyes, saying nothing of the cling of the fabric hugging each and every curve. And now she was a widow, on the prowl by the look of her! Was Jimmy over her as he insisted? True, he always had plenty of female company --- only he'd never settled down with any of them. Why not? He was a handsome, cheerful lad, and there had been no shortage of hopefuls over the years.

Lately he'd been hankering to make a new life for himself in New Zealand, well, once this war was finally and completely over. Since VE day, he'd made moves, planning the next step. Eliza could put the kybosh on all of this, and it would be such a shame. How could her nephew start afresh saddled with another man's children? Especially as there were three of them!

Lizzie looked Lil up and down, she was well aware of her friend's opinion. *"Are you going to sit your bum down then?"*

Lil was startled. *"Oh yes. Sorry love. Thank you."* She turned to Eliza. *"Hello stranger. What brings you over here? I haven't seen you for a long while."* Then relenting a little, she added, *"I'm so sorry about Thomas, how are you keeping?"* If she wasn't mistaken, the girl had been crying.

"Eliza made an effort to smile. *"It's been two years now, perhaps a little more, or thereabouts. I don't get out much. Dad brought me over on his bike; mam thought it would do me good. I dropped a few eggs and some other bits off at the church hall."* Her lip began to tremble. *"How are you and Patrick keeping? ---And Jimmy?"*

"We are all doing very nicely, thank you," bristled Lil. *"New dress? Nice colour."*

"Thanks, mam made it."

Lil couldn't help herself. *"Still pampering you, I see."*

Eliza blushed. *"I suppose. Only, it's not really my style to be honest."*

Ungrateful hussy thought Lil. *"It fits you perfectly, what more do you want? She's done you proud, most of us have to settle for serviceable, not your Paris fashions. There is still a war on young lady."*

Eliza glared; her blue eyes darkened. *"Is there? Well, I don't want serviceable, I want pretty."*

Lizzie looked from one to the other. She could see which way this conversation was heading.

"So, Lil?" Eliza challenged, *"You think I need reminding that there is a war on? Lore, you don't need to remind me. It damn well took my husband, didn't it? Left me a widow with three kiddies to feed and clothe."*

Lil wriggled her shoulders, stuck out her chin. Her look said it all. *"You're not exactly dressed in widow's weeds."* She couldn't help it, it just sort of spilled out.

"Now then." Lizzie chided. *"---Lillian! Whatever has got into you? This is my home---I'll thank you ladies to remember that."*

"Think I'm feeling a bit queerly," said Lil.

Lizzie tilted her head, considered. *"You're in a high dungeon about something, I can see that."*

Lil swallowed; her heart was thumping inside like a base drum. *"I'm sorry. --- Anyway, I called to bring you these no ten knitting needles that you needed, you see, to finish off that toy policeman. OOO, and here's some stuffing for it, I unpicked an old cushion."*

She turned red faced to Eliza, *"It keeps us busy. I've finished my policeman, only have to sew a couple of black buttons on his face----for his eyes. Do you knit Eliza?"*

Eliza stared. What was this woman about? One minute trying to put me in my place, heaven knows why, then jabbering on about knitting. *"No, mam does. I do like baking though---jam tarts---"* She found herself stammering. Drat. She jumped to her feet. She'd had enough. *"You don't like me, do you Lil? You never have. Are you worried I'll take your precious Jimmy from you? Is that it?"*

"Oh, crikey-o-reilly", mumbled Lizzie.

That did it! Lil could feel the sweat in the hollow of her neck. *"Alright then, being as you asked. You're not to my liking, never have been. You're a trollop. You can't help yourself, and I don't want you messing up Jimmy's plans."* She turned to Lizzie. *"I'm sorry about this Lizzie. I'll pop back later."*

Leaving the needles and stuffing on the table she dropped her friend a perfunctory kiss on the cheek and swept out, hoping that Patrick had managed to head Jimmy off.

"You did ask..." grinned Lizzie.

Eliza stared at Lil's retreating plumpness shoving out of the open door.

Lizzie laughed. *"Well, I think under the circumstances we could try the cards."*

Eliza watched closely as Lizzie unwrapped the cards from the purple cloth and shuffled. Concentrating, she placed them in sequence on the table. The clock on the mantle ticked, loud in the heavy silence.

Eliza's broke the silence. *"Who does she think she is? Women like her, they drive me silly. Don't they understand? This war has changed things for us women, we're not on an equal footing with blokes, not yet, only we have had a taste of independence, earning our own wage. What's wrong with looking nice, taking care of ourselves, expecting more? What exactly have I done to her?"* The tears welled and began to trickle down again. *"Oh, blimey, I can't do this anymore, it's too hard, I'm so------"*

Lizzie raised her hand, cut in quickly. *"Do you remember? In the early days when Belgium surrendered, and the German tanks had smashed all the way through into France? We all thought we were done for!"*

"Yes, of course. But where is this going Lizzie?"

"Here me out. They were dark days. Our men trapped on the beaches at Dunkirk---half of the cabinet were ready to surrender and leave them all there. If it wasn't for Winston Churchill's stubborn madness, they would never have even tried to get our troops away from that beach. But we did get them away, and I for one think it was a miracle. A lot of folks around these streets thought he was finished, scorned him, ready for the knacker's yard, too long in the teeth----- and Winston didn't care a jot what was said about him. And thank goodness he didn't."

Eliza stared.

"Are you giving in, after Tommy and so many others gave their lives for us? Listen, some folks have nothing better to do, and Lil's temper? She was rude to you. I'm sorry. It's not really like her, --- I'm sure there is something behind her outburst, only I'm not saying you should excuse it. I never had you down as a quitter Eliza."

Eliza protested. *"I'm not! Only, she's a bit of a cow, isn't she?"*

"Now then,"

*"Alright. Only, it was so uncalled for. I never did cheat on Tommy, not like some. Me and Jimmy are good pals. He was

the first boy to kiss me; we were only fourteen years old, so young. I haven't set eyes on him since Thomas died, well, only at a distance."

"Well then. You've nothing to worry about. It's words, just words, pet; and jealousy from some, I admit. Now, shall we carry on?"

"Yes, please Lizzie."

"Alright duck. Cut the cards."

Half an hour or so later the reading was over. Eliza sat back, eyes closed, slumped in the chair. The reading was good, Lizzie gave her comfort and hope. It was time to stop being soppy. Thomas was gone, but the future offered promise. It was strange---VE day celebrations had opened a floodgate, or a hornet's nest, of grieving emotions; sorrow, loss, anger, regret for unrealised dreams, and if she was wholly honest? Envy and spite.

Ruby was engaged to be married and soon to leave the UK with her Yankee officer. Frances's Joseph had returned to her after being missing for nearly three years, and they were starting up in business; and where was she? Stuck out in the middle of nowhere with three kiddies and her mum and dad.

Only it didn't need to be like this, not forever. The cards had hinted of better times. Opportunities. And they had acknowledged her sorrow and loss, her despair. The future was bright if she chose to celebrate survival and the joys in her life, for there were always joys and blessings if one looked hard for them. Lizzie confirmed that Tom was on the other side, that he had drowned, passed over quickly without being trapped inside the hull or burnt alive, as she'd dreaded.

What Lizzie had forecast from her palm and the lines in her hands---had positively overwhelmed her. Gawd help me; More children--- another two of them!

She watched as Lizzie folded the cards inside the silken cloth. Her hands were wrinkly and covered in brown liver spots, but her fingers were long and still had a certain sort of grace in them. *"Life is full of possibilities Eliza. Fear is a downward spiral, you must contribute, and yes, it will take discipline to move forward."* She looked up suddenly, her brown eyes peering at Eliza over her glasses. *"Meanwhile, I will give you a little something to put under your pillow to help you get a goodnight's sleep."*

Eliza nodded. She was penitent, ashamed of her outburst and sorry for the trouble she'd given her mam and dad over the last few days. But hearing that 'many were worse off than her' always filled her with rage. It was hard to explain her restlessness, her desire for something more. During the early years of the war, lodging with Frances and earning a good wage at the factory, she'd relished her independence. Knowing the boys were out of the way of the bombing, safe with her parents on their farm, had set her mind at rest, and she'd enjoyed having a free rein. Saving hard, she'd waited for Thomas to return, to resign from the Merchant Navy, and begin a new chapter in their life. Only it wasn't meant to be. It was time to accept it.

"Thank you, Lizzie, for the reading, and the kind words. You're quite right, I can do better; I think I'll cook something nice for them all tonight. Meanwhile, can I wait here for dad? He should be here about 4-ish. I'm going to turn over a new leaf---" her eyes shone bright. *"Can I do anything for you? You said you were a bit off colour?"*

"That's the spirit, bit by bit." Lizzie's soulful eyes looked directly into blue. *"I wouldn't dwell on Lil's outburst. Jimmy is like a son to her, you know that. I think Lil is at the latter end of the change of life. She's more than likely mortified by her little eruption. Anyway, yes, you can bring my washing in from the line, please duck. It will only get damp again if it's left hanging. Last time I left it out, it was full of earwigs. They'd dropped off from next door's tree."*

"Ugh. Right-o. Sooner said than done. I'll give them a good shake, I can't stand earwigs, they make me shudder."

Lizzie set to scraping out the ashes and resetting the grate with tightly coiled rolls of newspaper and kindling. The evenings could still be a little chilly, so she planned to treat herself to a small fire this evening with a few lumps of her precious coal, warm her old bones. Strange, she was always chilly these days.

Eliza bundled in, carrying the washing, careful not to hold it too close; the thought of earwigs dropping into her clothes was too horrifying.

"Is that it then? Lizzie? These clothes are still a little damp."

"I'll light a small fire later on, air them out."

Eliza smiled to herself as she draped the washing over the wooden clothes horse. Her friend was unlikely to catch a chill if she was still wearing these huge bloomers and long vests. Her amused expression didn't pass by her elderly friend.

"When you get to my age, you'll be more appreciative of warmth and comfort, instead of the fripperies the young ones have for underwear these days."

They both chuckled. Eliza glanced at her wristwatch, time to herself, wonderful! She was going to make the most of today, Lizzie was a tonic. Tapping her feet to the tune playing in her head she was alerted to a rap on the window. Both women spoke at once. *"Hello?"*

Eliza's stomach lurched. It was him!

Lizzie sighed. She knew it. Knew that when Jimmy heard his old sweetheart was here, he would be around as fast as a rat up a drainpipe. She was sure that Patrick would have done his best to head him off, warn him, only Jimmy wasn't the sort to take heed, whether or not he was aware of the kafuffle earlier between his aunt and Eliza. Jimmy didn't see the harm in anyone.

"Oh goodness, if your father turns up right now, he's not going to be best pleased, is he Eliza?"

Eliza paused, her mind working. *"Dad's temper isn't what it used to be; I don't believe he'd react badly. Please. Ask him in, I would love to see him, we're old mates, that's all."*

"Don't say I didn't warn you then."

"It won't harm none. Please?"

He stood in the open doorway. Eliza could feel the heat from the back of her neck spread around to her face. *"Hello Jimmy."*

The same smile, as broad and cheeky as ever, his brown hair an unruly riot of curls. Face? A little older.

Lizzie looked him up and down. *"Don't stand on the step then, you're blocking the day light. Come on in."*

He took a deep breath. Was it really her? At the sight of her he was lost for speech, struggling to swallow the huge lump of emotion that soared up through his chest. She was always with him, in his head, in the quiet moments. When he'd heard of her old man 'going down' with the ship he'd been genuinely sorry--- he'd liked, him, he was a good bloke. Over the last two years there had been a few passing fancies, but no one that excited him enough to give him cause to marry and settle down. He'd seen enough hasty marriages during this war; the blokes were away fighting before the marriage bed was even cold.

He had plans---New Zealand--- and now the war in Europe was finished, then it wouldn't be long before he could take his leave, from Uncle Patrick, Aunt Lil, and good old Blighty.

"Jimmy?" She breathed softly. *"Cat got your tongue?"*

He didn't look at her for a second. Kept his head down. He could feel her blue eyes drawing him in. Hold on Jimmy, he thought, she's got three nippers.

"Hello Eliza" He cleared his throat. Forced a smile. *"Look at you! As gorgeous as ever, in fact even more so, now you've got your figure back. You were a bit tubby last time I set eyes on you."* Crikey he thought, what did he say that for?

"Cheeky devil. I was carrying our Mary Rose as I remember. Anyhow. You can talk. Out in the afternoon in those old trousers and vest! What are you up to?"

He glanced downwards. Suddenly aware of the lack of a shirt. *"I've been with Joseph and Frances. They've had a delivery of huge crates and I stopped to give them a hand. Left my shirt there, sorry. You know they're setting up again only two streets away? A hardware store. Joe's leg was giving him jip, so me and Uncle Patrick were helping out. Then I heard you were here, and I rushed over—couldn't miss seeing my old pal, could I?"* You're rambling Jimmy, he thought.

Lizzie nodded towards a chair. *"Here, put your bum down Jimmy. You're making the place look untidy."*

Jimmy blushed. "Thank you, Lizzie, I will if you don't mind. Only I'm dusty from carting these crates and boxes. Have you a bit of newspaper I can sit on?"

"Don't worry lad, park your backside."

"Oh, if you're sure, thank you." He turned to Eliza. *"So, how are----?"* he stopped midsentence. How could he have forgotten how very lovely she was? Her hair was still the same luscious blonde----Her round blue eyes were fixed on him. *"Umm, how's your mam and dad, and the kiddies?"*

Before she could answer he shot upwards. *"Lizzie? Could I trouble you for a cup of cold water?"*

"Let the tap run for a minute Jimmy. Or I can make you tea?"

"No thanks, cold water's good."

"While you're at it splash your face, it's as dusty as your trousers." He caught the hand towel Lizzie threw at him, and without ceremony he ducked his head under the tap.

"Now listen," she whispered to Eliza. *"While he's out there in my scullery? A final word. It won't all be plain sailing, you will have troubles ahead of you—but they will be few and the blessings many, if you don't allow yourself to fall apart at the first hurdle. When things get on top of you? Remember Winston! Take yourself somewhere still, and a last word. Listen to your heart."*

"I don't have your gift, Lizzie. I don't see the signs."

Lizzie paused before answering, remembering. A gift! Some children kept quiet about the shadow people, she never had. Well, not until she'd began to notice the fear and the embarrassed laughter; then she held back a little, considered who she opened up to. Not that she was ashamed of who she was, that would be wrong!

"There are always messengers working to reach us, to help. If you only allow yourself the space and quiet, you will hear them, feel them, inside."

Jimmy emerged from the scullery, red faced and dripping water from his hair. *"Thank you, Lizzie."* He looked at Eliza. *"Still on your dad's farm?"*

"Yes, with my three children." She averted her eyes from his. *"Where else would I be?"*

His voice softened. *"Maybe I could pay you a visit? Take you and the nippers out for a little outing? I've got myself an old car, it's not much, but a bit comfier than that old bike I imagine. More room than a sidecar, I would think?"*

"That sounds nice," she hesitated. *"Only I'm not sure what dad would say."*

Jimmy gave her an encouraging smile. She noticed the gap in his teeth at the top right-hand side, remembered how he'd lost it in a scrap protecting her honour. Her mouth twitched; she couldn't help it. He took this as a sign of encouragement. *"What harm would it do Eliza? If you're worried people would talk, then bring your mam."*

Her blue eyes widened. *"Why yes, I'll ask her."* She stopped suddenly, hearing the sound of a motorbike engine spluttering to a halt outside. Her voice lowered. *"It's my dad."*

Lizzie heard it too. *"Round two"*, she mumbled. This is my house, she thought, if Sam starts something, then he will feel the sharp edge of her tongue.

Sam stood in the doorway, his eyes darting around the room, his presence was dark and grim. *"I should throw you out on your bloody neck."*

Jimmy met his stare, stood his ground. He could have dodged out the front door but chose not to. Eliza was not a child; it was two years since she'd been made a widow. Uncle Patrick had tried to warn him off, but he was determined to see her, needed to see her. He wasn't about to skulk about like a thief in the night.

"Now then," said Lizzie calmly. *"This is my house. There will be no chucking out unless it's by me! If you want to stay, I suggest you both behave like gentlemen."*

Sam sniffed. *"Gentlemen? He wouldn't know the meaning of the word. My daughter is in no fit state to have buggers like* him sniffing around. Sling your hook before I teach you a lesson you won't forget."

"Stop it dad, please." She could feel herself tremble. Clutching Sam's arm, she pleaded. "*Please, don't.*"

"*It's alright Eliza, leave this to me.*" Lizzie folded her arms in front of her. "*I told you, I'm not having this Sam. You're right, Eliza's been through a bereavement, only that doesn't mean she can't begin to enjoy life again and see her friends.*"

Jimmy stepped in-between Sam and Eliza.

"*Don't worry Lizzie. I'm not going to respond to his threats.*" His eyes were blazing. "*Teach me a lesson, old man? You always were a blinking tyrant. Leave her be. ----What are you trying to say? What do you bloody think is going on? This is the first time I've had the opportunity to speak to your daughter in two years. You've made damn sure of that, haven't you? Kept her busy on that farm of yours? Away from her friends?*"

Sam's face was puce. "*Why you! I ought to-----*"

"*Ought to what? Look at her. You shouting, stomping and throwing your weight around isn't helping, is it?*"

Lizzie tapped her hand on the table. She had very little patience with either of the men at this moment, the younger or the older. Sam was behaving like a territorial bull and Jimmy nosing around and ignoring the well-meant advice from Patrick didn't help any.

"*Enough. Sam. You may throw your weight about in your own home, but not here. Eliza didn't know Jimmy would be here. Patrick and Lil popped in; they must have mentioned in passing she was here. There was nothing pre-arranged.*"

Sam straightened up. *"I apologise to you Lizzie, only; Thomas is only two years gone and these VE celebrations have stirred a lot of emotions again. Kathleen and I want the best for Eliza and our grandchildren. Her mam has been downright worried sick about our daughter the last couple of weeks. I didn't expect the first time, the first outing, away from the farm, she'd be meeting that crafty blighter."*

Jimmy stiffened.

Lizzie placated. *"Enough Sam. This wasn't planned. Now both of you? Calm down."* She glanced at Jimmy. *"Maybe it's best you take your leave love."*

He turned to go, and then stopped abruptly, giving Eliza a wink. *"Be seeing you Eliza. Sorry Lizzie".*

Eliza blushed. *"Ta-ra Jimmy. I'm sorry about my dad."*

Sam made a move to follow him, and Lizzie caught hold of his sleeve.'

They listened as the gate banged shut and Jimmy's whistling faded into the distance, Eliza refused to look her dad in the face.

"I think it's time for you to be off then Sam." Lizzie waited, gave him a questioning glance.

"Yes." He plonked a jar of blackcurrant jam on the table. *"Only one left of last year's stock. Perhaps it will make up for my behaviour, do you think?"*

*"Get away with you Sam. No apology necessary. Only you're not getting any younger, it won't do you any good getting into a temper like that. He's not a bad lad really, despite his reputation. We all see that he's always been sweet on madam

here; I can see how it looked." Lizzie relented a little. *"Would you like a cup of tea before you leave?"*

Eliza shot to her feet. *"If you don't mind, we should be on our way dad? I'm missing the kiddies, Lizzie. This is the longest I've been away from Mary Rose since she was born. Can you believe it?"*

"Yes well, it's time to stretch your horizons. Staying cooped up isn't good for you. It's not good for anyone, although understandable; in the beginning."

Sam hung his head, sheepish expression on his face. *"Trying to do the best for her Lizzie, that's all I want."*

"That's right Sam, it's not easy. Here, have a bit of toffee."

He laughed. *"What's that for? Look at the size of it! You trying to keep my gob shut?! Thank you. I'll have it later."* He turned. *"Right then. Ready daughter?"*

Eliza's knees trembled. *"Ready dad."* She gave Lizzie an apologetic smile. *"Thanks for everything Lizzie----and I'm sorry-----"*

"No need to apologise. Off you go then. And remember what I said. Don't be a stranger Eliza. I'd love to see the children, when you can find the time the time, and Sam? Think on---" She stopped abruptly.

The whistler had returned.

Lizzy stopped, mid-sentence. *"Oh, what now? Lord Almighty!"*

Jimmy poked his head around the door. He'd donned a shirt and slathered a layer of Brylcreem over his curly hair.

"Don't forget, that offer of a trip out in my car still stands Eliza." He gave Sam a challenging look. *"You and the kiddies?"*

Sam roared. *"Why, you young rogue! Keep away from her. You will! Whether you like it or not. You turn up at my farm and you'll leave it with my foot up your arse."*

Jimmy laughed and sped off on his borrowed pushbike.

"Eliza," Sam hissed, *"Get your things."* He grabbed hold of Eliza's arm *"Not planned, eh?"*

Lizzie plonked herself down in her chair. *"Sam? Bugger off,"* she laughed. *"Don't know how your Kathleen puts up with you.*

The ride back home continued in total silence, other than the spluttering from the engine. Father and daughter entered the farmhouse softly. Kathleen eyed the pair over the top of her reading glasses. Little Mary toddled on plump legs over to Sam; his grim expression softened as he bent to pick her up into his arms. The boys were spread out on the floor at Kathleen's feet, engrossed in their jigsaw. Sam rummaged in his pocket and their heads snapped up in response.

"Grandad? What have you got there?" they chorused in unison.

"Chocolate, and a blinking big lump of toffee. You can share the toffee if you can bite it in half and give a tiny piece of the chocolate to your sister." Kathleen's eyes narrowed. *"Where did you find the chocolate Sam?"* She looked across to Eliza." Well?"

"Lord knows mother, he didn't offer me any. The toffee came from Lizzie. I think she was hoping it would shut his gob." With that Eliza kicked off her shoes and taking hold of her daughter she sat herself down on the mat and buried her face into Mary Rose's curls. Wrinkling her nose, the child held out her chubby arms. "*I want some toffee too.*"

Charlie reluctantly broke off a small piece of his sweet treasure.

Michael?" prompted Kathleen. He followed suit with a similar level of enthusiasm. The children now occupied with their sweets; her attention drew back to Eliza.

"Show some respect for your father. What happened? I thought it would do you a power of good getting away for a while--- but look at you! You look as if you found a penny and lost a shilling. Both of you."

Knowing the tears were threatening Eliza squeezed her eyes shut. She didn't want to alarm the children, although seeing the voracious rate that they were scoffing the chocolate, she wondered if they would be aware of anything else happening around them.

"Love?" Whispered Kathleen. She gave Sam a questioning glance.

He shrugged. *"Don't ask me. Lord knows, I've tried. Ask your daughter."* With that he stomped off, closing the door non too gently.

"Dad's a tyrant!"

"Don't be silly. He's a little difficult at times, I'll give you that. Want to tell me what's happened?

Eliza picked at the hem of her dress. *"No mam. There really is no point, he'll never change. Tommy loved me, understood me, ----he's gone."* She sighed. *"I can't see how things will ever get better."*

Kathleen knelt down beside her and took Eliza into her arms.

"Give it time pet, there's always a light at the end of a tunnel."

"Not this one, mam. It's all dark and there's no way forward. It's blocked by Dad. It's useless."

CHAPTER 4

It was a miserable wet morning. Black and grey and strangely silent, it did little to enhance Norma's mood. Here it was, the day Norma had dreaded---- June 12th, Reg's birthday. His 45th! Her eldest, Mary, was already fretting. At fifteen she was very aware of life's unpredictability, and she worried a great deal more about her dad than her three sisters. Reading the newspapers avidly, listening to the radio and gossip, whispers; she often regaled horrific tales of torture, barbarity, life in the concentration camps to her siblings, even young Margaret. Only last week she'd inadvertently came across her whispering a bedtime story to the young ones of some poor man having his throat slit from ear to ear. Well, fifteen or no fifteen, she'd tanned her arse. Sometimes Norma was at a loss what do with her. She'd resorted to put a stop on sending her on errands, for the stories she brought home with her after standing in the queues were hair raising, to say the least. She was sure that she took pleasure in embellishing and glorifying any gruesome snippet- safe in the knowledge that Hitler was finished, and they wouldn't themselves be at his mercy; Blighty was safe.

"Poor kids," she sighed, *"Let's hope we hear something soon."* Reg stared out at her from his photograph, his hair slated to his head with a tub of Brylcreem, chin held high, confident and proud in his uniform.

She clutched the frame close into her breast. *"Where are you Reg? I wonder if you'll remember your birthday. Know the date even?"*

Staring out of the window, she'd been unaware of time passing until the rain slowed to a stop, and a yell from upstairs reminded her of her motherly duties. It was time to make a move.

"Come on you lot, you need to get yourself outside for some fresh air. Find a thick cardigan, go and play."

Rummaging under the stairs she found a length of an old washing line and within minutes the girls had recruited others in the street to join in a game of skipping. The rope was stretched across the narrow street from kerb to kerb and the queue snaked along the pavements as the youngsters waited to take their turn. One by one they jumped into the middle as the rope turned, their little faces red with either cold or exertion, she wasn't sure. Socks slipped down from bony knees. Rationing was still in place and, although restrictions had eased off, food was hardly plentiful. Some mums were better at managing than others. She stretched to see more clearly. Mary was nowhere to be seen but she had a good idea where she was, more than likely she'd sloped off to Lizzie's.

Ah, there was Susan, her ringlets jiggling up and down as she bounced over the turning rope. At thirteen years she was tall for her age. Then there was Grace, pushing in and laughingly hopping into the centre. Only a year between Susan and Grace, that had been hard work-all those nappies! How she'd given Reg the sharp edge of her tongue back then. *"Careful? You? Reg Watling? I'll take the precautions from now on."* He'd sweet-talked her as usual, and then she had fell for little Margaret only two years later. 15-13-12-10. Four daughters. Thank goodness a word in the wise about a new family planning clinic had finally put them straight.

And there was her youngest, patiently waiting for her turn, bless her. She yelled out of the window. *"Margaret? Stop wiping your nose on your sleeve, you have a handkerchief in your pocket."*

It wasn't easy, being a single parent whilst Reg was away. Still, Mary was finished with school now; soon to start her employment with a local tailor. That would be a nice gentle little job for her, for she didn't want her daughter working in a factory. She would always be able to earn a little on the side once she'd mastered her trade. And she'd found herself a little cleaning job—charring for the Red Lion pub. All she wanted now was Reg home. When would that be? It was five weeks since his last letter. Reg and his blasted Eighth army! Where was he? Africa? Burma? Somewhere hot he said in his letters, that's all he would tell her. Heat and flies!

Holding the photograph up to her face she kissed his image. *"Happy birthday, duck. Come home to us soon."*

A wild roar of rousing shouts and black words broke into the once pleasant squeals and laughter of the bouncing youngsters. *"What in heavens name...?"*

Pushing his picture into her pocket she rushed to the front door. Screams and yells assailed her ears. The girls had abandoned their skipping and were darting about in all directions, scattering like shot from a gun.

"Quick, take cover!" yelled Susan, as she dragged the younger two siblings along with her. They bailed forcibly and heavily into the refuge of their mam's pinny. **Whoosh!** The impact of the panicking girls thumping into her knees knocked Norma backwards. **Wham!** She fell heavily onto her ample rear with a heap of arms and legs wriggling on top of her.

"What the…?"

"It's Malcolm Smith!" yelled Margaret, young face as reddened as an overripe tomato. *"Him and his snotty gang are causing all the trouble---- and the Sylvester street gang too, they've turned up here for a fight."*

Norma, finally righting herself from the wriggling mass, pushed her ducklings swiftly behind her.

At one end of the street stood Malcolm and his motley crew. Whistling a signal, he called out, provoking. *"Want a fight, you wormy scavengers?"*

He was met by answering cries from the leader of the Sylvester street gang. *"Baldy, Beaky? Got your head stuck in the mincer then?"*

Malcolm, an unfortunate victim of ringworm- black hair in tufts and his scalp adorned with white scaly patches, stepped up the war cry. *"Round arse! Tubby- barrel!"* he yelled, triumphantly. *"My gang will drive you back into Germany!"*

"I'm not German. My mam says my dad was Dutch."

Both leaders shouted out in unison. *"Come on lads. Squash 'em! Let's annihilate them!"*

The first stone slammed into Mrs Buckley's window, shattering the centre pane into tiny smithereens. Luckily for the assailants, she was out in her back yard pegging out her tea towels, oblivious to the mayhem out front.

"Gerry!" yelled Malcolm. *"Oy, Christiaan. That's not an English name, is it lads? Next time I'll aim for your head, and when you retreat, I'll get your fat arse."*

Christiaan turned his back to his adversary, swiftly yanked his trousers down and wriggled his rear. *"Kiss my fat arse, the lot of ya."* Pulling up his short pants he turned and gave a triumphant cry, *"At em lads!"* and loading his catapult in quick time, he hit his first target on the temple.

Their blood up, they ran at each other. Fearless, like the films they all devoured at the 'Penny Dreadfuls', they tore down the street. Stones and anything that would fit into a catapult, sticks, lumps of soil and grass began to fly in all directions, accompanied by *"ouch's"* and *"didn't hurt"* and *"gotcha"*.

Norma slammed her door quickly as a stone narrowly missed her front step. *"Stay here. Don't move, any of you."*

Smoothing her hair and straightening her pinny she made a dash for her back gate, racing around to Iris Smith's, three doors away and almost colliding with Iris. *"Your Malcolm..."*

Iris was a big boned woman, and she made a formidable sight as she slowly made her way, rolling her sleeves up for good measure. *"I know. I was having a little nap after my night shift. The little bugger. I'll tan his backside when I catch hold of him."*

Other mums, alerted by the noise, rushed into the middle of a skirmishing wresting mass of arms and legs. Homing in on their own, they grabbed hold of whichever body part or piece of clothing was more easily accessible.

Within minutes the street was cleared of the warring gangs and the girls were back out front with their skipping rope; Joan Buckley was having an angry discussion with Christiaan's mum about the origin of her son's name.

Norma's girls, well, three of them, were squashed either side of the dining table with a 1000-piece jigsaw of Scarborough harbour. It was the nearest they'd get to a trip to the beach this year. Satisfied it would keep their interest for a half hour at least she needed to find Mary. *"Susan? You're in charge. I'm off to see Lizzie. I'm sure I'll find our Mary around there. I'll send her back around sharpish, but until then, behave yourselves."*

They answered in unison. *"Yes mum."*

The comforting scent of lavender and beeswax assailed her senses immediately she stepped through the door. A sense of relief and calmness swept over her, soothing her jangled nerves, and lessening the impulse to light a Woodbine.

"There you are, Mary." The young girl didn't turn her head, she was lost in her dreams, whilst at the same time polishing the carved legs of the dining table, rubbing and dipping the cloth into a round tin of perfumed wax of Lizzie's own concoction.

Her elderly friend was sitting with her feet in a bowl of water, a towel draped over her head. Her face was hidden as she loudly breathed in the vapour from the basin of rosemary leaves and scolding water. Norma stopped short, folding her arms in front of her chest. Mary hastily explained herself. *"Hello mam. I've been telling Lizzie about my new job, with Mr and Mrs Hansom. I'm going to be a tailoress one day, aren't I? I'm so pleased I won't be starting in one of those horrible factories like Doris Wainwright. Mam says she'll have better wages- but mam says that's not everything is it, Aunty Lizzie?"*

A muffled agreement came from underneath the towel. Although not related by marriage or blood, the girls had grown up with Lizzie always being in and out of their home. She'd been friends with Norma and Reg since the early years of their marriage. The honorary title of aunty was an acknowledgment of this and the emotional ties that had grown between them from wartime necessity and familiarity.

Mary continued her frantic rubbing of the beautiful dark wood. *"I'm going to start saving as soon as I have my first week's wages. Mam's given me her old tea caddy to keep it in. Then, when I marry- I'll be able to sew pretty curtains and cushion covers to match."* She paused to wipe her nose on her pinny. *"My husband, he must be like my dad-kind-and a farmer would be nice; have his own farm, you know, like mum's friends, Sam and Kathleen. Eliza's really pretty don't you think?"*

"Crikey our Mary, do you ever come up for air?"

Lizzie pulled the towel away and put her finger over her lips, warning Norma to listen.

"We'll have a lovely farmhouse, surrounded by green fields and a huge front garden with a long winding path to the front

door. We'll have a chicken run and have eggs every day for breakfast, one each! I want a stable and those big horses to pull our wagons; you know? With the big hooves, and-pigs, spotted ones- they are so cute and funny. Can you imagine it? Bacon and eggs. Lovely."

Norma flopped into the armchair and smiled weakly. Lizzie vigorously rubbed her face with a flannel. The women looked across to each to each other. *"Sounds like you've worked it all out."* smiled Norma.

"Of course. An orchard would be nice too. Pears and apples. Mm- mm, apple pie-------I love apple pie, don't you? You can both visit, and Lizzie? Will you show me how I can make this wonderful lavender polish? I want two rocking chairs, one for each of us, and we'll sit by the fireside in the evening. He can smoke a pipe if he likes. Beehives for honey, and of course the wax for the polish. We'll have blackcurrants and gooseberries and mum you can make jam. Blackcurrant jam…heavenly."

Norma rolled her eyes. *"Finished?"*

"Nearly. We'll have two dogs, a big black one and a short white fluffy one, an-- and six children. Three boys and three girls. The boys will work the land with their dad and the girls will help me in the kitchen. Well, I can't do everything can I?"

"Heaven forbids it," laughed Norma. She looked fondly on her eldest, her little face so earnest, her whole life in front of her, bless her youthful heart. *"I hope and pray your dreams will come true duck."*

Mary was taken aback. *"Of course! And now this horrible war is over in Europe we'll be safe and of course, soon the Americans and everyone will beat the Japs and then they'll be sorry. Mam will stop shouting and be happy and stop smoking those horrible smelly cigarettes."* She gave the table a final flourishing swipe with the cloth and stood back, admiring her handiwork.

Lizzie smiled softly. *"You've done a grand job Mary, it looks beautiful, thank you."*

Norma frowned. *"Do I shout a lot? Anyway. Three boys and three girls? Just how will you guarantee that?"*

Mary reddened; she wasn't going to tell her. Mildred Green had explained to her how you could make boy babies and how you could make girl babies. No wonder mam hadn't any boys! She didn't want to talk about this stuff with her mum. This sort of thing was shared with the other girls, to be whispered and giggled about on the doorsteps and in the playground, away from the parents. *"Stop it mam."*

Lizzie pulled her feet out of the tepid water. *"Hand me a small towel Norma, please. There's one on the clothes airer."* Bending over was difficult, she didn't have much bend in her these days, drying her feet was a painstaking long job.

Mary crouched down. *"Does your back hurt? Shall I help?"*

"A little. No Mary, I can manage, but thank you. You're a good girl. You'll find a sixpence on the mantlepiece." Norma opened her mouth to protest. *"No Norma. I want her to have it. I've been trying to shake off this head cold, a bit of inhalation, and hot bicarb for my feet usually does the trick. Mary has been keeping me company."*

Lizzie smiled gently and Mary returned it with a wide grin.

"Well, as long as she's not been a nuisance."

"Mam." Mary protested.

"*Alright. Now then Mary, it's time to get along home now. I won't be long, hurry up, there's a good girl. And! Keep a close eye on your sisters, they've to stay put until I'm home. Just one more thing. If they're hungry then they can have bread with marge, or bread with jam, not with both.*"

Mary collected her sixpence. It was going in the tin. She shook her long braids behind her. "*All right mam. Thank you, Auntie Lizzie—ta-raa.*"

Lizzie's glance followed her out of the door, noticing how the young girl's flowered dress pulled tightly across her hips.

The door banged shut. "*She'll be needing some new frocks soon I think Norma, she's fair bursting out of that one.*"

Norma rubbed her neck in embarrassment. "*I'll have to pop down to the church hall jumble next week, see if I can pick up a bit of something to make into a couple of frocks. She was after me to cut off her braids too, wants a bob. Reg would raise the roof if he came back and found her with short hair. I think I'll get back Lizzie if you don't mind. Have a look through me wardrobe.*" She stood quickly.

"*Sit back down Norma. I didn't mean anything by what I said. The girls are a credit to you. We'll have a cuppa.*"

Norma hesitated. "*I don't want to bother you; I didn't realise that you weren't well. I'll pop back later. But I will make you a cup of tea before I go.*"

"*No Norma. Sit! I know why you're here.*"

"*You do?*" Her voice was high.

"*Yes. What I mean is. It's your Reg's birthday today. Your young one here, she was upset. Fretting about her dad. She *told me it's his birthday and he wouldn't have a cake or his usual two bottles of Guinness."*

Norma fiddled with her wedding ring. *"Mary has always kept things to herself, well, from me, at any rate. Although she does have quite an imagination! The other three have no idea it's his birthday. I didn't mention it because I didn't want to upset them."*

Lizzie nodded and handed Norma an ashtray. *"Here. Enjoy your cigarette, put your feet up. I suppose you heard the little blighters outside earlier?"*

Norma took a deep draw on her Woodbine. *"Did I ever."*

Lizzie considered for a moment. *"Listen. Have your smoke. ---- I'll brew the tea. Then we can talk of the good times passed and the good times to come. Take a leaf out of your Marys' book."*

Quietly getting to her feet, she left Norma alone with her thoughts and busied herself in the kitchen. Some days her home was as busy as the local railway station, a sort of nucleus of women's sharing: problems, secrets and regrets; she wouldn't have it any other way. Filling the kettle, she glanced out of the window; it was so wonderful not to have black out curtains everywhere, blocking out the light and the life happening outside in the street. Now she could look up at the sky any time of the day and night, and she did. A new moon, nights of blackness; a full moon and enough light to read a book by; a half moon and flickering shadows. She gloried in them. And in the fullness of noon, with no more black- out, she could see and hear every song and dance of life in the street, the sounds no longer muffled. It would be a very long time, or maybe never, when she dressed her windows with net curtains.

A sudden shiver took her by surprise. Right at that very moment the sky darkened, and the clouds became a heavy leaden grey. She swiftly pulled the window shut as a cold wind whipped up outside. '*Strewth, what genie brought this in?*'

"Norma? Have you washing on the line? I think we're going to have some rain, and it won't be a shower. By the look of this sky, we're in for a bit of a storm." There was no returning answer. Lizzie poked her head around the door. Norma was slumped in the chair, hands gathered together in her lap, cigarette smouldering in the ashtray. *"Never mind the washing duck,"* she whispered. *"I guess you've had a restless night, fretting on Reg's return, or non-return."*

Who could know? Reg's survival depended on a dollop of destiny and a smidgen of chance. She decided that today wasn't a good day to look into Norma's future, her friend's usual stoical nature was a little off kilter at the moment. She'd leave it a while; it didn't seem right.

Life was full of secrets, not everyone wanted Lizzie to share them, or for Lizzie to know of them. Some didn't even want to know of them themselves; it was too uncomfortable to own their darker shadow side. Some found it easier to turn a blind eye, others preferred to meet their fears head on. It was a responsibility having the gift of foresight and the knowing, Lizzie had learnt this the hard way.

"Well, it seems I'll be having this pot of tea to myself."

Her friend stirred, fidgeting, mumbling. Despite Norma's flushed cheeks- hot flushes of midlife, Lizzie suspected, also contributing to a bad night's rest- it was clear that Norma was troubled by other factors. Her eyes were puffy and swollen, as if there had been tears. Best leave her be, let her rest.

She'd just raised the cup to her mouth when there was a light tap at the door. *"Strewth"*, she breathed.

"Hello? It's me-Frances. I've brought you some sugar. Can I come in?"

"Come in."

"Oooo, did you hear that?"

"Yes, thunder. Sit yourself down."

Frances shivered. Her green eyes darted across to Norma and them back to meet Lizzie's brown eyed gaze. *"Whoops, is this a bad time?"*

"Now's as good as ever duck. Norma's having forty winks-it's a bit of a rough day for her. Reg's birthday."

Frances settled herself gingerly on the edge of a stool. *"My Joseph is in his element, setting up this hardware shop. We've been busy since 5.00am this morning. He's a slave driver."* She let out a hearty laugh. *"I wouldn't have it any other way really. But crikey, he's as a man possessed so I told a fib. Said you'd run out of sugar, and I would nip some around."* Kicking off her shoes, *"Do you mind?"* She wriggled her toes. *"My feet are killing me."*

Lizzie smiled. *"Make yourself at home. It's for the best, isn't it? Some find it difficult to settle back into civvy street. This new venture will be good for both of you."*

"I remember, when he first came home, 'he was 'soooo heavenly', and then? It all changed. He was pretty bad tempered, and it wasn't all down to his badly injured leg. He really struggled. Night sweats, nightmares. We shared a bed together, but it was like laying in single loneliness. I couldn't understand his moods, Lizzie. Why wasn't he glad to be out of it? And you listened to my troubles so often, didn't you? It's a wonder I didn't drive you crackers." She giggled. *"Anyway. I'm not going to brood anymore. It's done. We're on the mend, I hope."*

Lizzie squeezed her hand. *"Good. It's common sense; take charge of what you're able to control and the rest has a way of working its way out. And thanks for the sugar love. There are many like your Joe, out there, struggling to fit themselves back into family life. How can we ever understand what they've been through, what their eyes have seen, what they've had to do to others to stay alive themselves? Somethings are so terrible they will never be able to admit to themselves, let alone share with their wives; they're best left on the battlefield."*

"But it did hurt to be shut out, Lizzie. Joseph's nerves were shot to pieces, and only knocking pints back in the pub and talking to other blokes seemed to give him some relief. He'd never been much of a drinker, as you know. I dreaded him coming home sometimes, but then when he was really late, I feared that he wouldn't."

"And now?"

"These past two years have flown by. We can talk now, although I still feel he is holding something back. We love." She grinned, held Lizzie's gaze, *"a lot." He felt useless, guilty because his other mates were still in the thick of it. I didn't*

care about the others, about Adolf Hitler, about beating the Nazis. I thought, let the others do their bit now. Joe was home with me, that's all I wanted. His poor leg is such a mess, I could have lost him. Am I selfish? Bad?"

Lizzie considered. Her nut-brown eyes scanning Frances's face. *"No. I wouldn't say so, many would think the same. Only I wouldn't mention it to Norma, not at the moment. Let's hope the worst part of the war is over and those poor sods left fighting the Japs will be home soon. Now then. Let's pour ourselves another cuppa, shall we?"*

"Sugar?"

Frances gazed out of the window at the puddles gathering in Lizzie's yard. Norma stirred. *"Any news of Reg?"*

"Not a word. She's taken on a little cleaning job at the Red Lion, it's only a few hours but it's an early start. I came in with the tea pot and she'd flaked out in the chair. A little doze will do her the world of good. Mary's taking charge back at the house-fifteen years old already! Who'd have thought it?"

"I wasn't much older when I first set my cap at Joseph." She stretched out her long legs. *"He wants us to have the shop up and ready for the end of this month."*

"Well, that's smashing. We could do with a new hardware shop. I see you're still wearing the red lipstick. Dig your heels in, did you?" Lizzie yawned, set her cup down sharply on the saucer she put it aside on the table.

Norma stirred.

Frances raised her eyebrows. *"I certainly did. Men! All that fuss over a little makeup; it makes me feel better about myself, Lizzie. Pill box red, it's beautiful, isn't it? He said to me,*

"Your face is so lovely you need no adornment. Honestly! He thought he'd soft soap me. He is so jealous. I realised what had started him off though. Jimmy was helping us, hauling in those heavy crates. He'd mentioned how pretty I was. "Even wearing those baggy overalls you're still a smasher," he'd said. "Your Joseph's a lucky man." I didn't realise Joe had even heard him."

"That's Jimmy, all over," sighed Lizzie. *"Sometimes, I think he deliberately provokes- either that or he's genuinely stupid."*

"Mm-mm- Women love him. Well, you can't help but like him, can you? Only he does seem to get up the other blokes' gander a lot of the time. His aunt Lil worries about him, says he can't seem to settle down."

Lizzie folded her handkerchief on her lap. *"I suppose you heard about the ding-dong between Jimmy and Sam? The first time Eliza had visited me since little Mary Rose was born too."*

"Oh lawd, yes. Lil mentioned something. Poor Eliza. I can appreciate how difficult it all is though. Sam took it badly when Thomas's ship went down. He'd taken him to his heart, he was like a son to him." She stopped short, twisted her wedding band. She wished she'd made more of an effort to visit her friend after Thomas was lost, they'd grown quite close in the time they'd spent sharing lodgings when both their men were away.

"I think I've let her down a little Lizzie. I've been so wrapped up with my Joe the last couple of years. Only, the last time I saw her, she was in such a state-VE day had stirred up so much anger and regret in her."

Lizzie collected the cups onto the tray. *"Things gave a way of working out on their own Frances. Eliza will come out of this on top, I suspect. In a way, Eliza and Jimmy are two of a kind."*

Frances sounded hopeful. *"Do you think so? She always was one for pushing herself upfront- she was an incorrigible flirt, bless her., like Jimmy. There was never any doubt of her loyalty to Thomas, though I think she may have sailed close to the wind sometimes. It's two years since he's gone, hasn't it? And she can't stay on that farm forever. It might suit some, but not Eliza, she'd suffocate. Lil, Eliza, Sam, Jimmy, it's all around the street Lizzie. That Jimmy! My Joe told me he'd told everyone in the pub. Only, I still can't help thinking I could have done more, do you think I------"*

Lizzie cut in. She had no idea where all of this was going and Frances could be overly sensitive at times, it was her nature, she couldn't help herself. *"There aren't many secrets around these parts, it comes from most of us living in the one place for most of our lives, and Jimmy? He has about as much tact as a clacking goose."*

Frances smiled widely showing off her lovely white, even teeth; the red lipstick framed them perfectly. Lizzie always made her laugh, put things right.

Lizzy opened the window onto the street. *"The rain's stopped."* She took a deep breath. *"God's clean air, always so sweet after the rain. Isn't it wonderful?"* She turned to Frances. *"That lipstick really does suit you. Men! They'll never be a match for us women; in physical strength, of course, but emotionally, never. Don't fret anymore, leave it alone. Eliza will find a way."* She paused. *"Sam can be a bit controlling, he was a bit of a bully in his younger days; did you know? Kathleen has his measure, and she is a good mam; she's no fool and will find a way to help her."* She took a minute to gather her thoughts. Eliza has three children. Few men around here would take her on with another man's child in tow, let alone three.

"Jimmy dotes on her, always has. Do you think?"

Lizzie was about to respond sharply when Norma came to with a start.

"Lore, how long have I been asleep?" Her eyes searched the room, took in Frances, and Lizzie, then at the clock on the mantlepiece. *"Goodness, look at the time, and it's been raining!*

Lizzie stood quickly, in her haste catching her head on the corner of the open window. *"Ouch. Stay a moment luv."*

"No, really, I need to go." She gave a quick smile, *"Hello Frances".* Pulling her cardigan tight around her ample bosom, she gave Lizzie a quick peck on the cheek and disappeared. No sooner had she left then there was a slight scuffling sound outside.

"Forgot something?" said Lizzie as the door flung open, expecting to see Norma again.

Only it wasn't Norma. *"Hara!"* There she was, large as life, powdered, perfumed, lips shining with her favourite Poppy Red lipstick, auburn hair styled just so, the epitome of stunning glamour.

"Oh, Ruby, It's you."

"Hello darlings. John has a few days leave so I've taken time off to be with him." She leant forward and dropped a kiss onto

Frances's cheek and then gave Lizzie a squeeze. Taking a step backwards she looked Frances up and down. *"How super that you're here too Frances, you can help me with these tiring arrangements I have to make. It's going to take forever."*

Frances launched herself on Ruby, gave her a long hug. *"Soon to be Lieutenant John Parker's wife! How are you? Nervous? How have you managed leave? I thought they worked you hard on that American base?"*

"They do. And there's something big afoot. Can't say obviously." She kicked off her shoes." *I've had to stay on there for the last three nights, it will be wonderful to sleep in my own bed."* Turning to Lizzie she yawned. *"Is my bed made up Lizzie? Shall I pop upstairs and make it up?"*

"My lodger returns", sighed Lizzie. *"I put fresh sheets on your bed this morning, I was expecting you, somehow. I've aired it with hot water bottles, that room is damp even in June."*

Ruby threw herself down into the armchair. *"Your beds are a darn sight comfier than the camp bed that I have to put up with. Thank you, dear Lizzie, for taking such good care of me."*

"It's a pleasure duck."

Frances's eyes widened. *"Have you set a date then?"*

"We hope to do the deed during this leave. Thing is, do we slip quietly into the registry office-low key, you know, or have a celebratory bash? The truth is I'm feeling a bit rough."

Lizzie postured, hand on her bony hip. *"Did I hear a' right? Ruby Jones sneaking off for a quiet wedding? Come on now Ruby. Don't do us out of a knees-up. Or---hold on a minute"*

A flicker of concern creased Her brow, *"Unless? Is everything still…the pregnancy…. okay?"*

Ruby's pretty brown eyes shone. She patted her tummy. *"As far as I know, if this damn morning sickness is anything to go by. Thought it would have stopped by now. It's just that John's family are all across the water, and I haven't been in touch with my remaining relatives since I was a young girl; I wasn't sure, you see? How he'd feel?"*

Frances paused. *"Well, you both have lots of friends Ruby. I suppose you need to ask John."*

"That's just it, Fran. We've hardly had the opportunity to be together, alone that is. As I said, something's afoot, so these three days are all we have. Will you be my maid of honour? Please?"

Frances hesitated. Ruby pleaded, *"Be a sport, it would mean a lot to me?" And Lizzie? Will you give me away?"*

"Yes, I'll be proud to give you away. I'm not clear though. You plan to marry withing the next three days? You'll need a special licence. Gawd Ruby. I thought you said you and the yank hadn't managed to talk about it?"

"I did. Well, what I meant was, not at any length. So? There's no time to waste, is there?" Ruby glanced at Frances. *"You'll help, won't you darling? Be my maid of honour? Say you will? I know I can count on you both."*

Frances opened her mouth to protest, but one look at her friend's earnest expression and she changed her mind. This couldn't have come at a worse time-there was so much to be done, the shop wasn't nearly ready yet. What would Joseph say?

Ruby pursed her lips. *"What's your answer?" Please, pretty please?"*

Frances had mixed feelings. On the one hand she was delighted for her friend, on the other she couldn't help but feel cornered. *"Ruby, are you sure John will be able to obtain a special licence in time?"*

"Absolutely. He's hell bent on getting it. He's out there right now." She turned to Lizzie, *"We haven't discussed the finer details, dresses and guests- John's leaving that to me."* She theatrically wiped her brow. *"Whew! Can you believe this is all happening? To me?"*

Lizzie sat down heavily into her chair. *"If anyone can do it, you can."*

Frances raised an eyebrow, considering. *"Right then. A church wedding or the registrar? Wedding clothes? A suit or a white wedding frock? And, even if we chip in with clothing coupons, I can't see how I have time to knock up a wedding dress; in three days? Truly Ruby. You really are pushing your luck. I mean----"*

"Oh, don't be an old sour puss." Ruby launched herself across and threw her arms around her. *"I thought you'd be pleased for me?"*

Frances blushed, stuttered. *"I am, delighted. Only honey, you've no idea how busy we are, everything is totally topsy turvy at the moment. Me and Joe are up to our necks in packing cases, shelving, muck! Joe wants us to open shop as soon as we can. How am I going to be able to sew yours and my frock in time?"*

For a quicksilver moment Ruby allowed her mouth to droop. *"I see."* Turning and twisting, ostentatiously admiring her reflection in the mirror above the mantle she announced, *"We'll both find a nice suit instead. I mean really, bridal white is hardly appropriate for me, is it?"* she giggled.

Lizzie, recognising the forced bravado in her voice, reached out and gently took hold of Ruby's hand. *"Let's ask Norma. I'm sure she will help. She's such a whizz with that sewing machine of hers. She collects pattern cut outs from all of her magazines too. You must have your wedding dress Ruby; you're as entitled as any to wear white. John deserves to have a proper bride, veil and all. Frances? You won't need much material for your frock, there's nothing on you! You can have a short frock."*

Frances pretended to protest. *"Cheeky."*

Ruby paused, stood on tip toes to see better in the mirror. Patting her hair she smiled, widely.

Frances gave her a dubious look; her friend was so artful at getting her own way.

"If you're sure? It would be nice, I suppose."

Lizzie was no fool either. *"Hmm. That settles it then. Ruby? Dab up your clothes coupons. Frances? How are you fixed? I'll toddle over to Norma's, and then have a word with a few others in the street. They are always happy to muck in for a wedding, especially if they're invited; and when there is a yank involved, they can be sure of a good spread."* She scurried away, calling from the doorway, *"There's some cheese scones in the tin, help yourselves, only there's not a lot of cheese in them,"* she muttered.

"Shall we? I'm starving," grinned Frances.

Ruby patted her tummy. *"No thank you. I don't want to be a fat bride. I can't wear a foundation garment cause of the nipper."*

"Please yourself." Frances wiped the crumbs from her reddened stained mouth. *"Don't want to spoil my lipstick,"* she grinned. *"Mm, Lizzie bakes a lovely scone. You really should try one, they are splendid. One scone isn't going to make any difference, surely?"*

"Well. The truth is- I've already had something to eat, and I'm a little nervous. Too much grub always upsets my tummy."

Frances tossed her long black hair over her shoulder. *"Ruby? Are you having second thoughts?"*

"No. Not about John, exactly. I adore him. I'm sure he loves me-----He's a good man, I know he is, and kind."

Frances grabbed the seat of her chair, drew herself nearer. *"Then what is it? Tell me"*, she said softly.

"Oh, stories circulate on the base. It's not all honey and roses for the GI brides. Once over the pond, if it doesn't work out, then it can be difficult to raise the funds to come home. On the other hand, some are stranded here waiting for a passage, even though they have husbands, and some have babies."

Frances nodded. *"Starting a new life is scary, course it is. I'm surprised you listen to rumour mongering, though Ruby."*

"It's not all unfounded, Frances. Did you know? The American army do all in their power to discourage their men from taking a British bride? John waited almost twelve

months for official permission to marry me, even though he's an officer."

"Yet. You have it now, right? Surely, if you really want him, then all of this hubbub and form filling is worth it?"

"Listen. The Red Cross came here, to Lizzie's house. They asked me all sorts of personal questions-about my family-where were they and so on. Did my family approve of the marriage? Approve? That's a daft one, my dad---approve of me? It was horrid."

Frances gulped. *"Oh crikey."* She tried to make a joke of it. *"Lucky your dad's no longer around then. Lizzie, me, we are your family now, Rube. What did lizzie say at the interview? Did she behave?"*

"She was wonderful. She would never let me down. Dear Lizzie, she's the nearest I've had to a mother since grandma-mere died. They were very interested in the French relatives, you know, that side of the family. So many questions, you wouldn't believe it."

"Hmm, shocking isn't it. I can see how it's thrown you off course a little."

"Then John was asked how he would support me? Did his parents approve, even asked how much money he had in his bank account?"

"Nosey beasts."

"Routine. Apparently!"

"So? The red tapes done with now. You can both look ahead to your married life in a new country. Yours and John's relationship is hardly a moment of madness, like some. You *both love each other, that will get you both through the newness. It's time to celebrate. Come on old girl, chin up."*

There was no answer. Frances was puzzled, her friend didn't respond as she'd expected. *"Ruby? What is it?"*

Ruby chewed absently on her thumb nail. *"I'm not sure. I never saw myself falling for a Yank. Hadn't reckoned on falling in love- especially during a war. I've seen so many speedy marriages falling apart, I mean some hardly know each other. As they say, 'Marry in haste, repent at leisure."*

It's hardly hasty, John and yourself. You've been engaged for two years."

"What if?

"What? Come to the point. Crumbs. You can tell me anything." Frances's face took on a quiet earnestness. *"Do you want this man? Or not? It's as simple as that. All the rest is workable. Are you making excuses? Are you looking for a way out? because if you're not sure, then what the heck are you playing at, Ruby?"*

Ruby reddened. *"How can you ever think that? What on earth?"* she fired back. *"I am about to leave all that I know- give up a well-paid job too---leave you, my best friend, and lizzie, the nearest I've ever had as a mother, and sail thousands of miles across the Atlantic, to start a new life. It's damn well terrifying. God knows how long I will have to wait to join him- to get a passage on a ship. After this posting he'll more than likely be demobbed and returned back home; and I could still be stuck, waiting, over here?"*

Frances knelt in front of her friend. *"So, save up. Get yourself on a flight. John could send you money for a ticket."*

Ruby was stunned. *"A flight? Do you know the price of an air ticket?"* Then she laughed. *"Well, maybe---it could be possible. Oh, Frances, you wonderful thing, you."*

"Of course." Frances pirouetted in front of her. *"What next, Miss Scaredy Pants?"*

"Stop it. Next? My parents in law! John is very polite, charming, he comes from a good family. Crikey Fran, they own land, some sort of ranch. He has a younger brother at home too; wasn't able to pass the medical and he wasn't conscripted. I can't even ride a horse, never sat on one. John tells me the land has been in the family for over a hundred years!"

Frances roared. *"I can see you clinging onto the back of a horse wearing one of your tight skirts and a pair of high stilettos."*

"Oh don't!" Ruby moaned. *"Whatever shall I do? What will his family think of me?"*

The door creaked. *"Oh! It's you Lizzie. How long have you been standing there?"*

"In my own house? Long enough. Lord in heaven. They will love you, as John does, as Frances and myself do. You are going to have the life of Reilly, as you deserve—a family, children, the lot- all that your heart desires."

"Steady on Lizzie," Frances joked, *"You're making me jealous."*

Lizzie tutted. *"Righto. I have a bundle of clothes coupons in my pocket. You'd be surprised how talk of a wedding bucks everyone up. People around here like you Ruby, and the fact that you've chosen a Yank as your groom? There was hardly *a comment. The Americans are just like us, other than having smarter uniforms and sweeties for the kiddies. War, bad times, can bring out the best and the worse in us all, whichever side of the pond we originate from. So, is this wedding going ahead then?"*

"Heavens yes." Cried Ruby.

"Good." She rubbed her chin, smiled ruefully. *"I'll be reading the cards for half of the women in the street."*

"What?" asked Frances.

"Well, Ruby needed the coupons."

"Heavens. Oh, thank you Lizzie. No more carping! A couple of nights in my own bed, I'll be hunkey dory." Ruby took a deep breath in. *"I am about to wed the handsome Lieutenant John Parker and we will have the celebration of all celebrations."*

"That's the ticket. Although, we are going to have our work cut out," sighed Frances. *"I'll talk to Joe."*

Lizzie raised her eyebrow. *"Now don't you start Frances. If we hightail it down to Pettifer's, we can choose the material now. Norma was there yesterday and as luck would have it, they've had a new delivery. Things are appearing now that we haven't seen for years!"* She winked at Frances. *"And Joe? Let him cope for a day or two, absence makes the heart grow fonder. He's stronger than you give him credit for, don't start acting like his mother, that's not what he needs. Never stop being a wife, or you'll soon find yourself as a live- in housekeeper."*

Ruby rummaged in her handbag and pulled out a compact, reapplied her face powder, and dabbed a touch of rouge onto her cheeks. Lizzie grabbed her shopping bag and purse; she'd saved a few pennies and was going to enjoy spending them; she loved Ruby as her own daughter. Frances gazed thoughtfully at Lizzie, what did she mean? Don't become his mother? She would ask her later on.

They made a hasty dash for the door, three women on a mission.

CHAPTER 5

Lieutenant John Parker enjoyed a useful, productive morning. His status as an American Airforce Officer, along with his southern manners, charmed the Brits to full effect, and he took full advantage. His entrance to the dusty offices of the Registrar was an event; tall and undeniably handsome in his immaculately pressed uniform, he was aware of the glances from the women typists perched behind their desks.

"Like a film star", Doris Flaherty whispered from behind her momentarily still typing hand.

He'd planned to marry Ruby after the war, but what with this emergency posting, well, he had to move fast. The war in Europe was finished, good many men were already demobbed and back home with their sweethearts and family stateside. He'd expected to stay on at the base tidying up and closing down, he hadn't reckoned on this. Something urgent was afoot, a big push to finish the war in the east. There'd been grumblings back home. The newspapers were full of the losses, so many young American soldiers and pilots; the top ranks and American politicians were under pressure to wrap up the Jap fighting machine, pronto.

So, he guessed the time had come. Three days leave, and then a posting overseas. Hells bells! He wanted a wedding band on that gal's finger before he left. If anything happened to him now, his son would have the stigma of being called a bastard; his child wasn't going to be born out of wedlock, no way! Checking his wristwatch, he was surprised to see the hands set at 12.45pm- he'd hoped to buy a film for his camera, but it was proving to be a little more difficult than he'd envisioned. Red roses too, he'd promised Ruby she would have red roses in her bouquet. She had her heart set on them. *"Oh John,"* she'd pleaded, *"if you can only find me two or three- and maybe some greenery and spring flowers, it would be smashing."*

Pulling his cap down into place he climbed into the front of the jeep, how hard could it be? The engine spluttered and roared into action. He whistled a tune- he was about to find out.

Two hours and a warm pint of British beer later, he found himself tapping on Lizzie's door. It was slightly open, and he could hear muffled voices and giggles from inside. He coughed. There was no answer, so he tapped again.

"Hi, is anyone in there? It's Lieutenant John Parker. I'm here to see Ruby. Hi, ma'am?"

Ruby looked towards the door, hesitated. The sound of his slow southern drawl sent her pulse racing.

"Quickly," Lizzie whispered. *"You girls get yourselves up the stairs. I'll see to your man. He mustn't see your frock; it will bring bad luck. Now go, hurry."*

Without thinking Lizzie picked up the poker; opened up the door.

John's smile faded as he stared into a pair currant- brown eyes. They met his in a direct gaze. He stepped back.

"Eh, I'm here to meet my girl, ma'am."

"Come on in," Lizzie invited.

He didn't step forward.

"John?" Lizzie had a sudden epiphany, looking down at her hand clasping the fire hook in front of her, she chuckled. *"Lore. I'm sorry. I've got in the habit of never opening to a knock on my door without a poker in my hand. You see, most that know me, well, they just walk in. Come on in."*

Brits, he thought. Would he ever get used to their strangeness? He took off his cap, smoothed down his hair, and stepped inside.

"Now then! Please sit 'yerself' down, make yourself at home. You'll have to wait a little while for Ruby. She's up my stairs with Norma and Frances, cutting and sewing their frocks." Lizzie tilted her head. *"You didn't give your bride much time for wedding preparations."*

John's heart sank. All he wanted was a quiet hour with his bride before he returned to the base. He gave Lizzie a quizzical glance. *"Maybe I could shoot upstairs and see her?"*

She folded her arms. *"'fraid not."*

One look at John's downcast expression and she relented. *"Give her half an hour. I tell you what, let's have a game of draughts, while you wait?"* She smiled at him with enthusiasm, a smile that he had trouble returning. He wanted, needed to see his bride.

The scene upstairs was frantic. The three women were busily pinning and excitedly chatting and trying the materials against themselves whilst Norma was terrified of any rips that would make the patterns unusable. The dress designs that Norma had saved from her weekly magazines were so delicate they were a nightmare to work with. *"Be careful you don't tear them,"* Norma yelled. *"Place it flat against the tissue paper first. We need to make use of every scrap of material. Ruby, for gauds sake, be careful."*

"Oh crikey, I'm sorry, I've only caught the edge." She was mindful of John being downstairs waiting to see her and she didn't like it, she needed to see him. *"It's very quiet down there. I wonder what they're doing?"*

"Lord!" Cried Norma in exasperation, *"Will you keep still Ruby while I put these pins in."*

Frances could see Ruby's distress. *"I'll just have a peep."* She escaped to the top of the stairs and peered down.

There they were, sat across the table, the draughts board between them—Lizzie frowning in concentration and John squinting against the sunlight pouring through the window. He was tugging at his trouser belt; the British beer lay heavy on his stomach, and he was slightly queasy. Frances made her way back, swallowing her laughter. *"Lizzy has your John playing draughts."*

Ruby pressed her hand to her heart. *"Oh no! my poor John; I must rescue him."* She turned to Norma. *"Do you remember that time I had her kings cornered? She moved them back and forward for ten minutes before she would admit defeat."*

"If you want this dress finished, you'll stay put," Norma barked. *"Now then, where's my scissors?"*

Forty minutes later and Ruby's dress was ready for the final sew. They agreed that Frances would take hers home and make the final running stitches on the tissue paper and collar and pop it around to Norma's later in the evening.

Norma sighed. *"Give me a hand up off this floor, my knees are killing me."* She would be up all-night, whizzing away on her Singer sewing machine, giving it full treadle, and then have to leave sharp in the morning for her two-hour shift skivvying at the pub. They arranged to meet up again at hers at 11.00am. She was game though, all of this bustle had livened her up somewhat, she'd been going back over the years rather a lot lately; too much. Lizzie was right.

"Norma," she'd said, *"Hope is strength, remember this."* She didn't need to give too much thought about the girls' outfits, they all had their Sunday bests, she'd buy them a nice pair of white socks each and put their hair in ringlet rags the night before. As for herself? Well, her powder blue brocade two piece that she'd worn to see Reg off at the station was hanging in the wardrobe; she'd not worn it since that day. There hadn't really been the occasion to warrant it. It would have to come out for an airing. She only hoped she could ease herself into it.

Downstairs, Norma and Frances made a quick recce of the situation and made a hasty exit. Lizzie was a formidable opponent for board games, and they weren't about to be enticed into playing.

"Gotcha!" cried a triumphant Lizzie, *"You didn't see my King sneaking up on you this time, did ya?"*

"John folded his arms wearily. *"Well, no. You've soundly beat me-----again."* Meeting Ruby's gaze he silently pleaded.

"Hello gorgeous. We're finished now, for a while anyhow". She gave him what she hoped was a winning smile whilst her

eyes said, 'I'm sorry darling.' *"Lizzie kept you entertained, I, see?"*

"Ludo anyone?" Lizzie beamed; she was on a roll.

Hell, thought John, he didn't think he ever wanted to play this crazy dame ever again, not even at the point of a bayonet!

"Oh, they've gone" said Lizzie, puzzled. *"I was just getting into my stride."*

Ruby rushed over to John, planted a soft kiss on his forehead. *"Hello my love, miss me?"*

Lizzie was on a roll. *"How about you, John? Ludo?"*

He spread his hands in surrender. *"I'm done."*

Ruby giggled. *"He's exhausted----Look at him."*

Lizzie shrugged. *"Oh. I see. I'd better clear away now anyway. I'll leave you two lovebirds to it."* She turned to John, *"Maybe another time?"*

"Yes ma'am." smiled John.

"Ruby, did you finish what you needed to do?" asked Lizzie, as an afterthought.

"It's all tied up, so to speak, well, almost. Norma is finishing sewing my frock up right now and she'll finish Frances's when the girls are in bed. We're meeting up around hers at 11.am tomorrow. She's such a brick, I can't thank her enough."

"She's a good sort," agreed Lizzie. Turning to John she took hold of his hand, glanced down at his palm and then looked him up and down slowly.

Hell, thought John, what now?

She dropped his hand. *"Another time. Anyway. It's been a nice afternoon, John; we must do it again. I really must make a move. I've a bird soaking in cold water, I must get on."* She disappeared into the scullery, tightening her apron strings in readiness.

They could hear her muttering to herself as the cold water ran over her hands. *"Can't abide cleaning out a fowl,"* she yelled.

John's eyes followed the commotion of splashing and banging.

"It's a present off old Harold, Ruby," shouted Lizzie. *"It ran in front of his cart."*

"Interesting lady," whispered John.

"Hmmm." Ruby tilted her head to one side. *"How did you get on this morning?"*

"I pulled a few strings. Listen. Can we get out of here, honey? For a while? I need to clear my head." He checked his wristwatch. *"We've half an hour."* He took her hand, pulled her in close to his side. *"I'll tell you all about it as we walk."*

John hadn't planned on a lengthy visit with Ruby, but the pleasure of being with his love overruled his earlier intentions to have a quick catch up and then return to the base. The weather had blossomed into a glorious English afternoon. The sky above them was a magnificent deep blue, dotted with a melting of floating white clouds. Stretched out side by side the arms of the willow tree waved gently above them in the gentle, sweet-smelling breeze.

"John?"

He sensed her sudden restlessness. Pulling himself up on his side he leant over her. "*Hmmm?*"

"*Some around here think of me as a flighty piece.*"

"*What exactly does that mean, honey?*"

She turned to face him. "*I'm independent, always have been. I didn't accept the first man that proposed to me. My French grandmother raised me mostly, and my dad, when he was at home. I lost my mother at an early age. I suppose my upbringing was a little strange. And you've been raised in such a different, conventional way; two steady parents, a ranch, a younger brother------*

"*You never talk of your father.*"

"*I don't care to talk about him very much, I don't want to remind myself of him; we didn't really see eye to eye.*"

"*You had your grandmother?*"

"*Yes, for a while, I adored her. But I left home not long after I finished school, made my own way. You're not my first John, I've never hidden this from you.*"

"*So what? you've always been an open book, Ruby. Hell, we're not youngsters, I've had my fun, much more than I care to elaborate on. Now can we stop this? My parents will love you, as I do.*"

"*I do hope so. John? It's not only this. Women over here—this war has meant we can earn good money. Some of us are making nearly twice as much as the men were.*"

He was suddenly peeved. What was she about? He sat bolt upright. "*What are you trying to say?*"

"What will I do when I'm married? I mean, will we live with your parents and brother, on the ranch? What an earth will I do all day? Two women in the same kitchen, under the same roof? I like earning my own money---and hell; I've never ridden a horse—let alone sat astride one, and another thing..."

He stood, pulled her up onto her feet, turned away for a moment. She stared at his profile; he was handsome, more than handsome. Pale olive complexion, straight nose, firm chin, eyes narrowed against the sun. He swallowed, his Adams- apple bobbing slightly.

"He didn't turn to her. *"Do you want to pull out?"* His heart was banging, banging in his chest.

She gave him a broad, honest smile. Making a grab for him she pulled him into her. *"Oh. Don't be silly! How can you ever think that? I adore you, want you, forever. I'm scared----of disappointing you----of not knowing what to expect---what you will want of me, as your wife---your family."*

"Gee whiz. You had me worried. Listen. This is about you and me. If this damn war has taught me one thing, it's that being alive, and living are worlds apart. We will have our first home with my parents and kid brother for a while. I will teach you to ride, if you want to. And you need to hear this." He laughed. *"Ma isn't much of a cook—she's a rancher's wife, yes, but she's not tied to her precious kitchen. She takes some ribbing about her cooking skills from us men. We have an old Chinese guy as our cook. Dad realised he needed help early on in their marriage. When we had hands on the ranch, ma was out of her depth. He's part of our family now, been with us for years, you'll like him. As for your independence? It's one of the*

things I love about you—along with the French endearments you whisper to me when we make love."

"Comme-ca? Like this?" She undid the top button of his shirt collar, *"Embrasse moi Cheri,"* she whispered, pressing her lips into the hollow of his neck.

"Woo! Stop there. Anymore and I'll be ready for take-off!"

"Why? Pourquoi?"

He breathed in hard and gently pushed her away. *"The wedding's still on then?"*

"Mais oui, certainment."

"Ruby. Enough. Stop with the French."

"Alright," she laughed. *"Maybe I'll be able to teach your maa some of the French recipes that gran taught me."*

He raised an eyebrow. *"Ma? Don't hold out too much hope on that one. Maybe you could try them on our cook Bingwen! Anyway, I've something for you."*

"Oh, yes?" She eyed him up and down.

"You can be damn sure of that; later!"

She danced around him. *"What is it?*

"Sit here." He pulled out a ball shaped tissue. *"For you."*

Snatching it away from him she tore off the paper. *"Oh, my lord, an orange!"* Pressing it to her face she drank in the sharp aroma. *"OO, peel it for me, please?"* Propping her chin on her wrist she waited patiently as he carefully ripped away the outer covering and split it into quarters, licking the juice from his fingers, teasingly.

"Oh, give it here."

He laughed. *"Ruby, manners. You're like a child."*

Biting into each segment of cushioned flesh she made a pretence of swooning as the sweet, sharp juice squirted onto her tongue.

He wiped the corners of her mouth, his smile indulgent. *"Finished? Good, because I really do need to make a move."*

"Merci beaucoup. Oh John, that was lovely, and I didn't share any with you; I'm sorry. I haven't tasted an orange in such a while."

Leaning forward he took a kiss, tasting the perfume of her lipstick mingled with the sweet juice of the orange. The embrace lingered, neither of them wanting to pull away from each other. Suddenly a stone whizzed through the air landing hard against Ruby's foot; it broke the mood, along with excited children's chattering coming from the bushes alongside.

"Look at that yank kissing her. Ere, what's that she's eating? Him," another chuckled. *"Got any gum chum?"* they chorused. *"Any chocolate?"* squealed another.

"Ruby flushed. *"Clear off you little blighters!"*

John dug deep into his trouser pocket and held up an orange, in triumph. He tossed it amongst the bushes, and its landing was followed by hectic screaming and shouting. *"What is it?"*

"It's an orange," called Ruby.

Spilling out on top of them, they handed it back to John. *"Can you open it? It smells lovely."*

He pulled out a small penknife, slowly peeled it and cut it into segments, handing them each equal slices.

The couple strolled away, arm in arm, soon forgotten, the event of the orange having taken over the kiddie's interest. At the jeep they stopped, and he gave her a hard kiss full on the mouth, then swiftly turned and climbed inside, turning the engine.

"See you tonight honey. 8.30pm, for a beer. Or maybe I'll settle for a warm lemonade."

"Lemonade?"

"I'll explain later. By the way? I have a film for the camera, and red roses." Waving his arm out of the side window, he blew her a kiss.

Her stomach rose and fell. She settled her hand on her tummy. *"John's nipper."*

"See you tonight," she called, *"Missing you already."*

Ruby twisted to check her rear view in the long mirror. *"Are my seams straight Norma?"*

"You'll do. Where are you off to?"

She twirled a lock of red hair behind her ear. *"The Three Bells."*

Norma pursed her lips. *"Lucky for some. As soon as my little lot are in bed, I'll make the finishing touches to your frock. Mary can stay up a little late and help me."*

Ruby was aware of the slight reproof. *"Oh darling. I really can't thank you enough. It's only that, I'm hopelessly useless with a needle and thread."*

Norma raised a critical eyebrow. *"Maybe your mother-in-law will teach you."*

"Oh Norma, don't. I'm skittish enough as it is."

"Your life is about to change in a big way, it's understandable. Don't worry luv. I've been a bit of a moody cow lately, restless----sewing your wedding dress means I won't have time to brood."

Taking hold of her friend's shoulders Ruby looked directly into her eyes. *"Oh darling. Here I am, full of myself, and you're going through hell worrying about Reg."*

"If he'll ever return? Come home? Even if he's able, how do I know he'll want to? I mean, he's been gone a long time. Will he be the same Reg that left, four years ago? Take Frances's Joe for instance. He's crippled for life--- and she had a few difficulties other than his injured leg with him, if you take my meaning. Moods, and so on."

"Oh Norma. Reg won't stop at anything to come home to you and his girls."

"I wish I could be as sure. How do I match up to the foreign women that will have crossed his path? I can't be sure of him, he's a man, he has needs. I've heard so much gossip about them brothels out east, and the women throwing themselves at a soldier for a bar of chocolate or a pair of them nylon stockings. In truth. Who can blame the lads for seeking a little comfort?'

Ruby flicked her hair indignantly. *"Well, I would for one! You've been watching to many films love. Come on. This isn't like you."*

"Yes, it bloody well is. We can't all be stunning redheads. "Look at me. Dumpy with mousey brown hair. "

"Stop it. You are the mother of his four daughters, the wife he dotes on; an attractive mature woman who still has a lot to offer."

"Do you really think so?"

"I most certainly do." Ruby took hold of a lock of Norma's hair. *"You have wonderfully good, thick hair. Maybe a little permanent wave would cheer you up? I think it's strong enough to take it."*

"I couldn't afford it. The girls are shooting up like runner beans. Our Mary's already taller than me." She paused. *"A home perm, do you think? I could manage that."*

"Norma Watling! Do you think I'd let you make my wedding dress and not pay you? A professional perm for you; I'll arrange it and pay." Ruby wagged her finger, *"Definitely not a home perm. Do you remember when Lizzie tried it?"*

The memory of Lizzie's orange frizz was a sight neither of them would ever forget. Ruby started with a nervous laugh.

"Do I ever," grinned Norma. *"Crikey, she looked like she was wearing one of those tall fuzzy things, those regimental hats worn by the Welsh Guards. A Bear Skin!"*

"That's it." Ruby bent forward, squealing with laughter.

"Oh, my crikey, she was a sight," howled Norma.

"*Exactly. If your Reg returned home to see you looking like that, he probably would do a flit; well, to the nearest pub anyway. I will pay, I can afford it, my treat. Although you may have to wait until after the wedding, I'm not sure how busy they are.*"

"*Thank you.*" She smiled ruefully. "*I don't suppose I'll ever really know what Reg is getting up to.*" She sighed. "*What matters is that he comes home alive and in one piece. I'm being silly. Only, can you imagine it? A Bear Skin?*"

They both fell about laughing, weren't aware of a third person entering until a sudden shadow of a presence fell over Norma. She gave Ruby a quick look and then addressed Lizzie. "*Oh Lizzie. Why do you creep about like that? I didn't hear you come in.*"

"*I wasn't aware I was creeping! Oh, it's probably my new slippers. Anyway, it's good to see you both so merry; laughter, it's one of the best medicines in the world. So, tell me? What's the joke?*" She waited, eyes sparkling, eager to join in the fun.

Ruby's mouth twitched at the corners. "*Joke? Oh, nothing much really. Something silly really. Norma was trying to imagine how her Reg would look wearing one of those Bear Skins. She has a fancy for a soldier wearing one of those bear Skins.*"

Lizzie screwed up her eyes, clearly disbelieving them. "*Really? Anyway, listen to this. I've just been told, Lil Thompson? You'll never believe this. She is driving a crane! A crane! Can you imagine it?*"

Glad to change the subject, Ruby jumped in. "*I'm all ears, she worked as a barmaid at The Crown at one time, didn't she?*"

"'Sright." Lizzie gloated triumphantly with her bit of news. *"Can you imagine what will happen when her Teddy arrives home----he's due to be demobbed anytime now, I believe. And him? Always on his soapbox----- 'A woman's place is in the home---a man's not a man if he allows his woman out to work."*

"I remember. She was quick of the mark to get behind that bar though, wasn't she?" murmured Norma. *"He'll create hell."*

"She's a strong girl. I believe she'll hold her own." Lizzie pushed her specs up the bridge of her nose. *"But a crane! This neighbourhood is certainly seeing some changes."*

Ruby gave Norma a conspiratorial glance, *"What's the world coming to?"* they chorused.

John ducked his head, took a look around before guiding Ruby towards a seat. *"Let's sit at the window honey, it's 'kinda' dark in here. These country pubs of yours, they sure are poky."*

"They've been standing a long time; folks were shorter then. This one for instance, it's over a hundred years old."

He laughed. *"You don't say? I had to stoop to get through the doorway; nearly knocked my head off. It's cute though, has a sort of charm; kind of relaxing."*

"It will liven up later. Folks like to pop in for a quick drink after work. The licensee calls last orders just after 9pm--- closes at 9.30pm sharp."

"In that case, I'd better get out drinks in. The usual?"

"Can I have a bitter shandy please? I've such a thirst, and a packet of crisps?"

"Coming up." He leant forward, and gave her a long, slow lingering kiss, full on the mouth.

Ruby pulled back. *"John. Not in here."*

"Sorry honey. Couldn't help myself."

Ruby glanced around the room, acutely aware of the interest aimed at them since they'd entered. John leant on the bar, confident, easy manner, unaware.

"Blinking yanks. Who do they think they are?"

Glancing over her shoulder, she caught the spiteful eye of a young thin chap sitting in the corner. He tilted back on his chair, raised his cap, gave her a cheeky wink. Ignoring him, she fumbled in her handbag, took out her compact and checked her lipstick in the mirror. As she thought, smudged! Dabbing her lips, she smiled at John as he made his cautious tread back to the table, balancing two overfull glasses and her bag of crisps.

"Thank you." Deep in thought she took a long draw of the beer and lemonade. She was fed up to the back teeth with the comments, jibes, looks, that accompanied so many of her outings with John. Yes, America may have been reluctant to join the war, but they did, and thank God, because Britain had sorely needed them.

"What's all this? My girl is sad?"

Pulling her stool closer into him she whispered. *"Not sad darling. Daydreaming, about our new life together in the States, and about being your wife."*

"Mrs Ruby Parker, I can't wait to show you around home and introduce you to the folks. Ma is kind of shy with new faces, but you'll soon win her over."

"Oh, I do hope so. What does she look like?"

She's small, slim with long straight blue- black hair and sort of honey brown eyes; her father was a North American Indian, Sioux. Dad is a giant of a man, big voice, broad shoulders, thick red hair. My kid brother looks a lot like him---me? I inherited ma's bronze complexion and black hair, tall like dad but without his huge shoulders. Ma says I have a look of her father." He touched the tip of his nose, *"Long, straight."*

"I wonder who our children will feature," said Ruby dreamily. *"My grandmother was French, petit, with dark eyes and red hair, like me."*

"Our kids will be fine, the girls beautiful, and the boys? Who can say? Maybe red hair? Black hair? Big noses like me?"

Ruby giggled. *"Could be interesting."*

"Sure."

Ruby began to relax, tucking into her bag of potato crisps she glanced down at her waistline.

"Oh dear, I don't seem to be able to stop munching. Here John, you'd better finish these."

"Potato chips? No thanks honey, enjoy them, you look fine."

Ruby laughed. *"They're not chips, silly. Chips are what we eat from the fish and chip shop."*

"We call them fries."

"Whatever. Do you mind if I have another shandy, please? The salt has made me thirsty."

"For sure." He stood, paused. "*I wish these damn ceilings weren't low. I crick my neck every time I pass under these beams.*"

"Oh John, it's an old building, I told you."

Waiting at the bar he called back to her as an afterthought. "*In America one single state alone can be bigger than the whole of your England.*"

The darts game just finishing, his comment fell on a sudden hush.

Stan, the chap in the corner who'd been showing more than usual interest in the couple earlier, glared and made his way to the bar. Calling for a bitter, he deliberately jostled into John. "*'Ere, watch it, you've made me spill my beer.*"

"Sorry pal, let me buy you another. What will you have?"

"Keep your dollars mate." He raised his voice. "*Typical yank, throwing your money around.*"

"Hey, no offence meant sir. What can I get you?"

"*Save your money mate, you'll need it for your floozie in the corner.*" He turned to his darts partners, seeking approval.

John turned full on and faced him. "*Apologise to the lady.*"

The locals looked anywhere but at the two men.

Ruby jumped up, knocking her stool sideways. "L*eave it John. He's not worth it. Let's go outside. Please?*"

Taking note of Ruby's sudden flush, John relented.

"*She's right. You're not worth it pal.*" Slamming a handful of silver onto the counter he made a measured request of the landlord. "*Give the man whatever he wants, maybe he'll accept this instead of my dollar.*"

Ruby felt her pulse settle. "*Can we leave now. Please?*"

As he ushered her through the door a voice called out, "*Good riddance, sod off back home and take your tart with yer.*" Stan curled his lip. "*Yanks!*"

That did it. John gave Ruby a gentle shove. "*Wait outside honey.*"

"*Oh, my Christ, John, no. He's a bad piece of work, he's been inside. Leave it.*"

"*Ruby? Wait outside.*" He carefully closed the door behind her.

"*Let's see. Would you care to repeat that?*"

Stan pushed his face close into John's. "*She's a tart. What's wrong with our own men, that's what I'd like to know? Tart.*"

John caught him by the collar. "*You didn't apologise to my lady.*"

"*What are you going to do about it then?*"

For a moment John considered, then he suddenly released his hold and shoved him away. "*Ruby's right. You're not worth the trouble.*"

As he turned to leave, Stan drew his arm back and threw a fist at him. It caught him short. John was half expecting it, he turned sharp, and fist clenched, lashed out, hitting him hard and straight, full on the nose. The force put Stan flat on his back.

Heaving himself up he stared, stupefied. *"You've dam well broken my nose. He's broken my bloody nose,"* he said, looking around the sea of faces for sympathy. *"Ere landlord, what are you going to do about him?"*

The landlord came from behind the bar, pushing his shirt sleeves up. Stan sneered. *"That's right, throw him out on his arse."*

"I won't do anything of the sort. I've warned you before, you weaselly faced maggot. It serves you right. Go home to the missis. If she'll 'ave yer'. Now get out of my pub, you're barred."

Stan started to protest, *"But...."* A sudden gush of blood from his nose persuaded him to make a quick exit out of the side door.

The landlord sighed. *"Can I ask you to leave too sir, and your lady?"*

John made a show of dusting off his jacket, smoothed his hair. *"I'm sorry about him landlord. Heck though, he sure had it coming."* Grinning he addressed the room. *"We eat a lot of steaks back home; I guess these damn Yanks don't know their own strength."*

Ruby hadn't waited outside; she'd seen the whole episode. *"John?"*

"Honeeeey----I asked you to wait outside." Catching her around the waist he turned her towards the door. *"Let's make a move, I need some fresh air."*

"Your hand?"

"It's fine. I'm fine."

She giggled. "Tara all."

"Here, hold still," Norma muttered through a row of pins pressed between her lips.

Ruby protested. "Can I move now?"

"Last one. Yes, finished, in one minute!" She was pleased, and very relieved. It had been a long night.

Ruby twisted and turned, examining and considering her reflection, as Frances became more and more irritated. "This mirror is heavy Rube," complained Frances, "and you'll tip the stool if you're not careful. Stop fidgeting for one minute."

Ruby was oblivious to her friends complaining. "Is the length right do you think, Norma?"

Norma heaved herself up from her knees and took a step back. "Perfectly straight, and yes, it's staying where it is."

Ruby wiped a tear away from the corner of her eye. "Thank you darling."

"You're welcome, although, perhaps you should put your shoes on again and I'll check out the length, just once more!"

Frances handed Ruby a pair of two- toned cream court shoes. Slipping them on Ruby turned and twisted. "Thank you, Norma. The length is perfect, although I would have preferred a slightly thinner heel," she groaned.

Frances secretly agreed—she thought these shoes made her friends ankles appear a little thick. Should she say? It seemed she must. *"Oh Rube, they're not very flattering."*

"Hey," objected Norma. *"Don't change the height of the heel now, crikey- o- riley."*

Frances protested, *"Oh, come on Norma. It's not a day to make do, is it? Her wedding day?"* Turning back to Ruby she spoke calmly and reasoned, *"You don't have to wear cream to match your dress---and you really do need a thinner heel. What do you say, Lizzie?"*

"Step back up on the stool," Lizzie ordered. *"Hmmm---you're right Frances. These aren't right with your frock, Ruby. They make your ankles look fat."*

Frances gasped. *"Crikey Lizzie, I didn't say that."*

"It's what you meant Frances, and you're quite correct," despaired Ruby.

"For heaven's sake, you lot," cried Norma, arching her back to ease the stiffness.

"It will have to be my black patent heels then, the ones with the ankle strap and little pearl button, they have another one and a half inches to the heel. I knew the cream weren't right, but they match the dress, and I only had so many coupons, as you know. Hold on a mo. I'll nip back upstairs and fetch them."

"Ruby! Take off this dress first, now." yelled Norma. *"We don't want you tripping on those stairs."*

Lizzie took a hard long look at Norma. *"Sit down Norma, rest your legs duck. You've done wonders."*

Ignoring the commotion above their heads, they sat in silence. Ruby was clearly having trouble finding the shoes. Then---- a triumphant cry---and seconds later she appeared in front of them, brandishing her prize.

"Thank goodness. Put them on and get back on the stool before I lose the will to live," moaned Norma.

Frances slipped the dress over the bride's head and stood back. Norma made no effort to move from the comfort of her chair.

Lizzie raised an eyebrow, *"Very sleek. It's lovely how you cut it on the bias, Norma. It makes such a difference, and the long tight sleeves are very elegant. Perfect!"* She swallowed. *"You're beautiful duck."*

Ruby's eyes shone. *"Thanks' Lizzie! And God bless you, Norma. It's perfect. I didn't really want a dress down to my ankles, it's not so fashionable these days, is it?"*

"That's probably because folks can't get a hold of the material," nodded Lizzie.

"Maybe, and I hadn't given too much thought to my shoes, to be honest. The extra height makes a difference, doesn't it? I'm on the short side, don't have your long legs, Frances."

"Don't be daft," tutted Frances. *"Your figure is very shapely. Me? I'm like a bean pole."*

"When you've finished comparing your silhouettes, we still have a few odds and ends to sort out," complained Norma. *"Frances? You will need to press the hem of your frock---it's draped there, over the back of the chair. Ruby? There are a few lace daises still need sewing onto your headdress. Are you certain about not wanting a veil? I could knock up a short one? I have a scrap of white netting."*

"Lore, no thanks Norma. The little banded headdress is right up my street. We'll all be having a boogie afterwards at the pub, and I'm not going to change after the ceremony; a veil would look silly, don't you think?"

Lizzie moved quickly. *"Stay there Norma. Take the frock of Ruby---Let me hang it up before it creases."*

Frances helped tug the dress up and over Ruby's head. *"That's a beautiful under slip Ruby. Lace trimmed too. Is it part of your trousseau?"*

"Yes, it is. I've had to make do with three of everything. Couldn't manage the traditional six. I took this one out of the box because I'll be wearing it under my wedding dress, it fits nicely into my curves. I'll nip upstairs and take it off again."

"He's a lucky man, your John," mused Norma. *"Take a hint from me Ruby, I was shy when I married Reg. I insisted on switching off the light, and even now I undress in the dark."*

The three friends stopped short. Reg and his possible fate were a sudden elephant in the room.

Norma sighed. *"He never did see me naked."*

Frances took hold of Norma's hand. *"My Joseph says 'Lingerie maketh the woman'. I don't suppose Reg minded not seeing you naked."*

"Maybe not, but the times he stubbed his toe undressing because I insisted on keeping the light off," smiled Norma. *"Anyhow, if Reg ever does make it home----I'll do a blinkin' striptease, he can see the lot."*

Lizzie's sudden appearance with a tray holding four sherry glasses and a full decanter lifted the energy back into the room. *"I'll drink to that. Anyone join me?"*

They eyed the decanter. *"Parsnip wine?"*

"No. The real thing, well in a way. It's cooking sherry."

Lizzie did the honours. *"A small one for you Ruby. Raise your glasses."*

They held them high.

"To Ruby and John," they chorused.

"And let's have one more," They waited on Lizzie, *"One minute----- I know---"*

"To Reg's return. And to Norma's naked fan dance."

"To Reg's return," they hollered, *"and to Norma's naked fan dance."*

"My wedding day, Wednesday, 16th May 1945." Her voice echoed through the stillness of the room. She called out. *"Lizzie? Lizzie?"* No answer.

The house was unusually quiet. She was uneasy, nervous. Throwing back the bed covers she swung her legs out over the side of the bed and flinched as her feet hit the cold lino. *"Gawd."* A polite cough caused her to 'start'.

"Lizzie? Is that you?"

"It's me, yes. Who do you think it is? Can I come in?"

"Come in, do----Only I called, and you didn't answer."

"Can you open the door, Ruby? My hands are full."

She twisted the handle.

"You'll have to yank it hard, the woods warped, damp," came the advice from the other side.

She followed the instructions---the door flew open and there stood Lizzie, resplendent in hair curlers, face adorned with cold cream, holding out a breakfast tray in front of her.

"Here you are ducks. Hop back under the covers. Breakfast in bed."

For a moment Ruby was unable to speak.

Lizzie looked on, thoughtful. *"Hop in then."* She placed the tray across Ruby's lap.

"Everything changes today, doesn't it?"

"Only if you want it to," said Lizzie briskly.

"Oh, but I do. I love John. I really do."

"Good. Then sit up and eat your eggs. Don't ask me how I've managed to give you two, enjoy them."

Ruby cast a sideways glance. *"And butter? And Jam? What have you been up to? How?"*

"I just said, don't ask, didn't I?" laughed Lizzie.

Ruby took the teaspoon and tapped the top of the egg, cut across it with a knife and dipping the bread and butter into the rich yellow yolk, she popped it into her mouth. *"Mm-mm-delicious—blinking lovely."*

"Good," smiled Lizzie.

"Only, how did you manage this? Two eggs? bread slathered with butter. Is this fresh coffee? I insist, I really have to----"

Lizzie relented. *"If you must. It's from your soon to be husband. He knocked me up out of my bed a little after 4am this morning. Throwing stones at my back window, he was."* She raised an eyebrow. *"Seems he knows you sleep at the front of the house."*

"John? He did?"

Lizzie wriggled her shoulders. *"Haven't I said?"*

"I'm sorry," Ruby giggled, *"Here, sit on the bed. Share with me."*

"I've eaten. You don't think he'd leave me out, do you? I'll try a drop of that coffee please. It smells lovely."

"How did he?"

"He brought it in a flask. I'll fetch another cup."

Breakfast over, Ruby was taking a long leisurely soak in her bath, for once ignoring the ruling on the mandatory inches of water allowed. Even now it was early still, 06.30am. Laying fully back, she was luxuriating in the warm scented water lapping around and above her breasts, soothed by the thoughtfulness of her husband to be, and the comforting chat and coffee that she'd shared with Lizzie. The last few days had been so hectic, and at one point she'd thought it wouldn't happen---what with the special licence, her dress, flowers, rings, wedding breakfast, and then, to cap it all, that chap starting trouble in the pub.

She'd never really considered a religious ceremony; a civil wedding was fine. And so, like a miracle, it had all fallen into place: 11.30am at the registry office, them all around to the pub---opening at 11.30am. They would enjoy themselves until 3.00pm when the pub closed for a few hours. Perfect. Even with John's connections it would have been very difficult without the support of her long-standing friends and the goodwill of the neighbours 'dibbing up' the coupons. Dear sweet Frances, her Maid of Honour. Wonderful Lizzie, agreeing to walk her up the steps and give her away, and Norma! God bless her heart; she'd been an absolute brick. She couldn't thank her enough; her wedding dress was stunning. She smiled, she had a lovely surprise for her later, and hoped she would like it.

John had risen at daybreak, splashed handfuls of cold water over his face and head, and stood out in the air watching the sun slowly heralding his wedding day; 16th May 1945. A new dawn—the next stage of his life, to be shared as one, with Ruby. John and Ruby, Ruby and John. Without her love, none of this made any sense. The war? He'd never doubted being on the right side, never really considered they would lose. When he allowed it to, a slight nagging doubt he was being selfish; rushing Ruby through the marriage before this last leg of the war was over, well, it did unsettle him. The day Ruby told him she was carrying his baby, that had settled it. His baby would carry his name.

The first time he saw her he knew, every cell in his body seemed to recognise her, and he'd acted on those instincts and set out to win her. His pals wrote her off as some strange, crazy whim, teased him relentlessly, and then became slightly concerned. What was he doing? Getting serious over a Brit? They'd all tried with various lines of advice- come on John, you've seen how these relationships often turn out, romancing a little. Having fun? That's one thing, but you're waying in too heavy, etc, etc! He'd taken it in the spirit it was meant, and then ignored them. Despite her fiery independence, he sensed a tenderness in her that drew her too him. He hadn't held back, he'd pursued her.

Ruby had erred on the side of caution, kept him at bay for a while. She, more than any, was aware of the much-perceived stereotype, wartime female trying to hook herself up a passage to America.

His persistence eventually paid off. She began to look at him out, and that night of the air raid when he'd nearly ran her over with the jeep. That had got things on a different level. Yet still, he'd been reluctant to propose. The idea of rejection caused him to hold back until he'd lost patience with his weakness and decided he must have an answer, either way. Kneeling down in front of her friends and neighbours he'd offered her the blue sapphire ring, and hells bells, she'd accepted.

And today was their wedding day. Unable to settle, he'd skipped his shower, pulled on a sweater, and slacks, poured coffee into a flask and raided the stores. Would Ruby be awake? Would she change her mind? She'd been nervous, worrying about meeting his folks, giving up her life over here, and all of her friends. He wanted to see her, for a minute.

The drive over from the base had seemed interminable. Even though the sun was up and the birds noisily greeting the day, he had little thought for the passing greenery in which he usually delighted.

Grabbing hold of the flowers and brown paper bag and flask, he set himself outside Ruby's window. She was at the front of the house, right? Then he had second thoughts. No, he didn't want Ruby to see her bouquet yet. And he wanted to make her breakfast and take it up to her. He would see if there was a light on downstairs. Failing that, he was aware the old lady slept at the back of the house. He would try and rouse her.

 No lights on downstairs. He threw a couple of small stones at the back bedroom window. The sash window opened, and the old lady stuck her head out. *"Who is it?"*

He felt a little silly. *"It's me ma-am, John. I've got eggs. And the roses. Ruby's bouquet?*

Lizzie grabbed for her specs. *"Wait there, I'll be down in a minute."*

Pulling the door wide open she ushered him inside.

He handed her brown grocery bag, and she looked inside, then at him. *"Eggs, jam, butter?"*

"I've made coffee, real coffee. I thought we could have breakfast together. Is she awake? Can I see---?"

Lizzie cut in. *"See her? Yes. At 11.30am, at the Registry office—don't be late!"*

"But?"

"She's in the bath. Everything will be fine. Off you go. I'll make her a nice breakfast."

"Could I---?"

"No love. Thank you, you're very kind. I'll soft boil the eggs, take it up to her in bed."

"Oh, there's some for you too."

"Yes, lovely, thank you." Then she'd given him a huge hug, and a warm smile that lit up her brown twinkling eyes. *"Off you go then lieutenant. Drive safely."* With that she gave him a slight shove towards the open door.

He leaned back on the door, disappointed and a little dazed. What had he expected? Not this. That crazy old lady? Bad luck to see the bride before the ceremony, was that it? There was nothing else for it but to make his way back to the base, take a shower, shave, take a bite with Cameron, his best man, and get through the rest of the morning as best as he could.

Pancakes with maple syrup, a few games of bridge and the two set off: Cameron taking the wheel.

They'd made their way up the steps through the small group of wedding guests waiting to see the bride. He'd taken the banter in good humour, the usual sort of stuff; are you sure you want to do this? Get on the boat quick, etc. John was thankful to have some time to calm his nerves inside. The small room smelt musty. Cameron moved to position himself on John's right-hand side.

Despite his earlier misgivings, Cameron had agreed to be John's Best Man. He hadn't entirely altered his opinion, not 100%---American Service man, Brit bride; it was a risk. However, John was a good pal, and Ruby seemed genuine enough. So, what the hell, he would and did stand by him.

Lieutenant John Parker, officer in the American Airforce---quite a catch.

Grounded after his crash, John had a bad time of it, anger, frustration; guilt, the fact he'd survived when three of his crew had copped it. Then there was the adjustment from Pilot to Ground Crew Officer; it was difficult. Cameron, an older, enlisted man, an expert in hands on engineering, skilled in his knowledge of repairing and maintaining the aircrafts. He had been at the base since the beginning. He'd made a point of watching over him. Being an enlisted man, he'd not posed as any sort of threat, or been in any sort of position to make a judgement; he'd never been up in the air. John had gradually opened up to him.

Cameron, close lipped, practical, no nonsense; his inherited temperament from his Scottish ancestors; John—deep thinking, sensitive, both had one powerful thing in common. They were both longing to be back home in the State's, to leave this small island behind forever.

Yes. He would do this for him. Best man. Why not? He could sense John fidgeting beside him. He checked his wristwatch, nearly time. John nudged him. He turned.

"Where is she?" John mouthed.

Cameron grinned and twisted his head towards the open door. John followed his gaze, looking over his shoulder. His heart lurched in his chest. *"Ruby,"* he whispered.

And here she was. *"God, would you just take a look at her?"* he whispered to his Best Man. His bride. Stood in the doorway, holding onto Lizzie's arm---blushing, radiant, her warm brown eyes shining---his beauty. Turning, he faced her full on, and was met by a wide, happy smile—her shining red lipstick matching the red roses, precisely. As she walked towards him, his soul was brimming with such a tenderness for her that for an instant, he was unable to catch his breath.

The Registrar gave a polite cough, and John faced the front. Her perfume drifted towards him. He heard Lizzie murmur, and he looked to his side as Ruby joined him, and handed her bouquet to Frances, who then stepped back and took a seat on the left. *"Nudge up Joe,"* she whispered.

Ruby stood in close by his side, her head reaching to his shoulder. She gave him a quick smile and then turned to her front.

The Registrar made a short official statement and then invited them both to repeat after him---tipping his headfirst to John, and inviting him to repeat after him --- *"I do solemnly declare-----"*

The groom made his vows softly with his eyes fixed on Ruby—his slow American drawl intimate and composed.

The official adjusted his spectacles and nodded at Ruby. Smiling broadly, she looked into John's eyes and made her vows in a clear confident voice---*"I do solemnly declare---"*

Cameron looked on, stepped forward and handed over the wedding bands.

John's hand trembled as he slipped the gold ring onto his bride's finger; Ruby followed, pushing the ring onto John's finger with an ease and confidence *"A symbol of my eternal love,"* she whispered.

'Women can always find the words,' thought Cameron, 'ten minutes --- to change a life'.

They were ushered into a dusty backroom that smelt of mothballs. John, Ruby; Cameron and the maid of Honour as witnesses. John handed his Best Man the camera and he took their very first photograph as a married couple. The Registrar offered to take one of the four of them together, he seemed to think that Cameron and Frances were a couple. For some reason she didn't put him right. The four of them stood closely together, Frances, tall and willowy, stood behind Ruby's shoulder, John with his arm around his wife's waist, and Cameron at the back of John.

"Watch the birdie," called the official. Click-done.

John gave his bride a long kiss. Cameron shook his pal's hand and planted a light kiss on Ruby's forehead, hesitated, then tried for a swift peck on Frances's cheek. He aimed wrong and caught her on the tip of her nose. *"Whoops a daisy,"* she laughed. Cameron flushed.

The official made a pointed look at the clock on the wall. Within seconds they had joined Lizzie and Joseph and a few of the guests outside. Frances hastily handed the bouquet to Ruby and joined her man, a little guilty that she hadn't set the registrar right. Why hadn't she?

Cameron stood to one side, leaning against the brick wall, looking on at the small group of friends who were clapping and cheering and throwing confetti. He was a little envious, couldn't help wondering how it would be to return home with a wife. Maybe it would be kind of nice, although he'd never been the hearts and flowers sort of guy.

He was under no illusion; in his uniform he was presentable—but out of it? A short, stout Yank with bushy eyebrows and a crew cut that stuck out at angles because of his naturally curly hair. Marriage? No. he had things to do, people to see---ma, pa, sisters, nieces and nephews--- a garage business to set up. One day in the future? If he met the right gal.

"Hey, fella---come and join us!" yelled John. He walked into the opening semi-circle of friends, neighbours who were surrounding the newly married couple. All eyes were on him, and he was a little self-conscious. Stuck for words he uttered the first thing that came into his head. *"Pub open yet?"*

His comment was met with an encore of *"I'm parched—I'll say so---lead on."*

He couldn't help taking a quick glance at the bridesmaid, Frances; her jet-black hair cascading long and heavy across her shoulders and down the length of her back, his eyes darting down to her left hand to assess her marital status. Joseph stepped forward.

"She's taken mate."

"Can't blame a guy for wondering."

Joseph pulled at his collar. Frances reddened, aware that she'd possibly enjoyed the attention from Cameron a little too much earlier on. She made a silent appeal to Lizzie, who swiftly linked herself into Cameron's arm. *"Are we off to the pub then? I'm dead on my feet. It's been a long morning."*

"We can't have that. Hold onto me. --- Where's this pub?"

"Around the corner." someone shouted.

The hastily arranged wedding venue was situated at the back of the pub and was soon packed with close friends and coupon giving guests, eager to share good food first, and bless the couple with a toast of something sparkly. The landlord had squeezed in a top table and a long one other for the spread. Guests would have to take their chances grabbing themselves a seat and a place at the round pedestal tables dotted around the rest of the room.

John and Ruby sat in the centre of the top table, Cameron and Lizzie on the grooms right, and Frances and Joseph on the brides left. Much to Frances's relief this meant that her husband and the Best Man had a clear distance between them. What had she been thinking of?

Lil and Patrick were seated with their nephew Jimmy, and invited Norma to join them, who, having left the girls with Frank and Doris, two doors down, was luxuriating in her little bit of freedom. Arthur, Joanie, their son Gordon, and neighbour Kathleen were together at a table in the corner, Sam having volunteered to mind his grandchildren; he wasn't one for occasions.

Despite a good breeze, the crowded room was uncomfortably warm. Every now and then the celebration bunting hanging from the low ceiling shook wildly as it was caught up in the gusts of wind from the open windows.

Somehow, the landlord had managed to clear a small space at the far end of the room and push a rather battered piano into the corner.

Maybe it wasn't the smartest wedding venue, but for Ruby; it was perfect, her husband had 'done her proud'. Surrounded by friends, and Lizzie, who counted as family, she couldn't have asked for more. Her gaze wandered around the room, she was going to drink in every image, every happening, and carry it across the world with her. A hand touched her knee, and she touched his hand. *"I was always meant to love you,"* he whispered.

"And I will love you always," she answered softly.

His eyes filled with tears. *"Promise me you'll always feel this way about me."* Ruby was taken aback. *"The thing is, I've not finished my service yet Rube, you know that better than any. I've locked you into marriage with me and who knows if I'll come back, or if I do, in one piece."* Their eyes locked until the ringing sound of a spoon on the side of a glass broke them apart.

"Ladies and Gentlemen," announced Cameron. *"This dear lady,"* and he smiled at Lizzie, *"tells me it's time for speeches and a toast."*

The chatter in the room quietened. All eyes focused on the top table and the bride and groom.

"Raise your glasses to Mr and Mrs Lieutenant John Parker. To John and Ruby."

"To John and Ruby," they echoed. *"Is that what kept you up half the night?"*

"Speech," hollered Jimmy, followed by much hammering on the tables and whistling.

John smiled at Cameron. *"I do believe you're first in line, your duty as my right- hand man."*

He nodded. *"Okay folks, listen up."* Although a little keyed up, he was more than ready, eager to discharge his duty so he could relax. He had read through his words over and over again, it wasn't in Cameron's nature to do anything hastily, even though John's news of his wedding had taken him by surprise, he'd made a few enquiries of what was expected and was able to give a polished, competent oration, which belied his hidden anxiety. Relieved he turned to his pal. *"You're on!"* John stiffened; he was suddenly overwhelmed; Cameron gave him a jab in his side.

He stood, took a deep breath; *"Well, I guess my Best Man covered it all, so I'll just thank you fine people, for sharing in our day; and say what a lucky guy I am, and I hope you'll forgive me for snatching away one of your beautiful Brit women for my bride. Please enjoy yourselves."*

"Is that it?" Cameron protested. *"Is this what kept you up half the night?"*

Ruby laughed, and standing, she raised her hands; *"I'm going to follow the lead of my husband, who as you all know will be leaving to continue his duties shortly, and then I will be soon joining him overseas to start a new life. I believe Cameron here has done us all proud, so please enjoy the food and drink and music, we only have a few hours after all, before the pub closes. I love you all, and I couldn't have done this without you, you know who you are. England will always be in my heart, and I really do hope that when all of this is finally and completely over, some of you will take a trip across the pond and visit me. God Bless you all. Now, please, enjoy yourselves."*

Cameron whispered to Lizzie, *"What now? Am I expected to take charge?"*

"No, just keep your eye open, people can be silly when they have a bit too much to drink. When it's time for them to leave you may step in, help out, make sure it goes smoothly."

"Fine. I can relax for a while," he sighed. "I'm pleased my speech went well."

Lizzy put her head on one side. *"More or less, only you forgot to toast the bridesmaid."* He started to get up, but Lizzie caught him by the arm. *"No chick, you did well, best leave it now,"* and she glanced over at Joseph, she could feel his eyes boring into them.

Ted, the landlord, waiting on the side, moved in swiftly with heaped plates of food, and began to set out the wedding spread with the help of his wife and daughter. Within minutes the long side table was covered with a cold buffet and a small wedding cake placed at the centre. Glasses and bottles of something white and fizzy were shared between the tables.

"Lunch is ready," he bellowed. He didn't need to say it twice. Harold heaved himself up from his chair, and despite his bulk was first in the queue; pursing his lips he shrewdly perused the banquet.

Jessie had labelled each platter, she couldn't bear it when guests mauled the sandwiches and lifted up the corners to look inside, she took pride in her reputation of putting on a good spread. Harold was salivating. "*Gawd, where do I start?*" He hadn't seen this much meat since rationing had started. He pulled at his frayed cuffs. Extraordinary what these Yanks could get their hands on.

Lovely soft white batches, tiny, quartered sandwiches, tomato and cucumber, beetroot and radishes, roast chicken, pork and stuffing, potted meat, egg and cress, sausage and onion rolls, pork pie, pickled cabbage, peanuts and crisps; then the sweets----cheese scones, jam sponge, carrot cake, and small trifles decorated with a glace cherry in each centre. The wedding cake stood proudly in the centre on a round glass stand, models of the bride and groom already sinking a little in the thin white spread. Alice, the cook at the air base, was mortified, the icing hadn't really had time to set.

Harold wondered if there would be a fruit cake under the icing, I mean it was impossible for ordinary folks to get their hands on a few currants. He hoped so, he liked currants.

A barrel of beer stood in the corner of the room, courtesy of the groom, and a tray with dainty glasses filled with sherry, was being handed around to the ladies.

Maisie, the landlord's daughter mistook Harold's indecision for shyness. *"Here, let me help you dear. Would you like a little of everything?"*

In regard to food, Harold didn't 'do little'. He turned, reddened. *"It's alright, thank you, duck. I can manage. Since my missus passed, I've not had the chance to eat out; I couldn't decide what to go for first; spoilt for choice, I am."*

Maisie recognised that there was probably more to it than that, poor old soul, he looked a bit lost. *"I'm sorry. It must be hard, struggling on by yourself."*

"She's been gone, a few years back now, but I've never really got the hang of being without her. She always used to look after me at posh occasions such as this. Said she didn't want me to make a show of her by loading too much on my plate."

He bent over her, pulled a crumpled photograph from his jacket pocket.

Maisie made an instinctive move backwards; his clothes carried the familiar sweet mustiness of the many unfortunates who'd been bombed out of their homes, forced to make do with cramped, makeshift accommodation. He'd obviously made an effort, but his jacket needed a good airing. She sneezed. *"Dear Violet, and your lads, a lovely photo. Eric and Clive, they used to tease me."* She tucked him under the chin with her finger. *"Start at the beginning, and work your way along the table, take one of each, of whatever you like; then you can always come up again for seconds."*

He took her at her word, more or less. Rubbing his hands together, he hitched up his trousers and dived in, popping a sausage roll into the side of his mouth as he loaded up his plate. Mindful of her advice, he placed one from each serving dish onto his plate, then one more for good measure.

Cameron watched him make his way along. *"Would you look at him? You'd think he hadn't eaten in days."*

Maisie took exception to his comment. Placing a protective arm around the old man's waist, she helped him back to his seat, taking the precariously balanced heap of food. *'Big man with a big voice'*, she thought. Her gaze followed Cameron, travelled up from the brown polished boots, uniform trousers pressed to a knife edge, up and along his broad chest, and rested on his spiked brown hair.

"Foods haven't been as readily available for us these past few years—not like you lot," she glared.

He raised his eyebrows. *"No offence meant, ma'am. Just an observation, that's all."*

She flicked her black curls over her shoulder and looked him in the eye. He shrugged and mouthed, *"I'm sorry."*

Her mouth twitched, then spread into a wide smile. *"Have you ever tried a cabbage sandwich? Or marmite and grated carrot on toast?* she giggled. *"He's a lovely old man, a bit lost that's all. He lost his wife a few years back after their home was bombed out. He lives alone in an old caravan. Both his lads are still with their unit waiting to be demobbed and he's finding it hard. It's been tough for all of us, in one way or another; Bombing, food rationing—well, everything rationed, mostly. Black outs, not knowing where your loved ones are, whether they're dead? Then, our kiddies sent off to live with strangers, God knows where. I only hope his sons come home very soon, another winter in that caravan of his. Could finish him off."*

Cameron paused. *"At least back home our folks don't have to worry about food, but this war has been tough on them too."* He made a swift assessment of the elderly man; complexion reddened from spending much of his time out in the elements, grey curling eyebrows, dark brown eyes hooded with age, an off-white shirt and a creased tie sticking out at an angle from the inside of his waistcoat, an ample belly hanging over his corduroy trousers. *"He doesn't look as if he's been short of the necessities,"* laughed Cameron.

"It's about taste isn't it, not volume. At the beginning of the war, he used to rear a pig on his allotment, go around in his horse and cart collecting scraps from the mums in the street to feed it, and then it would be butchered, and we'd all have a bit of bacon. Always so resourceful," she sighed. *"He stayed with Norma for a while, but it didn't suit him; after his wife died, he found this old caravan. Lord knows what his daily*

diet consists of now, bread and dripping and cold corned beef more than likely. It's sad, him and Violet were a lovely couple; before the war they had a nice little house and two grown sons, and now his whole world has fragmented. Poor Harold. Violet used to say he wouldn't be able to boil an egg without burning it."

"Surely, he could eat out, have a meal in a restaurant?"

"We have a mobile tearoom down by the bus depot and once a week volunteers serve a dinner from the church hall, he could get a cheap meal there I suppose."

"I hear there are decent restaurants' in the West End of London?"

"Don't make me laugh. The West End? These places aren't frequented by the likes of us. What with twelve- hour shifts— six days a week, then queueing for everything. Eating out was, and still isn't an option, not for most of us. The Toffs? That's a different matter. For us common folk, living around here, we've grown whatever we can, wherever we can. I think you'll find class division is still very prevalent here in Britain, not like home in the good old USA. Still, I hope this next general election will improve lives for the better. If I could, I would stand myself."

"I see." Cameron was in awe. Intelligent and feisty, with eyes that drew him in; cute!

She felt his eyes following her and stopped abruptly. Aware she'd gone off on one, she turned, looked up at him. *"I'm sorry This isn't the time or place. My dad would be very put out if her heard me. Please forgive me. I'm quite a political creature, I'm afraid. Dad says it's not natural for a woman to be interested in politics. It's just that these toffs in Whitehall have little idea of the reality of the needs of the likes of us. Or, perhaps, little interest. Their sort doesn't mix with the man in the street; the likes of us."* Her porcelain complexion flushed to a pretty pink. *"I hear it's very different over there, in America. Please forgive my rant."*

He stood in front of her, his broad stance was powerful and confident, his brown hair standing up spikey from a high forehead. *"Nothing to forgive, honey. As for your question? Well, we don't have landed aristocracy as you have in England."* His mouth twitched as he glanced as the guests made their orderly way along the food table. *"You Brits always queue, for everything?"*

"Not quite everything," she laughed.

"I don't suppose? —then he stopped.

"You don't suppose?" queried Maisie.

"Would you like a glass of something? I mean, will your pa object If stand you a drink? Or are you supposed to be serving?"

"I'd love a glass of something, thank you. I've done my bit, helped mam set out the food, and I will clear away at the end of the afternoon. I'm free to join in the celebrations. Ruby is a friend of mine; I grew up with most of them here."

"Good. What's your poison?"

"I'd love a port and lemon, if I may." Making a quick adjustment to tidy her hair she caught the dragonfly comb holding back her black curls and it tumbled to her feet. They both bent to retrieve it. As they stood their faces touched. *"Whoops a daisy,"* grinned Maisy, *" bit of a collision there."*

He handed her the slide, mesmerised, coal black curls and a soft, welcoming English rose complexion. Her twinkling grey eyes met Cameron's brown eyes flecked with gold. They both felt the pull of instant attraction, an indefinable energy that drew them together.

"Port and lemon for the lady," he smiled.

Cameron was three deep in the queue at the bar. She considered him as he waited. *'He's nice, really nice,'* she thought. There was something about him, different. An American, of course, nice uniform; easy manner, broad shouldered and fresh faced, crew cut that didn't quite control his natural curl, and wonderful brown eyes. He was oozing confidence and masculine oomph. Only, it wasn't just the obvious attraction, she felt she had always known him, and she hadn't, of course. She was comfortable with him. A nice guy!

John watched his pal standing at the bar. He was aware that Cameron knew few people here.

"I'll be back in a second, sweetie." Ruby smiled. *"Go."* He'd not left his bride's side since they entered the pub.

He tapped Cameron on his shoulder. *"How's it going? I'm sorry if it's a bit awkward—you not being acquainted with many of our guests."*

Cameron stared ahead, sipped his beer thoughtfully. Turned. *"John. I'm fine. Listen. I have a question. Do you believe in love at first sight?* "He didn't wait for an answer. *"Because I think I do. hell---yes, I sure think I do."*

"Hell. How much ale have you swallowed, fella? The women here, they're all taken, or married, or long past wanting to

be." He quickly glanced over to Joseph and Frances, sitting with their heads together, engaged in conversation. *"Not the bridesmaid, fella? You've already had a near touchdown with her spouse."*

Cameron turned from the bar, raised his eyebrows slightly, made an almost imperceptible nod towards Maisie, who was busily engaged with her father in what looked to be a heated conversation.

"Nope. Not the bridesmaid. Listen. I'll catch up with you later." He made his way across the room towards her, carefully dodging the chairs pulled out from under the tables, and clusters of inebriated guests mingling and enjoying themselves. He could hear her voice, clearly protesting.

"Dad. Why do you do this to me? Don't shut me down, please. Why do you always shut me down? We owe Winston nothing. He's a hero, he'll have his dues for ever. He's done his job and he was a great leader, in war time. Our country needs change now. I' don't believe he'll make a good leader in peacetime. I have my vote and it's mine to use as I will."

"You should listen to me. Your ma listens to me, why won't you. Where is your loyalty---This war---Listen Maisie. I'm older, I'm your father. While you live under my roof you should do as I say."

"I can soon fix that! You and this war. It's all you ever talk about. Get real dad. My thoughts on this war are very different to yours. Winston and his sort are war mongers, they revel in the glory of it. I respect him, I don't much like his politics, that's all. We had to fight, we had no choice, but there is nothing romantic about young men being shot to pieces, or snotty nosed kiddies standing around with labels pinned on

their cardigans, wailing for their mams, wives working twelve-hour shifts and trying to keep their families together, missing their old men."

Ted's face was puce, his stance threatening as he pushed his face into his daughter's.

"Aar, smothering their heartaches, alright, with Yankee cigarettes and silk stockings and dancing the damn jitterbug—showing off their next week's washing."

She met her father's eye, didn't back down. *"You won't bully me like you do my mum. Leave it out, dad. I'm twenty- seven years old. I'm not a child. Please dad, stop it. All I'm saying, it's time to maybe listen to the other parties, give them a chance. Dad?"*

As Cameron stepped towards them Ted stopped short. A peal of laughter from across the room broke the tension.

"Dad?" whispered Maisie.

Ted appeared to relent, gave Cameron a rueful smile. *"She's a card, ---always been headstrong—nothing like her mam."* He sighed and moved away.

"Double port and lemon. Your pa?"

She nodded, swallowed." *Oooo, lovely, thanks."* Her fingers clutched the glass tightly. She looked away. The fine curve of her cheek was smooth and held a hint of pink.

"A bit heated there. Are you okay?"

"My dad." She shrugged. *"Yes, he's a bit of a bully sometimes, although he'd never hurt me. He can't understand why many of us younger ones want to change the old school*

domination in politics. He has these pathetic notions that we owe our allegiance to Churchill and his party. It's our men who put themselves on the line, it's their flesh and blood that was sacrificed. This country needs change—I believe the Labour party are the way forward. Dad can't accept it. I shouldn't have started it---stupid of me." She took a long drink from her glass and laughed. *"Blinking eke, I'll be sloshed."*

He couldn't help but notice the swell of her breasts as she took a deep breath to steady the tremble in her voice. His pulse quickened.

"You won't be the first not to see eye to eye with family. Religion and politics, always tricky. Listen. If it's okay with you? I'd like to know your name. I can't believe I didn't introduce myself. I'm Cameron." She looked at him. He repeated, *"Cameron."* She flashed him a wide smile. *"Cameron. That's nice. Cameron who?*

He faltered, smiled back. *"Anderson, son of Andrew, Scottish American. And you?"*

She was about to comment but the distinct soulful note of a clarinet took her attention.

"Hey, put it down. Carefully!" Ruby called out. *"I'll play later,"*

"Music." Ted shouted. *"Clear the tables to the side, let in some air."*

A frantic five- minute kafuffle and then the door onto the back ally was opened.

Harold sat himself at the piano and ran his fingers up and down the ivories; despite his age his fingers caressed the keys with agility.

John and Ruby stepped forward and danced a slow waltz in the centre of the room. The guests stood around watching; more than a few with tears in their eyes. They made a handsome couple.

Cameron put his hand on her arm. *"You didn't tell me your name?"*

"My name is Margaret Anne, but my family call me Maisie."

CHAPTER 6

"Ladies and gentlemen, make way for the bride and groom's first dance."

Harold ran his fingers up and down the keys, despite their gnarled appearance they were surprisingly nimble. He paused as John took his new wife's hand and gently led her onto the small space that was the designated dance floor. Harold's chest swelling with pride, he began to play a soft, tender waltz.

"Can I have this dance Mrs Parker?"

Ruby slid into the warmth of his arms. *"You want to dance with an old married woman?"*

He kissed the tip of her nose and swung her expertly around the room. *"For sure."*

"They make a handsome couple," whispered Maisie. *"No doubt about it, your friend's a beauty,"* agreed Cameron, all the time looking down on Maisie. *"Do you dance? Would you like to? Hell's teeth! Dance, I mean."*

She laughed. *"I would love to, thank you. I adore dancing, music. It's what gets us through the bad times, isn't it? The war---the ugliness."*

"Shall we dance, when they finish, I mean?"

"Well. Traditionally, the next dance should be the bride with her father—best man with the chief bridesmaid—only Ruby's father isn't here--- so?"

"And I can tell you. I may be the best man, but I won't be having a spin with the bridesmaid. That's for sure." Cameron pulled at his collar.

"Frances? Why? What's wrong with her?"

"Nothing, nothing at all. Her fella there? Joseph? He keeps her on a short rein."

"Oh, I see. Poor Joseph, he's not quite himself yet. He's not the only chap to return from his war a bit jittery."

Harold finished playing with a loud finale of chords, looking around the guests for an appreciative applause. Cameron gave John a questioning glance. Ruby, noting the uncertainty between them opened her arms and beckoned her guests. *"Well? Come on, aren't you going to join us?"* She turned to Harold. *"Play something lively please Harold."*

He took her at her word, licked his lips, and struck the keys down hard.

Ted rushed forward *"Wait."* Harold raised his bushy eyebrows, *"What's up?"*

"Listen", said Ted quickly, *"We can't have em boogeying in 'ere, it will be carnage. Play a foxtrot Harold, for gauds sake, not one of them Yankee free- for- all's."*

The pianist nodded his understanding, he ticked his ear. *"As you wish. Only, half a minute! Any chance of some lubrication? It's thirsty work this."*

"You play and I'll keep make sure you're well-watered—only it will have to be shandy mind, can't have you too inebriated. Remember what happened last time?"

Harold run his fingers up and down the keys. *"Right you are, chief."* Harold raised his bushy eyebrows. *"Maybe a tot of something stronger at the end?"*

Ted waved his hand up as he expertly wove his way through the tables, collecting glasses and looking in the direction of his missis who was chattering away to Lizzie in the corner of the room. *"Precious little help coming from that quarter then,"* he muttered.

Harold took the raised hand as a yes and hit the keys with gusto.

The younger guests moved forward in one, keen as mustard to join in the fun. Lizzie and company, including Ted's wife, spread themselves out amongst the tables, content to look on. He'd have a word in her ear later on!

Cameron and Maisie found themselves in close proximity to the bridal couple, so Cameron swiftly made a nifty move and swung his partner away to the left of them. John and Ruby were lost in each other's arms, Ruby softly humming along with the tune.

Ted looked on. Thank crikey he'd stopped Harold from playing one of them jive numbers, it would have been carnage if they'd started that GI Joe palaver, well, it didn't bear thinking on. He gave his trousers a tug, rubbed his chin, looked around the crowded room. He'd done his best, considering the short notice he'd had. Looking over at Maisie swerving around with The Best man—another yank, his mouth tightened. What did the women see in them? That's what he'd like to know. Well, apart from having plenty of money to throw around their damn swank. He huffed, waggling his neck like an ostrich. There will be a rush for the divorce courts after this war, all lust and excitement---Once these chaps were out of their swanky uniforms and back in their civvy overalls, these women would be down to earth with a bump. A marriage should be based on genuine affection, similar backgrounds and folks and so-on. What would happen then? Why they'd be scuppered. He felt a moment of panic. If he didn't do something quick, his girl could be one of them.

He pushed forward. "*Maisie? Maisie?*" She turned in surprise. "*Dad? What's wrong?*"

"*Haven't you anything to do? Shouldn't you be helping your mother?*"

"*Dad? Stop it! Mam's putting her feet up in the back room and I'm off duty until it's time to clear up. Everything is in hand. You know it is.*"

"*That's all right then.*" He started to walk away, the turned again. "*Well, behave yourself then, don't want you getting tipsy.*" He glared at Cameron. "*Some chaps can take advantage.*"

Maise giggled. Her partner tightened his arm around her waist, drew them to a holt. He stared as Ted stomped off.

"*Your old man? He sure is peeved.*"

"*Take no notice. I'm sorry, he was rude. He thinks you want to whisk me off to America,*" she laughed.

Cameron swung her around. "*Maybe I do.*"

Norma was quick to notice the exchange of words between Maisie and Ted. Sitting amongst the cluster of middle- aged women who were content to tap their feet and watch the dancing, she was itching to join in. She'd been asked, but somehow, it didn't seem right. Declining, politely, and slightly regretfully, she'd moved herself onto Lizzie's table. Ruby and John looked so happy, well, of course, it was their wedding day. She smiled softly at Joseph, sticking so close to Frances, clearly making his claim as her husband, but underneath, so very frightened of losing her. There were Eliza and Jimmy, over there sitting in a tight corner, heads together, talking like a pair of Guy Fawkes conspirators. Lonely in a crowd! How very true were those words.

Lil, Gordon, Arthur, Joanie, and Kathleen were all gathered around the piano enjoying a discordant, but enthusiastic singsong. Sam was at home with his grandchildren and by the looks of things Eliza was making the most of her free time. She couldn't help but feel there was something afoot with her and Jimmy. Joanie was glowing—her lad was home, safe--- one of them at least. Gordon hadn't allowed his injuries to stop him from moving on. Working as a teacher, following on in his father's footsteps. Arthur was very proud of him. She wondered what this girl was like that he'd taken up with. Joanie said her name was Gwendoline and her son was very struck on her. A Welsh girl, how lovely. And, James, their other lad, he was staying on in the RAF, but Joanie was expecting, or hoping, he'd be home sometime for a short leave.

Norma and her neighbours were close, very close, more like family in some ways. And now, with the war coming to an end, it should have been a time of happiness, only for her it seemed that everything around her was fragmenting. Yes, the last few days had been unbelievably hectic truth, be told she was more than a bit frazzled. Only the long hours sewing, planning, the sisterhood that she felt between herself, Frances, Lizzie and Ruby had been wonderful, precious even now that Ruby would soon be leaving for America. She could hardly blame Ruby for falling in love with John Parker, he was so very handsome. People said she and Reg had made a handsome couple on their wedding day.

Ruby suddenly looked up, as if she felt Norma's sadness; she caught her friends gaze and mouthed—*"Thank you darling, for everything."* At the same time John glanced down at his watch. *"Honey? Maybe we should take a break? I need to check on a few things before we leave. We only have tonight together before I leave."* He kissed the tip of her nose. *"Don't want my gal to be worn out; and little junior in there, is he okay?"*

Ruby blushed. *"John! Yes, let's sit this one out. Shall we join Norma and Lizzie? And hold on a second. Will you ask Cameron to bring the little gifts we bought for Norma and Frances and Lizzie? He's tucked them away somewhere."*

John glanced across the room, caught Cameron's eye. Tapping his wristwatch he called him over, Maisie tapped her foot to the music, waiting. Ted took his opportunity and pushed his way through to his daughter.

"Maisie"

"What now dad?"

He leant forward. *"You're a disgrace."*

Her eyes widened. *"I'm only dancing. Dad, what's got into you?"*

He couldn't say. It was irrational, he knew. A fear: his daughter slipping away from them, and he didn't like it. It wasn't about her having a fella, or her enjoying herself. *"We'll talk later."* He swung away from her abruptly. *"Right folks---half an hour! Time to drink up."*

Harold was resting his hands on the keys. It had been a while since he'd sat in front of a piano, but it had come back easily to him, like riding a bike. He sipped on the tot of brandy Ted had placed in front of him, it hit the back of his throat and made him cough. The room was slowly emptying, some of the guests had wandered into the yard out back. There was an air of anticipation as Ruby watched Norma and Frances very carefully opening their gifts. The pink tissue paper was so pretty they were loath to rip into it; habits of making use over the last five years were firmly ingrained. Lizzie, on the other hand had no such qualms, she tore at the paper.

"'Ere this is heavy. What on earth is it?" she cried excitedly.

"Open it and see," laughed Frances.

Balancing the weight on her knee she ripped off the last of the wrapping. *"A vase. A vase!"* She glanced at Ruby. *"Why, it's blinking lovely."* She had so many of them! It was a standing joke between her and Ruby that whenever she tucked anything away, she always hid in a vase. She quickly gathered herself. *"Red roses and butterflies. I've never seen one like it. I'll cherish it. Thank you, the both of you."*

Frances gave Ruby a conspiratorial wink and then looked at Lizzie. *"Why don't you look inside."*

"Inside?"

John and Ruby nodded. Lizzie looked at Frances, it seemed she was in on the joke. Tucking her hand into the neck of the vase she pushed down. *"Ere I'll get my hand stuck. No. wait a minute,"* her fingers touched on something. *"What's this?"* She pulled out an envelope. Stared at it. Studied it.

Ruby couldn't wait any longer. *"Open it then Lizzie."*

Lizzie carefully opened the envelope. *"It's a letter."* She held it up.

"Oh lord," cried Frances. *"Read it."*

She pushed her specs up her nose. *"For Lizzie. An I-O-U. A thank you from John and Ruby for all of the love and care that you've ever given me. An I-O-U for a return ticket to the States."*

Lizzie put the note down on her lap. Ruby jumped across and took her into her arms. *"When we are settled Lizzie, I want you to come and visit. John will post you a return ticket."*

"We want you to be at junior's christening," smiled John. *"We would like you to be his or her Godmother."*

"I don't know what to say," faltered Lizzie.

"Say yes," beamed John.

Pulling a handkerchief from her pocket she wiped her spectacles. *"I say, thank you, yes."*

"Now you Frances," said Ruby.

Norma leant forward. *"Hurry up Frances, let's see."*

Frances gasped. *"Oh, it's beautiful. An anthology of British poetry. Thank you both, how lovely."* She ran her fingers along the embossed cover. *"This will be my escape—my place of dreams."*

"I thought you'd like it, dreamer that you are. We've signed it so you'll remember out day and not forget us."

Frances swallowed. *"I will never forget you Ruby, and the things we've all been through together. I'll write about me and Joe, and I expect to hear about everything that you and John get up to."*

Lizzie looked at Norma. *"Come on Norma. Your turn. What have you got there?"*

Norma sat with the tissue paper folded carefully at her side. She was holding a small blue velvet box on her lap.

"Open it," whispered Ruby.

For some reason she was suddenly shy. Lifting the lid carefully she cried out. *"Oh, my goodness! You shouldn't have,"* she gasped.

"What is it? Take it out of the box," cried Frances.

Norma held a delicate yellow chain up on her wrist. *"It's a beautiful bracelet, and, oh, it has a pretty flower charm on it."*

"It's gold, Norma," smiled Ruby. *"And the charm? It's a blue Forget-me-Not, so you'll remember us."*

Frances clapped her hands. *"Oooo, put it on Norma."*

"My hands are shaking," laughed Norma.

John moved towards, her. *"Here, let me help you."*

"Goodness, it's heavy," she said, holding up her wrist. *"Thank you, it's beautiful. I don't know what to say."*

Ruby smiled, handed her an envelope. *"There's a little something inside for the girls, maybe, you can buy them something pretty. I'm afraid we ran short of time. You're an angel, you saved our bacon, darling."*

Ruby's eyes sparkled with emotion. *"I dearly love you all, so very much, and----"*

John glanced out of the window. *"Listen. I hate to cut in, but we really must shoot off, Ruby. Everything's arranged on a tight schedule. Cameron's waiting outside with the car."*

"No, he's not," called Cameron, just inside the open doorway, a suitcase in his hand. *"Time to be off, Mr and Mrs Parker. The car's waiting."*

"What's he say?" asked Lizzie, suddenly looking a little frayed at the edges.

Frances giggled. *"Had a few sherries' Lizzie?"* Her comment was ignored.

"Bride and Groom are off, folks," called Cameron. *"If you want to see them off, you'll need to come now."*

John took Ruby's hand and tugged her gently towards the door, pushing aside the scattered chairs with his knees and moving the odd glass or two that were balanced precariously on the edge of the tables in front of him. Outside the car was waiting for the, decorated with the usual paraphernalia of good luck slogans and tin cans tied to the boot. Cameron rushed forward and opened the front passenger door for Ruby and John quickly edged himself into the driver's seat.

"Wait a minute," said Ruby. *"I haven't tossed my bouquet."*

"It's getting late honey."

Ruby opened her car door. *"I must do this John, it's a tradition. Oh crikey, where are my flowers?"*

"They're on the back seat," said Cameron. He reached into the back and handed them to Ruby. *"Here y'ar."*

"Oh, thank you." Turning her back, she lifted her arm high, and threw the bouquet over her shoulder. Amongst the jeers and excited giggling, she heard a squeal of delight. Spinning around, she saw the precious roses land into the arms of Maisie. There was much laughter and good-natured jibes as Maisie clung onto them tightly.

"Is that it? Can we go now?" asked John, perplexed that the roses he'd had so much trouble finding for her had been thrown into the crowd.

"Yes darling." She wound her side window down; took a quick breath as a funny sensation like fluttering butterflies danced through her. She put a hand on her stomach to hold herself steady. *'This is it, Ruby. All done now, no going back!'* Looking out onto the long red bricked street that had been her home for these last years she was filled with a sudden ache of nostalgia. The local nippers were pushing and shoving for the coppers thrown by Cameron; the sky above was fading into a blue wash, and she rubbed her arms, suddenly needing warmth.

John frowned, *"Are you okay honey?"*

"Absolutely." She gave him a smile. *"Someone just walked over my grave."*

"What the…?"

Ruby started to explain, and John squeezed her hand. *"Well, you have me now, so they can scoot."*

As the wedding car slowly pulled away, a sudden cool breeze had drawn some of the guests back inside, only Frances and Joe, Norma and Lizzie were left outside, waving.

Ted ushered the stragglers outside. *"Time ladies and gentlemen please, haven't you lot got homes to go to?"*

Lizzie shivered. She folded her arms across her front. *"That's it then. Ruby never did play her clarinet for us, shame."* For some reason she didn't relish sitting alone in an empty house. Looking along the suddenly silent street, she stood, motionless, feeling the shadows collect around her. Someone touched her shoulder. *"All right ducks?"*

"Right as rain," she answered. *"Any of you fancy a cup of tea back at mine?"*

Lordy! She hadn't bargained on such a crowd! Frances and her Joe, Cameron, Harold, Eliza, Kathleen, Gordon, Arthur, Jimmy, Patrick and Lil. The last time her house had been so full was after Harold and Violet had been bombed out---what a day that had been. And then, Eliza's Thomas had turned up unexpectedly on leave and she'd announced there was another babby on the way, almost giving her mam a heart attack with the shock. Well, of course, they all thought she'd been up to no good, only thank the Lord that wasn't the case. Poor old Violet had slipped away to heaven from the chair in the front room, John had proposed to Ruby and the very same evening Frances's Joe had returned home from the twilight of 'lost and reported missing' after two years absence.

So much happened, sometimes it was hard to take in. And now the end of the war was all but over—Victory in Europe -8th May 1945—only the Japanese were still holding out. Ruby and John would start their married life with one evening for a honeymoon, and then the groom was to be posted overseas the very next afternoon. Some whispered the yanks had something up their sleeve. Back in the States there were rumbles. Though they were not willing to sacrifice anymore, young American boys to the stubborn resistance of the Japanese Emperor and his army. She wondered if John involved in some way with their plans.

At least she'd have Ruby for a little longer. She'd be staying with her until John sent for her, and she was jolly well going to cherish the few days or weeks they would have together. Sad, having to start their married life apart only--- this was war, it was the same for most newly married couples, bless 'em. Ruby had caught herself a very decent fella and he wanted his nipper to have his name and be born in wedlock, just in case. Just in case? No one talked of just in case. Six long years --she shook her head in disbelief, so many lives lost, so many changes. Those years had made their mark, the truth be told, she was completely washed out some days, bone weary; and the last few weeks, especially---Good ole Lizzie, always a laugh, always geeing everyone up---and now?

"Lizzie?" A soft voice broke into her musings. *"Shall I put the kettle on then? Only, you seem tired---Are you sure this isn't too much for you?"*

Lordy, had she dropped off to sleep? Lizzie shook her head from side to side. *"No,"* she answered, *"This is what I want. Good company. Think I drifted off. I don't want to sit here lonely and maudlin. Kettle? No. Bring the glasses in will you, please duck."*

A habit of a lifetime—she couldn't help herself, used to do it in the classroom, and got a few clouts around the head from her teachers if she remembered right. I wonder if I will drift off to heaven in my sleep like poor old Violet did. No, she'd more than likely leave this world with as noisy departure as her entrance had been. Her dad had always joked that she'd came into the world yelling as if she was being murdered and kept it up for three whole days.

"Here, shall I help you with these glasses?" asked Cameron as he watched Frances struggling with the loaded tray.

Joseph pounced. *"No need mate, back off."* Frances reddened, *"Joe!"*

Cameron met Joe's direct gaze head on. *"Hold on fella. No harm meant. Only, I was wondering if I can stay a while with you good folks. It's 'kinda' lonely back at the base now. Most of the guys have been shipped out one way or the other."* He paused, his expression hopeful. *"I've not come empty handed, have a few bottles?"*

Lizzie gave Joe a reproving glance. *"Cameron? You're more than welcome to join us. What do you say fellas?"*

"Any offer of booze is acceptable mate, and you're one of us now, you did a fine job for Ruby and John", smiled Gordon.

"That's right," ventured Harold, he didn't relish another glass of Lizzie's parsnip wine; it gave him terrible heartburn.

Arthur and Joanie were planning to give it half hour, their lad Gordon was obviously wanting to let his hair down and Joanie couldn't abide to see her son the worse for wear with drink.

"Well, if you don't mind, we'll have a cuppa and then scram, leave you young ones to it," laughed Joanie. *"Only, I'm halfway through clearing out the cubby hole under the stairs, six years of paraphernalia under there, Arthur will never throw anything away."*

Frances forced a grin; she was blinking annoyed with Joseph. Although determined not to let his moods spoil her day he was beginning to get under her skin. Making her way into the kitchen she ran the tap, filled herself a glass of cold water, anything to soothe her irritation. Joe scurried after her. *"I don't want to stay long; shall we shoot off home?"* He nuzzled in at the back of her neck, wrapped his arms around her waist. *"You looked gorgeous today, shall we sneak off?"*

She turned, unlocked his arms, and looked into his chestnut brown eyes, *"Joe,"* she pleaded. *"It's been a good day, let's keep Lizzie company for a little while, finish off the afternoon with friends, it will be nice."*

"Darn it, Frances. I'm tired, my leg's giving me jip."

"Then go and rest love. Only, do you mind if I stay a while? I want to catch up with Eliza, and Sam will be here soon with the nippers to fetch her and Kathleen home. We both need our friends Joe. When you were missing and I was waiting, not knowing if you were dead or alive? I'm not sure how I'd have managed without them."

He stood in the doorway, blocking her exit. *"No. Well, I can see that. Good friends? Ha."*

Her green eyes sparkled. *"What the hell do you mean?"*

"That Yank, hanging around you, ogling you, trying to give you a smarmy line. Is that what you like? Is that how you managed when I was away?"

She tried to push past him, and he gripped her shoulders. *"Get off, you're hurting me."*

"You're my wife and I say you're coming home with me. Do you hear me? I said, do you hear me? Can't you see how I am?"

She felt the tears stinging, ready to flow. *"Maybe I'm seeing you for the first time, you selfish bastard. These are my friends, you're friends. What's got into you Joe?"* she pleaded. *"Why so jealous? I longed for you to return. I was faithful, even though some said to forget you, to live; you were dead! Why can't you trust me darling? There's has only ever been you, but I won't put up with this, I won't have it. Do you hear me?"* She looked directly into his eyes. *"I only want you."*

His shoulders drooped. *"Hell, I'm sorry Frances. I'm being an arsehole."*

"You can say that again, although I'd put it a little more politely." She tried to laugh, relieved that he'd stopped the accusations. He'd never ever been violent towards her, and for a dreadful moment she'd been unsure, scared. *"What is it? We are getting along fine, aren't we? The shop, it's all going well?"*

He answered her carefully, his voice low. *"It's not the time or place to talk about 'it' luv. I bear the weight of deceit and it's eating me up."*

She felt the blood drain from her face. *"What? Tell me. Now."*

"*Alright. When I was hidden away—like a rat in a hole—I was in a lot of pain, agony. She cared for me, washed me, fed me, held my hand. We were shut down there for weeks. Then, when I was able, we looked out for each other, joined in operations with the rest of the group. She was so very brave Frances, she'd lost everything, seen her father and cousins murdered by the Gestapo. And while you were here, at home, amongst friends, in Blighty, I thought I'd never see you again, thought I'd die over there, in France. If the Gestapo had caught even one of us, it would have been the finish for all of us; no one survives their questioning, they all break in the end.*"

"*I never gave up hope Joe, but you gave up on me?*" She was angry, blindingly angry.

He caught her arm. "*The only hope I had at that point was if they got their hands on me, they'd finish me off, quick.*"

"*And?*"

"*We were lovers. ---I'm sorry---It was for comfort---I was never in love with her.*"

At that very moment she hated him. "*What was her name?*"

"*I won't tell you. You don't need to hear it. We knew it for what it was. I wasn't in love, and she wasn't in love with me. Her brother was somewhere fighting with the Free French. I'm sorry, so very sorry. Forgive me?*"

She didn't answer.

He thrust his head into his hands. "*Please, I need you to understand. Oh, God.*"

Pulling his hands away she looked deeply into his eyes, searching, then abruptly pushed him away. "*Joe! I understand *all right, I know how it works. I've seen it happen to others, over here."*

He tried to take her into his arms. *"No. don't touch me—not just now. I asked you to tell me. But why didn't you tell me when you were first home? Do you miss her? Do you dream of her? The nightmares? Are you crying out for her? Wanting to hold her? Kiss her?"*

"There are echoes, whispers of us together, I won't deny it."

Frances let out an anguished cry.

"I think of her, I think of them all." His dark eyes held a challenge. *"That Resistance group saved my life. You can't ever know how they lived, what the Germans did to them. Their bravery, the terror. I owe them my life."*

"Bugger off back to France then, go back to her," she spat.

"Frances, please? Listen! I don't want her, need her. It's you, the thought of you made me hang on, the need to hold you, be with you. When I first came home, I thought I'd be able to put it behind me, didn't want to hurt you; told myself, what good would it do?" He gripped her wrist, desperate to make her see, to understand. *"It plays on my mind though, a lot, and lately, when I see other blokes looking at you. I panic. I don't deserve you. Look at me, a bloody cripple. I'm bitter inside, and I take it out on you. Forgive me---Will you? can you?"*

"Let go, you're hurting me!" Her mouth quivered. *"Forgive you? Not now, not yet perhaps never."*

He groaned.

She looked down at her feet, her voice low. *"I will try---give me time."* Taking a deep breath in her green eyes held him with a steely stare. *"I won't be bullied though---this is your guilt---you have to deal with it and stop wallowing in self-pity. You made it home, you're not blind, deaf, burnt. Dammit, if you're really tired, then go home; or stay, as you wish, only if you stay? Behave."*

A polite cough stopped them short. *"Am I interrupting something? Looks like a serious conversation going on in here?"*

"Jimmy? No, nothing going on. My old man is leaving, his leg's giving him a bit of jip that's all. He's been pushing himself the last few days."

Jimmy was all concern. *"Sorry to hear that pal. I'm always ready to give you a hand in that shop, it should be a little gold mine, right now. You only have to give the nod, just ask."*

Joe was embarrassed, hoped Jimmy hadn't overheard. He coughed. *"A slight twinge. I might take you up on that offer at a later date though, thanks."* He tried to catch Frances's eye. *"I'm off home now, look after the missis for me, see her home?"*

Frances tried to lighten her voice. *"Joe, go. I can see myself home. I won't be long after you."*

For a moment he hesitated. *"Ta ra, then."* Giving Jimmy a quick smile he stepped awkwardly out of the back door.

Jimmie watched him leave. A slight twinge? Joe's face told another story. Not for him to speculate, but there'd certainly been something amiss between the pair of them from what he'd overheard. He wasn't a gossip though; they'd likely sort it out.

"Now then Fran. The yank- Cameron? He's just handed over this lot. Tins of ham, corned beef, soft bread, peanut butter. Want to help me cut some sandwiches? Lizzie has dropped off to sleep in there, and Eliza is in conflab with her mam up the stairs. They'll be down in a minute to help out, I'm sure--- only?" He gave Frances what he hoped was a winning smile. *"I don't want to disturb them. I think she wants to talk to her mam before her dad and the kiddies get here."*

"Okay dokey." She darted forward. *"Oh, blimey, peanut butter? Oooo, give it here."* She unscrewed the top and dipped her finger in. Jimmy laughed. *"You're like a big kid Frances."*

Frances made a theatrical swoon. *"Have you tasted this stuff? It's heavenly."* She put the open jar under his nose. *"Try some?"*

"Get off, it's disgusting."

Frances put her finger in her mouth and savoured its malty crunchiness, then ran her hand under the tap. *"What about Norma? Can't she give you a hand?"* She really wanted a few minutes to herself. Joe's behaviour and confession, the realisation that her worst fears were not flights of imagination? She needed to digest what had happened, how she felt. Her beautiful, gentle, quiet, Joseph and another woman. A Frenchie. He'd shook her world, the very foundations of her trust in him. The warm blanket of confidence and familiarity had been torn away from her in a few sentences.

"Say's she's not in the mood to butter sandwiches, "said Jimmy.

Distracted, and annoyed, she caught the inside of her cheek with her tooth. *"Damn and blast."*

Jimmy's eyes widened. *"Hold on a minute, Frances. No need for that."* He was shocked. *"No need for that, at all! What's got into you?"*

"Nothing's got into me, maybe ask my old man what's got into him!"

Norma was definitely not volunteering to make sandwiches, she was sweating like a don't know what, wishing she'd a bit more bicarb under her arms this morning. No, she had no qualms about declining Jimmy's request, as she was watching Harold, Gordon and Arthur play cards. She smiled to herself; Arthur was such a gentle soul but when he became embroiled in a game of cards, he became so competitive he threw honour into the wind. Patrick had dropped out of the game early on and was quietly in conflab with Lil. Lil's face was like thunder, she was never at her best when her nephew Jimmy was in Eliza's company, and the two had been in a close caboodle for most of the day. Although it had been a lovely wedding and Patrick and Lil had clearly enjoyed themselves earlier, the look on Patrick's face was certainly anything but jolly.

Norma's head was busy. Along with everyone around, she was aware New Zealand was at the forefront of Jimmy's mind and Eliza now being a free woman—a widow—yes, but free, well, Lil was really beginning to think Eliza would go with him if he asked her. Was that why Eliza and her mum were upstairs now? Was she telling Kathleen of her plans, now? Sam would be here to collect them any minute so in all likelihood she was dropping the bombshell at this very minute. Jimmy was certainly in high jinks; she noticed Frances and Jimmy were taking their time making those sandwiches;

Frances had looked a little peaky earlier, hopefully Jimmy's indomitably cheerful nature would work its magic on her. She'd noticed Joe leaving earlier, poor lad, people said his leg was a mess. She wondered, should she have a word with Lil? At that very moment Lil looked straight at her, as if reading her thoughts.

Norma nodded. *"Nice wedding, Lillian."*

"Yes, lovely. They make a handsome couple." Lil patted her husband's hand. *"I'm going to join Norma for a few minutes if that's alright with you?"*

It was more than alright with Patrick; he'd had enough of Lil's mithering this afternoon. *"Yes duck. I think I'll fall in with the chaps and have a game or two."* He sidled over to the table. *"Room for another? What are you playing then?"*

"Gin Rummy. Arthur's dealing. We can play as two partnerships." Harold shifted his bulk to make space for one more.

"I'll partner you Harold", said Gordon, "Patrick? You can partner dad."

Patrick rubbed his hands together, *"That alright with you Arthur?"*

Arthur winked in answer. *"Perfect. Let's begin, shall we?"*

Norma was about to enter the lion's den! She hesitated, not sure how to approach the subject that was obviously troubling her friend. *"Your Jimmy-------"*

"What about him?" snapped Lil.

She placed her hand over Lil's. *"I can see you're troubled. He's a good lad, nice natured. Look at him—always ready to give a hand. Oh, come on Lil, you can talk to me?"*

Lil looked down at her hands. *"Listen to them two in the kitchen. I don't know how many sandwiches they think we are going to eat; we've already had a nice lunch."*

Norma tried again. *"As I said, a nice lad, more like a son to you. You'll miss him sorely if he goes ahead with his plans and takes off to New Zealand."*

Lil hard eyed Norma. *"I wouldn't hold the lad back if that's what he wants. As you said, he may be my nephew, but he is more like a son to me. Patrick feels the same way too."*

"Well, if that's so, why so damned gloomy? You want the lad to have his chance."

"I 'spect I'm being difficult, and I really have had a nice day, Ruby and John make a lovely couple, I'm very happy for them both. It's, well, I have this terrible feeling that she's going to ruin his life, Norma. I'm sure of it."

Norma handed her friend a hankie. *"I won't insult you and pretend I don't understand. You mean Eliza, don't you?"*

Lil blew her nose. *"Yes, I blinking' do. They've had their heads together for most of the day, he's completely wrapped up in her. And now? She's up those stairs, with her mum, in conflab. Kathleen always spoilt her, that's why Sam overcompensated with his rules and curfews. I think he could see where his daughter was going, all right. What do I do?"*

Norma struggled to find the right words, not wanting to fan the flames, so to speak. In the end she decided honesty is always the best policy.

"Accept it."

Lil started to protest, and Norma's raised hand stopped her. *"No. Listen. Jimmy is in love with her, Lil. He'll never he happy with anyone else----and by the look of them together today it would seem he may be talking Eliza around to his way of thinking. She's a nice girl---been through a lot, like the rest of us. Losing Tommy at sea---they were a young couple—married very young. It's been well over two years since that U Boat blew Tommy's ship out of the water. Wish them well Lil, for heaven's sake."* Norma's voice softened. *"They've a lot of life ahead of them, don't begrudge them happiness."*

"Three kiddies? Another man's? It won't be easy," Lil sighed.

"If anyone can make it work, your Jimmy can. He's one on his own, I'll give you that. Many chaps would run a mile from this sort of responsibility. I do believe he's ready for it, after all, the children are only young and saw little of their dad because of this damned war. She is everything in his eyes, any fool can see it."

Lil pursed her lips in thought. *"He's never really settled with anyone else. He had some nice girlfriends though, only he always gave them the elbow."*

"There you are then. Listen, you're fortunate that Jimmy was in a reserved occupation and not called up for service, as most men were around these parts. Cherish the time you've had and still have left. You've done his mam proud, raised him well. Give them a chance, because you've no other choice really. Have you?"

Lil's face was stony. Norma gave her a prod in the ribs." *Lil? Don't be bitter, it poisons the liver."*

Lil's face spread into a broad smile. *"Aye? Never heard that one before. It's not only me. What's Sam going to say about all of this? I can't imagine."*

Norma laughed. *"Oh, I think you can. He'll go blinking ballistic."*

They chuckled, then heads together, they threw caution to the wind and allowed the laughter to take over, snorting and snuffling like a pair of silly teenagers. Patrick looked up from his hand of cards, *"First time Lil's smiled all day. Something's tickled her fancy, it seems."*

"Share the joke?" called Harold.

The pair were spared any awkward explanation as just at that moment Frances and Jimmy made their entrance from the kitchen. *"Ta-daa!"* said Jimmy," *Anyone peckish?"*

Harold threw his cards down and patted his ample stomach, *"I could manage a bite."*

Gordon protested, *"Hey, you're supposed to be partnering me!"* Then, giving his hand a quick glance, *"Oh, well-----"*

Arthur and Patrick cheered. *"We were thrashing you anyhow! A good idea, a little food will soak up the spirits we've knocked down us. What do you think, Arthur?"*

Arthur sniffed, looked over the top of his specs, *"I think I could manage a bite. Be a shame to waste it."*

Within minutes the cards were cleared, and the friends were making a good show of enjoying the goodies brought in by Cameron, who at that moment was finding the lady friend of Ruby's, Lizzie, a captivating spinner of yarns. Once Lizzie had recovered from her forty winks, she'd been firing on all cylinders, chatting away ten to the dozen. Cameron liked her and didn't understand what it was that John found strange about her… not until she opened his hand and began scrutinising it.

In the meantime, Eliza and Kathleen, after a very heated and emotional mother and daughter confrontation had wearied, as much from exhaustion as the alcohol they'd guzzled during the day, were sitting next to each other in contemplation.

"So," said Kathleen, arms crossed over her ample bust. *"You're going then?"*

"Yes," said Eliza," *Isn't this what we all fought for, mam? To live how we want? Make our own choices? To have a new and better future for our kids?"*

"I dread to think how your father will take it."

"Oh, I think we both know how dad will take it! Mam, Jimmy is a good man. I trust him. And, quite frankly, dad can stuff his comments up his jumper."

"New Zealand though," groaned Kathleen.

"Don't start again. We've already been over this. I appreciate how you and dad have helped me and the kiddies out, and yes, Thomas and dad were as father and son in the end. Dad won't like me marrying Jimmy, or any other man, let's be honest."

"You could marry and stay over here? Jimmy may like life on the farm, you won't know if he doesn't give it a go?"

Eliza raised her chin. *"This is what we both want. Jimmy is a brilliant engineer. It would be such a waste of his talent if he was buried away on a farm."*

"It was good enough for your dad," snapped Kathleen.

"Listen. For the last time, Jimmy has been offered work mam, highly paid work, not a dead-end job. He's highly skilled- why do you think he wasn't called up? New Zealand is a new country, well, compared to over here. We have been offered a house and the children will have a better life. Their dad has no other relatives over here in England. He was raised in that awful orphanage, so it's not as if they are losing any other family. This is the best I can do for my children. Jimmy and I have been friends since our early teens and he's a good man. Mam! Please, be happy for me."

"He's a good man? Is that enough?"

"It was enough for you and dad. Listen to me, I will never love any man as I did Tom, only, there are different kinds of love. I respect Jimmy, I like him—I like that he adores me, and yes, I do find him attractive."

"When you leave, I will never see you or my grandchildren again. How can you trust him?"

"Mam. What else do you want to hear? Blimey, I'm not like one of those GI brides, marrying for excitement, and because he has a sexy drawl and money jangling in his uniform pockets. We are sure. Me and Jimmy? We're well suited."

Kathleen listened, finally. What her daughter said, it made sense, only... Before this war started, she and Sam hade such expectations---Thomas would take over the farm one day, and they would live their last years surrounded by family, with their daughter and son in-law and their beautiful grandchildren. And now? Faced with the thought of spending the rest of her days alone with Sam, alone, on the farm; she dreaded it.

"Yes, alright then. In my heart I understand, and it wouldn't be fair to hold you back, you'd only resent me in the long run. It's hard to go against your family though Eliza, to stand up for what you want. And I take my hat off to you, I couldn't leave all the people I love, everything I knew."

Seeing Kathleen so upset was more than Eliza could bare. Flinging her arms around her mum, she tried to find words to comfort her. *"Oh, mam. Maybe we won't stay there forever. This new company of Jimmy's? They send them all over the world. If we do as well as he thinks we can, why, we could visit, or you could come over. Like Ruby said. They are going to buy a ticket for Lizzie to visit when they get settled."*

Kathleen had hope! *"Really?"*

"Yes mum. Jimmy is generous, he would want me to be happy."

"Oh," said Kathleen, brightening.

"So, you'll give us your blessing mam?

Kathleen slumped, she felt like she'd been put through the wringer. *"I will. I can save too. We're not paupers, me and your dad, we have land. Yes, alright, you have my blessing."*

"Now there's dad. He'll kick up a stink."

Kathleen patted her daughter's knee, *"Leave him to me. Now then. Shall we join the others? My mouth's as dry as a desert, I need a cup of tea."*

It's strange how alcohol increases an appetite," said Harold, turning to Cameron. *"Many thanks for this grub, lad. I shan't want anything else for days."* Frances leant forward and wiped crumbs from the corner of his mouth. She'd always had a soft spot for Harold. She gave Cameron a conspiratorial wink.

"Is that so Harold?" asked Cameron. *"It is,"* answered Harold, bowing his head, *"Don't much bother with food since my Violet went. It's not the same, eating on my own."*

Jimmy had a sudden thought. Scoffer would make short work of that ham bone he'd left on the kitchen table. *"Where's that dog of yours Harold? has he been on his own all day? Shut in the van?"*

"No, course not" said Harold, affronted. *"Joanie has taken him a nice walk down by the canal. I expect they'll be back soon."*

Arthur was alarmed. he'd been so engrossed in playing cards and the conversation he'd been oblivious to his wife's absence. *"Goodness! How long have they been gone? Scoffer's a big creature. He's too strong for Joanie. He'll likely to pull her into the canal."*

Gordon stood. *"Don't fret dad, she's likely stopped off, nattering. Mary Stevens lives on the canal, remember? I'll go and find them."*

Harold was put out, didn't like being a nuisance. *"She offered; said she wanted a breath of air."*

"I'll go and fetch them," said Gordon, giving Harold a gentle push back down into his chair. He caught his dad's eye. *"Mam probably needed to cool off after having one of her hot episodes,"* he said quietly.

Arthur cut in quickly, slightly irritated, Joanie wouldn't want her personal health discussed amongst others, and neither did he. *"Yes, well, off you go then lad."*

Harold's eyes fixed on Arthur, waiting until Gordon had closed the door behind him. *"Seems to be going on nicely, your lad. Such a pity about his hands."*

"It could have been a lot worse," said Arthur, knowing that the last thing his son would want was people pitying him. *"They did wonders in that special burns' unit. He seems to have settled in his teaching role, although he refuses to try for a post at one of the grammar schools or in a private education establishment. He doesn't seem to have the drive he had before the war, other than being involved in politics. The Labour Party. Can you believe it? I told him. Mr Churchill deserves our loyalty; Winston brought us through this war."*

Harold raised his eyebrows. *"He's not on his own, many have the same ideas. The young ones don't see eye to eye with these Tories; they think they're old school. All this talk of nationalising and a health service free for all, it's got them all fired up, and everyone knows that Winston isn't up for these changes. I like the idea of it all myself; although, I can't see how it would be possible. A pipe dream I suppose."* He paused. *"Only Arthur, I do like the idea of it."*

"Idea of what?" interrupted a brisk female voice.

"Joanie? Gordon? So, you found her."

Joanie glared. *"Arthur! You seem to think I couldn't find my way home. How long have we lived in these parts?"*

Gordon laughed. *"Come along mum. In this case, dad's right. There're some strange folks hanging around these days, I've seen them sleeping rough down by that canal."*

"Poor so and so's, Strange? They are to be pitied and helped, not judged", said Joanie, *"They've lost their bearings in one way or another, God help them. Although, I was glad to see you son, Scoffer was proving to be a bit of a handful. Once he put his shoulders forward there was no stopping him."*

Harold blinked, surveyed his dog, sniffed. *"Never gave it a thought, sorry."*

"I'll put Scoffer in the back yard, shall I Lizzie?" offered Gordon. *"He's a bit muddy- couldn't keep him out of the puddles. He nearly had me over on my backside a few times, I can tell you."*

Lizzie smiled and stroked the dog's head. *"Give him a bit of a rub down. Maybe he'd like that ham bone to gnaw at and a bowl of fresh water."*

Gordon grabbed the lead and tried to manoeuvre him around the chairs. Lizzie moved forward quickly, suddenly aware of the damage to Gordon's hands. *"Here, give him to me, lad."* The dog liked Lizzie, she'd always had a way with animals, they seemed to trust her. *"Come on Scoffer, me lad, see what Lizzie has for you. No, don't jump up,"* The dog stilled, looked at her expectantly. Yanking on the back door, she threw the ham bone out onto the yard and Scoffer disappeared after it. Rubbing her hands together she pressed the door closed with her bottom. *"Whew! He is a big beast---I'll leave him a few moments with his prize, let him enjoy it. You can nip out with some water for him in a while, Harold."*

"That's him settled then", said Gordon. *"Anyway, what were you saying? What do you like the idea of Harold, old man?"*

Joanie caught Lizzie's eye. The last thing she wanted was to be dragged into a discussion about politics. Why couldn't the men leave it alone for once? *"So, ladies, I'll think I'll join you all over there, leave the menfolk to their food. Where do they put it? I for one, couldn't eat another morsel. Eliza? Kathleen? How's the farm and your lovely children Eliza?"*

The women squashed up on the sagging sofa and Joanie found a spot next to Lizzie. The conversation was soft, their heads close together as they occasionally looked up at the men gathered around the table; Jimmy and Gordon, Arthur, Harold, and the newly adopted to their ranks, Cameron.

"I said, I like the idea of the national health scheme," answered Harold, finally. *"Only, I was saying to your dad, Gordon, I can't see how it will be possible--- what with Britain's war debts and all. I mean, we must owe millions to Uncle Sam."* He glanced quickly at Cameron, who didn't respond with comment.

Arthur took a long inbreath, puffed out his chest. *"Mr Churchill has his work cut out getting the country back on its feet, but if anyone can do it? He can."*

"What makes you so sure he'll be voted back in again?" asked Gordon.

Arthur's eyes bulged. *"Why wouldn't he?"*

"Because, father, this war has shaken things up a bit---the old school class system is outdated, and quite honestly, corrupt. The days of nepotism and privilege are coming to an end, and about time too."

Arthur gawked at his son. *"You really expect the Clement Atlee and his Labour lot to be up to the mark? I couldn't think of anything worse."*

Gordon touched Arthur's shoulder.*" Couldn't you dad?"* he said softly. *"This war has highlighted many wrongs. There's been a lot of talk in some circles about the state of some of the evacuee children--- undernourished, lice ridden, in poor health. Some middle-class families who took them in their homes were quite frankly appalled. We need representation for the working people of our country. They fought our war too, didn't they? And! I do not believe the Tory party will be able to do this."*

Nestled in the old brown sofa, the women looked over, startled to hear Arthur's usually mild-mannered demeanour changing into belligerent stance. *"Balderdash! Gordon, you are the son of an educated man, a man who taught boys from a privileged background, as you put it. I'm not rich, but I pride myself on doing a fair job of it. These men are educated to be leaders— to be in government. Without strong leadership, this country would not be the United Kingdom that rules over a huge part of our world. You yourself were in the RAF, benefiting from my position and a damn good education. What do you know of the manual working classes?"*

"Our neighbours and friends are working class, dad. I have eyes and ears and, because of mum's refusal to leave her roots, I've been raised amongst some of those who have little. Maybe it's not the East end, I'll give you that. I'm proud to teach at the local school. These children deserve a chance."

"I believe they do, son. I myself was a Grammar school scholarship boy and blessed to have parents that made sacrifices for my education. What I'm trying to say is this, it

can't all happen in a jiffy. The country has other, more urgent priorities."

Gordon pleaded. "*Father. What could be more important than children's health and working men to be able to look forward to retiring without dread? To have an old age that comes with a little income? A pension? Dad, you're a -----"*

Harold wasn't pleased with the way the conversation was leading. "*Now lad. I'm with your dad, I can't see how it can all happen at once. That's all we're trying to say."*

"*Let me explain then. The new Government will introduce a Social Security system where every working person will pay a stamp out of their weekly earnings, along with their taxes; it's simple. Free health care will mean children and adults will be healthier, this can only benefit the country. If they nationalise coal, power, iron, steel, transport, --- these companies will run more efficiently without the huge profits all jingling in their owners' deep pockets. Investment will be increased and working practices safer. You must see it could work?"* He turned to Cameron and Jimmy, held his hands open, appealed to them for support.

Jimmy was quick to answer. "*I'm not sure if I hold with the idea of nationalisation. This sort of thing starts in a small way, then it all becomes—well, we could end up as communists, commies. I prefer the idea of free enterprise. I'm not keen on this nationalisation lark, although the national health service? I could run with that."*

"*Do you think they'll be voted in?"* asked Cameron, "*To replace your Mr Churchill? I thought he was the Brits saviour? It wasn't so long ago when the crowds were mobbing his car as it drove along Downing Street. In an open car! The nation's hero!"*

"The V E Day announcement," tutted Harold. *"Just like Mr Churchill. Anyone could have taken shots at him. Bodyguards or not, some were climbing up on the running boards, desperate to reach him and shake his hand."*

Cameron decided to break in. *"When is this big event? This election?"*

Gordon leant forward, his eyes shining. *"Beginning on the 5th of July, and I believe the results will be held until the overseas squaddies have had the opportunity to vote."* He turned to Cameron, *"What's your view on this, as an American, looking on?"*

The last thing Cameron wanted was to be dragged into a discussion on politics. *"Not for me to say, other than, if I remember rightly, your Mr Churchill was seen as a risky choice by some in his government at the beginning of all this? And he stood almost alone in relation to Dunkirk until he could muster support for the evacuation, which was a miracle, by the way, don't you think? It seems to me; he was the man to see things through. Where would the British army have been if those thousands of fighting men had been left on the beaches? All I can say is, whoever is elected has a tough task ahead of them."*

Gordon persisted. *"So, what are your politics then?"*

"For me? My war isn't over. I'm off overseas in a day or two. I can't really see further ahead until this Japanese army is ground into the soil. My pals and many other allied troops are still over there, as you all are aware, and some of the stories reaching us about how the prisoners are treated are bad,

'real' bad. It's not over yet! So, forgive me, but I feel more than a little riled when it seems they are forgotten."

Norma's ears pricked up. *"I haven't forgotten!"* she yelled, from her across the room, *"My husband, Reg is overseas somewhere. Of course, they aren't going to be forgotten, are they?"* She looked anxious.

Harold did a struggling version of leaping to his feet. *"Never! Not on your life, Norma luv."* He glared at Cameron. *"Sir, they certainly aren't forgotten. But right now, this election means a lot to us too. It's exactly for these troops fighting that we need a new government, a change, so their lives can be better, in thanks for all they've sacrificed,"* said Harold.

"My apologies sir. I believe you have family overseas?" asked Cameron.

"No. My sons are stationed in Scotland now, they're due to be demobbed any day now."

Norma sighed. *"And yet, the war's still raging. It doesn't make any sense, does it? Why's it dragging on?"*

Arthur's eyes narrowed. *"Something's afoot, mind my words. Although, that Hirohito, he won't surrender easily."*

"Who's that?" asked Norma.

Lizzie heaved herself off her sofa, her knees were becoming more and more reluctant to support her without painful protests these days. *"He's the Emperor of Japan, Norma. Now listen."* Her voice was hoarse from the effort and pain. *"Let's remember why we're all here today. All this talk of politics— important, yes, only it's Ruby and John's wedding day."* She placed her hand on Cameron's arm. *"This young man here,* he's due to be posted overseas. Let's give him a good day, shall we?"

"Well, I have had wonderful time, thank you kindly," drawled Cameron. He looked at Harold. *"I'm sorry if I gave offence."* Harold dismissed his concern with a wave of his hand.

"That's right Harold," smiled Lizzie. *"Now, it's been a long day for me; I was up at the crack of dawn, and I'm not getting any younger, so I'll be heading up the wooden hill to Bedfordshire soon. Shall we have a toast and then you can all leave me in peace?"*

Norma struggled off the sofa, stumbled in front of Lizzie. *"I'll fetch the glasses, shall I?"*

"Thank you, duck." Lizzie tapped Frances on her behind with a newspaper. *"Shift your bum and help Norma; fill them to the top."*

There was a moments awkward silence, Eliza giggled, and Kathleen gave her daughter a sharp jab in the ribs. Lizzie didn't miss the raised eyebrows either. *"Alright. Not too partial to my home- made parsnip wines? Well, it has seen us through a few near misses; the dark days of bombing, and then those awful Buzzbombs, loss and hunger. We may still need its fortifying properties yet."*

"Can I have a glass of ginger beer please?" asked Cameron, already too familiar with the potent liquid refreshment about to be served up.

Frances gave him a wink of acknowledgement. They all waited as the glasses were handed around. Cameron grasped his tumbler and took a covert sip. Yep, ginger soda.

Arthur took charge. *"Let's raise our glasses to John and Ruby and-----"*

Jimmy moved forward, *"Hold on, I've some good news too."* He glanced at Eliza. A broad grin spreading over his face. Eliza looked like a deer caught in the headlights, mouthing, *"Jimmy. Noooo!"*

"What the...?" protested Arthur.

"Forgive me, but I thought we could make it a double toast. Eliza and me? We are off to begin a new life—me and Eliza, and the kiddies. We are off to the other side of the world. New Zealand."

If a penny had dropped none of them would have heard it. *"I've given my blessing,"* beamed Kathleen.

A round of cheers followed. *"When?"* asked Auntie Lil. *"Jimmy?"* Patrick waited, his heart in his mouth.

Jimmy took hold of Eliza's hand, looked at his Aunty and Uncle. *"In six weeks."* There was a gasp. Jimmy turned to face them all. *"I realise it's a bit of a shock. I have a good job and we have a lovely home waiting for us over there. It has to be now, they won't wait."*

Lil pushed back her shoulders, took a deep breath and walked over to Eliza. *"I wish you every happiness, love."* Eliza blushed and kissed Lil on the cheek, *"Thank you."* Patrick had watched the aftermath of this announcement anxiously, he stared at his wife Lil in amazement. Lil laughed. *"No. Patrick, it's fine, I do, really do wish them every happiness. It's a good thing."*

"What's a good thing?"

Eliza's dad, Sam, stood in the doorway. For a moment it was as if the air had been sucked out of the room. *"Dad?"* gasped Eliza." *We were going to have a talk to you, tell you."* She gave Jimmy a look, begging for help.

Sam looked from one to the other. *"Well?"*

"You'd better sit down," said Kathleen.

He pulled at his motorcycle gauntlets and sat down heavily. *"I think I can guess what's coming."* Suddenly weary he glanced at Lizzy. *"Could I have a cup of tea, please? I'm parched."*

Eliza stood frozen for a second, then asked Lizzie. *"Can I make dad a cuppa, Lizzie?"*

Lizzie nodded, smiled. *"You don't need to ask. Off you go, see to your dad."*

"Where are the children?" asked Kathleen.

Sam brushed his brow. *"Mrs Holton is taking care of them. The little 'un was fast asleep and the twins didn't want to stop their game of football."*

Frances followed into the kitchen. *"I'll make your dad's tea, Eliza. You need to stay with Jimmy and your mam, talk to your dad."* She glanced back through the open door, *"Your father looks tired,"* she whispered softly.

Jimmy dragged his chair up close to Sam, whilst the other guests kept a polite distance between themselves and the two men. Keen to diffuse the sudden tension in the room, they made sudden and overloud conversation. Eliza and Kathleen made a poor semblance of joining in whilst anxiously waiting for the inevitable explosion of words and emotion between their two menfolk.

"So, Gordon," burst in Harold, *"The Welsh girl, a nurse? Did you drop her a line? From the valleys I do believe?"*

Gordon found his mouth twitching in amusement at the almost desperate expression on the elderly man's face. *"I did write, and she answered. At first, I didn't want to seem horribly over keen, but it seems she likes me too. We've been corresponding ever since."* He leaned forward, lowered his voice in a mock pantomime whisper. *"I'm off to meet her family next week. Yes, she's from the Welsh valleys, a real smasher."*

Harold's eyes lit up. *"Live with her parents, does she?"*

"She does. She's a good girl and I'm very keen on her."

Harold raised his eyebrows and glanced at Joanie. *"Have you met her yet? This young woman who's stolen your son's heart?"*

Gordon gave his mother a hesitant smile. *"Mam? I thought perhaps---well---maybe you'd like to come with me, a bit of a holiday, some fresh air? Gwendoline, Gwen, would be thrilled to meet you, and we could take a train. What do you think?"*

"What do you think Arthur? I would like to, very much. Do you think you could manage without me?"

Arthur paused, pretending to consider. Joanie broke in. *"I mean, I'd like to go, if you could manage? Do you think?"*

"Go and enjoy yourself Joanie. The world won't stop if I have to knock up a few meals for myself. A few days away with our Gordon? I've no objection dear."

"I think I should." She looked at her son, a little anxious. *"I take it there is an invitation?"*

"Yes mam." Gordon was relieved, he'd expected a little opposition. His father wasn't one to give up on his home comforts so willingly. *"That's settled then. Thanks dad, I didn't relish taking the trip on my own. I've not met her family as yet, and they've invited me into their family home. I'll feel less awkward with mam."* He smiled ruefully. *"Yes, A grown man and all that! They're a close bunch these chapel goers. And my hands! I hope they don't think Gwen has saddled herself with a lame duck."* He reddened.

"Balderdash! You served your country," said Arthur, a sudden flash of anger shining his eyes. *"You served your country well, never forget it. This war brought a lot of work into these valleys- coal, steel; most of the menfolk are in reserved occupations. I wouldn't think their losses were as heavy as ours. Let nobody dare say different, my boy is no lame duck---she's lucky to have you."*

"Woah! Dad, keep your hair on! That community work damn hard and Gwen did her bit serving as a nurse in very difficult circumstances." Gordon's throat tightened. He really liked this girl and wanted his parents to like her too. If father was going to behave like this, it would certainly put the kybosh on his plans. *"Father! You'll like her, she's a good sort, really. Perhaps she could come back with mum and me for a little while and you can get to know her? What do you think?"*

Joanie was aghast. *"Arthur, what's got into you? You can't say a thing like that! Everyone in this war has borne losses in one way or another."* She turned to Gordon, *"Gwendoline will be more than welcome."*

Arthur made no response.

"Or I could find her lodgings?"

"No lad, that won't be necessary." Arthur rubbed his brow. *"I was offside. Your mam's right. We'd like to meet her."*

Harold rubbed his hand across his brow. How lucky Arthur and Joanie were to have Gordon home and their other son, James, still in one piece. I mean, what were the chances of that happening? If only his own two lads, Eric and Clive, were here with him. It was hard, being on his own, he had never really got over the loss of Violet and he didn't think he ever would. He had an ache in his heart that could only mend when he saw his lads alive and well.

Lizzie sensing his pain, made a cheerful attempt to engage him, *"Chin up Harold. Your lads will be demobbed soon, won't they? They'll soon have everything shipshape,"* she added brightly.

"I would like to think so. The caravan's not so bad really, and I'm accustomed to taking care of myself. Only, I won't deny I'm lonely sometimes. I don't think I'll ever stop missing Violet; she was taken so sudden, you see. She never did recover from losing her home in that way. I don't think it was the bomb as such. She was like a ship without an anchor, I think it broke her heart, losing our home like that. And the worry about our lads too."

"Where are they?" asked Norma.

"They're waiting for their demob papers. Up in the wilds of Scotland somewhere. Been expecting to be released a month ago. It sticks in my craw, why hang onto them?"

"Be patient, that's all you can do. Hang on," said Norma softly.

"Yes. I must be thankful I didn't lose them." Harold pointed his finger upwards. *"Maybe my Violet up there in heaven put a few words for them."*

"I'm sure she would have, no doubt about it; she lived for you and her lad. Prayers are answered, although not always in the way we want or expect," answered Lizzie.

"That's what worries me," sighed Norma.

"Try not to lose hope Norma," coaxed Lizzie. *"The storm doesn't last forever."*

Norma stood. *"It does for some, if it outlives them."*

"Stay a while, Norma, you're with friends." Lizzie was concerned, she didn't want her friend to leave in this low mood. She needed to find a way of comforting her, and at this moment the words wouldn't find their way to her tongue.

"No," answered Norma, decisively. *"I love you for caring Lizzie, well, all of you. I need to go. I'll be fine."* She turned around to face everyone. *"Ta-raa all. It's been a smashing day."* Without waiting for acknowledgement, she made her way through the back door. They heard Scoffer barking and the thud of the heavy gate, followed by a minute's silence from Lizzie. Her heart ached for her dear friend, and Norma was right, there were only so many platitudes one could listen to.

Taking a peek over at the other end of the room things seemed to be heating up. Lizzie decided, for once in her life, she would keep her nose out of it, but along with the other guests she was now unapologetically listening in.

Sam and Jimmy were faced up to each other like boxers in a ring, and Eliza's chin was raised in defiance. Kathleen threw Lizzie a look of helplessness.

"I've explained everything," protested Jimmy. *"Really Sam, what is it you don't understand? Security? I have a good career ahead of me- an engineering post with an established firm."* Jimmy's usual easy-going demeanour had disappeared along with Norma out of Lizzie's back door.

Sam was pushed to find any more flies in the ointment, but he wasn't about to allow this young man to drag his only daughter and his three young grandchildren to the other side of the world, not without being sure in his mind. *"You may be taking on more than you can chew. How can I be sure you are ready for this responsibility?"*

"For the last time, I love your daughter, always have, and I am more than able to take on the children; I'm no fly by night. There is a nice home waiting for us, plenty of space and clean air for the kiddies, a good education, a nearby school. Our family prospects are wonderful. The wages are better than I could ever expect if I stayed over here. They are crying out for skilled men." He looked at Eliza, his eyes pleading.

"Dad, I love Jimmy, and as this contract stands, we have to leave now." She wrapped her arm around Sam's shoulder. *"Please daddy, say yes. I'll go with or without—but I would prefer your blessing.*

Sam took a long drink of tea, wiped his mouth on his large, checked handkerchief. She hadn't called him daddy since she was a tot. Everyone was very still. To Eliza it was as if the air was sucked out of the room. It was a strange moment, even Cameron, who barely knew of these folks two weeks ago, waited with bated breath. Kathleen studied her husband's face.

Sam reached out and took Eliza into his arms. *"You shall have my blessing duck."* He scowled at Jimmy. *"You put one step wrong with my family though lad, and I'll swim all the bloody way to New Zealand and sort you out."*

Kathleen rushed towards her husband at the same time as Eliza, and they all fell into each other's arms. Jimmy pushed his way in and gripped Sam's hand. *"Thank you, brilliant! You won't be sorry."* He rushed over to his aunt Lil and Uncle Patrick, squeezed them so tight Lil protested, then followed around the small room shaking hands with the rest of his friends. *"Steady on lad!"* laughed Arthur, *"You'll have something over in a minute."*

Scoffer had finished his bone and, sensing the commotion inside, barked his intention to investigate.

"Oh, I quite forgot him," smiled Lizzie. *"Harold? Let him in, he wants to share in the good news."*

"That's that then." Lizzie pulled the heavy curtains across the front room window. This had been a long day and she was too weary to examine or try to make sense of the turmoil of emotions that were spinning in her breast. She was quite alone, and content to be so, for the present.

Lighting the candle, she stood back, delighting in its' warmth and glow. Today she lit it purely for pleasure, embracing the sense of other worldliness it brought to her. She remembered the gas lighting in her childhood home and in a way, it was so much kinder than the electrical lighting that now replaced it. She'd been careful to always keep a store of candles in her pantry where she could lay her hands on them, for during these war years it was prudent to keep one or two in, along with a full box of matches and a jug of water in the scullery. There had been more than a few burst water mains and burnt-out electric cables over these years, not to think about the gas main that blew up after the buzz bomb dropped out of the sky, killing eleven in the explosion.

As the candle flame flickered in the draught from her open kitchen window, she looked out at the darkening sky, celebrating in the newness of unclothed windowpanes. She'd hated the blackout blinds that had dominated her views, or lack of views, since the war had begun. The sun hadn't totally set in the sky. The oranges were fading and blending into streaks of purple and indigo, bringing a deep sense of tranquillity and reminding her of her tiny part in all of this. The lonely cry of a neighbourhood cat made her shiver and she felt edgy, realising how hungry she was. Strange, despite the wonderful wedding fare, she had hardly touched the lovely food.

"Make yourself a cup of cocoa Lizzie." If she took a bite at this time of the evening it would lay on her tummy like a brick.

Carefully treading the stairs, one at a time like a toddler, and balancing the tray holding a mug of steaming cocoa and two arrowroot biscuits, she nudged the bedroom door open with her elbow and kicked off her slippers. How come the linoleum was always cold, even after a warm day? *"There you are bed,"* she sighed, *"and you are so welcome."* Placing her tray on the bedside table, she pulled down the candlewick bedspread that

Ruby had bought for her at Christmas. She ran her fingers over its fluffy stripes of softness, admiring the deep pink peony flower embroidered in the centre. Plumping up her pillows, she slipped off her best frock and undergarments. Although it was warm enough to sleep in her full slip, she still pulled her winceyette nightdress over her head; it was comfy.

Leaving her bedroom curtains open she climbed inside the covers. *"Oooo, lovely."* Well, that was it, Ruby and John were married, Gordon and his mam Joanie, off to Wales to meet Gwen's family, Frances and Joseph? She was sure things would work out between them, and maybe the good Lord would grant Frances her wish for a baby. Now Joseph had finally opened up to Frances? She was sure her friend would understand and forgive him, in time. Harold's sons, Eric and Clive were due to be demobbed any day, although it wasn't as straight forward as first in, first out, she was sure of that; things didn't run so easily. Eliza and Jimmy and the kiddies soon off to begin a new life in New Zealand, with Sam and Kathleen's and Lil and Patrick's blessing. And Norma, God bless her, and her Reg? in the hands of fate although she had an inkling, well she'd see. Cameron, that nice young American? She'd not long met him, but the cards indicated a romantic outcome.

She reached for her cocoa. Propped up on her pillows she looked up to the heavens, the sky had darkened and was dusted with stars. *"So very beautiful,"* she smiled. *"Yes, all in all, a nice time was had by all."* The faint outline of the wedding gift from Ruby and John stood out against the wall behind her dresser. The thought of the IOU for a flight ticket to America tucked inside the vase filled her with a warmth. For a fleeting moment, she wondered about Ruby, how would she find it, living across the sea in America? When would her husband be free to send for her? What if? After all, he was being posted and the war in Japan was not over. And when did she start talking to herself?

"Enough." Her eyelids became heavy. *"Tomorrow will bring whatever it brings. Tomorrow will be a good day."*

CHAPTER 7

Ted heaved himself from the comfort of his bed and took a good, long stretch. It was 6am and the sun was already shining its warmth through the thin curtains, reminding him he'd laid in his bed for too long. He was expecting this to be a really busy day, Friday the 27$^{th\,of}$ July. Yesterday the election results had been announced, shocking or thrilling, depending on which side they'd voted. The Labour lot, led by Clement Atlee had won a landslide victory. *"Who'd have thought it?"* he moaned. He pulled the curtains open and looked out onto the cobbles outside, scratching his head. He wondered if he could escape his duties at the drill hall tonight. It wasn't his evening to patrol so it shouldn't be too difficult to swing an excuse by the Home Guard Leader. He was expecting the squad would be disbanded, but they were still waiting for the word, so until then, they carried on.

The clatter of a dustbin lid in the back alley made him take a closer look. A ginger tom was hanging out from the bin, pulling out the papers from their chip supper last night. *"Oy, scram!"* It had taken three weeks for the overseas votes to come in, delaying the results from the 5th of July voting. In his neck of the woods, people's expectations had been that Churchill's party would get in. His daughter was cock-a-hoop with the result. There was no doubt Maisie was a smart girl, but on this occasion, he couldn't agree with her. He scratched his head. Where did she get her stubbornness from? Must be her mam's side of the family, for he saw himself as a reasonable type of chap. Well, never mind, it was over, done. The Tories slogan, *'Let him finish the job'*, had seemed a winner- shame. Instinct told him to expect a bit of trouble downstairs today. Once the chaps had got a few beers under their belly there would likely be some heated exchanges.

He pulled on his dressing gown and took a quick look at the missus- out for the count with her head under the covers. It amazed him how she could sleep like that; how could she breathe? He crept out of the bedroom. Another hour in bed wouldn't do her any harm; she was looking a little peaky. He'd have a quick wash and shave in the scullery. Friday always meant a packed pub and today there would be celebrations and drowning of sorrows. He would have to be on his mettle. The wireless was already playing in the kitchen---that would be Maisie. She was like him, an early riser. She greeted him with a smile, singing away to the radio without a care in the world. He planned to have another word with her today, for she needed to watch her step with that Yank! If he had to, he would put his foot down. Not just now before the pub opened its doors, it wasn't the right time, and besides, she had a knack of ducking out of his company if she thought something heavy was afoot. He'd have to pick his moment.

Maisie heard his quiet tread on the stairs. He had a way of creeping up on her and she was expecting another lecture about either her interest and support of Labour policies, or her acquaintance with the American officer. She would have to be nifty to avoid anything too difficult. Bright and breezy then, that was the way to go!

"Morning dad! Looks like we'll be having a scorcher today. There's tea in the pot and I've made you a couple of rounds of toast, so I'll leave you to have breakfast; I need to get on."

Ted sat gingerly on the edge of the dining chair. *"My back's giving me jip already. Listen, Maisie? Don't rush off. I'll have a quick wash; I need a quick word."*

Maisie swallowed, sensing what was coming. *"Lord dad! Not now. Can it keep for later? We've a delivery already on its way, as you well know and I promised mum I'd give the tables and the snug a going over, and the 'lavies' need freshening up too. Mum is looking tired dad; don't you ever look at her?"* That might distract him, she thought, make him feel guilty.

"What do you mean by that? I've told her to pack that WVS lark in. She takes on too much; only she insists on helping out at that damn clothing exchange. Let someone else have a go, I said to her, only she swears she must do her bit. I left her in bed this morning, although more than likely, she won't thank me for it. She'll be all hustle and bustle when she realises the time."

Maisie nodded. *"I'll just----"*

He grasped her shoulders, pushed her down into a seat. *"Now then, sit for a minute. That's all I'm asking, a few minutes with your old dad?"*

"Alright," she said, her voice flat.

"Listen love. The last six years, well it goes without saying, they've been tough. I can understand, you being young, you want a bit of excitement, a change---No. really, I do. Only you don't need to hang onto a Yank's coattails to find it. It seems you were right. This election, who'd have thought it? There will be lots of changes happening soon, opportunities for the likes of folks like us now!"

Maisie's eyes widened. *"You've changed your tune."*

"Well, I've been thinking on it all, I suppose. It's only natural you want to spread your wings."

"Yes, and you want to clip them," she retorted. *"Oh dad, can't you understand? I like him, I really do, he's nice and so sincere, not like some of the fellas around here; just after one thing. Since Ruby was married, well, we've spent quite a lot of time together. What with John having to report to duty the day after their marriage, Cameron was at a loose end, so we tugged him along with us. Don't think badly of Ruby, she's a very genuine sort dad and we've become good friends. Everything is very much speeded up in wartime dad, you must see that. What is so very wrong in wanting to see life?"* She opened her arms, *"Escape the known, and venture into the unknown?"*

"No need to make a blinking speech luv," laughed Ted.

"So, he's American, so what? Isn't this what we've learnt from the war? Don't judge a person by their creed, religion, nationality? If there's one thing we should have learnt from these awful times is, we are all human beings, both good and bad."

Ted sat; his brow furrowed. How could he get through to her?

She dotted a kiss on her father's cheek and made her escape. *"That's it then, you've had your minute. I must get on, really."*

She was not in the mood to listen to her father droning on, or for the sideways looks from her mam, snide comments from the pub's customers or from neighbours who she'd grown up with.

Ted caught her hand and tried to pull her back. *"Maisie--- People around here have strong feelings about women who hook up with American soldiers, and with good reason. It's not all bigotry love, some of it is sound common sense. I don't want you to learn the hard way. Sweet talking, sharp uniforms, little presents and promises, and then they bugger off home and leave them in the family way, without a bye your leave."*

"Any man is capable of that sort of thing, not only Americans. Look at Meryl Dawson down the street. She was left in the lurch, and the father was our local bank manager."

"Yes, and he will be brought to account. There's not much chance of that happening when the chap responsible is a Yank and protected by the army. I'm not saying they're all bad, it's easy to get carried away; lonely, missing home and all that. Maisie, I'm your dad, and I'm trying to put you right. It's my place to do so."

"Dad, it won't happen to me."

"That's what they all thought too. A bit of a lark! Now look where it's left them- up the creek without a bloody paddle."

"I can swim!"

Ted's morning assessment was spot on; lunchtime, and the pub was already packed full.

"What can I get you?"

Jimmy leant on the bar, *"I'll have another bitter please Ted, and you had better pull a pint of your best for that lot sitting back there."*

Ted raised his eyebrow.

"It's on me," Jimmy laughed. *"I'll have a family to support soon so this won't be happening too often. Look at them. A right miserable bunch this morning."*

"No work today?" asked Ted.

"Aunt Lil was driving me mad, she's inconsolable. Crying and weeping that we've betrayed old Churchill. I'd already cleared it with the foreman, needed a day to tie up a few preparations; as you must be aware, I'm off overseas pretty shortly. Anyway, my gaffer, he's a good sort. Pressures off a bit now to be honest, well, on the work front that is." Jimmy gave Ted a wry grin.

Ted nodded, then looked over to the corner of the room. Sam, Harold, Arthur, Gordon, and Patrick were squashed together on the side seat. Joseph was perched on a stool.

"Bad show Arthur? I take it you're not too happy with the election results then?" called Ted, his grin contradicting his statement.

Arthur didn't rise to Ted's banter. The truth was he was absolutely devastated.

Ted leant over the bar to Jimmy. *"Looks like he's lost a tenner and found a shilling. Do you feel the same?"*

He shrugged. *"I'm not too surprised by the result, it was in the wind."*

Maisie gave Jimmy a warm smile, *"Not long now then before you all set sail?"* She didn't wait for an answer. Wiping her hands quickly on her pinny, she winked at Ted. *"Go over dad and join them, you've been busy all morning."*

Ted didn't wait for a second offer. *"Well then, I'll take you up on your kind offer, my little pidge."*

"And dad? I'm sorry I was short with you earlier. I understand you are looking out for me, really, I do. Oh dad? Can I have your bath water? It's not much of a bath is it, five inches of hot water."

Ted laughed. *"Thought there was a catch. You do understand it's supposed to be shared between the family? Go on then, I'm happy with a strip wash."*

"Thanks dad. Mam can use it after me, she won't mind. Anyway, surely, we can ease up a little now?"

"Soft soaping your father Maisie."

"Oh mam? I didn't see you there. Soft soaping? Only a little."

Jessie considered. *"I won't mind you going in first, but only if you leave me a little of that nice, scented soup your American friend gave you. It's as rare as hen's teeth around here."*

Maisie raised her eyebrows. *"You smell nice mam. Are you wearing my Evening in Paris, again?"* She was met by a decidedly shifty expression. *"Oh, never mind."* She turned to her dad. *"Will you carry these beers over to the table?"*

Jimmy stayed at the bar, watching Ted balance the tray expertly over to the waiting recipients amidst murmurs of thanks. He turned to Maisie. *"Perfumed soap? I take it you're still seeing the Yank then?"* He waited, carefully sipping the froth off the top of his beer.

She looked up—her eyes holding a challenge. *"You mean Cameron? He does have a name. Yes, as a matter of fact, I am."*

Jimmy held up his hands in surrender. *"Whoa! Hold your horses---making polite conversation that's all."*

"I can read you like a book. That Yank! I've had all this from my father already today. I wish folks would mind their own business."

"He doesn't want you to come unstuck, I suppose. Your dad, I mean. It happens to the best of them, if you get my meaning?"

Maisie tossed the bar cloth at him. *"Oh, I understand your meaning all right, Jimmy. I suggest you concentrate on sorting your own life out."* She sighed, *"Although it seems as if you have. Off to New Zealand with Eliza and the children. You always wanted her, didn't you?"*

Jimmy thrust out his chin. *"Yes, I did. Won't deny it. It doesn't mean I wished Thomas the fate he met though, poor sod. Can't think of much worse- being torpedoed by one of them Jerry U Boats. It's sad, but he wouldn't want her to be left on her own. I'll take care of her, and his kids. I'll do right by her and him; I owe him that."*

"Oh Jimmy. I'm sorry. I am happy for you all, I really am, although I can't imagine how you managed to swing it by her old man."

"It was touch and go," laughed Jimmy.

Maisie reached out, took his hand. *"Cameron's nice, Jimmy. he's a good decent man."* Her eyes pleaded.

"Are you sure he's not married?" Jimmy's eyes narrowed. *"He's no spring chicken, is he? I'm sorry Maisie, only this is happening regular around here. Romancing our women and all the time they have a missus back home. ------- Don't look at me like that and leave that dishcloth where it is! All I'm saying is, be careful!"*

She still threw the bar cloth at him. *"Jimmy? Just bugger off."*

"Hey! That's twice! Keep your hair on. He seems a decent sort I suppose. No offence meant." He wandered back to the table and planted his pint down amongst the others. *"Shove up, Harold mate."*

Ted's eyes widened. *"What are you saying to my daughter?"*

"Oh, something and nothing, landlord. You know women!"

"I do," grinned Ted, looking over to his wife and daughter, both now engrossed in a lively conversation behind the bar. *"Couldn't do without them though, could we?"* He laughed, giving Arthur a nudge with his elbow.

"Come on now, Arthur. It's not so bad. It could be good for us. Shake things up a bit."

"He's worn out I should think," added Joseph. *"It's a shame though. Can't help feeling for old Winston. Full respect to him and all that, but age will tell."*

"Six years of leading our country through thick and thin would finish any of us off---never you mind, at his age!" bristled Harold.

"I reckon waiting for the troops overseas vote done the Tories in. Our boys didn't want to be faced with mass unemployment

and poor prospects like the lot returning from the First World War," added Ted.

"The Tory party sat back on their laurels, I'm afraid. Their campaign revolved around Churchill as a war hero and not enough of putting the country right. I can see how it happened now," sighed Arthur.

"Even so, a landslide victory for Clement Atlee; cunning bugger! Churchill wanted the alliance with Labour and the Liberals to continue on until Japan's defeat. Atlee would have none of it, point blank refused to carry it on. He was ready for a fight, weighed up the people's mood. Got it right, spot on the nose," added Jimmy.

"Atlee and his party focused on the workers' rights, housing, full employment, cradle to grave healthcare. Who wouldn't want that?" said Gordon, finishing the dregs of his beer and wiping his mouth decisively.

"Come on," said Harold, his eyes bulging, *"That's never going to happen is it lad? I mean, Churchill was straight forward, honest. The new government won't be able to meet these promises. There are war debts to be settled, factories and houses to be rebuilt, schools, hospitals; gawd help us, I can't imagine how much we owe the Americans."*

"Cradle to grave healthcare?", said Arthur softly. *"Sounds wonderful. I can understand why the young ones voted for it; as I said, an improbable utopia."*

"Come on, dad," Gordon encouraged, *"It isn't impossible, surely not. A government taking responsibility for the well-being of its citizens? It's not a new idea. Look, the beverage report goes back to 1942—it proposed the creation of the welfare state a long time ago. If this government goes ahead*

and nationalises the major industries such as coal, steel, transport; why? The profits won't be leeched out by the 'Top Boys' anymore. Imagine! It's not improbable, it's possible. The National Insurance stamp will cover the cost, everyone chipping in." He paused for comments and was met by a stony silence. *"What's wrong with you chaps? I for one, am over the moon. Never dared to think it could happen. If they roll their sleeves up as promised, we will all benefit- men and women."*

"I think you'll find the women will be pleased to return to their place at home after this little lot is over and done with," muttered Harold.

"Go back to the kitchen sink?" laughed Gordon. "Balderdash, that's never going to happen." He held his glass up in a challenge. *"Here's to the new Labour party and a new beginning for our country."*

Jimmy was the only one to join in the toast. Sam glared at Jimmy, wondering why he was so enthusiastic, considering he wouldn't be in England to benefit from these so-called changes. He tightened his lips, kept his counsel.

"Still have to defeat the Japs yet," said Ted.

"I hear things are starting to go our way," added Joseph. *"The poor devils—out there still,"* he whispered, more to himself than anyone else. For some reason, Joseph's particular demeanour didn't encourage any comment. Since he'd returned from his war in France, he sometimes had an odd, faraway look in his eyes that didn't invite ease. Apart from the obvious physical injuries, there were some who secretly wondered if he was a damaged in a way that had left him what they called, 'bit touched.' How could he share his torment, the ghosts that occupied his days; the beaches and waves that

swallowed the struggling and buried the dead; the screams that filled his dreams.

"Harold?" asked Sam, attempting to fill the sudden awkward void of silence. *"Any news of your Eric and Clive yet?"*

"Waiting to be demobbed."

"Smashing," said Jimmy, *"When?"*

"Any day, I do believe. They've lost their mam to this war, their childhood home bombed out, and their old man living in a caravan that's seen better days. I haven't the heart to take care of our small holding now, not without Violet to keep me on my toes. Still have my horse, there are a few nice fat chickens scratching about, and Scoffer's good company. As for me? I think I'm about ready for the knackers' yard myself," he sniffed, *"and Scoffer will probably follow close behind me."*

Joseph leant forward, his gaze intense. *"They haven't lost their lives Harold, and they haven't lost you. Buck up now. You have your land, so sit tight. While you have your caravan on site, you can keep your eye on it. You have water and facilities? That piece of land could be worth a bob or two. If you have no interest in working it, then there are thousands of houses that need to go up. Sit tight and wait for your sons. They'll need you when they return, be sure of it."*

"Do you think? I won't be a burden to anyone, especially my lads."

Gordon clapped him on the back. *"Buck up Harold. Scoffer's lucky he wasn't taken off to the vets like most of the neighbourhood cats and dogs were at the beginning of the war."*

"Getting maudlin, am I? Lord, the lads would never have forgiven me if I'd euthanised their dog, and yes, I suppose some thought it the kinder thing to do, what with the bombing and food shortages and such. Violet would never have agreed to it either, she had a kind heart." He brightened. "Yes, as Joseph says, I have water and the soil is good. The old house is still partially standing. Can't bring myself to have it demolished, not just yet, although I've been advised it's unsafe. I'm forever chasing the kids out of it. I swear, they're almost feral, some of them."

"Running wild, poor little scrappers. It's only to be expected, isn't it? Women at work, absent fathers, little schooling, family's broken up. Doesn't make it right though. We've a lot to make up to them," sighed Gordon. "That's why teaching is important to me. I feel I can do some good." He glanced down at his scarred hands.

"Now who's being maudlin?" asked Arthur.

Sam gave a hard laugh. "*It's not a day to be exactly jolly, is it? I mean to say, this Shangri-la promised by Atlee? How does he propose to bring in all of these sweeping changes? And I for one, do not believe it's these promises of a better life, that gave the Labour party the upper hand in this election. Consider,*" he pointed his finger. "*The British public have not forgotten how Neville Chamberlain negotiated with Hitler and signed that 1938 Munich agreement. Yes, sanctioning Germany's annexation of parts of Czechoslovakia—so desperate for peace, at any price he was, bloody fool!*"

"*Churchill didn't have any part in that. He wasn't in power at the time, he was brought in later,*" argued Arthur. "*It wasn't so long ago we were all standing shoulder to shoulder against a common enemy, now it's all turned to politics. This war is not fully over yet. I fear we've made a huge mistake; we should have kept Churchill at the helm."

"I'm inclined to agree," acknowledged Sam. *"Chamberlain was a member of his party though, and they are still resented for their part in it; many hold them responsible for mismanagement of the situation leading up to the war. It gave that bloody Kraut lunatic the idea we are weak and would roll over for him. I voted for Churchill's lot, but I can tell you, this was forefront in my mind, I seriously considered the options. In the end it was my respect for old Winston that was the deciding factor."*

Ted looked across at his daughter. *"Should have kept the coalition for a bit longer. Look at our Maisie, she's all in favour of this new government."*

Sam studied the contents in his glass. *"My Eliza too, says it's time for a change. I suppose you've all heard about Jimmy here? He's taking her and the children to the other side of the world, off to New Zealand. My dreams of passing on the farm have gone for a burton. None of the grandkids will be here."*

Jimmy fidgeted in is seat, dreading that Sam was going to try and coax a change of heart. He pulled at his collar, the heat rushing up his neck to his face was not unnoticed by Sam.

"No Jimmy don't fret. I've given it a lot of thought and I've come to the decision you're doing a good thing for them all. A good job, excellent prospects, a nice home waiting for you all. My daughter and grandchildren wouldn't have all of that if they stayed here."

The interest in Jimmy's plans lifted the mood and he spent the next half hour answering the many questions, eagerly promoting his ideas and plans. He was keen to ensure Sam's continued approval. Finally, topic exhausted, Jimmy altered the tide of interest towards Joseph and Gordon.

"*So, how's the hardware business Joe?*" asked Sam.

Joseph wiped his hand across his forehead, it was clammy. "*Going on nicely, thank you. Although it's early days, of course. Frances is a trouper, thrown herself into it with gusto.*"

"*How about you Gordon?*" asked Jimmy, winking. "*I've heard you've found yourself a Welsh beauty from the valleys?*"

"*By golly, I have,*" beamed Gordon. "*She was a nurse during the fighting, but she's packed it in now; exhausted! She is back home with her family, recuperating. In fact, mam and I plan to take a little trip, meet her family.*"

"*You may be in for an interesting visit,*" said Harold.

Gordon tensed. "*In what way?*"

Harold took a sip of his beer. "*They're a close community, those Bevin Boys. Everyone in those valleys knows everyone else, or they're related. Chapel going, are they?*"

"*Gwen's filled me in on certain issues already. I really must meet her parents. And I'm a little concerned. What about these?*" Gordon held his hands out in front of him. "*I don't want them thinking their only daughter is being lumbered with an invalid. I'm set in a teaching post and I'm sure I can provide for her. I want her to join me here when we marry. It would have been unheard of before the war, her leaving the bosom of her family and all that; but with her being away from home for most of the war, I'm hoping they will be more amenable to it.*" He sighed.

"Got some sweet talking to do then," said Harold.

"That's why I'm taking mam. Have her at my back, so to speak," frowned Gordon.

Arthur sighed. *"You served your country. Any girl will be lucky to have you, son."*

"What about your other lad, James?" asked Jimmy.

"He's staying in the RAF. Still in action at the moment, although he doesn't tell me much. Well, he's not allowed to," said Arthur, his mouth tightening. *"Still, the life suits him. He loves flying and now the pressure is off, I'm thinking he may be having a bit of a hoot; out of service hours that is. Can't say when I'll see him. Writes to his mother."*

"I would have liked to see him before we leave for New Zealand," said Jimmy.

Arthur was about to answer when he was cut short by a piercing whistle.*" What the…?"*

"Cameron," smiled Maisie. *"I didn't think you could make it today?"*

Giving his new friends a nod, he walked casually over to the bar. *"How could I keep away from that beautiful smile of yours?"*

"Gawd," muttered Harold. *"These Yanks have all the charm in the world. I was just--------"*

The heavy clamp of a hand on his shoulder stopped him short.

"You were just what dad?"

The two men stood behind him, tall and broad, dark hair cut very short, and one sporting a moustache.

"Christ Almighty!" he turned. *"Oh, my Gawd!"* He clutched his heart. *"Clive? Eric? When did you get back?"* He stood, held out his arms. *"My sons everybody!"*

"How do you do?" they said in unison. *"We've just come away, from home I mean, what's left of it that is. Crikey, dad. You didn't tell us the house is in ruins. You said it needed a bit of work. It needs a bulldozer to clear it. And the small holding?"* Clive pulled a crisp note from his wallet. *"Get the beers in Eric, for all of them."* He sat down by his father. *"How long have you been living in that old charabanc? I thought you'd moved in with neighbours?"*

"It's a caravan! We stayed with Norma, but when your mam passed it didn't seem right." His shoulders drooped.

Clive's eyes crinkled with laughter. *"Don't worry dad. Here, give us a hug, you old rogue. And by the way, Scoffer nearly knocked us over when he saw us. What have you been feeding him on?"*

Harold looked shifty." H*e's had lots of walks."*

"Really?" laughed Clive.

"Harold stuttered. *"Well, Scoffer's always enjoyed his food. If I've been short, then he's the last to go without. He doesn't have as many good walks as he should have; I'll give you that." Harold* turned to Sam. *"Not as young as I was, and the bugger pulls me over."*

Clive changed tack, concerned for the conditions his father had been living in and feeling more than a little guilty. *"Never mind dad. We have some work to do, and you have us here with you now."* He paused, taking in Harold's appearance. Dad had always been so hardy, nothing like the ropey specimen in front of him today. He swallowed, a sense of desolation sticking in his throat. Coming home was harder than he thought it would be. He turned to avoid his dad's eyes. What or who was his brother up to at the bar? *"Hurry up our Eric, my mouth's as dry as the Sahara Desert."*

Ted jumped up and rushed over to the bar. *"Here, Maisie. Let me."* He moved her aside, expertly taking hold of the pumps.

Eric was sipping his beer. *"Coming!"* he yelled, making no attempt to move.

"Thanks dad. That was a long half hour." Maisie gave Ted a sly glance, fully aware that it was the presence of Cameron and not his eagerness to serve that had prompted his move.

Ted gave Cameron a surly look. *"I can see you aren't here just to talk about politics."*

Cameron cocked his head to the side. *"No sir. I'm here to court your daughter."*

The two men locked eyes. *"Dad,"* pleaded Maisie, *"Please, don't start again, not now, not in full view of our friends and customers."*

Cameron passed a note over the bar to Maisie. *"I can see your busy, honey, I'll catch up with you later."* He nodded at Ted and made a swift exit, giving a jaunty wave of acknowledgement to the men in the corner.

"See what you've done now dad?" Maisie's heart thumped in her breast. All she wanted was to run after him, but she fought the impulse, aware that there were enough curious eyes looking her way.

"Who's that then Maisie? Your new beau?" teased Eric.

She looked straight past him, her focus on the open door, listening for the engine of the jeep. Eric studied Maisie's face, then his gaze flickered along down to her feet and back up again. The young girl of his childhood had blossomed into a strikingly beautiful woman. Totally unaware of his scrutiny, he tapped on the bar to gain her attention.

"Maisie? Gone deaf from the bombing?"

She gave a start. *"Oh, goodness. Eric, how very rude of me. You and Clive, home, and in good shape from what I see. Thank goodness, it's wonderful to see you both again."* She tilted her head. *"You haven't changed a bit, either of you; a little thinner perhaps."* Her smile lit up her face, *"A little older too,"* she laughed, *"or maybe that's the moustache."*

He clutched his hand to his breast. *"Insulting a man back from war?"* he joked.

Maisie reddened. *"No. I mean, it suits you. Gives you a sort of debonaire charm."*

"That's all right then, and you've certainly bloomed." He leant towards her, *"Your dad being a little tough on you, is he?"*

"It's a little awkward, that's all." She blushed. The last thing she wanted was to share her private business over the bar, so she quickly changed the subject. *"I'm so pleased your dad has both of his boy's home. He's had it rough since your mother died."*

Eric looked across the room at Harold, his eyes haunted. *"Yes, it was a rum- do. We couldn't be at mam's funeral, obviously, it was all over and done with before we received dad's letters. The years certainly show on the old man's face; he doted on* mam, and she on him. I hope I can meet someone and have a good marriage one day, like they had." He gave Maisie a wink.

"Are you coming with those beers, or not?" yelled Clive.

"Hold your horses, I'm on my way," laughed Eric.

Joseph made room. *"So, what are your plans now you've been demobbed?"*

"No idea mate," answered Eric. He pointed to his brother. *"Not sure about Clive. All I want for now is, to catch up with my old mucka."*

"Hey." Protested Harold.

"Sorry. I mean my dad and buy myself a decent suit." He stuck out his trouser leg. *"Look at this demob clobber, it's shocking. I'll never find a nice girl at the dance wearing stuff like this,"* he laughed.

Jimmy howled. *"Blimey. Look at those trousers! You could fit two legs in the one."*

Harold scowled. *"Ere, don't take the micky out of my lad. He's been away fighting for his country."*

Jimmy winced. The fact that he'd been turned down for active service on account of a medical condition would always be a thorn in his side. Thank crikey it hadn't damaged his chances for New Zealand. *"No offence meant."*

Clive sensed Jimmy's discomfort. *"Come on father. Where's your sense of humour? These suits are dreadful. One size fit all."*

Harold stuck out his bottom lip. He stared at Jimmy a minute too long. *"You were never called up?"* he challenged. Jimmy reddened.

"Now Harold, that's below the belt," said Patrick, banging his fist on the table. He'd been fairly quiet up till now, carefully listening to the arguments about the election results, holding his opinion inside. He believed a person's views on religion and politics were best kept to oneself. The truth was he was poleaxed about the prospect of his nephew soon to be going overseas, and more than likely, he wouldn't see him again. He'd been careful to hide his upset rather than dampen the lad's excitement. Lil had been a handful since she'd known, and it wouldn't take a lot to start her off again. Jimmy was doing the right thing for himself and his ready- made family; nothing was going to spoil it for him. The friendly atmosphere took a sudden chill. Clive's beer paused between his chin and his mouth. Ted looked over, alarmed, checked his watch. They'd been here all morning; good for trade but not so good for tempers! *"What are you trying to say?"* demanded Patrick, glaring at Harold.

Jimmy squeezed Patrick's arm. *"Leave it alone uncle."* He looked from one to the other, pleading. "Is this always going to haunt me? I couldn't serve. I wanted to, to do my bit. I was kept in a reserved occupation and joined the AFS. That was no picnic, I can tell you. Ask Arthur." said Jimmy, his eyes shining. *"It was him and me dragged your missis out of your bombed house, Harold."*

"That's right. Got a short memory Harold? He's bloody colour blind, and also a dammed good engineer," said Patrick, stabbing the air.

Harold gave Jimmy a hard stare. *"Ever saw a man killed, standing right beside you Jimmy?"*

Jimmy didn't answer. Joseph's eyes took on a strange glint; so many pals dead, or left for dead on the beaches, never to see the shores of England. They gave their lives, and he'd made it back, he couldn't help but wonder, why me? Why was I saved? His leg hurt.

"Lord. What's got into you, dad?" gasped Eric. He gave Joseph a quick glance; the man was ashen! *"Jimmy was pulling my leg."* He forced a laugh. *"Ha- ha, my leg, do you get it? My trouser leg?"* There was an uncomfortable silence. *"Apologise father, I mean it."* He turned to Jimmy. *"I'm so sorry mate, really, I don't know what to say."*

Harold tugged his non too clean handkerchief from his trouser pocket and made a trumpet like noise with his nose. *"I'm sorry Jimmy. I can't think what came over me. I'm sorry Patrick. Too many beers for an old man. Violet always kept me on an even tack."* He blinked back the tears that were stinging the back of his eyes. It had all been too much for him today. Winston's defeat had knocked him for six, then Clive and Eric turning up out of the blue; his heart was full. He'd overreacted. What would Violet have made of today, he wondered? And what was worrying him was, where are the lads going to sleep?

"Say no more about it, Harold. I think we've all had our fill; it's been a peculiar sort of day." In one way Jimmy was glad he was making a new life overseas; this would not be the last time he was reminded that he hadn't served in the forces if he stayed around here.

"*It's time to drink up lads,*" shouted Ted, relieved, he hadn't been sure of how that could have ended. Eric began to protest, and Ted held his hands up. "*Sorry. Brewery rules, we close at 3pm. We're open again this evening.*"

Joseph was nauseous. He could feel a slight tremor taking hold. He needed to leave, and smart. He stretched out his damaged leg. "*Time to make a move. Frances will think I've gone AWOL.*"

Ted snapped his knuckles. "*Come on then, finish your pints, let's be 'avin yer'.*"

One by one the little group said their goodbyes and made their leave. Harold and his sons the last to make a move. Harold stood and promptly slumped back into his chair.

Ted had a sudden thought. "*Where are you all staying?*" It would be more than a squash, and non-too clean in the caravan that had been Harold's home for the last few years.

Harold's chin began to tremble. "*I—you see---*" Eric cut in. "*Dad,*" He turned his gaze to Clive for a moment, then took his father's arm. "*We've made arrangements.*"

Harold swallowed in relief. "*Really?*"

"*Yes. Get your cap on. Lil has offered us a couple of rooms for now—until we get fixed up.*"

"*Let's hope she doesn't change her mind when she hears about your behaviour this afternoon,*" said Clive. "*She thinks the sun shines out of Jimmy's backside.*"

"*Oh gawd, I didn't mean it,*" moaned Harold.

"It's all fixed up dad, don't worry. Jimmy won't say anything, and Patrick was fine when he left. When we found where you were living. We popped around Lil's for a cuppa and she offered us a roof until we've fixed us up. We've left our bags there and then we came to see you here at the pub."

"What about the dog?"

Before they could answer, the door flung wide open, and a large hairy beast came barrelling in followed by a breathless Jimmy. *"Aunt Lil's got the table set for us and she doesn't like waiting."*

"Did you tell Lil?" Asked Harold tentatively.

"Naw," laughed Jimmy. *"Come on."*

Ted rolled his eyes. *"Come on, you horrible lot, before that hound knocks off these empties and demolishes my pub."*

They made their leave, waving and shouting their thanks.

"I feel sad," said Maisie.

"Why so?" asked Ted.

"The last few years we've all pulled together—now it seems that we're all scattering in the wind."

Ted didn't answer. He pulled the shutters down and bolted the doors.

"Dad?" Maisie's voice shook. *"I will miss you, if I go. I'll miss you and mum."*

He turned to face her, swallowed the hurt. *"I know love. I know."*

Chapter 8

"What in the blazes?" The frantic hammering on her front door gate crashed into Lizzie's sleep. Painfully dragging her reluctant body from the fuzz of sleep, she tugged at the sash window and popped her head out into the street.

"Who is it?"

Norma moved away from the step and looked up. *"It's me Lizzie, Norma. Please can I come in?"*

Fumbling for her spectacles she pushed them gratefully onto her narrow nose. *"That's better. Oh, it's you Norma. I'll come down and let you in."*

In her haste, she forgot to move the draught excluder away from the front door. She dragged the little peg rug away with her foot and undid the bolt. Norma tripped, fell into her arms. Seeing the fear in her friend's eyes she didn't need to ask why she was here. *"Ducks?*

"A telegram!" Lizzie propelled her into the nearest chair.

"My Reg----" her eyes were wide in fear. *""Oh gawd, Lizzie."* She* heaved; a wave of nausea engulfed her.

Lizzie moved fast. Well, for an old woman that is. Pushing Norma's head between her knees she made soothing strokes on her friend's hand, her own heart hammering away in her chest. They sat in silence until Norma lifted her head up.

"Please Lizzie? I can't."

"Open it? You want me to open it?"

Norma thrust the crumpled paper into her hand. Lizzie froze like a rabbit in the headlights.

"What's going on?" Ruby's soft slippered tread had not alerted them to her presence.

"Norma has a telegram." Said Lizzie.

Ruby lay a protective hand across her belly. It had become an unconscious habit –holding onto the precious life inside her. She moved across the room and knelt at Norma's feet. *"Darling, you have to open it."*

"I can't. Will you?" Norma turned to Lizzie. *"Or you?"*

Ruby took the envelope from Lizzie and opened Norma's hand. *"No. You must open it. Take a deep breath. Now! 1-2-3. Rip it open."*

Norma felt the vomit rush up into her throat. Her hands trembled. *"We are here with you darling",* whispered Ruby.

Lizzie wrapped her arms around her friend, tightly; Ruby stayed on her knees, not sure of her own reaction to the enclosed news.

"Right then. 1-2-3." Norma's hands tore at the paper. Ruby stared, eyes fixed, wishing with all her might for a miracle,

The telegram fell at Ruby's knees. Norma gaped blankly in front of her.

"Norma? Norma?"

In answer, she catapulted herself at Ruby, pushing her back onto her rear end and pulling Lizzie over the top of the chair with her. *"He's alive!"* she screamed. *"My Reg--- the bugger's alive!"*

Ruby pushed herself forward. Lizzie plopped herself onto the nearest chair.

"He's in military hospital. A letter's following. How peculiar. Why didn't they let me know?" She re-read it, her hands shaking. Laughing wildly, she swept Lizzie into her arms, then tugged Ruby to her feet. *"Sorry luv."* She kissed the paper in front of her. *"Thank the Lord. He's been very ill with dysentery and malaria, it says. How lucky I am. How very lucky is he?"*

Ruby smiled. *"Dysentery and malaria? Don't think Reg would consider himself lucky, do you Lizzie?"*

"On the contrary, I think he would----very-very lucky."

Frances watched as Joseph busily stocked the shelves with nails, screws, raw plugs, springs- the varied paraphernalia that made up the stock of a hardware emporium. He was so engrossed he didn't turn when the bell above the door tinkled a warning.

Dear Joseph, oblivious to her presence. Frances took in his dark hair curling over his shirt collar, his broad shoulders, the brown overall coat that he donned each morning for work hanging loose on him. Strange, despite her lovingly prepared meals, he'd not yet filled out to his once broad muscular self. The constant nagging pain he suffered wore him down. He tried to hide it from her but some days it was clear, it was getting the better of him. She couldn't help wondering if the army surgeons should have amputated his leg when they had the chance.

How she adored him, loved him. She had begged and bargained with God, *"Send my husband home to me and I'll never ask for anything, ever again."* And she wouldn't. Despite his recent confession of infidelity, her love was strong, although tinged with sadness. For better or worse—they were together.

He didn't realise, in confessing his guilt, he'd placed the weight of torment squarely onto her shoulders. It wasn't in his character to live with a lie, to leave his wartime misdemeanour buried behind the lines. He was working so hard, determined to make it up to her. Building up a successful business was a part of his commitment.

She tapped him on the shoulder. *"Frances?"* He swivelled around. *"How long have you been standing there?"*

"Not long."

"Blimey. Damn doorbell didn't ring. I'll need to take a look at it."

She laughed. *"Oh Joe. It rang! You were lost in your own little world. I've been watching you."* She smiled. *"I like looking at you."*

"Oh, do you? Come here."

"What for?" she asked coyly.

"Come around this side of the counter and I'll show you." Lifting up the countertop he made a grab for her, pulling her into the storeroom. Frances squealed. *"Joe, stop it; someone may come in."*

"I'll soon put that right." Sweeping past her, he flipped the open sign to closed. Returning to her, he pulled her onto his

lap. She pushed her face into his shoulder, inhaling his scent. *"Oh Joe, I do love you so very much."*

He nuzzled into her neck. *"Why don't you show me?"* He reached behind and pulled the clips from her hair. Its darkness tumbled down in a heavy sheet of coal black glory.

Back at Lizzie's little terraced haven of kindness, Ruby was sorting through her wardrobe. She stretched to relieve the ache in her lower back; the little codger inside her was making his presence known. Heart burn, big knickers, breasts the size of melons and the need to make frequent lavvy trips just a few signs she had to deal with. She was sure she was carrying a boy and Lizzie had seen a blue layout in her crystal ball. For a moments relief she sat down on the end of the bed, rubbing the middle of her back. How she wished John was here with her. The honeymoon night seemed a long time ago.

As promised, he'd sent her the airline tickets for America- 25th August 1945. Today was the 3rd. In 22 days, she'd be sitting in an aeroplane flying over the Atlantic. Dr Wilson had assured her she'd be quite safe to fly. Earlier on or to- near the birthdate could be a little risky, but she wasn't unduly concerned. Ruby wasn't really one to worry, never had been. A little company would have been nice---never mind—she would take a book, have a sleep; she only hoped she wouldn't be too cramped.

Seeing her beautiful wedding dress hanging inside the open wardrobe door she smiled, patting her tummy, *"You were there with mummy and daddy, little un."* Heaving herself up she swished through the coat hangers and pulled out her outfits, inspecting them one by one, then setting them into two neat piles- these to go into her suitcase, and the second pile for Norma and her daughters. Norma was skilled with the needle; she would make good use of them.

Looking down at the shiny newness of her wedding band, she wondered if her husband would be there to meet her off the plane? Or would it be a man she'd never set eyes on before- his younger brother? Could it be possible that John would have completed whatever it was he was involved in? Well, he wouldn't be flying again, he'd been grounded after his crash— but—oh well, she'd have to wait and see. Heaving her weight from the bed, she plodded down the stairs. Lizzie was sitting very still, enclosed in the cushions of her favourite floral armchair, her gaze unfocused.

For one awful moment Ruby thought----- *"Lizzie?"*

She smiled. *"Yes duck? Have you finished up there?"*

"Almost. I'm whacked, don't know about you?" She brushed her hair back from her face. *"What a day! And Reg! Such wonderful news."*

Lizzie nodded. *"I hadn't expected the worse, although one can never be sure. Best to keep somethings to myself, would have been very wrong of me to build up Norma's hopes."*

Ruby raised an eyebrow. *"You saw him in the cards?"*

"No duck. In the crystal ball. He was wearing pyjamas." She gave Ruby a wink, her brown eyes full of laughter.

"Oh Lizzie, I do love you. I'll really miss you darling. In three weeks, I'll be in a plane flying across the Atlantic. You will join us, won't you? When we're settled?"

Lizzie averted her gaze. *"I 'speck so. Anyway, are you hungry?"*

"Am I ever. Is there any blackcurrant jam left?"

Lizzie scurried into her kitchen. *"I'll get it. One round or two? Don't answer, you're about to tell me you're eating for two."*

There was something comforting about sitting here, listening to her friend humming and pottering about in the kitchen. What would she do without her dear, dear friend? She realised Lizzie may have given her the brush off just then, changing the conversation to food; only she would not give up. By hook or by crook, Lizzie would use the tickets to America, absolutely, and then she would talk her into staying!

"Love you Lizzie," she called out.

"Do you want the crust?" She didn't wait for an answer. A tear trickled down her cheek. Ruby was like a daughter to her, the daughter who she had lost as a child, and often since wondered what sort of a woman she would be now. She hoped and prayed that when she passed over it would be her precious Dorothy Ann there to meet her.

"Are you OK, Lizzie?" called Ruby.

"Yes love. Put the wireless on luv, I'm coming in."

Arthur studied his son's face. Despite the protested assurance of his wellness, he often seemed preoccupied, and today was one of those.

"How did it go son?"

Gordon pushed his hair back from his forehead. *"To tell the truth, it was a little awkward at the outset. Gwen and her mother did their very best to welcome us—only…"*

"I believe you and your mother would have been more at ease if you'd stayed in a guest house, it can be difficult staying in a stranger's home."

"Gwen's not a stranger dad."

"I stand corrected," answered Arthur.

"We couldn't have been made more comfortable in relation to our rooms and so on. Anwen, that is, Gwen's mother, she lay clean towels in our rooms every morning and she and Gwen cooked us a jolly good breakfast each morning. It took a while to break the ice with Gwen's dad. He really didn't seem to enter into small talk, although Gwen insists her father has always been a quiet, serious sort of chap."

"I see." Arthur took a moment refilling his pipe, considering, tempering his reaction. *"Did you achieve what you set out to do? Or did he deliberately keep you at arm's length, do you suppose?"*

Gordon's eyes lit up. *"Mam is a trooper. I didn't realise she could be so artful. She totally charmed him, even to the point of showing an interest in his pigeons."* He grinned, *"Our mam and pigeons, you should have seen her."*

Arthur's eyes opened wide. *"Pigeons? Your mother?"*

"Yes. Apparently, Anwen can't abide them. She dislikes the mess they make."

Arthur drew on his pipe. *"Where are they kept? In the yard? No woman would tolerate that."*

"Certainly not. Gwen's mother keeps her home spick and span, like a new pin. He has an allotment, grows all sorts of veg. Come to think of it, dad, they kept a marvellous table. David, that's his name. He wouldn't take a penny from us; said he would be insulted if mam kept insisting."

Arthur nodded in agreement. *"Proud fellows, miners. Tough, dirty work. He has my full respect, as long as he respects my son."*

"He's not grafting at the pit bottom now dad, his health isn't too good. You're quite correct though, most of her family are working in coal or steel, apart from Gwen's maternal grandfather. He was a vicar! It didn't hold well when Anwen, you know, Gwen's mother, married a miner. She worked as a teacher in the village school and met him whilst taking the children carol singing. Love at first sight, apparently---can you believe it?"

"I can. Take their singing seriously, the Welsh, powerful voices! The men in particular. Church of England and chapel? How did that work out?"

"Anwen took on her husband's chapel. Said she preferred it. She carried on teaching until Gwen was born, although it was a while before her father came around, so to speak."

Arthur leant forward. *"And so? Is it settled? Are you accepted? Gwen is his only daughter!"*

"Yes. I wouldn't have accepted anything less. Didn't take on the Luftwaffe to surrender to some Welsh man. No seriously dad, he gave me a thorough interrogation; I was embarrassed,

and then I got my gander up. He'd taken me for a look around his allotment and his damned pigeon coops, whilst mam and Gwen and Anwen were supposedly sharing recipes." Gordon raised his eyebrows.

"What were his objections?"

"What I had expected, I suppose. My disability, my Englishness, I suppose, the short time we had known each other. Then, above all, he didn't want her to move away; her being his only daughter. Understandable. I managed to convince him that my intentions are honourable, and he agreed, finally."

Arthur slapped him on the back. *"Well done son. Reason and rational can win an argument if one hold's their temper."*

"Well, that, and I suppose Gwen threatening she'd marry me anyway, with or without his consent, and that he and her mother would see a lot more of her if he agreed and stopped being so archaically stubborn."

Arthur was quite frankly relieved. *"When is it all happening? When are we to meet your future bride?"*

"Today," answered Gordon with triumph.

Arthur's eyebrows almost pushed to the top of his hairline. *"I beg your pardon?"*

"Now. Today---she's out back with mother. They got caught up with Mrs Watling. It seems she's had news of her husband, Reg. A bad deal by all accounts. Malaria and dysentery, poor chap. Anyhow—"

The door swung open, and Joanie presented a beautiful, blushing, petite young woman. *"Arthur? This is Gwendoline, our soon to be daughter-in-law. Gwendoline, meet Arthur, Gordon's father."*

"*How do you do?*" whispered Gwen shyly.

Arthur took her hand. "*I do very well, thank you, young lady. Welcome to our family, Gwendoline.*"

She gave him a tentative smile. "*You can call me Gwen, if you like.*"

"*Thank you. Gwen it is, then. You can call me Arthur.*"

Maisie watched in anticipation as the postie sauntered along the street, her heart hammering inside her breast. Crikey, can he walk any slower? Please let there be something for me. Cameron had finally been posted home to the States and he was in her thoughts from morning to night. Whirlwind romance her mam had called it, and it was clear her dad was mightily relieved when Cameron was shipped home. She counted back on her fingers.

Ruby and John's wedding day, the sixteenth of May, and two weeks before that she had glimpsed Cameron for the first time, only really meeting him properly on the day of the wedding. So, now it was August, they'd spent three months packing in every possible moment together. And then, he'd gone!

She'd never forget his proposal. He'd knocked on the door, well, hammered, to be precise, in the darkness of the night. Then he'd added insult to injury by throwing a stone up to the bedroom window, her parent's bedroom window, at that. She gave a little giggle. Dad was furious. She'd realised immediately it was Cameron. Pulling on her dressing gown, she'd flown down the stairs and unbolted the side door, not even stopping to straighten her hair or check in the mirror. Hurtling into the darkness she threw herself into his arms. *"What is it?"*

"Oomph. Hey, can I come in?"

Ted hung out of the bedroom window. *"What the blazes?"* She remembered her mum pulling him inside, talking softly, trying to coax him back inside. *"Ted, it's Cameron, maybe he's had an urgent posting. She's really keen on him, let her say her goodbyes."* Her dad poked his head out of the window, like a tortoise out of his shell. *"What time do you call this? I'll give you say goodbyes. Why not come around at a decent hour?"*

Within seconds he'd been down the stairs, out of the open door and prodding Cameron in his shoulder. Well, dad was a good bit shorter. Maisie giggled again. Luckily, he'd already whispered his proposal of marriage to Maisie. Romantic, magical words she'd never forget. She filled with warmth at the memory.

Thank the Lord for her mam, forever the peacemaker. Why, she'd calmed down numerous near punch ups in the pub, all four foot ten inches of her. Within ten minutes, Jessie had the three sitting at her kitchen table with a mug of cocoa placed in front of each of them. Cameron looked like hell! It was clear something was happening.

He'd had orders to leave the next day, a flight would be ready at 0900 hours. He couldn't leave without speaking to his girl. His eyes met Maisie's across the scrubbed kitchen table. *"Now?"* he mouthed silently. She'd nodded.

"Sir, can I have a word?" She'd giggled. Ted was well aware what was coming, and he tried to make excuses. Jessie was

having none of it. *"Let the lad speak,"* she'd ordered, taking her daughter into the scullery.

"Maisie!" Cameron shouted. They rushed out. *"Your father has agreed. He will give me your hand in marriage."* She'd cried with relief. Jessie nudged Ted. *"When did he propose then?"* She'd turned to her daughter. *"Well?"*

"Outside, just this minute." She'd pointed to the damp patches on the knees of Cameron's trousers. *"He knelt down, right in a puddle from that leaky guttering."*

Ted had roared with laughter. Unknown to the others, Rodger, their pet bulldog had a late-night call of nature just in that spot just before he'd locked up. Cameron saw the funny side of it, fortunately!

That night, or early hours of the morning, Ted and Cameron had said goodbye on seemingly good terms, and Jessie told Ted to leave the couple to say their goodbyes in private. Looking back, she suspected Ted thought nothing would come of the proposal, that once the Yank had gone, it would be the last his daughter saw of him. She wrapped her arms around herself. She relived these moments over and over again.

That was three months ago. As much as she wanted this letter, she was a little apprehensive. Maybe her dad was right?

The postman tilted his cap. *"Post for the house."* She made out to snatch it from his hand.

"It has to be posted through the box. It's not a telegram."

"Give it here, Larry Thompson. We've grown up together. Don't be daft."

"Having a bit of fun, that's all. Here."

"Thanks." She sat down on the step and ripped it open. *"Dear darling Maisie-----"*

"Mam!" she yelled, *"Mam!"*

Jessie's heart missed a beat. Pulling her apron over her head she rushed outside.

"Whatever is it?"

Maisie pushed her letter under her mother's nose. *"Look!"* she screamed.

Jessie sat down beside Maisie on the step, but before she read the letter Maisie snatched it back. *"Oh lore, he's sent me money for my ticket."*

"Ticket? Here, let me have a read then?"

"I'm off to America!" Maisie squealed. *"I'm to fly with Ruby on the 25th of August."*

Jessie pursed her lips. *"How's he managed that then?"*

"I have no idea mam. Isn't it marvellous?" She grasped Jessie by the wrists and pulled her up, swinging her around.

Jessie didn't think it was marvellous, in fact, she couldn't have heard worse news. But, despite her feelings, she couldn't help but laugh at her daughter's irrepressible joy.

Maisie put the letter to her face, breathing it in, holding it close. "I'd better run around to Lizzie's and tell Ruby." She gave a loud whoop and, waving it above her head, she skipped along the street, calling to any who were out and about. *"I'm off to America!"*

"*Right then*," breathed Jessie. She fixed a smile on her face. Time to face her old man.

It should have been a jolly afternoon tea back at Sam and Kathleen's place. It was supposed to be a celebration of a new start in life for Eliza and Jimmy and the three children. In a way it was, but there was no denying the occasion was tinged with sadness. The children seemed oblivious to the undercurrent of apprehension and were driving everyone crazy. The twin boys were dancing the conga, their younger sister clinging on as best as her little chubby legs would allow. They'd been obsessed with it ever since they'd seen the grown-ups dancing on the day of the street party. "*We're all going on a big ship,*" they chorused.

Little Mary Rose sensed something was afoot, only it was all too much for her young mind to fathom. Considerably unsettled and unusually clingy, her mother was too distracted to offer her the sense of security she was craving. Grannie bore the brunt of her insecurities and if she disappeared from view she would erupt into high-volume tantrums; her screeching setting the cat off into a frenzy of spitting and careering around the house. It was bedlam!

If it hadn't been that Jimmy's disposition was so interminably good natured and cheerful, Sam and Kathleen would have been seriously concerned. Eliza didn't doubt him for a second. Her perceptions of people were extremely sharp, always had been since she was a young girl. It was clear that Jimmy adored her and luckily her kiddies as well. As far as she was concerned, she was doing the best she could for her and Thomas's children. In her eyes, New Zealand had everything to offer that poor old Blighty didn't. Jimmy was aware that

Thomas was her first love and would always own a little corner of her heart. Luckily for Eliza, he didn't have a jealous nature. If he had, she would have had serious reservations, aware that jealousy can penetrate every facet of a relationship until it destroys it.

Jimmy's uncle Patrick and Aunt Lil were devasted but hurting those around her couldn't be avoided if they wanted to take this opportunity; an opportunity that they may never come across again. Unable to have their own child, they had raised Jimmy since he was a young lad. Losing him would be a big wrench. She'd no idea why her parents had limited their family to one child, although she had an inkling it was down to her father's selfishness, wanting her mother to himself. No! She refused to allow their sadness to spoil the chance of a better life for them all.

Jimmy was torn at the sadness in his Aunt Lil's eyes, but not so much that he would reconsider. Aware of the undercurrents of anxiety and regret amongst the elders, he was doing his very best to reassure and placate, almost to the point of desperation.

"Anyone for more cake? Try this one Aunt Lil? No? Uncle Patrick? Sam? Kathleen? Old Lizzie baked this especially. It's real chocolate icing. Can you believe it? A perk from Ruby and her friends. Anyone? Cake?"

There were no takers. He turned to Eliza, his eyes bright. *"Can the children have another slice, love? Or would you? It's corking."* Crikey, he wished they were on the boat now, this was agonising.

"Son. I think we've all had enough cake," said Lil, smiling gently.

Eliza took his arm. *"The kids are crammed to the hilt love."*

Lil caught her husband's eye. How they would both miss him. And it would have been so nice to share his life with his new family. Eliza wouldn't have been her first choice for her nephew initially, although the young woman had grown on her, and Patrick liked her----well, most men did!

"Jimmy, sit down. Stop worrying. Your uncle and me? Sam and Kathleen? Of course, we will all miss you, a lot, at the beginning, only, this is the way of things. It will be a good-while before this country gets onto its feet. You have been given a wonderful opportunity. You're a clever young man, and I believe- yes! - I do believe Eliza will make you happy. She's a wonderful mother too, I'll give her that. When you've all settled in your new country, home, job, life, she may give you a couple of nippers of your own."

Eliza rolled her eyes. *"Steady on, Lil."*

Jimmy blushed to the ends of his ears. *"Aunt Lil, please!"*

Sam coughed. *"Hold your horses Lillian, give the girl a chance. She's three youngsters already. They'll need a bit of breathing space."*

Patrick leant back in his chair, folded his arms across his paunch, and gave Sam an apologetic glance.

"While she's young and healthy. Nothing wrong with that," said Lil, glaring at Patrick.

"She's my daughter, and she'll be the other side of the world, without her mam to jump at her every whim," said Sam, his eyes fierce. *"It's only right I have a little concern."*

"Dad, you gave me your blessing. Remember?" pleaded Eliza.

"That's correct—I did, and I still do. Only, I have to admit, I still have my reservations."

Jimmy leant forward, perched on the edge of his chair. *"I understand your concern, and I give my word. I will take good care of your daughter and your grandchildren."* He turned to Aunt Lil. *"It's much too soon to think of Eliza giving me children, aunt. She's not a brood mare. As I see it, these children are mine and Eliza's. Well, as soon as she marries me. It's the decent thing to do, for us all. The children can take my name, or keep their father's, whichever Eliza sees fit."*

He looked into Eliza's eyes. *"Whatever she wants, that's how it will be."*

"Well said lad", said Patrick. *"Lil? Look what you've started. This is meant to be a nice get together. We should be making the most of our time together, there isn't much time before they sail."* He took her hand, a kindly twinkle in his eyes. *"Come on pidge, buck up."*

"I didn't mean to throw cold water on the occasion, I'm sure," huffed Lil. *"Didn't mean to cause offence."*

Sam tutted.

Kathleen glared at him. *"None taken Lil."*

Eliza gave Jimmy a meaningful glance. *"Shall I put the kettle on?"* Without waiting for an answer, she pulled him behind her. *"By the way, if any of you were wondering, we are being married on the ship."*

Sam frowned. *"Is that legal?"*

"Yes," called Jimmy from the safety of the kitchen.

Kathleen raised her eyebrows. *"Well, I never. "*

"She never fails to surprise me, our daughter," grumped Sam.

The boys looked from one to another, sensing the tension in the room. Mary Rose climbed on her grandmother's welcoming lap, thumb in her mouth, eyes wide. Kathleen hugged her close, began to hum softly, her face sad.

Patrick took a deep breath. *"Well, nippers are resilient,"* he said, handing a bag of toffee to each of the boys. They scampered away before their mam confiscated it. Their sister was too sleepy to demand her share of the prize.

"Marrying on a ship then?" bellowed Patrick.

Eliza and Jimmy's giggling reached them from the kitchen.

Lil began to snivel. Patrick dug in his trouser pocket and handed his wife a big, squared handkerchief.

"Whatever will you think of me?"

"Hurry up and wipe your eyes Lil, the lads are looking at you."

Lil made a valiant effort to smile. *"I'm sorry Kathleen. After all, it's worse for you, they're your grandchildren. It's a splendid opportunity, of course it is."*

The room throbbed with silence, interrupted thankfully by the appearance of Jimmy, red lipstick smeared on the side of his face; valiantly bearing the weight of a tray carrying a huge brown teapot, milk jug and a plate of macaroons. Eliza followed closely behind him, humming, a hand behind her back.

"*Lord are they what I think they are?*" gasped Lil.

Eliza touched the side of her nose. "*Ask no questions, hear no lies,*" she laughed. Leaning forward she pulled out two small bunches of pink marigolds. "*Here mam, one for you, and one for you, Lil. It's not much, but flowers, aren't they beautiful? Little posies of sunshine. Let's all remember this little tea together. Me and Jimmy, we love you all, so very dearly. We should try, for the kiddie's sake. Make it easier for them, don't you think?*"

Patrick gave Lil a warning glance. She responded. "*Marigolds? Pink? I can't remember when someone last gave me a bunch of flowers. Thank you.*" She buried her head in their fragrance.

Kathleen beamed. "*Beautiful. Look, Mary Rose.*"

The little girl pulled at a petal. "*Pretties.*"

"*Here,*" said Lil. "*Jimmy? Sit down, I'll pour.*"

"*So, when do you plan to sail?*" asked Patrick, in between slurps of hot tea.

Lil gave him a warning glance. "*Patrick, manners.*"

Jimmy answered quickly. "*It's the 25$^{th\ of}$ August.*"

"*The same day that Ruby and Maisie fly to America. Can you believe it?*"

"*That's a fluke. Who would have thought it?*" gasped Lil.

Sam stood. "*Kathleen? Fetch the decanter and best glasses. We need something a little stronger than that weak tea*".

Sam stood first, his tall lean figure towering over Patrick's stoutness. Kathleen had a twin on either side of her, as Lil held onto little Mary Rose's hand. Jimmy had his arm wrapped around Eliza's waist, his fierce love of Eliza and joy at a dream come true threatening to burst out of him in a flood of very unmanly tears.

"*Raise your glasses*," commanded Sam. Lil, Eliza and Kathleen held up their green tinted sherry glasses, Sam and Patrick and Jimmy had tumblers of a rough whiskey that had been hidden under the kitchen sink; the children had milk.

There was so much to be said and little time to say it. Eyes bright with excitement, hope, regret. They raised their glasses in unison.

"*To new beginnings,*" said Sam.

"*New beginnings,*" they chorused.

As day closed and darkness fell, Jimmy made his way home with Patrick and Lil. Kathleen cleared away, and then sat with her knitting, Sam at her side.

Eliza tucked her children into their beds, then gazed out of the window at the night sky. "*Tom,*" she whispered, "*If you are looking down on me my darling, please know you were my first love, and I will always hold you in a corner of my heart. Every day you live on, in our children. Please watch over them darling. Jimmy is a good man. Wish me luck darling.*" She fixed her gaze on the brightest star she could find. "*May God bless you and keep you, Tom.*"

"*Eliza.*" Kathleen's voice called up to her. "*Cocoa?*"

She blew a kiss to her first love, turned.

"Coming mum. Coming."

Chapter 9

Harold was occupied.

"What's that you're reading, dad?"

He didn't answer. He pulled off his spectacles, folded the broadsheet and threw it on the chair beside him.

"Dad?"

"I can't believe what I'm reading, that's what!"

Eric picked up the newspaper, read through the headlines. *"They were warned dad. 'Little Boy', let's see, the first atomic bomb, dropped on Hiroshima."*

Clive gave his brother a cautionary look. *"Dad? Why read it over and over again?"*

"It was the only way to stop them father," said Eric.

Harold thumped his fist on the table. *"But it didn't stop them, did it?" They dropped another, what was it? That's it, 'Fat man,' only three days later. Nagasaki. My gawd. We wiped the poor buggers out!"*

Clive's words were measured. "They were asked to surrender on the 26th ^{of} July---they refus*ed to give an unconditional surrender."*

Harold stared ahead. *"The Americans certainly let em 'ave it. Can't get it out of my mind."*

"President Truman wouldn't have made a decision like this on his own. You can bet the British and the Ruskies were involved," answered Eric. *"It was the only way to put an end to the fighting in the Pacific---the conflict with Japan would have carried on for ever! I think, good on them. The Japs will surely surrender now, and our lads can come home. I for one celebrate it."*

"No son. It troubles me. Messing with nature. I couldn't sleep a wink last night."

"Well, stop reading the damn papers then," said Clive. *"Come on, join us for a lunchtime pie and a pint."*

"When Japan surrenders, then I'll thank the Lord for the end of war, but I can't rejoice at the way it was achieved. Look at these pictures!"

Eric shot forward and snatched the newspaper. *"I've a few pictures in my head that I'll carry with me for the rest of my life! It's war. Don't you think they'd have used it on us if they could? Have you spoken to anyone that's been a prisoner of the Japs?" They're no push over; they're brave and proud to the point of fanatical."*

Harold pulled at his collar. *"Maybe so, but we're not like them. Who could live with themselves, making this sort of decision?"*

The brother's looked at each other in exasperation.

"Father," said Clive, wearily. *"The weight of leadership is heavy. Look how Churchill's health has gone down the pan over the last six years. We've all lost. We've lost our mam, only the war spared our old man. So, enough. Make us all a good strong cuppa, and then we'll take Scoffer for a nice walk*

down by the canal. We've a busy day ahead of us, we need to make a visit to our council to arrange the planning permission and paperwork for your bungalow."

Wiping a tear from his eye he looked at Eric, then Clive. *"My sons! I'm proud of you. And your mother? How she looked forward to the war ending and having her lads back home. Went to church every Sunday and lit two candles for you. Strange how she passed. It was------"*

They didn't want to hear the story of Violet's 'passing', not again. *"Dad, no, please,"* they begged.

It was to no avail. *"Fell asleep in the chair in Lizzie's front room, and I was playing cards! We thought we'd leave her asleep, see?"* Harold looked from one to the other. *"It was the bombing of her home that done her in. She survived the bomb. It was all too much for her old heart, bless her. And there she was. Slumped, her arm hanging over the side of the chair, cold, an---"*

Clive couldn't bear to hear it all over again. He'd seen death, a lot of it, only this was his mum. *"That's it, father, enough."*

"I feel guilty," pleaded Harold. *"Do you think there's anything? Up there, I mean? I'd like to think she is up there, watching over us."*

Clive stared ahead. *"I like to think so dad. I had some strange experiences when we were over in France and Germany. In some way it's a comfort, thinking mum is still around somewhere."*

"That's what Lizzie says, and your mam always believed in---what did she call it? ---"

"The afterlife, dad," interrupted Eric. *"As for me, I prefer to get on with this one. We've places to go, people to see; so, put your cap on father, let's skedaddle and we might make some progress."*

Harold heaved himself up from the very comfy armchair. *"One thing. How long do you think we will be lodging here?"*

"For as long as it takes to clear the rubble of the house, clear planning and for the building work to be complete."

"Well Eric, you may not be too pleased with me. I've done something daft."

"Crikey- oh- riley father, what now?"

"Did you see those pedigree puppies? The boxers?"

"You mean Mrs Smith's? Her Trixie's litter?" Eric's eyes narrowed.

"Father! You haven't!"

"I was lonely. I couldn't resist them, they're smashing. I've bought the biggest in the litter. Such a beauty! It will be good company for Scoffer---give him a new lease of life."

The boys began to laugh. *"You are simply incredible father, what's the landlady going to say about this?"*

"I didn't think."

"Right. Put your cap on. We'll pay a visit to Mrs Smith and try and sort something out. Maybe ask her if she will keep him a little longer, or maybe Clive can sweet talk our landlady, offer her a few more Bob for the inconvenience."

"What have you called the pup?"

"Violet," said Harold, proudly." *It's a she."*

Clive roared with laughter. *"You've named the pup after our mother?"*

"That's right," grinned Harold. *"Good aint it? What do you think?"*

Lizzie had slept heavily and was decidedly groggy, so she'd taken her morning routine more slowly than usual. Despite keeping her bedroom window open, her bedroom was unbearably hot. She trod softly down the stairs in an effort not to wake her lodger. Ruby needed her sleep more than ever right now.

Opening her curtains, she sat herself down on a hard backed chair at the kitchen table and looked out onto the yard. The sky was a dazzling blue with only a few wispy clouds marring its unbroken glory. For some reason, or no reason, she expected some sort of happening, but what was it? Ever since she could remember, she was disturbed by premonitions- some clear, some not so, and more often than not, they held no valid explanation, although in time they always became apparent. It was strange, these sensitivities, a trouble or a blessing, were not declining in equal measure to how her physical self was fading.

She'd survived this war, although like many, it had taken a lot from her. She'd aged and was very aware she would never make use of the airline ticket sitting in the bottom of her vase. She glanced down at her fingers, puffy, and her wedding band was uncomfortably tight. Why the good Lord had spared her and taken so many of her friends she didn't know---- Hitler gone--- Germany defeated, What of Japan? The bombing!

What would happen now? The good side does not always win---- Hitler was an evil fanatic--- only, there must be good and bad on all sides. Surely… Fully occupied in her thoughts, the sudden appearance of a face at her kitchen window gave her an unpleasant jolt and her head swam as past and present collided in a dizzying crash.

"Oh! It's you Frances." Putting her hand to her breast she could feel her heart hammering. *"Come inside."*

"I'm so sorry I startled you Lizzie" Rushing forward she took hold of her friend's hand. *"Aren't you well? I peeked through the window, and you were so still?"*

Lizzie's nut- brown eyes twinkled, *"Thought I'd popped my clogs, did you?"*

Frances smiled. *"Well, for a moment, yes, I did."*

They both chuckled.

"I've had a rotten night, Frances; the truth be told. Couldn't sleep. No air coming in the window, it was stifling. My nighty's soaking. Only to be expected I suppose in the middle of August. Is it late? I'm usually out of my bed at the crack of dawn."

France's helped Lizzie gently into her armchair. *"Can I pop the kettle on? Make us a brew?"*

"If you will, duck. And while you're at it you can tell me why you're around here so early? Shouldn't you be helping you husband to open that shop of his?"

"It's all over the early papers," Frances called out from the kitchen.

Lizzie twisted her head around in the direction of Frances's voice.

"What is?"

"Harry S Truman, America's President, announced Japan's unconditional surrender to a group of reporters at the White House on the 14$^{th\,of}$ August 1945."

"That was yesterday! Good Lord."

"Isn't it splendid? My Joe, he read the headlines to me, not half an hour ago. I had to rush around to see if you'd heard. Isn't it absolutely stunning?" squealed Francis.

"Hallelujah! Does this mean it's all over?" Lizzie's eyes brimmed over with tears. "Did you bring me the newspaper?"

"Must be over, surely! Sorry, didn't bring the paper with me, Joe hadn't finished with it."

"Never mind. I'll pop around the newsagents in a while, I don't think I'll believe it until I've read it with my own eyes. No offence."

"None taken," yelled Frances. "It's all over the front pages. Let's have a nice hot cup of tea first, and then I'll nip pick you one up. I should rest awhile if you're not feeling too lively."

The women drank their tea quickly, both of them strangely lost for words. Frances's cup trembled in her hand. "This is it, Lizzie. I can't quite take it in, can you?"

"It's been a long time coming."

Frances suddenly shot to her feet, pulling Lizzie into her arms. "Oooo, you smell of lavender." She gave Lizzie a hug.

"Hey, mind my old ribs!" shouted Lizzie.

"Whoops. It's over then. It's finally damn well over. We won! My Joe, and all the others who fought and gave their lives, it wasn't in vain." She gave a whoop of delight.

"Yes. Eliza's Tommy, Norma's Reg, Ruby's John and his friend Cameron, Harold's Clive and Eric."

"And Arthur and Joanie's lads, Gordon and James, and so many more," said Frances. "All of our brave men and women, it wasn't all for nothing." She sat down quickly. *"Think I'm hungry, I'm a bit lightheaded,"* she laughed.

Lizzie eyed her friend. *"Forget the biscuits, this is a day to celebrate. Let's have that bit of chocolate cake in the tin, I'm sure Ruby won't mind. Top shelf of the pantry."*

As if on cue at the mention of her name, there was a querulous call from the upstairs bedroom. *"What's all the shouting? What time is it?"*

"Time you were out of bed Ruby," said Frances, winking at Lizzie.

Ruby made her way slowly down the steep stairs, treading warily and slumped heavily into an armchair. *"Frances?"* She looked from one to the other. *"What's all the noise about? What time is it?"*

Frances didn't rush to answer. She handed her a cup of lukewarm tea. *"Sorry, it's a bit stewed. You don't seem too chipper this morning?"*

"Hmmm, you could say! This little one inside here has been playing basketball all night." She sipped the tea, *"Ugh, I can't*

drink this, it's nearly cold!" She drank it anyway, quickly. *"So?"*

"Japan has surrendered".

"What? When?"

"Yesterday," answered Frances, *"Hurrah!"* She gave a twirl. *"Isn't it a blinking triumph? It's all over the news, An unconditional surrender."*

Ruby found herself unable to speak. The cup and saucer shook in her hands. *"John…"* she whispered.

"Steady on," said Lizzie. *"Take a breath."*

Frances leant forward. *"Are you alright?"*

"Alright?" Ruby felt the colour rushing back into her face. *"Yes, and I'm absolutely stunned, and shocked, and gloriously happy!"* Catching hold of Frances's hands, she pulled herself up from the sagging chair. *"Sorry. Move out of the way, pregnant lady. I need a pee."*

For the next few minutes, they sat in silence, apart from Ruby's singing from the outside lav.

A sudden slamming open of the door gave them both an unwelcome start. *"Dammit Frances, we've got a queue."*

"Joe!" She slammed a hand over her mouth. *"I forgot all about you, and we've a delivery due."*

She looked at her husband, his black wavy hair standing up from his forehead as if he'd had some sort of shock. She giggled. *"Sorry darling."* She waved her way through the doorway.

Joe gave a sheepish smile. *"Sorry about my entrance Lizzie. Good news, isn't it? I can hear Ruby singing from the outside whatsit! I take it she's heard?"* he laughed.

Frances rushed back inside. *"Come on Joe. I thought you were busy?"*

He tapped her bottom with his newspaper. *"Tara then. Oh. I brought my paper."* He threw it onto Lizzie's lap and followed his wife outside.

Lizzie took hold of the paper and spread it out on her lap. *"Where's me reading glasses?"* Fishing down the side of the cushion, she pushed them onto the end of her nose and scanned the headlines. Ruby was still singing in the lav. This was it then. Thank God! Peace. At long last, the final surrender. Closing her eyes, she placed her hands together in prayer. She struggled to pray; her head was all over the place. These bombs, so terrible; had brought an end to the conflict. So many from all sides had paid a very dreadful price. These atomic bombs had brought in a new era of warfare, championed by some, hated by others. Surely it must have been a last resort? Although people talked of compromise and negotiation, this requires movement from both, or all parties involved? *"Oh Lord------"*

Ruby bustled her way in. Seeing her friend in prayer, she sat and placed her hands together.

"I'll join you."

Chapter 10

Reg had travelled back to a British port on a rusting converted troopship, listed and registered as a hospital ship under the Geneva convention. In between fever stoked hallucinations and bouts of disabling stomach cramps, he'd eventually reached home, where he had been collected by a military ambulance and taken to convalescent home for soldiers on the coast, namely one of his and Norma's favourite holiday resorts, Brighton.

Once there, he'd spent six weeks recovering from dysentery and malaria, a common enough malady amongst the troops who were fighting in North Africa. The usual medications and jabs had played their part, but he still had a long way to go for recovery and it had been decided he'd have a better chance back home. His genetic hardiness, the good nutrition, and medical treatment soon had him feeling more like himself. Following a minor altercation between the matron and the chief medical officer, in which the M.O.s assessment was upheld, it was decided he was well enough for home.

Reg's sudden transfer onto the hospital ship meant Norma had no idea of his whereabouts until his confused state had settled. He confided in a young nurse that he was worried his missus had found someone else because he'd not had word from her since he'd been in Brighton. Investigation proved there had been some sort of mishap in communication and so a telegram had been dispatched at full speed to his wife.

Ever since he'd disembarked on British soil, he'd had a strange sense of not belonging which continued even when his confused state improved. For the last five years, he had shared his physical and personal life with the other squaddies; the levelness of each day now was oddly unsettling. Hearing nothing from Norma had increased his sense of loneliness and at times he feared he would never be quite right, or the full shilling as his mother put it.

The damn nightmares were still bothering him, even in the afternoons when he was trying to doze. In his thoughts and daydreams, he was back there in the sweltering heat, eaten alive by stinging, biting flies, with a raging thirst. The water always tasted lousy because of the chemicals added so it was safe to drink, and the belly cramps never left them. Worst of all, the fear of being captured was always there with him, even now.

Maybe the matron was right, he would make a better recovery at home with his loved ones. Only, how could he expect Norma to put up with this shadow of the cheery confident chap that had left to fight for his country? He'd missed the first draft, but when the age limit was raised to 51yrs, he'd been keen to do his bit, and he'd joined the Royal Engineers, later to be amalgamated into REME. It was a special unit incorporating technicians, mechanics and electricians, their job being to keep the army moving in all areas and facets of warfare. He'd been proud to be part of this vital unit, responsible for the maintaining and building of vehicles and weapons, building bridges, or blowing them up, and anything remotely mechanical or technical or electrical. He'd seen his fair share of fighting, hands on and otherwise. Legions of men, dead, left for dead.

For him it was the heat and sickness that had nearly finished him off, not the enemy, and yet the sea air and the ocean, at first so wonderful, now filled him with a vast and empty dread.

It was the morning of his discharge, and his state of mind was far from euphoric. In an effort to take a grip, he'd taken great care with his morning ablutions, shaved until his face was as smooth as a 'baby's bum', corrected his tie umpteen times and thanked all those who had any part in his return to health before climbing into a taxi, driven by a women driver!

The 9am train was twenty minutes late. He'd pushed his hat on straight, dusted down his grey pinstriped demob suit, clutched his suitcase, and climbed aboard.

Norma brushed the heavy lock of hair away from her forehead, making a promise she'd give it a nice wash in the rainwater from the water butt when she'd finished her chores. The three youngest were playing two- ball in the entry. Mary, her eldest and soon to be out from under her feet earning her living, was hanging out the sheets and towels she'd just put through the mangle. For a second, Reg's face flashed through the forefront of her mind. What would he think of his daughters now? His eldest, now a lovely young woman; what would he think of her?

These years without Reg had been a struggle, and they'd left their mark on her face. The constant fear for him, God knew where? Keeping the household running on rations and little else. Growing a few veg, borrowing and bargaining, keeping the girls safe from the bombing; and then the fiasco of evacuating her girls and her decision to bring them home. Not forgetting the daily fight to make them carry their gas masks, the youngest two bedwetting every night at the start of the air raids, water mains blown up, black outs, and trying to keep them decently dressed. She sawed at the loaf of bread, well past its freshest, but beggars couldn't be choosers. It would be fine after a soaking in cold tea, one egg, a little margarine, a spoon of sugar and a few precious currants thrown in; a wholesome bread pudding to fill the girls ever empty bellies. Baking always cheered her, no matter how frugal the ingredients. The warmth from the oven, the springy dough and the yeasty aroma, or the crispness of pastry well made, was one of life's simple pleasures.

It was a beautiful August day, the early morning sun already generous with its heat. She'd started the wash early, wanting to get the bedding dry and folded before the evening set in. The cries and whines of the playing children was music to her ears. Mary's humming whilst she pegged out the last of the washing, the sudden sense of freedom from the fear and privations of the last five years gave her a boost of energy and hope.

Japan's long hoped for defeat and surrender, and the wonderful, miraculous news of her husband, was almost surreal. Mary's tuneful song reached her from the yard and Norma picked up on the last few bars, remembering how Reg loved to lead them all in a singsong after a well-earned couple of beers down at the local on a Sunday morning.

 The thought of Reg returning filled her being with a sudden wave of nerves and excitement, like a swirl of butterflies on a late afternoon. She wanted him home, in her bed, at the dinner table red faced, beer breathed, carving the Sunday roast. And this new Labour government, with their promises of health care without worry, old age without hardship, a fairer world for the working classes; by Jove, there was every reason to be hopeful. Her girls would have so many opportunities their parents would never have believed possible.

The world was going to truly be a better place, and the men and women who had fought with courage and determination against all odds, defeating Hitler and his cronies; bye crikey, they deserved to return to better prospects and a fairer world. She felt for Old Winston though, his defeat must have been a kick in the belly for him. Only the people had voted. A shake up in the old establishment was what they wanted and a fair deal!

Dear Mr Churchill, he would always be remembered for his valiant stance against the dark forces, and he'd pulled them through the dark times, no doubt about that. He'd done his bit. Time for him to have a very deserved rest and to enjoy the respect of the British people, and of the many all over the world.

Her Reg, and the returning men and women, were returning to a new playing field, where they could enjoy the prize of victory. And it was about time they sent him home to her!

Rolling up her sleeves, she squeezed the soggy bread, dropped it into her brown mixing bowl, then added the mixture of margarine, dried egg, currants and a little sugar. Rations were still on, so this was about as luxurious a treat as she could manage. Dropping it into the baking tin, she slid it into the oven. She wiped her hands on her apron, satisfied with her labour.

Glancing out of the open window onto the yard she surveyed her mornings work; the washing hung bright and fresh smelling, it should dry nicely.

"Mam?" called Mary, her voice muffled from behind the sheets, *"Can we go to the park for a while? Please?"* Her request was followed with a profusion of pleading. *"Can we mam? We promise we won't get into any scraps; our Mary will take care of us? Can we? Mam?"* They rushed to the window.

She smiled indulgently at the row of expectant faces. Reg's girls, Mary, 15yrs, serious, leggy and lean; Susan,13yrs, feisty and a little demanding; Gracie,12yrs, placid dreamer, freckled, with thick curly hair, like herself, and little Margaret, 10yrs, dark haired and shining brown eyes, blessed with a joyful, cheerful disposition, favouring her father in looks and temperament so very much.

"Wait a moment…" Leaning forward, she threw a small paper bag out of the window. *"Mary? Catch! I've been saving these, but you may as well them now. And try not to spread it all over your faces."*

"Sherbet and liquorice torpedoes," cooed Mary.

"That's right. Be off with you then and behave. Mary? Have them back before teatime, I'm baking something nice."

Within seconds, the yard was in silence. Wandering into the front room, she relaxed into Reg's armchair. They'd hardly used this room since the war. The wallpaper was needing a freshen up, the paintwork had worn a little better though, and the sideboard always held a beautiful shine due to her frequent wax polishing. Two young smiling faces beamed out at her from the silver framed wedding photograph, stood at the centre of the mantlepiece. She traced her finger over their image, taking in every detail; his eyes crinkling at the corners with laughter, his arm wrapped around her shoulders, possessively? Protectively? And there she was- young and quite pretty, gazing up at her husband adoringly. A lifetime ago! Before their daughters or this damn war was ever thought of. She kissed the glass. When he comes home, she would tell him how much she loved him, how much she'd missed him every day. *"Remember how we loved Reg?"* She whispered. *"Will you?"*

Reg pushed the gate open, noting it was hanging lose on the hinges, and took a step back in an effort to manage a sudden wave of anxiety. The scene of domesticity- wet sheets flapping on the line, a few marigolds sprouting amongst some lettuces in a narrow strip of earth dug out under the window, a skipping rope and small rubber balls dropped in haste in the corner of the yard- brought on a terrible sadness for all the years he'd missed. A wet pillowcase slapped him in the face, and he stumbled. *"Bugger!"*

At last. Here he was. Home. His girls, his missus. He began to whistle a tune.

Norma's heart stopped. She froze, listened. Sure enough, there it was. It couldn't be, could it? Hers' and Reg's tune, the one he always sang to her to get into her good books after losing at the bookies or staying too long in the pub.

She flung open the door and then stopped. Visible below the line of washing were a pair of suited trouser legs ending in army boots. Silence. Gawd, was she going mad? The whistling began again.

"Reg?"

The shoulders of a man's grey pinstriped jacket appeared; the head caught up in a wet pillowcase. A ghost, behind her washing line?

A deep voice. Reg finally emerged. *"So?"* He opened his arms wide. *"Finally, I meet my love."*

Norma's knees buckled. He caught her in his arms and lifted her to her feet, then with a roar of laughter he dropped her down again.

"Blimey girl, what you been eating?"

"Reg? My Reg." Wrapping her arms around his neck she pressed into him, inhaling the familiar, comforting scent of tobacco and minted shaving soap.

He laughed. *"Watch me specs."*

She pulled back, tilted her head. *"I like them, you look sort of, distinguished."*

"Come here." He pulled her into him, buried his head in the softness of her hair. They stayed put for many breaths, neither of them wanting or able to release their hold ---allowing their spirits to feel and feed upon one another.

Norma was the first to let go. *"Is this a dream?"* Her eyes locked into his, she smiled, gently. *"Reg Watling, you are beautiful."*

He was suddenly shy. *"I think I'm supposed to say that to you."*

"What? Reg Watling, you are beautiful?"

He chuckled. *"Damn it, Norma, come here"*. He grabbed her. *"You haven't changed one bit, just as lovely as ever. Bit more of you to cuddle though."* He raised his hands in a surrender. *"And I've no complaints mind, none at all. You're my lovely little pumpkin."* He kissed the tip of her nose.

She looked deeply into his face. *"Was it so very bad, my darling?"*

"Couldn't abide that damn heat. Wore me down a bit."

The truth was that the past few months had been a torture of humiliation, uncontrollable bowels, the stench of contaminated body and clothing, sweats and chills and muscle cramps. It was ironic, he'd survived the fighting and then almost popped his clogs with a double whammy of malaria and dysentery.

"Reg?"

"I'm not the man I was, like, before I went away."

Taking his hand, she turned and pulled him in closely behind her. *"You'll do for me,"* she added softly.

"I've been so lonely," he whispered, his voice low.

"Me too. Come inside." She kissed his cheek. *"Your home Reg, and you're my husband, my fine, brave, husband. I will cherish every bone of you, and as long as I live, you will never be lonely again."*

The news of Reg's homecoming was passed from door to door, window to window. After the train journey he'd meandered along the terraced row of houses, smilingly acknowledging a young lad kicking a ball about and half a dozen girls playing hopscotch. This was the street where he'd lived all his married life, and where his wife had borne their four daughters. He took in the bombed-out spaces between the once red bricked terraced houses, now wearing the soot of war; blown out windows, still boarded up, the waste ground on the corner. Each narrow house front sporting various efforts of growing vegetables; even in the small window boxes there were what looked like radish and carrot tops. He'd removed his hat and thrown it up into the clear blue sky. The sun shone down a welcome.

His arrival at the top of Brinklow Street in a taxi had caused a stir and he knew his hope of sneaking home unseen were dashed. A black cab was a rare sight around these parts. Digging deep into his trouser pocket he'd pulled out two silver shillings and pushed them into the driver's hand. In thankful amazement at the generosity, he'd insisted on accompanying Reg and carrying his luggage, be it only a small battered brown suitcase, and kaki holdall. Reg waved him goodbye at the gate.

Lizzie was the first to call. Still a little unsure of her welcome, she tapped on the door.

"That's Lizzie's knock. Come on in Lizzie."

She peeked in. They were sat at the kitchen table, a large brown teapot and a plate of untouched scones set before them. They nodded, acknowledging her presence.

"*So, it's true then. You're home, Reg Watling.*" Her eyes brimmed with tears.

"*Fraid so Lizzie. It's me. Large as life and as hairy as ever,*" joked Reg. In an odd way, it might help, to have a little company, well, Lizzie; he didn't want a crowd. It all seemed a bit awkward.

"*Hello Reg.*" She noted the yellowish tinge of his complexion, the sharpness of his cheekbones and jaw line, the troubled shadow in his eyes. She took his hand. "*It's good to have you home, Reg.*" She gave Norma a quick glance. "*The girls? I came to collect the girls, thought you'd both need a little time to catch up?*"

"*Oh. They're at the park, not long gone. Thanks for the thought though.*"

"*I see. I'll be off then.*" She gave them a wink, turned to leave.

"*Where are you off to, gal? Stay,*" said Reg hurriedly.

Lizzie gave Norma a questioning glance.

"*Yes, do. Have a cup of tea, share in our good fortune.*" The scones are not long out of the oven. I've made a bread pudding too.*" She patted Reg's knee. "*Your favourite.*"

Lizzie hesitated.

"*Sit,*" said Norma.

Lizzie sat down heavily on a hard backed chair. *"If you're both sure."* She took hold of Norma's warm, cushioned hand, then reached for Reg's, it was dry and papery.

Reg wiped his specs; Norma poured the tea.

Lizzie peered into his eyes. *"How are you Reg?"*

"I don't mind telling you, things were a bit grim. Still, that's all behind me now." He glanced at Norma. *"I was worried sick about this one here, and the girls."*

"We're all fine. I have to tell you, though love. I'm not sure how we'd have got through without Lizzie. There were times, well, things got a bit on top of me---and Lizzie was a godsend with our girls. It was terrible having to send them away on that Pied Piper evacuation nuisance. The girls were so unhappy, so I took a risk and brought them home. Poor Harold and Violet bombed out, and then Vi' suddenly passing. Eliza lost her husband. Then VE day, and the men started to trickle home, and I hoped, and then nothing, your post stopped! I thought, I thought-----"

"Thought I'd had it, caught an unlucky one?" Reg's smile didn't quite reach his eyes.

Norma swallowed. *"I did."* She turned to Lizzie. *"Will you cut the scones please? I need to fetch my hankie."*

Lizzie sliced through the soft thickness and spread a thin layer of blackcurrant jam on each slice. Placing it on a dainty china plate, she offered it to Reg.

He lifted a morsel to his mouth and stopped halfway, giving her a rueful smile.

"Can't seem to manage food too well just now."

"You've been very ill, it's only to be expected luv. Take a day at a time, don't rush yourself and then, you'll see, one day, that everything has slotted into place."

He shrugged, fiddled with his plate.

Lizzie took his hand. She was usually good with words but for some reason she wasn't able to link her brain with her mouth at this very moment. He was so very thin, and his brown eyes seemed almost black against his yellowy pallor. The sounds of Norma opening and closing drawers upstairs told her she was probably getting her bedroom tidied, ready for Reg.

"You'll feel better when you've had a little breather. Anyway, I really must get on." She stood up too quickly, knocked her elbow on the table.

"No, please Lizzie? Wait for Norma, she'll find it odd if you up and leave without saying tara."

Against her better judgement she stayed, sitting awkwardly on the edge of the chair she looked up at the ceiling. What was Norma doing up there for goodness' sake? *"The girls will have a few questions for you when they see you. Norma's done a good job with them, they're little smashers. When you need a little peace and quiet from them, and you will, send them over the road to me. Ruby is soon to be off to America, so I'll have the house to myself again."* She sighed. *"It will be strange."*

Reg tried to feign a show of enthusiasm, but the truth was he could only vaguely remember a mention of it in one of Norma's letters.

"Ah yes, recently married."

"That's right. An American officer, John Parker. Anyway, there'll be plenty of time for you to catch up, as I said earlier."

He laughed. *"Time! Can't really say time passed in the blink of an eye. I have to admit, I was in a bit of a state; Gallipoli gallop, well, that was bad enough, but malaria? Didn't know if it was night or day, they had to pin me down on the bed or I'd have landed them one. Shameful! They were a wonderful bunch; nothing was too much for them. Those medics and nurses pulled me through, that's the truth of it."*

"What's the truth of it?" asked Norma, joining them, her face blotchy.

He gazed at her intently. *"I did a lot of thinking in that hospital. There really is no death."*

Norma looked upset. *"How can you say such a thing Reg?"*

"No, hear me out. I mean, no death as most of us think of it. The things I heard and saw. The chaps that died in my arms. I became convinced when it came to my turn, I would find a way for some part of me to return to you. What I feared most was being taken prisoner. I was as sure as hell if it came to that, I'd have put a gun to my head."

Norma bit her lip, fighting back the tears.

"Struth." She wanted to slap him. *"Reg Watling! How can you say such a thing?"*

"Well, I didn't, did I? I'm here now, you silly article."

"Yes but-----" She stopped short. *"What was it like Reg? The fighting? Did you? ----"*

"Please don't ask me that----I did my bit."

She searched his face. *"Doesn't it help to talk?"*

"Sweetheart?" he coughed, twice. *"I don't believe it will. I left the thinking to the likes of our officers. I followed orders, ate, slept--- when I could, took aim, dodged---each minute, each hour, day and night. I shan't talk about my war. I shan't constantly dwell on it, there was no glory in it for me."*

"I see."

Reg leant forward, took his wife's hand. *"Come on, gal. I'm with you now, and I'm never going to leave you---ever again."*

He gave Lizzie a wink. *"Have a scone, Lizzie."*

"Don't mind if I do, only I'll take it home with me." She smiled, pleased to see a little of the cheeky chappy that had left for war.

"Ta-raa then. Thanks for dropping in," smiled Reg.

Norma blushed, looked the other way.

They listened as the back gate clanged shut. Reg fiddled with his plate. *"When do you expect our daughters' home?"*

"Another hour maybe, they're led by their stomachs."

"We could have a little lay down, do you think? It was a bit of a journey?"

She took his hand, kissed each finger. A minute passed in silence. Reg coughed. *"Don't know if I'll be up too much though."*

A ray of sun shone through the open window, highlighting the greys in Norma's hair. He touched an escaped curl. *"Shall we?"*

They climbed the creaking stairs. She pushed open the bedroom door and pulled the curtains across. *"Sit on the bed, I've something I want to show you."* She pushed him down onto the mattress.

His eyes widened. *"Aye up."*

She undid her dress, slowly, then yanked her under slip over her head. He watched, stupefied.

"I made a promise to myself; if you returned home to me, there would be no more lights off. Ever heard of the fan dance, Reg?"

Chapter 11

Silence. Despite the jumble of emotions fighting to be expressed, the small group found themselves locked in a verbal straight jacket.

Jimmy, Eliza and the three over-excited nippers, had embarked on the ship amongst a loud flurry of ta-ra's, tears, hugs and waves. They were eager to begin their dream journey to a new life that would not include the loved ones who had been an integral part of their existence for most of their life, and certainly their main support network during the last six years of war. There were many waving goodbyes that day. Jimmy and Eliza weren't the only ones needing to shake themselves free of post-war Britain. New Zealand, according to Jimmy, was a magnet for those seeking adventure and new horizons. The war over and the oceans safe to travel, there was nothing to stop them.

Up the gang plank, a quick wave, and onto the ship. Eliza was clear, she did not want the parents to wait and watch the ship sail. The children were fractious, and she needed to settle them. She never could bear lengthy goodbyes, and this could well be the last time she would see them again; she wanted to remember them happy.

But despite her warning, they'd waited, their expressions as miserable and grey as the early morning sky. The mizzle soaking through their clothes, glistening on their faces, mixing with their tears.

Patrick was the first to make a shift. In a sudden flurry of movement, he pulled his wife up and away from the holding support of the barrier. She dropped her new brown handbag at her feet. *"Patrick! Careful."* He ignored her protests.

"That's it then, they're off. 25th August 1945. A day I shall always remember. I never really believed it would come off. He's always had a hankering to travel, only I hoped, when he and Eliza got together, he'd change his mind."

He took a clumsy hold of Lil's arm. *"Come on, let's find somewhere we can have a cup of tea."*

She pulled away. *"No. Not yet."*

Patrick sighed, looking to Sam for help. Sam was staring straight ahead, his face grim. Kathleen gave him a gentle shove. *"Jimmy loves her Sam; I do believe she loves him back."*

"I don't doubt it, but did he have to take her halfway around the world to prove it?"

She took his hand, and they started walking, followed by Lil and Patrick.

"There, on the corner," said Patrick, *"Let's go inside."*

It was no warmer inside than out. The dampness saturated the walls and furniture. The metal chairs were cold and uninviting, the few tables were bare, except for half empty sauce bottles. Over in one corner, a young couple sat with heads closely together, engrossed; they didn't make the customary good morning greeting.

Sam settled Kathleen at a table and moved briskly to the counter at the back of the café, rapping briskly on the Formica top. *"Service?"*

Out came a plump woman with frizzy hair and a smile as wide as a sunbeam. Her presentation at odds with the bleak coldness of the establishment.

"What can I get you duck?" She carried on without waiting for an answer. *"You wouldn't believe it's August, would you? The damp comes straight in here off the water. And then? Within a couple of hours, the mist clears, and I'll have to pull the shutters half down to keep the heat out."*

Sam stared, his head a riot of emotions. She tilted her head. *"Tea? Anything to eat?"*

Patrick's short stocky bulk appeared at Sam's shoulder. *"Four teas please, and if you've any sugar, then one in each. Oh, and a few biscuits wouldn't go amiss."*

She looked from Patrick to Sam. *"Oh, I see, your ladies are over by the window? Right-O. Sit yourselves down and I'll bring them over."*

Patrick struggled to squash his bulk into the small chrome chair. Sam grinned, *"A tight fit!"*

He ignored the comment. *"His new employers paid their passage. Skilled you see,"* he said, pushing out his chin. *"They're keen to have young men like our Jimmy, he's been tinkering with anything mechanical since he was knee high."* He looked to Lil for affirmation.

"He has. And, of course, he has his papers. Five long years it took him. Did you know?"

Kathleen nodded. Oh yes, she certainly did; Lil was never shy of boasting of her nephew's accomplishments. She tapped her fingers on the table. Today she'd watched her daughter, and three grandchildren leave for another country, to sail across the world, and in all likelihood, she would never see them again. She turned her head away.

Lil carried on, oblivious to Kathleen's distress. *"He's like a son to us. I'll miss him, terribly."* She blew her nose on her best embroidered hankie.

"Now then, Lil," soothed Patrick. *"We've both agreed----it's a fresh start. He's been offered a wonderful opportunity and there is many a young man who would snatch at this offer."* He looked at Sam and Kathleen. *"Why----What an adventure they have in front of them. I wouldn't be------"*

A tray holding four large mugs of steaming brown tea appeared on the table in front of him, followed by a plate loaded with thick slices of thick toast, oozing with what looked like, and smelt like, real butter.

The waitress beamed, *"Toast is on the house----thought your ladies needed a bit of cheering up."* She wiped her hands on her apron and gave Patrick a wink. Lil glared.

Kathleen looked up. *"Thanks. That's very kind of you."*

She bounced out, calling over her shoulder, *"It's not marge, it's real butter. Tuck in."* She disappeared through the green door behind the counter.

Patrick's eyes followed the ample hips swaying under a tight red frock.

Lil scowled. *"I only wanted a biscuit."*

"Drink up Lil, don't look a gift horse in the mouth." He took a long gulp. *"Blimey, this tea will put hairs on your chest."*

Lil took a sulky sip. Kathleen handed round the plate of toast. They all dived in, munching quietly. Patrick used his sleeve to wipe the grease running down his chin. *"You wouldn't think a slice of toast could taste so good."*

Kathleen wiped her hands on her handkerchief. "S*he's right. It's real butter. I mean----we're fairly strictly monitored on our little farm. How can they be so lavish?*

Sam's lips tightened. *"There's a lot of skulduggery goes on in these sorts of places. There aren't enough bobbies to stop and search every sailor who comes into dock."*

"The black market has always been around Sam."

"Yes, wife, for those that can afford it."

"I didn't see you refusing it," added Lil. *"Rationing should easy up now--- hopefully."*

Sam frowned. *"That's not the point. Some lost their lives bringing food over to these isles."*

"Leave it Sam please," begged Kathleen. *"Not today-----"* She bit into her lip. *"I'm going to miss them terribly---and how is my daughter going to manage three kiddies cooped up in one of those cabins?"*

The waitress returned, slamming a plate of assorted iced biscuits in front of Sam, who stared at them in amazement.

Lil snatched up an iced shortcake. Sam shook his head, Patrick shrugged.

"*She has our Jimmy with her,*" said Lil, at the same time crunching on her biscuit. "*They packed the snap cards and half a dozen crayoning books and pencils, jigsaws, bedtime story books. Mary Rose has that new rag dolly you made her, Kathleen. The children are all very excited. It will be fine.*"

"*Our lad will be a good help. He'll read to them and play with them, up on deck,*" said Patrick. "*If they're allowed. They are sailing on a great liner and there will be wonderful ocean views. By crikey, I envy them, I do---really.*"

"*I believe the upper decks are for first class passengers,*" added Sam.

"*From what Jimmy said, they will be allowed up on the main deck, weather prevailing, and when the ship has to restock with fresh food and fuel, the passengers can step off and have a look around.*"

Lil smiled at Kathleen, encouragingly.

"*I suppose,*" added Kathleen, biting into the edge of a wafer biscuit. "*Let's face it. Your Jimmy's always had the devil at his heels.*"

Lil looked as if she was about to protest.

"*No Lil. I mean no offense. I like him, I really do. He has a good heart. They're both suited in this respect. Our Eliza could never really settle.*"

Sam raised his mug. "*The very best of luck to them all. Let's wish them a safe passage and a happy healthy life.*"

They snatched up their cups.

"*To Eliza and Jimmy and their little family.*"

"*To Eliza and Jimmy and kiddies,*" they chorused.

"*God speed*", added Kathleen.

"*God speed.*"

Ruby yanked at the sash window, stuck her head out, and glanced up and down the long street. It was strangely silent, and chilly, maybe the long sunny spell was coming to an end.

Breakfast had been served on a tray, and despite Lizzie's encouragement, all she'd managed was a slice of toast with a scraping of blackcurrant jam, washed down with a cup of strong tea sweetened with a spoon of sticky condensed milk.

Her soon to be flight companion, Maisie, had made a valiant effort to push down the slice of bacon and the fried egg put in front of her, but the grease lodged in her throat.

Ted had watched her toy with her food with irritation. He'd woken in a strange humourless mood, waking a good sight earlier than suited him, and the way his daughter was picking at her breakfast as if it was something the cat brought in didn't help. Jessie had given Maisie the last thick slice of bacon; what he wouldn't do for a crispy rasher on a bit of bread dipped in the bacon grease. He'd had to make do with a bit of fried spam!

He lowered the newspaper he'd been thumbing through, cleared his throat and sniffed. His mouth watered. "*Ere, if you don't want it, give it here. Your mam had to queue up for half an hour for that yesterday.*"

Maisie pushed the plate in front of him. She looked at Jessie. "*I'm sorry mum, I'm really not very hungry.*"

Ted beamed. *"If you're sure?"* He didn't wait for an answer.

Jessie looked at her daughter, her grey eyes troubled. *"Are you certain duck? It's not too late to change your mind."*

"I am sure mum, never so sure of anything in my life. Really." She gave her mum a gentle smile. *"A little nervous---flying----me---who'd have thought it?"*

"Is that all that's bothering you?" asked Ted, a slice of bacon halfway to his mouth.

Maisie stared at the bacon grease on his chin. One thing was for sure, she couldn't see her future stretched out in front of her here, in this pub, seeing her dad grow more belligerent with age and her mam slowly fading from hard work.

She nodded. She was not going to admit any qualms; her father would see it as an opening for another tirade of reasoning of maybe's and let's wait; try to tip the balance again. Who wouldn't be scared? She had little idea what would happen when she stepped off the plane, other than Cameron promised he would be there to meet her off the flight. In a way she was relieved it would only be herself and Cameron, rather than be thrown in the deep end with relatives who would probably be wary of her.

Maisie didn't envy Ruby, beginning her married life on a ranch in the middle of nowhere; beautiful, exciting; but nevertheless, facing a way of life completely alien to her. Cameron had found a modern two-bedroom apartment and he'd promised she would have the fun of furnishing it---mistress of her own home, with all the American mod cons.

She could do this, of course she could. The thought of the new outfits hanging in the wardrobe gave her a new burst of confidence. Her fiancé had sent her a parcel: two pairs of tailored flannel slacks and three beautifully cut shirtwaister blouses in powder blue, primrose yellow and a pale green with a daisy print collar. She was a lucky girl, with the way it was at the moment, well, with clothing coupons and such, she would never have been able to buy anything as beautiful as these.

She pushed her chin out, tried to look chipper. All she needed was a few moments to collect herself.

"Father! You've got egg running down your chin."

Ted wiped it off with his shirt sleeve. She raised her eyebrow.

"Listen, please, both of you. This is my chance to be with the man I love. I'm a little scared, who wouldn't be? I will miss you both. Only please, don't spoil it for me. No more questions." She pulled her chair back from the table. *"Try to understand, there is nothing for me over here."*

"Charming," huffed Ted.

"Dad!" she yelled. *"Please be happy for me."*

She ran up the stairs two at a time.

Jessie glared at her husband. His eyes widened, *"What?"*

"The taxi will be here for me and Ruby soon, it should be here in about an hour," shouted Maisie from the bedroom.

"What time's the flight?" bellowed Ted.

"Oh dad. You have all the flight details down there on the sideboard. Mam? Show him." answered Maisie, her voice muffled.

Ted scowled. *"Do you think she deliberately set her cap at him?"*

Jessie shrugged, not sure how to answer. Her daughter was smart, not one to overlook an opportunity---and God knows they had been few and far between in this neck of the woods. It was clear the American was a decent enough chap, and he was clearly besotted with her. She believed her daughter honestly thought a lot of him. No reason for her not to have both, love and a better future.

"What makes you think anything different Ted?"

"Maisie is a looker, and she's always been one to want more than a little house and her own fireside. She will wrap that poor bugger around her little finger. But marriage is a big commitment, it's important she likes him enough to make a good go of things. I'm worried----- "

Jessie cut in. *"I believe they have a chance, as good a chance as any during these times Ted. I see the way she looks at him, she wouldn't go all that way with a man she didn't have some feelings for. She's interested in all sorts of things; she's always been a little different and head strong too. There in a big city, I'm sure she'll find work, maybe in one of those big political organisations they have over there. Our Maisie has always been so clever at organising and such. And she can type!"*

"What about Cameron? He's a fair bit older than her, he's likely to want children as soon as they're wed," Ted protested.

"Stop it now Ted. She's going to have a really good time, I'm sure of it."

"Hmmm. Our daughter's never been one to do as she's told, is she? When she thinks she's right, she digs her heels in."

"She knows who she is and what's right and wrong. Nothing wrong with that."

Jessie frowned. There was a long pause. *"Ere, what's all this about? What are you trying to say Ted?"*

He shrugged.

"I do not want her upset, not today, especially today. Listen. She's bossy, like you! It's in the blood." Jessie was on tenterhooks. Her daughter was brave enough to take her chance, and she was damned sure that her old man was not going to stop her, not now, not at the very last minute. She stared at him. Just what had he got up his sleeve?

Walking over to the window Ted lit a cigarette, gazing into space.

"We won't see her again. Do you realise? It could all go bloody wrong."

"If Maisie being happy, means there's a price to pay, and I shan't see her again---as her mam, I'll gladly pay it."

Ted took a long draw on his cigarette. *"I hope to God this won't turn out to be the biggest mistake of her life."*

Jessie moved towards him and put her arm in his. *"Be proud of her Ted. It's a courageous decision."*

He swallowed. *"I'm going to miss her. Do you think th------?*

"Shush, she's coming down."

Maisie placed herself in front of her parents, eyes shining with excitement.

Ted swallowed. *"My gal."*

"Well? Will I do?"

"You look beautiful duck. Me and your mam, we wish you all the luck in the world."

Maisie's brown eyes brimmed with tears. Jessie passed her a hankie.

"Oh, look what you've made me do, dad," she whispered.

Ted sniffed, moved awkwardly around her. *"I'll fetch your baggage from upstairs."*

Maisie threw her arms around Jessie's shoulders. They stood in the embrace until Ted clambered down the stairs.

"Ready then?"

She pulled away. *"As ever. The taxi should be here any minute. I'm sorry, I hope you don't mind but it's easier saying goodbye from here."*

Jessie struggled to control the tremor in her voice. *"Don't be sorry pet. Be happy—write lots---"*

"I will. I promise."

This was it then. Ted looked at his watch.

"Let's have a nip of something, together, 'fore you leave the house."

Jessie nodded; she didn't trust herself to speak.

Maisie took hold of her mother's well-worn hand. *"I'll make good money over there, mam, much more than I could ever do over here. I'll save up and send for you."*

"Don't you worry about me love, I'm fine. I'm where I want to be." She winked. *"I can handle your dad. ---Ted, best brandy, mind, best glasses; it's an occasion. We'll have it in the front room."*

Maisie took a look around the tiny parlour. So many photographs---all of her, well, mostly. School photos, sports day; days at the seaside; last day at school busting out of her uniform; standing proudly wearing her Red Cross uniform. The brown velvet cloth on the table she'd bought for mam from the vicarage jumble sale, the garish striped knitted cushions that they'd knitted together from unpicked pullovers, flimsy crocheted covers over the back and arms of the sofa, the polished brasses over the fire. She shivered. *"It's cold in here mam."*

"The sun doesn't warm it until the afternoons I'm afraid. Never mind, let's sit together on the sofa."

Here was Ted with the silver tray and three cut glass tumblers of amber liquid. *"Here we go then, bottoms up."*

"Crikey Dad, if I swallow that lot they won't allow me on the plane," laughed Maisie.

Ted ruffled her hair, *"What? A landlord's daughter can't hold her drink?"*

Jessie eyed her glass. Ted snorted. *"Can't say the same for you duck. Maybe you'd have been better with a sherry?"*

Jessie gave him a defiant stare and downed half the glass in one go. The heat rushed up her chest and around her face and the back of her neck.

Ted squeezed himself between the two women. *"Budge up."*

"I guess this is it then. What shall we drink too dad?" Maisie leant her head on his shoulder for a second.

"How about…?" Ted's mind was suddenly blank. *"Righto. Hold your glasses up. Here's to happy and prosperous new beginnings."*

"Happy and prosperous new beginnings," they chorused. Jessie's voice was croaky. They all laughed.

Outside they could hear the children playing. The sun began to shine its warmth through the window and the dust moats danced on its rays. The clock ticked. A ball thumped the outside wall. They huddled together; Jessie in dread of hearing the taxi pull up outside and honk its horn, Maisie wondering if she should nip out to the lavvy for another pee, and Ted? Rueing the day that Yank stepped inside his pub and romanced his only daughter away.

Ruby had done with speculating and worrying. Already married to her American lover and carrying his child, she was more than ready to embrace her new life.

Her future in-laws had written to her many times with warm welcoming words that showed an eagerness to meet their son's British bride. The letters wrapped her in an American hug of words and black and white photographs of their homestead. Other than the regret of losing Lizzie, she was more than ready to join them.

John was now discharged from the Airforce. She tried to picture him wearing civvies, she'd only ever seen him wearing uniform. Would he wear one of those cowboy hats- Stetsons? Like the ones they all wore in the movies? That's what they wore out West, wasn't it?

She looked down at the small silver framed photograph in her hand, begged from Lizzie only this morning. *"I want to take this with me Lizzie, please?"* It would travel with her in her small clutch handbag, a sort of safety talisman. There she was, Lizzie as a young girl, before life had taken its toll and left her childless and a widow. Even then there was an unfathomable something shining out from those brown eyes --- wisdom above her years, innate goodness. Lizzie knew folks around here whispered, liked her or shunned her as a healer, or witch!

Lizzie's words last night came back to her. *"Life is a flickering light and shadow; you can't grasp it in your hand, it's not solid, we have to dance in its light and not cower in its shade. You'll be alright duck, he will always love you and the nipper, he won't let you down."*

She denied having healing powers as such, *"Me duck? No. I understand the power of listening, kindness, prayer, the properties of a few plants and herbs, that's all."*

"But your crystal ball? The cards?" Ruby challenged.

"Well, yes. I can read the signs. They are there for all to see. Maybe God has given me an extra-long radio antenna." She hadn't laughed about it, mindful a gift from God was to be acknowledged and treasured. Her silver cross was always worn discreetly inside her blouse of dress. She didn't wear it as a badge.

A sudden draft and the scent of lavender alerted Ruby. Lizzie had a habit of treading so softly, as if she appeared in a puff of smoke, like a genie from its lamp.

"Almost time." Her wrinkled olive face was so close it seemed the image had jumped out of the tiny photo frame and magnified into the present.

"I'm glad I said my goodbyes last night, Lizzie. Eliza and Jimmy and the children will be well on their way now, won't they? What an adventure for the kiddies, sailing on a big ship. Norma, Frances, all our friends and neighbours, I'll never forget them, or you, especially you and what we've been through together. I used to be afraid of what would happen to us all when this war finished; daft isn't it? Only we were all so very close. Why would I, or anyone, want to cling onto those terrible times? Doodlebugs, V2 rockets, squashing up in the shelters, wondering if the house or even the street would be standing when we crawled out; the madness of it all."

Lizzie considered. *"I shall miss my siren suit; it was handy to pull on over my nighty when the raid was on. I think I'll keep it to wear when I'm doing a bit of gardening."*

Ruby roared. *"Oh Lizzie, Noooo. They are awful, nothing but an old boiler suit."*

"Winston Churchill wore one," protested Lizzie. *"Anyway, at least I gave you a laugh. Today is not the time for the doldrums. There were enough tears last night."*

"We were awash with them, weren't we?" smiled Ruby.

Lizzie folded her arms in front of her, gave a little push on her bosoms. *"Shall we have some tea? Do you think the nipper* will be alright if we have a teaspoon of something in it? Or not?" She waited for an answer.

"Better not. Or maybe; where did you get your brandy from anyway?"

"It was left over from your wedding do, a tiny drop at the bottom of the bottle, that's all," called Lizzie from the scullery.

"That will be rather special. Today of all days. Yes, please then. The little scallywags been kicking my insides out since the early hours of the morning. He, or she, is very active, wouldn't have thought it possible." She rubbed her swollen belly. "People are so rude, always commenting on my size."

Lizzie looked up as the cuckoo popped out of the clock. *"We've about half an hour before Bert and his taxi arrives."* She stopped short of hinting to Ruby that her size may indicate she was carrying twins, the signs were all there. Shaking her head, she decided to hold her counsel.

Ruby was momentarily confused. *"Lizzie? Why are you shaking your head? Isn't it a good idea? The brandy?"*

Lizzie waved her away. "Half a teaspoon? Don't be daft. I remembered something I needed to do, that's all."

She placed the two bone china cups and saucers carefully down in front of them. Ruby noticed the slight tremor in her elderly friend's hands; she didn't mention it, she'd seen it before.

"Bottoms up!" chortled Lizzie.

Ruby sniffed the tea. *"The smell of brandy is as good as the taste."* She sipped it delicately.

Lizzie tipped her cup back and finished it off in one go. She reached across and took Ruby's hand. *"I'll ask Bert to bring your suitcase down when he gets here. Where are your flight bag and papers?"*

"It's all here." The flight bag was at her feet.

"Good. Finish your tea then. When Bert arrives, I'll see you in the cab and wave from the door, just as we agreed. You'll be at the airport in an hour and another hour later you'll be on your way." She squeezed Ruby's hand.

Ruby finished off her tea, touched up her makeup for the tenth time and sat tapping her foot. They had talked for hours last night, deeply and tenderly; a nostalgic, spiritual conversation. Today was about seeing it done. They were keeping to pleasantries.

Despite her effort at control, Ruby made a dive for Lizzie and gave her a desperate hug.

Lizzie patted her on the back. *"Now then. I don't want you getting upset. You are to go forward with determination and hope---like we agreed. Bert will be here in 10 minutes. Why don't you pay a visit to the lav? It might be a while before you have another chance."*

Lizzie opened the front window and stuck her head out, looking up and down the street for Bert's taxi. It pulled into sight as Ruby came bustling back, straightening up her coat.

Ruby's heart thumped. This was it then. Lizzie opened the door. Bert, his stout figure filling the narrow doorway, tipped his cap.

"Ready then?" He looked from one to the other.

"As ready as ever," joked Ruby.

"*Ere, Bert. Can you bring the suitcase down the stairs? It's on the landing.*"

Ruby's eyes brimmed with tears. Lizzie took her in her arms and kissed her cheek.

Bert side stepped around them and trundled past them, loading the suitcase into the Boot of the taxi.

They followed him outside. "*Come on love, in you get.*" Bert glanced down at Ruby's shape. "*Another GI bride,*" he thought. He pulled the door open wide and guided her onto the back seat; waited as she made herself comfortable.

"*Don't forget, Bert, one more to pick up, at the pub. Maisie, remember?*" shouted Lizzie.

He straightened his cap and gave her a crooked smile. "*Right you are, missus.*"

The taxi slowly pulled away. Lizzie stood in her open door, her wispy hair blowing in the breeze. Ruby looked back at her, waving her hankie. She had a sinking feeling. Lizzie had been the nearest to a mother she'd ever had. The baby kicked and she glanced down, when she looked up again the doorway was empty.

"*It's here.*"

Maisie's stomach knotted.

Jessie made a grab for her daughter and Ted made his way to the door. The engine stopped.

Bert was at the open door. "*Ready?*"

Ted bundled the baggage through the open door.

Maisie pulled away from her mum, gave her dad a hasty hug and climbed in besides Ruby. Pushing her clutch bag down at her side, she gave Ruby a nervous smile.

Bert slammed the door shut.

Maisie took Ruby's hand. *"All set Rube?"*

"As ready as I'll ever be Maisie."

They giggled; nerves and excitement overwhelming them.

Bert slid the dividing window open. *"Here we go then ladies. Ready for take-off?"*

"Ready Bert," laughed Ruby.

Maisie paled and twisted around to wave to mam and dad. Jessie was leaning heavily on the doorframe then she disappeared inside. Ted stood for a few seconds longer and joined her, closing the door behind him.

Ruby handed her companion a lace handkerchief.

"Airport then?" yelled Bert.

"Just go Bert," they chorused, *"just go."*

The soft breath of morning caressed Frances's cheek as she lay in the pearly light. Jo had been restless last night, and his murmurings and fidgeting had made it impossible for her to sleep well. The heat and closeness of his body was making her uncomfortable, and she carefully tried to pull away. Murmuring, he threw his arm over her, his head rolling onto her pillow, his black wavy hair clinging to his forehead in damp sweating tendrils. She lifted his arm and rolled on her side. Unable to summon enough energy to swing her legs out of bed, she stretched out for the letter laying open on her bedside table. There was just about enough light to read Ruby's scribbles from her second and latest communication from America.

She wrote of her in-laws and how everyone was so welcoming and friendly. How John treated her like a queen and refused to allow her to take on any sort of chore or exercise whilst they waited for the birth of Junior, who was frustratingly late to arrive. Honestly, she was not missing home in the slightest, although she worried about Lizzie and begged Frances to make regular calls on her, apologising because she realised her and Joseph would be extremely busy in their new business venture. She asked of Eliza and Jimmy and reminded Frances to please send on their New Zealand address when she had it. Ruby had finished the short letter with love and all the best, and PS, don't forget to write.

It was just over two months now since Ruby and Eliza had left the street, and although Frances gave them both an occasional thought, she and Jo had been so busy with the shop. She was, of course, also trying desperately to move past the momentous affect Joe's confession had had on their relationship. Consequently, she hadn't written. Sliding carefully out of the covers so as not to disturb Jo, she resolved to make time to answer the letter after teatime, and to pay a visit to Lizzie.

The lino was cold on her feet as she crept into the small kitchen and filled the kettle ready for an early cup of tea. Looking around for matches, she was disturbed by a tapping on the back door. Hesitating, she wondered whether to answer it. The tapping became louder, insistent. She popped her head around the parlour door and took a peek at the clock on the mantle.

Just five am. Who could it be at this time of the morning? Maybe it was the milkman caught short again- seems he was having a bit of a problem? She moved closer to the outside door, it was locked and bolted. Jo said they couldn't be too careful, what with the shop out front and all the stock they carried and everything.

"Who is it?"

"It's me, Fred."

As she thought. The milkman! Sliding open the bolt, she unlocked the door. The lavvy was out the back, he didn't need to ask.

She began to speak, *"Fred, you don't need to-------"*

"I'm sorry Frances, but do you know this gentleman? Only he was sitting on the wall out the front when I passed, and he asked me if I knew where your Joseph lived?" Fred looked concerned, *"And this little nipper was with him, and she looks fair done in, God bless her."*

A tall lean man stepped forward, his face eager and at the same time anxious. *"Joseph? Joseph Will—i—ams? Pardon madame. Je suis ----looking for Joseph Will-iams?"*

Fred dithered, stepped forwards, then backwards. Just at that moment Joe called down the stairs.

"Frances? Is that the door?" Before she could answer, he came racing down and pulled the door wide open. He stared, open mouthed. *"Bloody hell! Alain?"*

A wide grin spread across the visitor's face. *"Oui. Who else?"*

A soft cry, almost sounding like a miaow, came from behind him. He smiled and reached his hand behind him, pulling forward a small child. She clung onto his mackintosh. He coaxed her softly. *"Josephine ma Chere"*.

The little girl pouted. Frances gasped; she was named after Joseph. *"Joe?"*

Alain glanced at Frances, then at Joe. *"This is Josephine; ta fille,"* he coughed, *"Your daughter."*

Fred made a hasty exit. None of his business. After all, he heard and saw some strange things in his line of work.

Frances moved first. She bent down to the child's height, looked into a pair of huge hazel eyes. She put out her hand.

"Hello, my name is Frances."

The child stared, and then held out her hand. *"Je m'appelle Josephine."* Frances took the small hand and smiled softly. She was rewarded with a sweet, toothy smile.

Joe swallowed. His daughter? She was a tiny little thing. She had a mass of black curls held either side of her face by a pair of pink slides. Her delicate features were so finely carved, she had the look of a child who was undernourished or who had not long recovered from an illness. Her pale olive skin had none of the natural rosiness one would expect in a healthy child.

He still hadn't recovered enough to speak. He gaped, lost back in another time. She had her mother's eyes. Colette's eyes. Huge hazel eyes.

Frances stood, looking from father to daughter, then directly at the visitor. *"Please, sit down both of you. Forgive us, this is all rather a shock."* She turned to Joe, her eyes pleading. *"Joe?"*

He groaned. *"My little girl."*

Frances was about to pull Joe forward, then hesitated. She turned to the stranger. *"Please sit, Alain. I think my husband is finding this all very difficult."*

"Thank you." He sat down awkwardly on the edge of a chair and lifted the child onto his knee.

He gave Frances an apologetic smile. *"She was a surprise for me too."*

Frances looked at her husband, he was frozen to the spot. She put out her hand to the child and pointed the men into the parlour.

"I'll make her some food; I think you two have some talking to do."

The child hesitated for a moment. Frances clapped her hand to her brow. *"Oh goodness, how stupid of me. Alain? Can Josephine understand any English?"*

"Yes. Une peu. She was cared for by the nuns in the orphanage, some were English." He turned to his niece. *"Ma Cherie, this is Frances. Stay here for a moment. She'll look after you."*

"J'ai tres faim," the little girl whined, rubbing her tummy.

Alain smiled an apology. *"We haven't eaten. But then she's always hungry."*

Frances melted. *"Oh, my darling. Come. See what we can find."* She nodded to the men. *"Go."*

The child ate enthusiastically, her little face bulging with apple and cheese and bread. Frances couldn't tear her eyes away. Joe's child! She looked to be around the age of about three. It was 1946; from call up in 1939, Joe had been away for two years, then missing for just over two years, with the Resistance. He'd returned around the end of 1943. He clearly didn't know of her, so she must have been born while he'd returned to England. This must be the child from the French woman. Where was she? Why would she let her child away from her side? She had so many questions. She could hear Joe and Alain talking inside the parlour.

The little girl coughed. *"J'ai soif."* She pointed to the milk bottle on the table.

Frances gently wiped the crumbs from around the small mouth. *"Would you like some milk?"*

The black curls bounced. *"Yes. Lait. Milk?"*

She watched as the cup was emptied and then proffered again. *"Un de plus? One more? Please?"*

Frances refilled the cup. The child gulped it down and then smiled, hiccupped.

'The child is starving.' She didn't want her to guzzle too much and bring the food back up, it was clear she needed its goodness. *"Enough just now, you can have more later."*

Josephine nodded, fidgeted.

Frances had a sudden thought, the little one may be needing the lavvy. *"Josephine? Toilet?"* Well, Alain said she could manage a little English.

She bobbed her head, slid down from the chair. *"Yes."*

When Frances flushed the lavatory Josephine's eyes widened. *"Water?"* She gaped into the bowl. *"Water?"* She giggled. *"Again?"* Pointing to the cistern she tried to reach up to pull the chain. *"Again?"*

Frances began to laugh. What on earth? She lifted her up and Josephine yanked hard and watched in awe as the water flushed again. *"Encore! Again?"* Frances nodded her head. *"No."* The child wriggled down from her arms.

"Come on sweetie. Let's go inside, see what your uncle Alain and Joe----- your---- father has to say."

My Lord. Joe was a father. He was able to father a child, only not to her. ----- It must be her fault! They hadn't had a child between them, despite their doctor's reassurance that all was in order. She must be infertile! A shiver ran along her spine. Did Lizzie know? Had she seen this in the cards?

Josephine tugged at her dress. Frances swooped down and picked her up into her arms. *"Let's go inside pet."* She was as light as a bird!

She sat her on the old sofa in the corner of the kitchen whilst she tidied away the remains of breakfast, and then sat down beside her. The child climbed onto her lap. She began to hum softly to her, stroking her beautiful black curls. *"Joe's daughter,"* she whispered. Withing minutes she was asleep, curled into Frances's breast.

Alain and Joseph shook hands.

Alain was soon to be returning to his ship in The Free French Navy where he'd served most of his war since France fell. He'd served in the auxiliary force alongside The Royal Navy in the Atlantic, only returning home for a short while in early '43 when he'd came across the Englishman, Joe, who was being hidden by the Resistance in his home village.

On returning home just three months ago, he'd found his sister Colette and her Resistance Unit were all dead- wiped out by the Gestapo after a disastrous raid which went horribly wrong. The women in the village had told him of a child, his sister's child to the Englishman who had been with them during '42 and '43. They'd been unable to feed her; reprisals had taken the men from the village and left them all short of food. In desperation, they had taken the girl baby to the local convent and begged the nuns to raise her.

He'd immediately made his way to the convent and met with the Mother Superior. She had given him a letter written by Colette, left with one of her neighbours. She'd instructed the nuns to hold onto it, and in the possible event she didn't return, they were to give it to her brother Alain on his arrival back in the village. The letter was clearly written in hast, but it contained Joseph's full name and whereabouts, the town and street but no number, along with his mother's crucifix and a couple of photographs of his sister as a child and a teenager.

He had taken his niece and rented a house in the village. It was clear the French and English nuns had very limited resources and it was imperative he found her father in England before he returned to his ship. And so here he was! He hadn't thought of the impact this child may have on Joseph's life; he hadn't considered it for a second. Josephine was his sister's and the

Englishman's child. She was in need, and it was his duty to see her settled with her father.

They found them both fast asleep, the child wrapped in Frances's arms.

Joe sat Alain down at the table and placed a slice of ham and a hunk of bread and cheese in front of him. Alain would be able to stay for a further ten days to help settle the child, and then he must leave. He ate hungrily, deep in thought; 'his country free but in upheaval. The Vichy government now dispersed and its leader, Marshal Philippe Petain, arrested as a traitor. De Gaulle's Government had returned and established back in Paris. He threw his knife down on his plate. How could a Petain, a hero of the First World War, collaborate with the Germans, stripping thousands of French Jews of their nationality and condemning them to their death? He felt no mercy for the French men and women who'd followed Petain, who'd openly collaborated with the German soldiers. They deserved all they were getting. The war may be over, but the slate wasn't wiped clean. It was good that his niece was safe from this bitterness and chaos. These English were good people, he could see that. Of course, he would have liked to keep her close, but it was impossible. Maybe one day.

Joe watched and waited for Frances to wake. They needed to talk. He wanted to explain, apologise. He knew Frances would be hurt, but he also hoped her innate goodness would get them through this, and surely, she would not reject his child? Thank God, he'd told her about Colette. He was saddened but not shocked to hear of Collette's unit's death by the hands of the Gestapo. The only mercy was they'd all been shot in an ambush and not been held and interrogated.

He'd planned to take Frances to the south of France after the war to meet the wonderful friends who'd hidden him and saved his life. Now, they were all gone! He hadn't any idea Colette had been carrying his child; their affair had been intense, born of need, and short. One day he would take his daughter to see her mother's home and her resting place. He would tell her how brave her mother and her friends had been. He hoped she was buried in a proper grave?

There would be further heartaches; Frances may not be able to carry her own child. But this wasn't a forgone conclusion, was it? Time would tell.

Alain finished his food and made to leave. He put out his hand, shaking Joe's vigorously. *"Thank you for your understanding, and your offer of hospitality. I hope ta femme will be sympathique? I must hurry and collect our things and be back before my niece wakes. I left them at a house on the corner."* He nodded towards Frances. *"I'm sure you and she will need to talk."* He stepped outside and pulled the door behind him.

The click of the door broke into France's light doze. She sat upright with a jolt. Joe leapt forward, panicked.

"Fran? I'm sorry! Please don't leave me. I wouldn't want to live if you didn't love me."

Frances was calm. Joe looked frantic. She smiled at him and kissed his cheek gently." *Did you know?"*

"No. I promise, I had no idea."

"I believe you. We need to talk."

He kissed her full on the mouth. *"Yes."*

He waited, braced himself. The child murmured in her sleep. *"When?"*

"Not now. She's beautiful Joseph, your daughter, our daughter. So, like you."

Joe looked at her in speechless amazement. *"Fran?"*

"We are a family now Joe. I love you. I'll never leave you. She needs us. We are alive, we've survived this war and we owe it to her mother to raise her in a loving home. And her mother?"

"No. She's gone. Dead." He looked towards the door. *"I need to explain. Alain should be----"*

"Not now. By the way, I took her to spend a penny and she wouldn't stop flushing the blinking lavvy?"

"What?" He couldn't believe she was taking it so calm. *"Frances? Are we alright then? Are we going to be alright?"*

"Yes Joe."

"Oh. I'm a lucky man."

She stroked the child forehead, dropping a kiss on her brow. *"Yes, you are."*

"Anyway, The lavvy? They have earth toilets in their village."

Frances laughed. *"We're going to have some fun."* She looked at her wrist. *"I'm staying with Josephine; you can open the shop!"*

EPILOGUE

It was one of the loudest, most joyful parties that had been held in The Three Bells since Ruby and John's wedding. The friends and neighbours celebrated with determination. The daily newspaper headlines warned of a country in debt, a massive rebuilding programmes was needed, a world still in chaos.

They had lived for each day for the last six years, not daring to hope or look too far ahead. Now they were talking of and facing the future; a future some grasped eagerly with hope, or a future that was unsettling or downright scary. This was the peace they had all longed for, and yet the world was still in a state of upheaval; the winning powers squabbling and taking their slice of the vanquished territories like a greedy child at a birthday party. Rationing had eased very slightly but Britain owed a massive war debt to America. Bombing had destroyed much of the housing, and what remained were damaged or needed modernisation. The new Labour party boasted there would be a great modernisation programme- indoor bathrooms and toilets for all, providing work for those returning. The opposition scoffed; impossible! Women did not want to give up their jobs and return to the kitchen and although rationing eased, it still continued. Old Harold stopped his order of 'The Daily' in protest; *"I mean how much doom and gloom can a man take over his morning cuppa?"*

But today, none of this mattered. One of their own had returned home, back from the land of the dead, or presumed dead. He'd knocked on the door at an unearthly hour and given the household the fright of their life. Young Bertie, sticking his head out of the bedroom window and seeing the shadowy figure of his father, screamed at the top of his lungs, *"Mam, there's a ghost trying to come in the house!"* The whole household had tumbled downstairs, their mother at the front of her squealing brood bearing a rolling pin, just in case.

Once the shock had subsided and the story shared, Dennis and Milly Goodall sent their brood flying down the street with invites to a knees-up at The Three Bells. Almost everyone accepted, even the vicar. It was an invitation too good to miss.

As usual, Ted had rose to the occasion, and his wife Jessie pulled in a few favours and managed to make a reasonable spread. Of course, it was nothing as lavish as Ruby's reception but then, she'd married a Yank! And so had their Maisie, her letters were full of her new life with Cameron and the wonderful opportunities for women in America. Why, she'd already secured a post as a PA to some Yank politician; and she had a woman who came in twice weekly to clean their apartment. Unbelievable!

The celebration of Dennis Goodall's return had been going on since opening time at lunch, broke for pub closing, and continued again at opening this evening. The host and hostess had eventually made their way home with the littlun's, after leaving a kitty behind the bar. The party was still going strong. Dennis's tale of his escape from captivity and being on the run in Germany would be a story to engage his family for a long, long time. The fact he'd been selective with some of the details, and the dates didn't quite follow, wasn't lost on his wife, but she chose not to dig. It was a miracle he was home. That was enough. That evening, over a cup of cocoa, he told his story again to the rapt audience of his kiddies, before sending them up the wooden hill to bed; and then sat in wonderful comfort on the sofa with his plump adoring missus. His tale would expand in danger and daring over the years, and he would enjoy many a free beer on the strength of it, as he'd already found. Life was good.

Reg and Norma were making the most of a beautiful early evening and they sat with their four daughters in the pub yard, the girls each eating a bag of crisps and making bubbles with their orangeade and straws. Norma wore a floral dress with a sweetheart neckline. Softly blossoming under her husband's tender loving attentions, she sipped her shandy and Reg savoured a pint of draught. Leaning forward, he kissed her gently full on the mouth. The girls giggled. He smiled, gazed down at her protectively. He had all he wanted and ever needed in front of him. Home! The warm blanket of familiarity and belonging wrapped around him. He'd done it! Bloody survived.

The music was blaring out into the open air. The voices were loud and raucous, the cigarette smoke thick and heavy, drifting out into the early evening air. Some couples were dancing to Harold's personal renditions of Big Band favourites and then later in the evening they'd sing along with the sentimental, haunting wartime melodies that had seen them all through the darkest days of war.

Arthur and his wife Joanie shared a table with their son Gordon and his dark haired, stunning Welsh fiancé Gwendoline. It was clear to all who had eyes that the young couple were very much in love. Joanie would have hoped for her other son, James, to be here, she had to be content he was doing what he loved, serving still as a pilot in the RAF, be it across the other side of the world. Never mind. Gwen was lovely, she couldn't have wished for a lovelier daughter-in-law, and they'd given the newly married couple their own little sitting room and bedroom in with herself and Arthur so they could save a little; their home for as long as they needed. She hoped it would be a while before they moved out!

Across the room, Lizzie sat with Frances and Joseph just inside the door, whilst the curly haired little girl with the red ribbons who'd recently joined and changed their world, was playing ball outside, well within the periphery of their anxious supervision. Little Josephine was proving to be a confident child who showed few signs of impairment following her recent upheaval and sudden migration from a convent in France to a small home in England. She had settled contentedly into her new family- the only family she'd ever known; with a tall quietly spoken father, and a stepmother that clearly, blindly and hopelessly spoiled her. Her strange preoccupation, hiding bread under her pillow, speaking volumes of her early years when she'd been tucked into bed whilst hunger had gnawed at her little stomach, was gently overlooked. Joe had tentatively shown her the photographs of Colette her mother, ready to answer what he anticipated as a tirade of questions and tears. The child held them for a while, ran her finger over them and then handed them back to him. She clambered on to his lap. *"Papa? Where is she now? Why has she left me?"* With her huge hazel eyes staring up at him, he'd answered best he could, promising to take her back to the village and convent when she was older. Joseph's time in France and Josephine being raised by French and English nun's, meant communication was fairly easy. The little girl enjoyed teaching her new mother her first language, whilst of course, with a little teasing in the process.

Was Frances jealous? It wasn't in her nature, and when she'd found she was expecting Joe's child just a few weeks after Josephine's arrival, she'd wondered. *"Did you see this in the cards? Did you know?"* Lizzie smiled artfully and answered, *"Some things are best left unsaid."*

Eric and Clive were enjoying the celebrations, stood at the piano, chatting to 'The old man' and surveying the local talent. They had every intention of dancing the night away, well, until the landlord called time. They'd been given the nod, planning permission to build on their father's land would be soon forthcoming. Hardly a surprise with the local council's push to build as many homes as they could, and quickly.

Patrick and Lil were there; everyone was. With a nod from Patrick, Harold changed to a slow number and Patrick took Lil's hand and pulled her up for a dance. She laughed and tried to sit down again but he insisted, and so she hung on around his neck while he led her on a slow stumbling waltz. She'd been a bit low since Jimmy had taken off with Eliza to the other side of the world. Well, until she'd taken up a part-time post as a tea lady with the local council that is, and now there was no holding her. Women's keep fit, swimming lessons and flower arranging were all enjoyed now, and she was styling her hair in a new way. Patrick was enjoying this new side of his wife.

Sam and Kathleen looked on from their shared table. The four of them had kept in touch since the young couple had emigrated; a mutual interest being the letters from their daughter Eliza and her now husband, Jimmy. They met up every couple of weeks for a game of dominoes at each other's house, taking turns to provide supper and a few beers. This being the turn of Patrick and Lil to host, they'd brought Sam and Kathleen along to the party. Patrick couldn't pretend that Sam was easy company, but they rubbed along, and the two women hit it off. A change fast of tempo and Patrick and Lil re-joined them, Lil relieved to have a sit down, her new patent shoes were pinching her toes.

They watched as Harold's lads whirled the two sisters from no' nine around the dance floor. Ted shouted a warning. *"Oy, be careful lads, this isn't a ballroom, you know. You'll have the chairs over."* Sweating and laughing, they lifted and swivelled until even Harold became concerned. He watched as they tumbled outside. Maybe his bachelor sons wouldn't be bachelors for long.

Harold was flagging, so Bert Williams took over the piano and Harold made his way across the room to refuel and sample the strawberry jam tarts brought along by Kathleen; they'd had a bumper crop this year.

Mrs Rodgers, buoyed up by three sherries, made her way over to the vicar and stood herself directly in front of him. The vicar gave her a wry smile. She held out her hand. *"Would you like to dance vicar?"* Turning a red that would have enraged a bull, he pointed to his wristwatch, muttered something incomprehensible and made a hasty retreat.

Harold found this highly amusing until she made her way over to him. His face was a picture of mixed delight and foreboding. She led out her arms. He hastily swallowed the remains of his third jam tart. *"What me?"*

"You're not going to refuse a lady?" she slurred.

Eric and Clive, returning to the fray, were amused to see their dad waltzing Mrs Rodgers sedately around the floor, his partner looking up at him coquettishly. Who would know where this opportune request would take them both?

And so, the sun began to slip down into the sky, making its orange, purple and indigo farewells, and the friends and neighbours made their leave and drifted off, arm in arm to their homes. Homes and lives left standing despite the worst that their enemy could throw at them; these were the survivors.

Lizzie stopped off at Lil's before turning in to share the photographs of Ruby and her twin boys. Yes, Ruby had a long and painful labour, but, with the aid of her new American mother-in-law, the bonus of not one, but two, babies had made the effort worthwhile. Lizzie knew in her heart she wouldn't be using the ticket tucked inside the vase. Ruby had started afresh and had a wonderful man with a lovely family who welcomed her. Lizzie would stay here in Brinklow Street, doing the things she always did, and Ruby's disappointment would fade as she embraced her new life.

Ted and Jessie locked up, sent the bar staff home, and wearily began to clear away the left-over food and empty glasses. All in all, it had been a good day. Good for Dennis and Milly Goodall and their kiddies, and good for Ted's profits. He couldn't complain. A great get together for all.

War is a cruel, vastly destructive deed, and yet sometimes there seems to be no other way to solve a dispute, settle a grievance, or stop a bully.

Some say there is always a solution to a problem, but for a satisfactory solution, there requires compromise, from both, and all parties involved. If there is willing and movement from only one, then this means victory for the unyielding, and complete capitulation and loss of hope on the part of the first.

And so, will mankind ever achieve a forever peace?

I really don't know.

I hope, and pray it is so.

Betty Rose